DOUBLE EXPOSURE

A SPY THRILLER

THE EXPOSURE SERIES
BOOK ONE

KIRK VOCLAIN

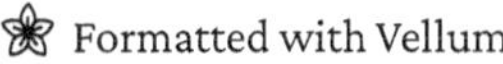 Formatted with Vellum

DEDICATION

The idea for Double Exposure came to me over 35 years ago, during an unforgettable moment with airport security. They pulled me aside because they thought my tripod was a gun. The absurdity of the situation gave me the idea for this novel.

Throughout my 40+ years in the photography industry, this story lived only in my imagination, being written and rewritten in my mind.

I want to thank my wife, Tammy Voclain, for being my preliminary editor and my sounding board through this entire process.

I owe a special thanks to Scarlett Gauthier, my daughter, for creating the name of the main character, and my grandson, Reed Sawyer Gauthier, whose spirit and determination continue to inspire me every day.

PRAISE FOR KIRK VOCLAIN

Double Exposure is a high stakes thriller featuring a shadowy covert organization, and one man who rises to the challenge of exposing and bringing them down. My preference in spy novels leans more Jason Bourne than James Bond... this was right up my alley!

— MYRA N, REEDSY DISCOVERY

Double Exposure is a razor-sharp spy thriller that delivers high-stakes action and cinematic suspense, following rogue agent Reed Sawyer as he races to clear his name, uncover a global conspiracy, and prove that sometimes the most dangerous weapon is the truth you weren't meant to see.

— NEWINBOOKS

This is not just another book, it's a deep piece of an artist's love for his art and how it has shaped his life.

— EDDIE S. BARR

Reed Sawyer's cover as a photographer is clever. It adds atmosphere, scale, and originality to every scene. The spycraft is grounded and believable, and the tension builds up naturally as Reed is forced from a trusted operative to hunted fugitive.

— STEPH

This is a perfect example of a story inspired by real life experiences. The best stories come from what the author knows and has done.

— GILBERT SAITO

A NOTE FROM THE AUTHOR

If you found this book during a promotion, thank you for taking a chance on my work.

If you enjoyed *Double Exposure*, I'd truly appreciate an honest review on Amazon or Goodreads. Even a few words can help other readers decide if this story is for them.

You can find more at **KirkVoclain.com**, where you can join my list for updates on new stories, bonus content, and future promotions.

PROLOGUE

You can sneak a prohibited item through airport security easier than you think.

It's not about gadgets or technology. It's about beating people, their instincts, their assumptions, their patterns. Security loves predictability. Break the rhythm, shift the focus and you create your own opening.

Confidence is the key. No hesitation, no second looks. They don't screen for contraband; they screen for fear. A confident man with a camera in his hand rarely registers as a threat. He's a professional, a journalist, an artist. The world makes room for people like him. Smile at the agent, crack a joke. Let them see what they expect: another traveler trying to make their gate before the boarding call.

But distraction, that's where the magic happens.

The shiny advertisement cards are scattered at the entrance of security: *"FREE COFFEE AT GATE C13."* Simple, enticing. Who wouldn't grab one? The promise of coffee during a morning rush. But no one thinks about the layers in that cardstock. No one thinks about the tiny bit of lead embedded between the fibers. Just a little trick of the trade. When scanned, those cards throw a shadow.

Now thirty passengers are holding identical cards. Some are in carry-ons, others in purses, all going through the checkpoint at the same time. The machine beeps nonstop, panic sets in and security scrambles to figure out what's going on. It's perfect chaos! And perfectly harmless. At least for them.

And while they're sorting out the mess, the real magic happens. A disassembled weapon hidden in the layers of a camera bag. Tripods, lenses, filters, cables, nothing out of the ordinary for a photographer. Not worth a second look. Cameras are the ultimate cover. Expected. Familiar. Invisible.

That's the trick: disappear in plain sight. Don't hide the act, hide the intent.

It's not about the tools; it's about the illusion. And when done right, an illusion becomes reality.

1

THE FRAME

Reed Sawyer glided through the terminal like a pro, blending in with the stream of travelers. Camera around his neck, bag over his shoulder, he looked like every other person scanning the crowded expanse ahead. But Reed wasn't here for vacation or business. And he wasn't alone.

The Louis Armstrong New Orleans International Airport was alive and loud and busy, a whirlwind of sound and motion. Normally that chaos made Reed feel safe, invisible in the crowd. But today was different. There was something off in the air, a vibe that made his skin prickle.

He turned and wandered into a magazine shop, positioning himself behind a stack of travel guides, his eyes scanning the terminal with slow, deliberate sweeps. That's when he saw him.

At Gate C13 to Washington, a man stood out, too dressed up for this time of day. His slate-gray suit was perfect, unwrinkled. He carried no bag, just a phone held loosely, like a prop. But he wasn't looking at the screen. He was looking at Reed.

Reed refocused, nervously flipped through a magazine without looking at it. He took short, quick breaths, forcing his body to calm. One wrong move and he was done. This was what all his training was for, the discipline that kept him still as he turned another page, while his mind spun through scenarios.

Had he been made? Reed thought to himself.

The **Professional Photographers Institute (PPI)** looked like a legitimate organization, a global entity dedicated to education, networking and resources for photographers. But beneath that respectable façade lay PPI's true purpose: The **Private Protection Initiative**, a covert intelligence agency that used photographers as operatives. Their cameras more valuable than any weapon. Photographers were invisible, a fixture at events, ignored by most, and allowed to move freely, even in places others couldn't get to. It was the perfect cover: slipping through embassy checkpoints, blending into private events, wandering restricted areas with the excuse of adjusting a lens or tweaking the lighting. But now, in his own city's airport, something was off.

Reed moved, set the magazine down and stepped back into the terminal flow. The man in the suit was still there, watching. Reed's instinct told him to move. He turned to the coffee stand, wove into the line and let the crowd of travelers and families hide him.

A few minutes later he took a look back. The man was gone.

Reed made his way to the line for the flight to Vienna, Austria. The flight was heading through Washington Dulles International Airport. He joined the stream of passengers and moved along with them, pretending he was in a group of people anticipating their vacation. He was blending in like he always did.

The journey to Dulles had passed with surprising speed. Altogether, the journey added up to just over two hours in the air, followed by a two-hour layover on the ground. But for Reed, there was nothing to be concerned about, assuming the man in the slate-gray suit had taken a different flight and wouldn't be showing up again.

At last Reed was getting on the plane to Vienna. His eight-hour plus flight ahead did not concern him. He was too focused, too committed, on the mission. Yet the man in the slate-gray suit would not leave his mind. He hadn't seen the man in over four hours, but the thought of him made Reed's mind work overtime. Reed had been taught by PPI to trust his instincts. And his instinct was saying that guy was not a coincidence.

Reed settled into 17D, stowed his bag under the seat in front of him and scanned the cabin. Everything looked normal, parents wrangling strollers, a man typing away on his laptop, a teenage girl glued to her phone, oblivious to the world. Reed breathed out slowly, relaxing into the seat. Maybe he'd overreacted.

Then he saw him.

The man was dressed as a flight attendant now, dark pants, white shirt, navy vest. The slate-gray suit was gone, replaced by the calm, professional uniform of the crew. But Reed's mind caught on the familiar face: the sharp jawline, the dark, obsidian eyes that seemed to record everything. Recognition hit him instantly. The man moved up the aisle, checking overhead compartments and greeting passengers with the detachment of the job.

Reed's heart raced but he kept himself calm, moving naturally. As he adjusted his camera lens, the action was cover to sneak another look. The man stopped a few rows ahead, smiled at a passenger struggling with a seatbelt. To the naked eye he was just another flight attendant. But Reed knew better. This man wasn't supposed to be here.

Their eyes met for a second, a flash of recognition on the man's face before he turned and continued down the aisle, expression blank as stone.

Reed sat back, fighting the urge to act. PPI had warned him about these moments, when the line between his cover and reality would blur, when the role of the "photographer" would be tested. He'd trained for this, but training was nothing compared to the raw feeling of being hunted, of knowing someone was closing in while he was in character.

What did they know? How had they found him?

The man disappeared behind the curtain to the crew's quarters.

Reed leaned his head back, his mind spinning. There was no backup, no signal to guide him. Just him, his camera and his instincts honed over years of work. And those instincts were screaming this was no coincidence. Whoever this man was, he was after Reed.

As the plane rolled out, engines purring, he closed his eyes and attempted to calm his breathing. But his mind wouldn't shut up. Who was this man? And why now?

A vibration buzzed in his pocket; was it a message? He shouldn't be doing this, but he pulled out his phone anyway. It wasn't a text or an email. It was something else entirely. It was as if the cellular network had been hijacked and words were appearing on his screen:

"Reed, we need to talk. Now."

No signature, no indication of who had sent it or how. Just six words.

His gut clenched. PPI contacts never contacted him like this, especially not directly. Communication was always through Pro4u-M.com, encrypted and buried behind multiple layers of misdirection. This kind of message was unheard of. Whoever sent it either didn't know the rules... or didn't care.

The plane lurched as it lifted off and he switched his phone to airplane mode. Reed's grip tightened, his eyes fixed on the screen, the message frozen in its final moment of connection. This wasn't a warning. Someone was watching him and playing by their own rules. Someone who knew his real name, his true purpose.

As he was trying to process what was happening, the flight attendant returned. Moving down the aisle with a tray of drinks. He stopped at Reed's row, his smile polite but his eyes icy. He leaned in, his voice almost a whisper.

"Hope you're comfortable," he said. "It's a long flight."

Their eyes met, the man's gaze challenging him to respond. Reed kept his face neutral while his mind raced beneath the surface. This was more than just a tail; this was a deliberate signal, a warning delivered in person. Reed was being followed and whoever was behind it was closer than he thought.

As the man walked away a new kind of fear crept in, more intense than any he'd ever felt while handling a lens. This wasn't mission thrill; this was fear of being exposed, vulnerable. And for the first time in years Reed Sawyer had no idea what was coming.

The plane hummed along, a constant reminder of Reed's unease. His mind spun, fully aware of his situation: cornered thousands of feet in the air, with no backup, no exit strategy, and worst of all, no weapon, not even a pocketknife. Just a bag full of camera gear. He felt like a sitting duck.

Reed pretended to relax and let his hand wander over his gear. As his fingers touched the cool metal of his telephoto lens, an idea crystallized. In the right hands these weren't just cameras. They were weapons, ready to be used if need be.

The thought of using a tripod as a blunt instrument flashed through his mind, a sharp and unwelcome mental image. He forced it away.

Then he thought: what if the man wasn't alone?

The calculated smile on the "flight attendant's" face and the message on Reed's phone were not adding up. Could there be another operative on the flight, someone blending in like him, hiding in plain sight?

The passengers around him looked different, his gear seemed heavier. Reed was no longer just a tourist with a camera; he was a hunter armed and ready to defend himself.

As soon as the plane's Wi-Fi came on, Reed pulled out his laptop and connected. He logged into Pro4uM.com. The homepage loaded, filled with PPI Sales Info and other ads for "professional photographers". The site was PPI's perfect cover. Reed had been lured in by this very disguise years ago; it was his introduction to the world of espionage.

To the casual observer Pro4uM.com was just another photography site, with "educational resources" on lenses, lighting and editing. But Reed knew it was a clever disguise, with layers of coded messages and hidden links masquerading as photography articles.

To outsiders it was a community of photography enthusiasts. To insiders it was a tightly controlled communication channel for PPI agents.

Reed had stumbled upon Pro4uM.com by accident, drawn in by the promise of "exclusive techniques" and "advanced education". It didn't take him long to realize something was off, posts at odd hours, strange phrasing in comments, occasional redirects to encrypted pages. Cracking one of those codes had been an idle curiosity but it hadn't gone unnoticed. A few days later he got a message from PPI inviting him to a meeting. He had no idea why or what the meeting was about, but he felt he had to go.

And that's how it started.

Now, years later, he was back on the site, not as a professional photographer but as a covert operative. Reed logged into Pro4u-M.com with ease, navigated to the private area. Once there he typed in the cryptic message he'd received: *Reed, we need to talk. Now.*

The screen went black for a moment before lines of encrypted text appeared. Reed's heart kicked hard. This wasn't how Pro4uM worked.

Then a single line appeared at the top of the page:

Look closer, Reed. You're in the frame.

Reed squinted, the words eating at him. "In the frame" wasn't a casual phrase, it was a warning.

Then another line appeared:

Section: 3. Page: 16. Code: 105-B.

He furrowed his brow as he glanced at his gear. He knew the drill, "in the frame" meant the answer was in something he carried. But he hadn't received a physical package from PPI in months.

Before he could do anything, another message appeared:

Someone's watching. Play your part.

Reed's throat constricted. Whoever sent this knew he was being followed and knew more than he was telling. The numbers in the message could refer to a hidden document, an embedded file or something in his camera or an archive from a past mission. But one thing was clear, "play your part" meant keeping his cover, playing the photographer.

He closed the laptop and the message felt like a weight on his chest. He looked around the cabin. The man in the flight attendant uniform had disappeared behind the curtain but Reed knew he wouldn't stay hidden for long.

The message echoed in his head: *Look closer, Reed. You're in the frame.* A warning, layered and menacing. The numbers, Section 3, Page 16, Code 105-B, tugged at his brain, a puzzle he had to solve. It had to point to something specific, something he'd seen before.

He pulled out the telephoto lens from his bag, pretended to clean it, his fingers tracing the notches along the metal barrel. This lens had a hidden compartment, a trick PPI agents used to store micro-film or compact storage drives. It wasn't likely what the man behind the curtain was after, Reed hoped not, but it would give him a second to react if things got hairy.

The plane rumbled as the passengers settled in, the cabin was quiet. Reed shifted, angled the lens to peer through the glass and catch a reflection in the window. The man reappeared. He slipped out from behind the curtain, scanned the rows with a practiced air of nonchalance. His eyes flicked to Reed for a second before moving on.

Reed's mind was racing, connecting the dots fast. If he was "in the frame" it wasn't just surveillance, it meant he was the target of whatever was happening. Was the man PPI or an outsider who'd cracked Pro4uM.com? Either way was bad.

He had to move.

Reed stood up, camera in hand and walked into the aisle as if to the lavatory. Space, he needed space, a vantage point, somewhere he could think without the eyes on him feeling like a chokehold. He'd barely stood up in the aisle when the plane hit a patch of turbulence and the man in the flight attendant uniform blocked his path with a tray of drinks.

"Can I help you with something, sir?" The words were friendly but the look in his eyes said otherwise.

Playing the part of a passenger caught mid-walk Reed said, "Just stretching my legs," and added a smile that didn't reach his eyes.

The man nodded slightly. "I think you should sit down. It's about to get rough."

Reed saw the subtle tension in the man's stance, the way his fingers gripped the tray ready to drop it at a moment's notice. The threat was silent but clear.

"I'll take my chances," Reed said, shifting his weight, his fingers wrapped around the camera body. It wasn't much but it was something.

As he waited for whatever was coming, the tray shifted, and a narrow gap opened for a second. Reed caught the seat marker out of the corner of his eye: **16B**. The seat was one row up, to his left. The occupant, a middle-aged man in a crumpled suit, had his head back, looking like he was asleep. But under the seat in front of him was a small, unassuming case. Most would miss it, but not Reed. This was no ordinary case, it was a PPI covert camera case, designed to be invisible.

Adrenaline surged through Reed, sharpening his focus and giving him a renewed sense of purpose. He forced a smile and nodded like he was surrendering.

"I'll sit back down," he said, moving into the aisle and letting the flight attendant step aside. But his eyes never left 16B. He was no longer just observing; he was preparing for what was to come.

Reed's brain kicked into overdrive as he slid back into his seat, his eyes scanning the passengers to focus on the man in 16B. He watched as the middle-aged man shifted slightly as if he knew Reed was looking at him. The case under his seat, so invisible a moment before, now seemed to glow. Reed had to get closer, to figure out if this man was the key or just another complication.

Reed adjusted his camera again, angling it to keep 16B in the frame of his telephoto lens. The act of taking pictures was the perfect cover for him to observe without drawing attention. He zoomed in, noting the worn edges of the case, the tapping of the man's fingers on the armrest.

As Reed focused his lens the man opened his eyes, shifted slightly to push the case further under the seat. 16B turned his head to the right and their eyes met and in an instant the man's expression changed from fake sleep to full alert.

A small nod. Just enough to confirm what Reed knew. This wasn't a random passenger. He was involved and he knew Reed was too.

Reed stood up, stretching like he was loosening his muscles. As he walked by 16B the man spoke without turning his head, his voice low and even.

"Check your case," he said, the words almost lost in the drone of the engine.

Reed kept walking, acting like he hadn't heard but inside he was reeling. The man in 16B had either just given him a lifeline or set a trap. The air in the cabin seemed to thicken, every second dragging.

He glanced back and caught the flight attendant's eyes, narrowed in on him like he hadn't missed the exchange. The plane dropped slightly and Reed slid back into his seat, holding his camera.

Look closer, Reed. You're in the frame. The message echoed in his mind. *Check your case.* Whatever was in his own case was part of the puzzle and he was in deeper than ever.

The numbers ran through his mind again: *Section 3. Page: 16. Code: 105-B.* It couldn't be just random numbers; it was a key. Reed's eyes drifted to 16B. The man sat with a calmness that only a trained operative could achieve. The message from Pro4uM.com wasn't a warning. It was a lifeline.

Reed tried to settle into his seat, the drone of the engines a constant buzzing in his ears. His mission had seemed simple, at least at first: photograph Secretary Lucien Kessler, one of the most powerful men in the U.S. government, at an exclusive event in Vienna. The press pass, courtesy of PPI, was his cover. A routine assignment, or so it seemed. But just minutes after he received the mission its true scope came into focus. The real task was embedded in the shoot itself: pass on a coded sequence hidden in a routine photo op. The mission was two-fold, get a picture of Secretary Kessler and confirm the code was received.

It was supposed to be easy. Almost *too* easy. Too easy to have extra operatives on his tail now. Reed's confusion grew. And now that plan felt shaky. The man in 16B was the missing piece, ally or threat unknown.

Reed looked at his bag, pretending to dig through it. *Section 3*, could it be a chapter in his camera manual? And *Page 16*? Maybe it wasn't a literal page but an image or technical reference within Chapter 3. PPI often hid messages in the mundane, using the complexities of photography as cover. Camera manuals were perfect for this: dense with diagrams, jargon and obscure details, ideal for hiding something in plain sight.

105-B. To most, it was just a description. To Reed, it was a code, a directive only a trained PPI operative would understand. The beauty of hiding codes in camera manuals was that no one read them in detail, which made them the perfect hiding spot. PPI's cryptographers were experts at embedding these hidden triggers, so agents had access to secret instructions where no one would ever think to look.

He felt a surge of excitement as the pieces started to fit together. If the answer was in the manual, then the next step was in his hands.

Play your part, the Pro4uM message had said. Reed sat back, his fingers running over the worn edges of the camera manual. The familiarity of it calmed him as he opened it to *Section 3, Emergency Alerts and Error Messages.*

His chest thudded as he turned to *Page 16* and flipped through it quickly. There it was, an image of emergency alerts for his camera. Beneath it, *Item 105-B* read:

Flash unit that does not support red-eye reduction attached, and flash mode set to red-eye reduction or red-eye reduction with slow sync.

To most it was technical mumbo jumbo, the kind only a photographer would notice. But to Reed it was a code song. It meant an operative, or unit, working without support, a PPI agent in the field using improvised means to signal presence. Flash mode meant need for subtle synchronization without drawing attention.

Reed's heart rate steadied, confusion giving way to clarity.

Reed kept the manual open, his eyes scanning the page as if lost in technical details. But now it was more than a manual; it was a roadmap to survival. And the man in 16B wasn't just a coincidence, he was Reed's lifeline.

The flight attendant emerged from behind the galley, his eyes like razors. Reed's heart missed a beat, but he covered it with a small smile, keeping his cover.

He had time. Now he just had to live long enough to act, get to Vienna, and finish the Kessler job.

2
THE CLICK

A surge of turbulence jolted Reed awake. Overhead lights flickered, casting shadows on worried faces. A murmur rippled through the passengers as the plane rocked again. Reed blinked hard, shaking off the fog that clung to him like a shroud. The last thing he remembered was leaning back in his headrest, his eyes heavy from exhaustion after 24 hours of no sleep.

He had been posing as a photographer at the Governor's daughter's wedding, one of those New Orleans affairs that bleed into dawn, a chaotic mix of flash, fast adjustments, and the city's crazy revelry. He hadn't planned to sleep on this flight to Vienna, but the fatigue was absolute and he was under before he could resist.

He stretched his legs out and looked down, his pulse kicking up. The camera manual, a thin booklet that had fallen from his fingers while he dozed, was perched precariously on his lap. He breathed a sigh of relief as he snatched it back. This wasn't just a manual; it was a lifeline, disguised as a book.

Reed looked around the cabin. 16B was still sitting there, eyes closed but motionless, like he was sleeping. The flight attendant who had been watching him with an interested gaze earlier was nowhere to be found. For now.

The plane lurched again and the captain's voice came over the intercom. "Ladies and gentlemen, we're experiencing turbulence. Please remain seated with your seatbelts fastened."

Reed barely registered the announcement as he was too busy wondering what he might have missed in the manual. If this was PPI's way of guiding him, then there was more to this than a covert photo shoot. The mission to photograph Secretary Kessler and get him the code was suddenly secondary, a cover for something bigger.

Vienna was still hours away but now it wasn't just about getting there. It was about survival.

His eyes snapped to the overhead lights as they flickered on, followed by a crackle from the intercom. The captain's voice came through, steady but with an edge that made Reed's gut tighten.

"Ladies and gentlemen, due to unforeseen circumstances, we will be making an emergency diversion to Bratislava, Slovakia. Please remain seated with your seatbelts fastened." A murmur of confusion spread through the cabin as passengers shifted uneasily. Reed felt the tension hit all at once. Bratislava? This wasn't on any of his contingency plans. He looked at 16B who was now fully awake, eyes alert. And slowly turned his head in Reed's direction. Their eyes met, and Reed knew: this wasn't a coincidence.

The captain continued over the intercom, "Your safety is our top priority. Arrangements have already been made to secure transportation to your final destination. You will receive more instruction once on the ground. Customs and Immigration agents will be providing additional information. Thank you for your cooperation."

The flight attendant emerged from the galley; his smile gone. His gaze swept the cabin like a sniper before landing on Reed. Another jolt of turbulence hit the plane and Reed's grip on the manual tightened.

He leaned back, pretending to be interested in the pages. The coded alert replayed in his mind, a signal from an out of sync operative calling for subtle coordination.

"Unexpected, isn't it?" a voice muttered across the aisle. Reed turned just enough to see a pale, worried-looking woman clinging to the armrest. Her knuckles were white. He nodded reassuringly, hiding the storm inside.

Bratislava meant delays, missed connections and a complete overhaul of his escape plan. Vienna and Secretary Kessler seemed further away with each passing second. But this diversion wasn't an emergency change of plans; it was deliberate.

Reed looked at 16B again. The man was staring right at him. "Looks like a bumpy ride," the man said, his voice low and casual. He looked at the camera then back at Reed. "You must be a pro with that kind of gear?"

Reed blinked but kept his smile in place. "You could say that."

The man reached into his jacket pocket and pulled out a card, passing it to Reed with a nonchalant air. Reed took it, looked at the clean design and tucked it into his pocket. Box Gallery it read. The tagline below said An Eye for the Unexpected. The address and phone number were unmistakable, coordinates every PPI operative knew by heart. This wasn't a gallery; it was a PPI safe house.

"Good eye." Reed said, making the exchange seem like small talk. The man in 16B nodded once, a small smile playing at the corner of his mouth. The plane jolted again and 16B sat back, closed his eyes as if the moment had passed. But for Reed the revelation had landed like a weight in his chest. This wasn't just an unexpected diversion or a suspicious flight attendant, it was bigger. He was a pawn in a larger game and Vienna wasn't the end point. It was the starting point for something much more complex. The man who gave him the card was connected, how deeply Reed didn't know.

The plane started its descent and the captain's voice came over the speakers. "We'll be landing in Bratislava shortly."

Reed's heart skipped a beat as he closed the manual and tucked it under his arm. Whatever was waiting for him in Slovakia he needed to be ready.

The plane began its descent into Bratislava, the engines humming as the murmurs in the cabin grew uneasy. Before Reed could think his next move, the flight attendant emerged from the galley and strode towards him.

"Mr. Sawyer," the attendant said, his voice clipped and professional, "I need you to step aside for a routine PPI inspection."

Reed's mouth opened in shock. The phrase sounded harmless, but to him it meant something far more sinister. Why PPI? Was the attendant hinting at Reed's connection to the organization? Or was this something else entirely?

Reed stood slowly; camera instruction manual tucked under his arm. "Of course," he said smoothly, letting a hint of compliance show as he stepped into the aisle.

"We'll need to verify a few things," the attendant said, his tone firm as he gestured Reed towards the galley. Leaning in, his voice dropped to a whisper. "PPI checks are essential, but not all forums are secure."

Reed's mind raced. The "forum", a clear reference to Pro4uM.-com's dual nature? It was known that not all intel on the site was trustworthy. The warning was subtle but clear: even trusted procedures could be traps.

"Mr. Sawyer," the attendant said again, his calm cracking. "We need to do this before landing."

"I'm ready," Reed said, though the question remained: ready for what, and for whom?

Reed had taken five steps when the seatbelt signs flashed on and the intercom came to life: "Ladies and gentlemen, we've begun our descent into Bratislava. At this time, we'd like to ask everyone to please return to your seats, fasten your seat belts, and ensure your tray tables are stowed and seatbacks are in the upright position. Flight attendants, please prepare the cabin for landing and take your seats."

The flight attendant looked at Reed. "Please return to your seat. We'll continue the inspection after landing."

As Reed turned back, he caught the briefest of glances between the flight attendant and 16B. It was swift, so quick it might have gone unnoticed by anyone else. But Reed's training kicked in.

Years behind the lens had taught him to catch the smallest changes in a person's expression, the faintest flicker of recognition, a hesitation in the eyes. This was one of those moments. The glance wasn't just a glance; it was a signal.

Are they working together? The thought shot through Reed's mind, colliding with cryptic clues and coded warnings. The flight attendant's professionalism, the PPI reference, and now this glance, it all felt like pieces of a puzzle that didn't fit. Reed's training came back: *Trust no one completely. Even the familiar can betray you.*

Was 16B orchestrating this with the flight attendant? Was this diversion to Bratislava part of a bigger plan that was set in motion before he even boarded? Or were they both agents manipulating him from different angles?

Reed's mind spun with questions. On paper the mission was straightforward: fly to Vienna, photograph Secretary Lucien Kessler at an exclusive diplomatic event and subtly pass on a coded sequence hidden in the way he directed the session. It was classic PPI, an exchange masked as routine. But now with the diversion to Bratislava and the cryptic interactions on the flight, Reed felt the weight of what wasn't being said.

Settling back into his seat Reed went through the mission file in his head. Every detail was committed to memory: expected lighting conditions, attire, the address to pick up the equipment.

Wait.

The address.

His hand shot to his pocket, and he pulled out the card 16B gave him. He looked at the printed address. It matched.

Relief flickered, brief, fragile. A confirmation they were on the same side. *Or were they?*

The question hung in the air, uncomfortable and persistent. What was bothering him were the omissions, the unspoken elements

PPI was known for leaving in its instructions. The gaps felt deliberate, calculated, as if designed to leave room for the unexpected. Now with 16B's involvement and the flight attendant's cryptic warnings Reed felt like he was assembling a puzzle he never knew existed.

Is this still the PPI I thought I knew? The question surfaced, unwanted but refusing to be ignored. He remembered when PPI first recruited him, presenting itself as a silent guardian, stepping in where bigger agencies failed. It had promised honor hidden in secrecy, serving without recognition but with the knowledge justice was being done.

A memory flashed: training days at PPI, shadowy rooms filled with agents speaking in code and sharing stories that walked the line between truth and myth. He had been so eager then; driven by the belief he was joining an organization that protected without the politics and red tape. A mentor, Hudson, once told him, "We don't get the glory, but we make sure others do. We're the difference between a headline and a footnote." It was like being a commercial photographer. Nobody remembered the photographer who shot car ads for Toyota; he was just a footnote, an anonymous craftsman cashing a check.

Reed's thoughts froze. Was that still the PPI he was with? Or had its noble mission twisted under ambition, shadowed by the corruption it vowed to defeat? The diversion, 16B's cryptic message and the PPI-trained flight attendant's obscure words pointed to a mission that was far from straightforward.

The idea of Kessler as a decoy began to take shape. If the Secretary was just a lure, the real target was deeper, hidden beyond what PPI trusted him to see. The thought stung, biting like a betrayal.

Reed exhaled slowly, forcing clarity into his thoughts. He'd joined PPI to be on the right side, to do meaningful work without getting caught up in the big games of world powers. But now with the pieces moving around him like chessmen in someone else's game he couldn't shake the feeling he was a pawn in a game beyond his control. He looked down at the camera instructions, open in his hands. He reminded himself who he was, an operative trained to see beyond the obvious, to capture what others missed. If PPI's purpose had changed, if their true intentions were compromised, he knew he would have to play this out on his own terms.

For the first time he wondered if the operative in 16B was as in the dark as he was, another pawn in a game they both didn't fully understand.

Reed's resolve hardened. Whether he was being set up or not, he would see this through. He would get to Vienna, confront Kessler and find out the truth. If the mission had deeper motives, he would do what PPI trained him to do, adapt, survive and uncover the real story hidden in plain sight.

The descent continued, Bratislava airport lights twinkling through the small window, a promise of safety or the start of a new trap.

His muscles tightened as the landing gear engaged, the plane shaking to a stop. This was it. Time was up and the game was about to get serious.

The tires screeched on the tarmac; passengers jolted into their seats. The engines roared as the plane slowed, noise masking whispers. Reed felt the pressure closing in.

In the chaos 16B turned his head, his eyes on Reed. His lips moved, almost inaudible over the confused noise of the aircraft. "They know you're here," he said, each word sharp.

The engines purred as the plane taxied. Reed's eyes bounced between the flight attendant, standing rigid by the galley, and 16B, sitting up straight, eyes forward. The cabin lights flickered, as if on the verge of failure. The captain's voice came over the intercom, calm but hollow: "Welcome to Bratislava, Slovakia. We caught some strong tailwinds, so we've landed ahead of schedule despite the diversion. Please remain seated until we reach the gate."

An hour early. Reed's hand went to his phone, still in airplane mode, silent for 12 hours. There had to be a message, an update, something from PPI or someone else. His fingers itched as he turned it on, eyes on the screen as notifications downloaded. One message jumped out: *"If Kessler falls, it's failure. Watch the shadows, but move only in the light."*

Reed's breath hitched, almost a groan, as the message sank into his chest. The airport lights shone outside the window, casting long, dark shadows. He held the camera instruction manual and the phone, his muscles coiled as the plane stopped moving. The world outside was dark and full of question marks.

3

THE FLASH

The 787 Dreamliner buzzed with anticipation as it taxied through the Bratislava night, its 63-meter-long fuselage pressed against the tarmac. Over 300 passengers shifted in their seats, the tension building since their diversion from Vienna. Despite its size and fancy design, Reed knew chaos was only a heartbeat away.

As Reed scanned the packed cabin, he noted that every seat was full. Families, businesspeople, solo travelers crammed into the big yet somehow cramped space. Getting off this plane alive was priority one. Panic and the unknown would be on his side, but he needed to spark that.

A distraction was needed, no, it had to be more than a distraction. It had to be an event that would command attention, create the smokescreen to get him out.

Reed's mind flashed back to the familiar pre-flight safety script. Every passenger had heard it at least a dozen times: "If you have any lithium batteries, e-cigarettes, or other prohibited items…" The warnings had become background noise to most but Reed wasn't most. Digital cameras ran on lithium batteries, powerful and volatile in the right conditions. And in his camera bag he had a dozen spares. Sacrificing two for his survival was an easy trade.

The plane jolted to a stop, the lights of the airport casting a cold glow through the oval windows. He kept his eyes steady, sneaking glances at the flight attendant by the galley.

He couldn't put his trust in 16B, not yet. The passenger's cryptic message was too thin a lifeline to bet on. No, Reed's only true ally was the training he'd received at the Private Protection Initiative, or PPI. To the outside world PPI was an elite organization offering resources, training, and networking for top tier photographers, professionals who needed access to the far corners of the globe. But beneath that façade it was something far more sinister. PPI agents were masters of surveillance, extraction and intelligence. They moved like ghosts, blending into crowds, slipping across borders, using their photographic cover to penetrate the highest levels of security. Reed had been one of their best, recruited not just for his skills behind the lens but for his instincts and adaptability. This mission was no ordinary assignment; it was the culmination of every shadowed lesson, every coded message, every silent observation. And now he'd have to use it all.

The overhead chime sounded and the fasten seatbelt sign went off. The cabin erupted into movement as passengers unbuckled themselves, grabbed their bags and waited to get out of the plane. This was it, Reed's moment to act.

His fingers dipped into his camera bag, feeling the cold parts of the lithium batteries.

Reed's fingers moved quickly with the batteries, paper clips and gaffer's tape. The improvisation reminded him of his early days as the 'MacGyver Photographer', always finding solutions in unexpected places. But this was no artistic challenge. This was survival. His movements were methodical, honed from years of working on the fly with whatever tools he had at hand. He bent the paper clips to bridge the positive and negative terminals of the batteries and secured them with the gaffer's tape to prevent the clips from slipping. He knew he had only a few minutes before the makeshift device would react, sparking a burst of fire and smoke intense enough to create disorder in the cabin.

Reed watched, muscles coiled, eyes on the flight attendant. The plane's door finally opened, letting in a wave of thick, stifling air and the smell of jet fuel from the tarmac. The murmurs of passengers waiting to disembark filled the air, each voice another layer of sound to hide his plan. This was it. He slid one battery forward, let it roll under the seats ahead and one back into the narrow space behind his row. The paper clip bridges were holding, sparks were imminent.

The seconds ticked by, each heartbeat louder than the last. Then with a hiss and a pop, the forward battery spat out a small burst of smoke. A grey plume curled into the aisle, tendrils of acrid smoke stinging the eyes and nose. Passengers gasped and recoiled as the second battery cracked with a deeper, muffled *thud*, releasing a sharp, metallic smell and dark smoke that quickly filled the cabin. "FIRE!" Reed shouted, putting just the right amount of panic in his voice. He leapt to his feet, waving his arms wildly to add to the chaos. "GUN, HE'S GOT A GUN!" he bellowed, eyes locked on the flight attendant who froze, caught in the sudden mayhem. Passengers screamed, abandoning their seats, some kicking over armrests and each other in their panic to get out of the perceived danger.

Pandemonium broke out. Luggage fell from the overhead bins, adding to the noise and confusion. Feet stamped, elbows jostled and voices screamed, blending into a din of terror. Smoke swirled in thick, choking clouds that blinded and suffocated. The flight attendant's eyes went wide with panic and one hand instinctively went for his pocket, but he was swept back by the human tide, unable to maintain composure or control.

Reed didn't wait. He slipped into the surge, angling his way towards the door with practiced stealth. The crowd was perfect cover, each panicked thrust and shout helping him escape. He kept moving, shouting "RUN, RUN!" to nudge the stampede and keep attention away from himself. The fire alarms wailed, the shrill noise piercing the mayhem, telling everyone to get out, get out fast.

He slid past the shouting flight crew and down the exit ramp, the smoke and turmoil hiding his escape. Behind him the pandemonium continued. Ahead was uncertainty, but at least it was on his terms.

Reed was out, but freedom was temporary. The key was to keep moving. Whoever had planned this had been very good. They had managed to get 16B on the flight and a fake flight attendant past enough scrutiny to blend in. The level of detail and coordination pointed to someone high up in PPI, a puppet master with access and power.

The diversion from Vienna was strategic. Someone knew about Reed's signature weapon cache system, loaded guns hidden in everyday objects in major airports worldwide. His reputation at PPI was built on such innovations. In Vienna's Terminal 3, behind Jamie's Italian restaurant, a gun was waiting in the tissue compartment of the men's room. But now the diversion had cut him off from his own failsafe, leaving him exposed. Whoever had planned this knew his playbook inside out. His mind was buzzing as he tried to put the pieces together. How deep did this go? If PPI were willing to do this, Reed knew he wasn't dealing with a simple mission gone wrong, this was something much darker.

He needed answers, and he needed them now. The smoke and bedlam behind him were clearing into the heavy, damp night air. Reed tightened his grip on the camera bag and took a deep breath.

4

THE EXPOSURE

Reed weaved through the crowds in Bratislava's airport, trying to go unnoticed. He knew the agency's eyes were every-where. Security cameras, guards, and even ordinary passengers could be operatives ready to report his movements. As he scanned the terminals, he spotted a flight attendant entering the men's room. An idea formed.

Reed followed him in, approaching the sinks where the attendant was washing his hands with a faraway look. Reed slipped into role easily. "Long layover?" he asked casually, looking in the mirror.

The attendant nodded, looking at Reed through the reflection. "Yeah, heading to Atlanta eventually. Have a couple hours to kill first."

Reed nodded back, looking thoughtful, his mind already racing. An ID badge was clipped to the attendant's uniform, giving him access to the next available flight. For Reed, it was a ticket to Vienna. He knew how to play this.

As the attendant dried his hands, Reed reached for his camera bag and swung it up, bumping into the attendant just enough to snatch his ID badge. "Oh, sorry about that! Guess I'm travel-weary."

"No problem," the attendant said, barely looking down.

As they exited, Reed smiled and said, "Safe flight!" The attendant waved, none the wiser.

Reed reached into his bag and pulled out a thin, customized sticker, a photo of himself, one he kept just for situations like this. He pressed it over the photo on the stolen ID badge, instantly turning himself into his temporary alias: "Evan Taylor."

Reed blended in with the airport traffic. He walked fast, bypassing the chaos of the main gates and heading toward the tarmac access door marked "Crew & General Aviation." He scanned the digital flight monitor on the wall.

Flight 72X | Private Charter | Destination: Vienna (VIE) | Status: Departs 10 mins

Perfect. A repositioning flight. Empty planes often hopped between the two close capitals to pick up VIP clients.

He mentally noted the attendant's uniform he'd seen earlier: white shirt, navy pants. Reed pulled the white shirt from his bag, slipping it on over his t-shirt. It wasn't a perfect match, but with the stolen ID clipped to the pocket and a confident stride, he believed he could pass.

He stepped out onto the warm tarmac, the smell of jet fuel hitting him. A sleek Gulfstream G650 sat idling nearby, the pilot doing a final walk-around.

Reed approached, flashing the badge. "Hey, Captain. I'm Evan Taylor. Dispatch said I could hitch a ride with you over to Vienna? I'm working the outbound flight for the Ambassador, and the rail line is backed up."

The pilot barely glanced at the ID, more interested in his landing gear. "Hop in. We're wheels up in five. Just don't eat all the catering."

Reed climbed the stairs, the door sealing shut behind him with a heavy thud. As the jet taxied past the main terminal, Reed looked out the window. He could see flashing lights and emergency vehicles swarming the gate he had just fled.

While the Flight Attendant and 16B were trapped in the lockdown he had created, Reed was already airborne. By the time they cleared security, he'd be on the ground in Vienna, a ghost in the wind. He was getting closer to figuring out PPI's real game.

As he settled into the plush leather seat, Reed understood that every move from here had to be precise and calculated. He had only a short time to stay hidden.

With the plane's Wi-Fi, Reed logged into Pro4uM.com under a private network, erasing all digital footprints. He knew the site's rule: every operative had to use their real, full name for accountability, a rule strictly enforced.

The administrator, Tammy Stark, was someone Reed knew well. They'd dated briefly, although it was more about strategic positioning, a calculated move for a situation exactly like this.

Reed thought back to the time they had dated. Tammy was gorgeous with long brown hair and a shapely figure. Reed looked at himself in his phone's darkened screen and was under no illusion about himself. He wasn't handsome or memorable, average height, average build, average face. Nothing distinct, nothing that would linger in someone's memory. And that, he reminded himself, was exactly what made him perfect for this job.

The only distinctive feature he'd ever had, bright red hair in his youth, had long since faded to a dull red and white mix, a result of years of stress and the duality of PPI life. Even his beard, hovering between goatee and full beard, was the same dull color. His appearance was the epitome of unremarkable, which was exactly how he liked it. Reed knew he needed a different approach to get Tammy's attention. So, he became an active listener, remembering the small things, her favorite coffee order, her sister's upcoming wedding, her childhood dream of being a concert pianist. He asked thoughtful questions about her photography, praised her artistry, and feigned interest in the technical aspects of her work. While other men might ogle her beauty, Reed made her feel seen and understood. He never mentioned Pro4uM unless she brought it up and carefully cultivated the image of someone more interested in her mind than her position. Every remembered detail and spontaneous gesture of kindness had been orchestrated but to Tammy it had all seemed genuine.

Tammy was precise, capable and dedicated to her work, but Reed had noticed she trusted easily. Early on he started building on that trust. He suspected Tammy was not a PPI agent; instead, she was likely another innocent pawn on the board, managing Pro4uM.com with a well-meaning diligence she thought was just for networking among photographers.

One evening as they had dinner, Tammy left her phone on the table and got up to go to the bathroom. Reed had been waiting for this moment. Over their past few dates, he'd been watching her unlock pattern, always the same four digits, 8-2-9-4, tapped out unconsciously whenever she checked her messages.

In that window of opportunity Reed acted. He entered the code and as he'd expected her phone's password manager had stored all her login credentials including her access to the Pro4uM admin panel. Within seconds he'd created a covert login under the bland alias "John Smith". Unremarkable, forgettable and camouflaged among thousands of other monitored accounts.

Reed had never used this account before, he'd saved it for a time when going undetected would mean the difference between staying hidden and being caught. Now was that time. He logged in as John Smith and scoured the hidden threads and encrypted channels of Pro4uM, knowing this was where PPI operatives and admins hid mission-critical info behind innocuous sounding photography discussions. Each post looked normal on the surface, titles like "Best Lighting for Portraits" or "Posing Tips for Professionals" but Reed had trained long enough with PPI to recognize certain phrasing, strange responses at odd hours and unusual terminology held a much deeper meaning.

As Reed clicked through the coded posts his gut tightened. Thread after thread subtle messages emerged, he hadn't noticed before, each one hidden in bland-sounding posts. So many pointed directly at him, posts scattered across the forum in such a way only an insider would recognize. In a thread on "Models" he found a series of cryptic phrases, each one tied to dates and times that eerily matched events in his current timeline. This was no coincidence. Each post left behind subtle breadcrumbs, a method he recognized as classic PPI misdirection meant to disguise info from anyone not trained to see it.

A familiar name caught Reed's eye: Barry Cox, known within PPI as "The Architect". An exceptional photographer from Tulsa, Cox ran his portrait studio with military precision. His knack for orchestrating complex ops and managing resources made him essential to the agency. He didn't just take photos, he built things: plans, networks, careers. And he made sure every outcome was perfect.

The more Reed thought about it, the clearer it was: Barry Cox was the architect of this whole web, pulling the strings that had ensnared Reed from the start.

The forum posts followed a familiar pattern, hiding in plain sight under threads any photographer would casually scroll past. But Reed recognized the outline of a hidden message, invisible to the untrained eye. It was classic PPI strategy: sensitive intel buried in plain view, accessible only to those trained to sift through the mundane to find the hidden.

One post stood out, a seemingly innocent tutorial on posing hands. But coming from Barry Cox a man who dealt in power plays not posing tips every word carried weight. The post's date matched the Kessler assignment. Reed decoded Barry's metaphors: 'thumbs back, fingers forward' meant keep calm and move slowly under surveillance; 'touch only at fingertips' meant minimal contact; 'if you lean on something lean on it, don't hug it' meant don't form attachments. The message was clear: stay isolated, trust no one, keep distance. Classic Barry, sensitive intel and buried directives in plain sight while preparing Reed for a solo mission.

But why take such care to isolate him? The answer hit Reed like a punch: Barry wasn't protecting him, he was setting him up.

Reed continued to dig through Pro4uM.com, sifting through

posts layered in double meanings. Another thread caught his eye: "Composition Tips for Event Photography". At first glance it seemed to cover the basics, how to get candid shots, manage lighting in large venues and other general advice for event photographers. But as Reed read further, he found a post from Barry Cox about a specific piece of equipment: the Kessler Crane.

The post started with a technical description of the Kessler Crane and how it allowed photographers to have smooth and precise movements and get the perfect vantage point for capturing large events. Cox had written, "A Kessler Crane lets you control every angle, keep the whole scene in front of you even when your subject moves. It's all about setting the right perspective while staying out of the picture yourself."

To an untrained eye it was just equipment advice, but Reed saw through the lines. The crane's purpose was clear: it allowed someone to direct focus without being in the frame. This was all part of a calculated op where someone high up was manipulating the angles, controlling the narrative and keeping their own involvement hidden.

Further down in the post Cox expanded, "For best results position yourself above the crowd where you can see everything, yet no one sees you. This vantage point gives you complete oversight without interference. The Kessler Crane is perfect for those times when you need to manage the scene without becoming part of it."

Reed shivered. The words matched his assignment. His role at Kessler's event wasn't about the photos at all, it was about creating a controlled environment where something else could happen. Reed was meant to be the Kessler Crane, controlling the angle, giving PPI the perfect cover for a covert op that couldn't be traced back to them. In the last line Cox had written: *"Sometimes it's not what you capture, but what you keep hidden that tells the real story."*

Reed couldn't keep up with the avalanche of thoughts as the pieces fell into place. PPI didn't need Kessler's event photographed. They didn't need Reed to pass a message. They needed him as a distraction, an expendable pawn while they facilitated an intel leak under the cover of diplomacy. And they'd done it all without him knowing it, casting him as the "crane" in their composition. If he was caught or killed PPI would brand him a traitor, their hands clean, their narrative airtight.

This wasn't a mission, it was a setup. And Cox or someone was pulling the strings.

But realization brought resolve. Reed's mission wasn't about objectives anymore, it was about exposure and survival. Now it was his chance to flip the script before the puppet master cut the final string.

Reed had an epiphany: if Barry had built such an elaborate web its structure could be turned against him. Pro4uM, once a liability, could now be used as a tool, a stage where Reed could rewrite the script.

Knowing he was being watched, Reed began to plant misinformation. He created ordinary looking posts on Pro4uM hiding coded hints that would only stand out to PPI operatives. Each post was bait: a mention of the "golden hour" near a Vienna landmark, a lighting setup for "urban shots". Casual photographers would see nothing; PPI would see breadcrumbs leading to a specific time and place.

He even mentioned the "Box Gallery" a supposed safe house tied to his cover. Everything pointed to controlled meeting points designed to pull Barry's attention to where Reed wanted him.

When he hit post he felt a sense of satisfaction. For the first time he didn't feel like a pawn being moved, he was a player playing the game. Every word every phrase was a thread in his own web giving him time and space to stay ahead.

The student had become the master.

Barry Cox had been more than a mentor. Reed had wanted to be him. He admired his mastery of light, his flawless execution of every scene, his tactical brilliance in the field. But now that admiration had turned. Every lesson, every shared secret, every earned bit of trust had been used against him. Barry had spent years training the perfect fall guy: someone skilled enough to be useful, loyal enough to follow orders, yet dumb enough to miss the trap until it was too late.

As the plane landed in Vienna Reed logged off and stowed his laptop. Stepping off the plane with practiced calm his movements were smooth, but his mind was moving ahead.

First step: get the weapon from Terminal 3. Then use everything Barry had taught him, every technique, every shadow game, to dismantle the trap piece by piece.

Barry had built a complex web. But he'd made one critical mistake: he'd taught Reed too well.

5

THE DARKROOM

Reed glided through the terminal wearing a cloak of calm, his heart thudding underneath. He'd tried to wipe his digital footprints from Pro4uM, but he knew better than to think he was completely invisible. Pro4uM's eyes were trained, and Barry, if Barry was behind this, had the resources and reach to catch him off guard.

Every stare from a security camera, every passing airport employee, or every wandering traveler could be another set of eyes on him. Reed's instincts were honed to a fine point.

He walked into Terminal 3 and made his way to the bathroom at the back, not looking over his shoulder too often, not breaking stride. He passed the row of stalls and headed to the last one at the back wall. He knew the spot by heart. Months ago, he had hidden the gun, wrapped in gaffer's tape and concealed in the compartment for extra tissue rolls.

Reed reached up into the compartment and felt nothing but smooth cold metal. His heart skipped, a sickening moment of doubt that made his pulse stutter. Then his fingers brushed the familiar bumps of the tape. Relieved, he pulled it back and felt the weight of the Walther PPK with the silencer. A gun designed for discretion, small enough to fit in his hand like a trusted friend. He slipped it into his camera bag, amidst his equipment.

Exiting the restroom at the same pace, Reed's thoughts turned to Secretary Kessler. Should he involve him? Kessler's public position made him a powerful asset, a guy who could be used to draw attention away from Reed. But the man could just as easily be another pawn in Barry's game, manipulated like everyone else, unaware of the dark undercurrents pulling the strings. Reed had to be careful; using Kessler as a decoy was tempting, but without knowing PPI's true intentions it was a gamble.

More questions than answers swirled in his head. His hand went to his pocket where he felt the card he'd been given on the plane: Box Galleries. A "safe house" in name but Reed knew better than to trust the promise of sanctuary from an organization that had seemingly brought him down. Box Galleries was on the edge of Vienna's old town, a warren of cobblestone streets and ancient buildings. It presented itself as a high-end art space, but Reed knew it for what it was, an artifice, a place where PPI operatives met, where secrets were as carefully curated as the photographs on the walls. It was Reed's next move, his chance to get answers.

Approaching Box Galleries, he felt that familiar unease. It was like stepping into a shadow of David Tompkins Fine Art Photography back in New Orleans, a gallery deep in the French Quarter, draped in the same quiet, too-perfect stillness. No curious tourists, no patrons browsing the photographs on the walls, just one person at a desk in the back, barely looking up as he entered.

He couldn't shake the comparison. In New Orleans, David Tompkins Fine Art Photography was an open secret, a place everyone knew was a front for the mob. Not a single photograph ever left those walls, yet every day the gallery logged huge cash deposits, hundreds of thousands, all in cash, through the books without a single sale. Photography as cover, art as a shield for something far darker.

Box Galleries felt the same, culture as a mask for its true purpose. This was no ordinary safe house. Every detail, the perfectly arranged prints, the minimalist decor, the silence, seemed to be carefully crafted to lull, to mislead.

The air was scented with varnished wood and archival paper, an odd comfort to Reed but also a reminder of the carefully constructed illusion.

Reed's eyes swept the young woman behind the desk, taking in her relaxed posture and her absent expression as she scrolled through her phone. Early twenties, brown hair, black blouse and jeans. No obvious signs of covert work. But he couldn't be sure. Sometimes the most invisible people were the most trained. He'd have to test her to see how aware she was. Reed ambled over to a large black-and-white photograph of a wharf, framed in a minimalist border. Another cliché, every fine art photography gallery seemed to have one. He leaned in close, studying the image, and adjusted his stance as if examining some hidden detail.

He glanced over his shoulder to see if she noticed. Nothing. She looked up, met his gaze for a beat, then went back to her phone.

Time to try another approach. Reed turned to her, smiling. "Do you know the story behind this one?" he asked, his voice smooth with a hint of curiosity.

She looked up, surprised, then shrugged. "Not really. I think it's supposed to be solitude or something. Lots of people say it's peaceful?"

Reed nodded thoughtfully, showing a glimmer of interest. "Interesting. I thought it might be one of Tompkins' originals. You don't see many of those around here."

The name-drop was intentional, a way to gauge her reaction to a high-profile art connection back in New Orleans, an art dealer everyone in Reed's circle knew was mob-connected. If she had any PPI experience, even peripherally, it might trigger a flicker of recognition.

But she just smiled politely. "Tompkins? No, we don't carry his work. Mostly local artists here."

Reed nodded slowly, maintaining the innocent tone. "Local talent. That's nice. So, do you get many private viewings? Special showings in the back?"

She hesitated, looked unsure, then nodded. "Yeah, sometimes. If a client is interested in something specific, we, uh, take them back there."

Her wording was hesitant, confirming she wasn't in the know about PPI's operations. This was just a job to her, the same as working at a coffee shop or boutique. She probably didn't even know why the gallery had a private back room. Reed let the conversation die, nodded thanks, and moved back to the wharf photograph. Now he had a better sense of the woman's role, he felt the tension ease in his shoulders. She was no operative, no hidden threat. Just a minimum-wage employee who let certain people into the back when they asked the right way.

For a moment he felt a pang of sympathy for her, trapped in this strange world without knowing it. But that passed as he focused on his goal. With his cover secure, he looked back at her. "How much for this one?"

She answered almost mechanically, as if reciting a line. "$210 thousand."

That was the phrase Reed had been waiting for. He took a breath and delivered the rehearsed response, the one that meant nothing to a casual visitor: "The tonalities remind me of *Le Violon d'Ingres* by Man Ray, and it sold for 12.4 million. Do you have something like that, something a little more exclusive... something in the back?"

The woman blinked, her expression changed, and for the first time, her gaze sharpened. She looked him over with a glimmer of recognition, or perhaps just awareness, flickering in her eyes. Without a word, she slid a keycard across the desk. "Room 5... it's locked," she murmured, almost as if testing him. Her eyes held a hint of challenge as she added, "But I bet you already knew that..."

Reed smiled slightly, pocketed the keycard and nodded. She didn't seem surprised, but there was an edge to her calm now, as if the mention of Man Ray and the back room had flipped a switch. He took his cue and headed back. She didn't look up.

As Reed made his way down the narrow, dimly lit corridor to Room 5, the air was thick with the scent of old wood and faint metal.

The soft lighting cast a warm glow over polished wood floors and carefully placed art. He knew from experience every detail was calculated, down to the art-gallery lighting, which kept faces in soft shadow and identities ambiguous. Standard PPI procedure dictated Room 5 would have all the camera gear he'd need for his current job. Lenses, stabilizers, lighting setups, everything he'd need, or so it seemed. But Reed also knew this setup came with strings attached. Any gear in Room 5 would be rigged with tracking devices to monitor his every move under the guise of support. At this stage, he couldn't use any of that equipment. He'd have to come up with a work around.

The gallery's backroom layout interested him. He'd only been cleared for Rooms 4, 5, and 6. Each room was purposefully designed. Room 4 was storage and prep, always stocked with basic gear and disposables he could use and leave behind. Room 5 had mission-specific gear. Room 6 was the strategy hub where agents would gather for briefings and review intel.

But Rooms 1 through 3 had always been off-limits. Reserved for higher-ranking operatives or special assignments. Their contents were a mystery. Reed had never questioned them before, but now, with the full weight of the setup against him, he found himself drawn to the secrets they might hold.

As he approached Room 3, his mind spun. The message from the plane had come through an unusual channel: *Reed, we need to talk. Now.* This wasn't PPI's style, nor was it Barry's. PPI communicated exclusively through coded *Pro4uM* channels. A deviation like this couldn't be ignored. Then there was the message that had saved him before: *Section 3, Page 16, Code 105-B.*

Could it be that simple?

He felt a rush of adrenaline as he punched in 1-6-1-0-5. The hallway fell silent as the door to Room 3 creaked open, a sign of the unknown ally who had risked everything to send that code. As the door swung open, Reed's heart beat faster. He had no idea what he'd find behind this door, but he was certain it wouldn't be protocol. Inside, the room was different from the other back rooms he'd seen on previous assignments. Unlike Rooms 4 through 6, which had the functional setup of equipment storage and briefing spaces, Room 3 had a more private, detailed design. The walls were lined with file cabinets, sleek and built into the room itself, each drawer labeled only by numbers and dates. A large central table was empty except for a dim reading lamp and a stack of old-fashioned notepads. Reed noticed how it differed from the high-tech gear in other safehouses, as if Room 3 served a unique and more confidential purpose.

He stepped inside, his eyes scanning the room. A framed photograph hung on the wall, the kind of scenic shot that would belong in a gallery. But to Reed, the scene looked all too familiar. It was a landmark in Vienna, a location he'd been briefed on during another mission, a sign that this room was designed for those with inside knowledge. Was this a strategy room for high-level operatives? Or a private vault of some kind?

The realization hit him that whatever secrets PPI kept in Rooms 1 through 3, they were for top-tier agents, like Barry Cox. Reed wasn't authorized to be here.

He steeled himself and approached the file cabinets. Opening one carefully, he found files marked with dates and mission codenames, info that if uncovered by anyone outside PPI would destroy years of covert operations. He realized this room held more than intelligence. It held leverage and information that could expose PPI's inner workings.

He reached for a folder with a familiar codename, one tied to his current mission. As he flipped through the contents, a cold fear crept into his chest. This wasn't just a dossier on Secretary Kessler; it was a meticulously designed plan to discredit the operative. Strategically timed leaks, fabricated cover stories, carefully chosen scapegoats; it was all there, laid out with precision.

And Reed was the main subject.

The documents painted a picture: Barry Cox's fingerprints were all over every decision, every thread of the operation. His control was so fine-tuned it was like a photographer adjusting a shot, every detail framed to tell one story. Reed wasn't surprised. Barry's "composition" was far more meticulous than he could have ever imagined. But one thing cut deeper. In the margin of a page, written in ink, were the words: *"Remove Kessler. Frame Sawyer. No loose ends."* Below it, a signature, sharp, deliberate, and unmistakable: *Barry Cox, Director PPI.*

Reed froze. He wasn't an agent on assignment, he was bait. A carefully placed pawn to take the fall if things went sideways.

A cold knot of adrenaline tightened in his stomach as he read the note again. Each word seared into his brain. Every mission Barry had given him over the years, every piece of guidance and advice, in hindsight, it all added up to something sinister. Had every assignment been a stepping stone to this moment? Was every nod of approval, every piece of advice, just another thread in the noose Barry was tightening around his neck?

Reed's jaw clenched as the weight of the betrayal hit him. This wasn't just professional, it was personal. The cold precision of Barry's plan, combined with the intimacy of years of grooming Reed for this role, hurt more than any operational betrayal ever could. And now the truth was in his hands, written in Barry's own handwriting.

He strained to keep the anger from boiling over. Barry might have framed the shot, but Reed wasn't going to let him finish the story. Whatever advantage PPI thought they had; Reed now had a piece of leverage. Whoever had helped him had known more than they were letting on, guiding him here with the knowledge this file would change everything.

He turned on the reading light, angling it to capture the pages.

With practiced efficiency, he lifted his camera and took photos of each page, making sure every word, name and code was captured. Shadows danced as he moved the light, revealing more of the room.

Reed set up his camera's Wi-Fi, transmitting the files to his computer. While the files transmitted, he glanced around the room, his eye caught on a description on the bottom of the filing cabinet. "Lyt Meeter." He knew the misspelling wasn't a mistake. It was a signal or misdirection; a clue for those who would know what it meant.

He got up and opened the drawer. Inside, a neatly organized space held ten slots, each one exactly the same size as a light meter. Nine of them were empty. The tenth held a single device, its sleek casing bearing faint scratches as if it had been handled many times. Reed picked it up and turned it over in his hand. This wasn't a light meter; it had a code generator with a secure cellular link, hardwired to Pro4uM's private channels. He realized this was a direct line to the organization, disguised as photography equipment.

But he couldn't take it, not without raising alarms. A new plan formed in his mind: the equipment in Room 5. Standard PPI protocol meant his next instructions would be there, along with a set of supplies for his mission. He could swap this device with the standard light meter in that room, and no one would ever know. Satisfied, Reed put the folder back where he found it.

Exiting Room 3, Reed felt a new sense of purpose. He wasn't just on the run anymore; he was armed with the truth that could blow PPI's corruption wide open. And as he headed for Room 5, he knew exactly where he was going.

In Room 5, Reed saw the fully loaded dolly with camera gear, right on protocol, neatly arranged as if to give him everything he needed for the assignment. If he left the equipment behind, someone would notice and wonder. He had to take it with him, no matter the risk.

He moved through the equipment with deliberate slowness, his hands casually inspecting each item. Among the neatly stacked gear, his fingers brushed against something familiar, the standard light meter. Under a stack of lenses, he felt the usual tool everyone expected, perfect for the swap. He wheeled the dolly out of Room 5 and past Room 3, glancing back to make sure he was alone. In one swift motion, he placed the light meter in the drawer and swapped the "Lyt Meeter" into his camera bag. The weight of the device in his bag felt heavier than the original, a reminder of the stakes.

Now armed with the "Lyt Meeter", Reed felt the weight of its importance. This was no ordinary device; it was a tool that could blow everything wide open if used correctly. But he knew it was as dangerous as it was valuable. One misstep, one wrong move and it would show his hand as clearly as if he'd set off an alarm. As he continued down the hall, Reed's mind spun with the possibilities, and risks, of having PPI's secrets in his hand.

Reed took a deep breath, quickly assessing his options. Standard protocol was to exit through the side door where a car would be waiting to whisk him to a hotel, no doubt bugged and monitored. But because he was an hour ahead thanks to the Bratislava diversion, the car service wouldn't be there yet. He had a window of opportunity.

As he wheeled the dolly forward, Reed's thoughts raced. The dolly creaked under the weight of the gear, cameras, lighting, and lenses, all PPI-issued and no doubt bugged. Every piece of equipment felt like a shackle, binding him to the mission, to their control.

And then it hit him, like a bolt of inspiration. Photography rental shops. Neutral ground. A place where gear came and went, no questions asked. Reed smiled at the simplicity of the idea: swap out his PPI gear for clean, untraceable rentals. The move would sever the surveillance without raising an alarm.

He pulled out his phone and searched for the nearest rental agency. Top result: *Lenscape Photography Rentals*. Reed tapped the address without hesitation, his instinct telling him this was the way to go. A quick ride share later, he was on his way.

As the ride share van wove through the congestion of downtown

Vienna, the midday traffic crawled. A drop of sweat rolled down his neck as he remembered the code generator in his bag at Box Galleries. The persistent code, *Section: 3. Page: 16. Code: 105-B*, had haunted him like a ghost, each time revealing more of PPI's nasty plan. Maybe now the code was once again the key to flipping their strategy. He pulled out the generator and typed the letters and numbers, *S3P16C105B*, he watched as the screen flickered to life, its circuits spinning before a line of text appeared. The name 'Barry Cox' appeared in a bold, unmistakable font.

Then the words read like an execution order: *"Sawyer must die. PPI will be clean. Operatives in place. Plans in motion. Kessler is the disguise. P4M code 'Chubby Senior.'"*

Reed's hands shook as he read each line, his brain ticking fast to keep up with the brutal clarity of the plan. This wasn't just a setup; it was a takedown. Kessler was just a smokescreen, a "disguise" for PPI's real goal. They'd created a perfect cover to make Reed a turn-coat, a threat to international security, a ticking time bomb to the public. By discrediting him as a traitor, PPI could protect its own dirty secrets, sever ties with Reed in a way that left no room for his survival or his reputation.

The van felt claustrophobic, the air thick. The walls closed in, the weight of betrayal crushing him down. He'd known he was a pawn, but now he saw the full extent of the game, and the depravity behind it. His fingers clenched on the code generator as his resolve hardened. If they thought he'd go down quietly, they were wrong.

He could disappear, slip off the grid and let PPI claim victory, live the rest of his days as a ghost, always on the run, always looking over his shoulder.

But the idea turned his stomach. Running was surrender, acceptance of the fate they'd written for him. And Reed Sawyer had never been one to let others write his story. He felt a fierce determination rise up in him. PPI had trained him well, and now he would use every trick they'd ever taught him to unravel the system that had brought him down.

He didn't hesitate. He would take back his story, use every piece of information, every skill, every contact he'd made along the way.

As the van pulled up to Lenscape Photography Rentals, Reed's heart rate slowed. He'd made his decision. He would set the trap, lure them in and expose the web they had spun for him. He wasn't just in this to live anymore, he was in it to win.

6

THE LENS

Reed got out of the rideshare van and took a look around. Lenscape Photography Rentals was tucked away in a quiet neighborhood, far from the touristy part of Vienna. The shop's exterior was as unassuming as the row of small businesses lining the street, a bakery, a shoe repair shop, and a bookstore with dusty window displays.

The neighborhood felt lived-in, the cobblestone streets dappled with afternoon sun through the branches of the tightly packed trees. It was the kind of place locals went to, where conversations lingered and the occasional cyclist zoomed by. There was a sense of calm in the air, stark contrast to the overexposed chaos of his own thoughts.

Lenscape was a single-story building, the front modest but clean. A large display window showed off a curated selection of cameras and lenses, their shiny surfaces positioned to catch the light. The shop's name was painted in clean sans-serif letters on the glass door, with the slogan: *Focus Where It Counts*.

Reed scanned the street again, his instincts on high alert. Nothing out of place, no idling cars, no lurking figures in trench coats, no glint of surveillance lenses. But experience had taught him danger often hid in the ordinary.

Reed opened the door to Lenscape Photography Rentals and the soft chime above went off. He looked up at the logo etched into the glass panel beside the entrance. A clean circle, the PPI logo with its seven-bladed aperture. Seven blades. The mark of legitimacy, the symbol for PPI's surface-level operations that dealt with photographers and their craft.

This was different from the logo at Box Galleries. But the difference was as distinct as night and day for those who knew. Six blades meant covert ops, the underworld of PPI's world where intelligence, espionage and danger lived. The subtlety of the distinction was genius, invisible to outsiders but glaringly obvious to insiders trained to see it. Reed liked it for what it was, a clever signal to separate the hunters from the prey.

But seven blades on the door didn't necessarily mean Lenscape was safe. He'd learned long ago not to take anything at face value. He stepped inside, moving slow and deliberate, every nerve on high alert as the door closed behind him. The interior was bright and functional, the kind of place that put photographers at ease. Rows of shelves lined the walls, stocked with lenses, tripods, and lighting kits. A faint smell of plastic and metal hung in the air, mixed with the hum of a nearby printer. Behind the counter, a young man looked up briefly before going back to his computer. It was all so ordinary, so boring, but Reed's instincts were still ticking.

He scanned the space, making mental notes of the exits, the security cameras and the rental equipment. On the far wall, a sleek sign hung with the company's name and slogan: *Lenscape Photography Rentals, Focus Where It Counts.* The tagline felt weirdly normal. He hoped the shop was exactly what it seemed, a legitimate photography rental store and nothing more.

He needed clean equipment, gear without bugs, tracking devices, or hidden microphones. The equipment from Box Galleries sat like dead weight in their cases, every piece a tool of surveillance. He had to ditch them before his next move.

Reed approached the counter, his camera bag slung over his

shoulder. The young man looked up again, his polite but distracted smile giving nothing away. "Need some help?"

"Yeah," Reed said. "I need a full lighting setup for a high-profile shoot. Reflectors, softboxes, stands, the works, stills, video, and audio. And a couple of lenses for wide-angle and close-up shots. Something reliable."

The young man nodded, his fingers already typing into the computer. "We've got you covered. Any specific brands or models in mind?"

"Not picky," Reed said, faking nonchalance. "Just need it to handle a fast shoot."

The man typed a few keys on the keyboard, his eyes flicking between the screen and Reed. A moment later, the printer behind the counter went off, spitting out a neatly formatted list of equipment. He grabbed the paper, scanned it quickly before handing it to Reed. "Here's what we have. If anything catches your eye, let me know and I'll pull it from the back." Reed looked at the list, nodded thoughtfully and met the man's gaze with a smile. "Great. I'd rather take a look at the equipment first if that's okay, save you the trouble of pulling it out and putting it back if it's not what I'm looking for. Can we head back and take a look?"

The man nodded, folded the paper and set it aside. "Sure, this way," he said, gesturing for Reed to follow him.

As Reed trailed behind, weaving through the narrow aisles of neatly arranged gear, his mind raced. Was this place really as normal as it seemed? The 7-blade logo suggested legitimacy, but PPI's reach had taught him that appearances were often carefully constructed lies.

As the clerk pulled items from the shelves, each one felt like a step further away from PPI's surveillance, a step towards reclaiming some control. Just as Reed was about to look at a lens, the bell above the front door went off.

The clerk looked up and set down the lens cap he was holding.

"This will only take a minute," he said with a smile, brushing his hands on his apron. "I'll let them know I'll be with them shortly."

Reed nodded, forcing his face to remain neutral as a shiver ran down his spine. He kept his hands steady, focused on the lens in his hand as the clerk walked towards the front.

"Can you give me five minutes?" the clerk asked.

"No problem," the other man replied. "We're not in a hurry."

Reed froze. His breath caught and the lens slipped in his hand. That voice. He hadn't seen the man, but he knew the tone, the inflection of it. His heart kicked hard in his chest as he tensed, peering cautiously from behind the shelves.

Through the gap between two cases, he saw them. 16B, leaning against the counter, and the flight attendant beside him. Both were dressed in plainclothes, jeans, neutral jackets, but their presence in the shop made Reed's alarm bells go off. What were they doing here? Coincidence was a concept he no longer believed in, not after everything that had happened. If they had followed him to this quiet shop, then his plans were coming apart faster than he'd thought.

Reed crouched behind the shelf, muscles tense, his mind calculating. Could PPI have orchestrated this? His rational side rejected the idea. He'd had at least an hour's head start, even counting the slow ride-share and traffic jam. And Lenscape wasn't a place you stumbled upon by accident.

Reed forced himself to focus, to clear his head of paranoia. If this was intentional, there would have been breadcrumbs leading here and he would have seen them.

But there weren't. No whispers on Pro4uM, no coded messages. That left only one conclusion: coincidence. A genuine, unscripted event.

Reed exhaled slowly, his tension easing just enough for clarity to kick in. A PPI unplanned encounter. If it wasn't part of their plan, then it could be used. Advantage Reed.

He crept closer to the front counter, positioning himself behind a stack of equipment cases. From here he could see 16B leaning against the counter while the flight attendant examined a display case full of filters and adapters. Their body language gave away nothing, but their conversation was another story.

"...just doesn't add up," 16B said, his voice low and agitated. "We're given one set of orders, then halfway through it's like the whole mission flips. And now we're here with nothing but a vague directive and no target?"

The flight attendant shook his head, his hands on his hips. "I know. They've always been tight-lipped, but this feels different. Like we're not supposed to know what's happening. Almost like we're being tested."

Reed's heart was quickening. A test? They were as confused as he was, which confirmed what he'd thought since Bratislava: even operatives like them weren't in the loop.

"Do you think it's Sawyer?" the flight attendant asked. His tone was cautious, as if saying the name itself was a risk.

16B's jaw clenched, his face darkening. "If it is, they're playing us. Either he's rogue or they're setting him up as one. Either way, we're the ones on the block not him."

The frustration in their voices, the underlying distrust, said it all. They were just as lost as he was. PPI's maze was targeting not just him but them too.

He could feel the gears turning in his head, recalibrating. If they were confused, doubting their orders, then they weren't the threat he thought. They might even be allies, caught in the same web of deceit.

Reed's heart pounded in his chest as he listened more. The words between 16B and the flight attendant had already shifted the narrative in his head, but he needed more. A single phrase, a slip of truth, to confirm they weren't part of the setup to frame him.

The flight attendant sighed in frustration, crossing his arms. "I'm telling you, something's not right at the top. I've seen how PPI handles rogue agents and this isn't it. They're using us to clean up a mess they don't want traced back to them."

16B growled. "And what if Sawyer isn't rogue? What if they've set him up because he knows too much? You've seen Barry's playbook. He always works an angle, always finds someone to pin it on when the heat is on."

The flight attendant shook his head. "Then we're all expendable, aren't we? If this goes south, we'll be tied to it, just like Sawyer. They're burning the bridges and we're standing on one."

16B looked around, lowering his voice further, but Reed caught the words: "If I thought for one second that Sawyer wasn't what they're making him out to be I'd back him. Heck, he's one of the best operatives they've got. But we don't even know where he is or if we can reach him before it's too late."

That was it. They were questioning everything, doubting the very orders they'd been given. They weren't on Barry's payroll; they were as lost as he was. In their confusion, Reed saw opportunity. Reed pressed himself against the shelf, he ran scenarios. Should he approach them now? If they could be swayed, if they could trust him, then for the first time since this craziness began, he wouldn't be alone.

Reed took a deep breath and stepped out from behind the shelves, moving slow and deliberate. His voice, low and firm, broke the silence. "Start gathering that equipment. I'll take it all."

His gaze snapped to the two men standing nearby. "Seems like PPI's got us all working different angles. Or maybe... just one."

Both men spun around, their eyes wide with surprise. As Carter, the flight attendant, reached for his jacket, a reflex learned from training, Reed raised his hands slightly, palms out. "Easy. If I wanted a fight, you wouldn't have seen me coming."

16B narrowed his eyes, his body tense. "Sawyer?" he muttered, his voice low and full of suspicion. But something in Reed's calm demeanor made him hesitate. "How in the world..."

"Does it matter?" Reed cut in, his tone steady. "We're here now. And by the look on your faces, you have as many questions as I do."

Carter exchanged a wary glance with 16B then stepped back.

"You're not... running?" he asked, his tone a mix of confusion and grudging respect. "After that move at the airport I would've bet my life, you were bailing. That was genius."

"I could ask you the same thing," Reed said. He gestured towards the front of the shop. "But we're wasting time standing here. Either we figure this out together or we keep walking into Barry's trap."

The mention of Barry's name made both men flinch. That was the crack Reed needed. He moved closer, his gaze steady. "I know enough to know we're all being played. And I think you do too."

For a long, tense moment no one spoke. Then 16B nodded, a small but telling movement. "Let's talk," he said, his voice losing some of its edge.

Carter looked towards the front of the store. "Five minutes tops. That clerk will be coming back." He turned to Carter and 16B. "More than enough time. Start talking. What's your role in this?"

16B's jaw clenched, his words sharp and precise. "Protection detail. My assignment was to follow you, no contact, no interference. Orders were to step in only if your life was in danger. Beyond that I was left in the dark." He paused, his gaze steady. "I broke protocol when I gave you that safe house card. I was hoping you'd realize we're on the same side."

Reed frowned. "Protection from what?"

16B laughed, a humorless sound. "That's the million-dollar question, isn't it? PPI doesn't give details. Just orders."

Carter crossed his arms, his brow furrowed. "My orders were different. They told me to watch you for... suspicious behavior." He looked at Reed, the weight of his words hanging in the air. "I thought you'd gone rogue."

Reed's stomach churned but he kept his face neutral. "And now?"

"Now?" Carter's voice was laced with frustration. "Now none of it makes sense."

Reed let their words hang in the air, each piece falling into place like shards of a broken mirror. PPI wasn't a network of support, it was a machine of manipulation, one that thrived on isolating its operatives, keeping them uncertain and expendable.

"Barry's not just pulling strings," Reed said finally, his tone deliberate, his words cutting through the tension. "He's orchestrating something bigger, something designed to keep us in the dark while he tightens the noose. This isn't about Kessler or the assignments they've given us. It's about power, control. And if we don't figure out how to break that hold, we're not leaving this alive."

16B's jaw clenched again, a flicker of understanding crossing his face. He didn't speak but the subtle shift in his stance said it all. Carter exhaled sharply, shaking his head before nodding. "Alright," he said, his voice tinged with frustration. "But what's your play, Sawyer? Because right now it feels like we're still chasing shadows."

Reed turned, his eyes scanning the shelves as if the answer might be hidden among the rows of gear. "We move like nothing's wrong," he said, "I finish the gear run, and you two keep watching me. PPI, Barry, whoever, they only see us sticking to protocol, doing our jobs. Whatever Barry's building, it's got cracks in the foundation. We find them and we bring the whole thing down."

16B crossed his arms, his brow furrowed. "You're talking about taking on PPI's golden boy. You know how that ends, don't you?"

With a sharp edge of defiance in his voice, Reed replied. "This only ends one way, together. Barry's long game isn't perfect. He's meticulous, sure, but he's not untouchable. He's counting on us to follow orders, to play by his rules. But if we pool what we know we'll find the thread that unravels everything. And when we do we expose him for what he really is."

For a moment the weight of Reed's words hung in the air, unspoken questions passing between them. Then 16B nodded, his reluctance replaced with determination. Carter hesitated a second longer before adding his own quiet agreement.

"Alright," Carter said, his voice steady. "We follow the thread. But we'd better move fast, because if Barry finds out we're working together he'll cut us loose before we have the chance."

Reed held his gaze, his face resolute. "Which is why we don't rush. Two objectives: first, gather irrefutable evidence, something that ties Barry Cox directly to this setup. Second, ensure Secretary Kessler's safety. Whatever Cox is planning we can't let it play out. If Kessler's the pawn, then he's also the key."

"Alright," 16B said, his voice short. "How? What's the play?"

Reed's eyes moved to the back of the shop, scanning the rows of shelves and cases filled with gear. "We use what's here," he said, his voice measured but sure. "Cameras, lighting rigs, audio setups, they're more than tools for a shoot. We turn them into instruments of evidence. Every shot, every mic, every setup, they'll all work for us. And for Kessler." Carter glanced again at the door, his unease clear. "And the shoot itself?" he asked. "You're going to use it as a staging ground?"

"Exactly," Reed said. "It's our best shot. If we set this up right, we can expose the Architect's hand before he knows we've flipped the script."

Before Carter could respond, the soft sound of wheels on tile announced the store clerk's return. A dolly stacked with gear rolled into view, the clerk's eyes flicking between the three men with mild curiosity. "Everything you asked for," he said, his voice polite but with a hint of skepticism.

Reed stepped forward, his face blank. "Perfect. Let's get started."

As the clerk began checking the inventory Reed adopted a casual tone. "Quick question," he said. "Who handles buying equipment around here? I have a few items I want to move."

The clerk paused, tapping the counter with his pen. "That's my boss. He's not in though, he won't be back until next week."

Reed smiled politely, his mind already working two steps ahead. "No problem. Can I leave the gear here with you? Once he's back you can contact me for an estimate."

The clerk hesitated, his brows furrowing as he considered the request. Then he shrugged. "Yeah, I can do that."

"Great," Reed said, nodding toward the gear. "Let's get another dolly."

The clerk nodded and disappeared into the back. Moments later he returned with another dolly. Together Reed and the clerk began moving the gear from Box Galleries onto the dolly. Cameras, cases, everything, all neatly stacked onto the dolly as if they were just buying new equipment.

Each item added to the pile felt like shedding a layer of surveillance, a silent unwinding of PPI's grip. Finally, the clerk wheeled the loaded dolly into the storage area, none the wiser to what he was taking away.

Reed turned to 16B and Carter, his mouth twitching into a small smile. "If they're trying to track me or listen in all they'll get is silence now."

Carter chuckled low in his throat, his unease easing. "Good move."

"Necessary," Reed said, his voice sharp. "This has to be perfect. No mistakes, no oversights. The Architect's meticulous but we're going to have to be better."

The three men looked at each other, a silent understanding forming. Trust wasn't there, but need had created something stronger, an unspoken agreement.

Manipulated as they had been, their individual skills and fragmented knowledge were now tools to dismantle PPI's web of deceit.

Reed moved forward, his presence commanding yet calm. "Here's how this works," he said, gesturing to the gear. "Every piece serves double duty. Cameras, lighting rigs, they're not just for the Secretary's shoot. They're our surveillance, our evidence. If Cox is involved these will catch him."

"Every lens, every angle, they're witnesses. If there's something we're not supposed to see, we'll get it."

16B leaned against a nearby shelf. "And the Secretary? If this blows up he's the one in the crosshairs."

Reed answered, unshakeable. "Then we make sure it doesn't

blow up. The photo shoot isn't just a setup, it's our safety net. What-ever Cox has planned it stops with us. The Secretary stays alive. That's non-negotiable."

The room was silent as his words hung in the air, binding them together with an unspoken agreement. Their fractured alliance now had direction, a purpose stronger than the distrust between them.

They turned to the shelves, poring over the rental agency's inventory with precision. Cameras, lenses, tripods, every piece of gear was scrutinized for its surveillance potential. Reed's expertise proved invaluable as he flagged items that could be modified for surveillance or intel gathering. Each selection was a small win, a tangible step towards unraveling Cox's control.

The quiet work had an unspoken understanding. Together they were up against a force that had manipulated every move they made, spinning lies and half-truths to keep them in the dark. But now, with each calculated decision, they were clawing back control.

Reed looked up, a small smile on his face. "Well, I suppose it's time we got to know each other. You know me, but who are you?" 16B straightened, his posture deliberate and offered a firm hand. "Keith Kranch," he said, his voice dry. "Freelance muscle, occasional babysitter for rogue photographers, and apparently, the guy who needs a crash course in spotting setups."

Carter chuckled, the sound releasing the tension in the air. "Craig Carter," he said, bowing low with a flourish. "Photographer, jack of all trades, master of none, but I make it look good. Here to help, or so I tell myself."

Reed nodded. "Nice to meet you both. Now, what brings you here? A rental shop, of all places?"

Kranch shrugged, gesturing to the shelves of gear. "Blew out a softbox on my last job. Thought I could get a good deal on a used one here."

Carter jumped in, a grin on his lips. "Needed a polarizer for this outdoor shoot, some 'artsy' nonsense. Figured I might as well pick up some good glass while I'm at it. After what you did at Bratislava

Airport, we knew we had to get to Vienna fast. So, we hopped on a train, thinking that's what you'd do. Found this place after a quick Google search, first photography shop on the list. And, surprise, you're here."

Reed raised an eyebrow, his mind working as he processed their answers. Coincidence? Blind luck? Or the invisible threads they couldn't see yet? Whatever the reason, here they were, the three of them, in a rental shop, of all places, with just enough common ground to start fighting back.

Reed stepped back, his eyes scanning the gear. "This is it. The tools we need to turn their game against them."

"Let's hope we're better players," Carter said, with a small smile.

Kranch cracked his knuckles. "We'd better be. There's no second chance here."

Reed leaned against the counter, his tone light but inquiring. "So how did you two get into this business?"

Kranch grinned. "Logistics turned into something... bigger. Let's just say PPI knows how to find people with 'hidden potential.'"

Carter shrugged. "Same here. They start you out in photography, probably like you, then show you what's underneath, the espionage, the surveillance. It's all layers of secrets, wrapped up in a camera strap."

Reed nodded, his smile fading. "And Barry Cox is at the center of it all, pulling every string."

They finalized their plan quickly and called a rideshare van to take them to the hotel where Secretary Kessler's photo shoot was scheduled. The location would be crawling with surveillance, bugged rooms, hidden cameras and layers of covert operatives. This wasn't paranoia; it was protocol. To avoid suspicion, they would have to arrive separately, staggered in time, each staying in character. Reed knew the drill well, it was standard PPI tradecraft: blend in but keep all connections invisible.

As the van pulled away from Lenscape Photography Rentals, Reed looked back at the small storefront. The irony struck him: this unassuming place, found by accident, was the key to his mission. PPI's carefully laid plans hadn't accounted for this moment, this alliance.

They'd been manipulating every move, every pawn for years. But this unplanned turn, this little bit of unpredictability, was something PPI hadn't seen coming. Reed was going to make it count.

As Vienna's city lights rose up ahead, Reed fingered the Lyt Meeter in his pocket. The road ahead would be rough, the fight brutal. But he wasn't running anymore. He was setting himself up for the takedown of a lifetime.

7

THE SETUP

The hum of the rideshare van filled the silence as Reed, Carter, and Kranch sat in tense quiet, their thoughts as heavy as the Vienna skyline slipping past the windows. Protocol dictated that they keep their cards close, stick to their roles, and avoid unnecessary communication. PPI thrived on isolation, operatives compartmentalized, missions fragmented. Trust wasn't just discouraged; it was dangerous.

Reed's gaze settled on the glowing screen of his computer as he logged into Pro4uM.com. The interface was sterile and efficient, every icon and message a cog in the invisible machinery driving PPI's operations. He entered the codes he'd obtained from Box Gallery, each keystroke deliberate. His assignment details appeared, unchanged: photograph Secretary Kessler, maintain cover, await the delivery of special codes for the Secretary, and above all, avoid complications.

Beside him, Carter's fingers danced over his own screen, his brow furrowing as he scrolled through his directives. On the surface, everything looked routine, but something gnawed at him, a feeling Reed could sense but didn't comment on. Kranch sat in the far corner, reviewing his orders. Each man worked in silence, connected by the invisible thread of protocol yet divided by the barriers PPI had carefully constructed.

Suddenly Carter's screen pinged, a notification. He frowned, tilting the device closer. A cryptic update glowed against the dim light: *"Realign objectives to accommodate operational flexibility."* The phrasing was vague, open-ended in a way that sent a ripple of unease down his spine. PPI's instructions were rarely this ambiguous.

"What in the world does that mean?" Carter muttered under his breath, forgetting himself for a moment.

Reed glanced up sharply, catching the words. "Something wrong?"

Carter hesitated. Protocol said to keep quiet. Sharing updates, especially out of turn, was a breach that could cost more than just trust; it could trigger consequences from above. But the weight of the message made him decide otherwise. He turned the screen toward Reed and Kranch. "I just got this," he said. "Tell me that doesn't feel off."

Reed leaned closer, his expression darkening as he read the words. Kranch followed suit, his lips pressing into a thin line. "Realign objectives?" Kranch repeated. "That's... not exactly standard."

"No, it's not," Reed said quietly. His mind churned, dissecting the words. PPI didn't make allowances for 'flexibility.' Every step, every move, was calculated. This update wasn't just odd; it was unsettling. It hinted at something shifting in the shadows, something even they weren't meant to understand.

Carter leaned back, his voice quieter now. "I don't like it. It feels like... a setup."

Reed exchanged a glance with Kranch. The unspoken tension between them cracked slightly as they recognized a shared doubt. Carter breaking protocol to share the message wasn't just a risk; it was a step toward something unexpected, trust.

"We need to figure out what this means," Reed said. His voice was steady, but the edge in his tone betrayed the storm building beneath. "Because if PPI's changing the rules, it's not in our favor."

Reed waited until Carter and Kranch were fully engrossed in their Pro4uM tasks, the soft glow of their screens casting faint shadows over their focused faces. Quietly, he retrieved the Lyt Meeter, keeping his movements slow and deliberate. He didn't need their questions right now, not yet.

The cryptic update Carter had received earlier, *"Realigning objectives to accommodate operational flexibility,"* gnawed at the back of Reed's mind. After he keyed the phrase into the device with steady fingers, he could feel the vibration of its processor. For a long moment, the Lyt Meeter seemed to hesitate, as if weighing the information. Then it flashed a response, its simplicity more chilling than Reed had anticipated:

"Speak directly with Marty Grimes."

Reed's grip on the device tightened as the directive sank in. Marty Grimes. Who is Marty Grimes? It was a name that hadn't surfaced in his assignments before, at least not in a way that mattered. He slipped the Lyt Meeter back into his bag, masking any sign of the unease twisting in his chest.

"Hey," Reed said casually, leaning back in his seat. "You ever hear of Marty Grimes?"

Carter's head snapped up first, his brow furrowed. "Grimes? Yeah, the name's familiar. Saw it in a couple of reports. He's not high-level, though. Why?"

"Humor me," Reed replied, shrugging. "Check him out on Pro4uM."

Carter's fingers danced over his keyboard, Kranch leaning in slightly as the search yielded a single post by Marty Grimes: *"Posing the 'Chubby' Senior."*

Carter read aloud, his voice tinged with confusion. *"Remember, as a photographer, your job is to make your subject look the best they can look!"*

Reed froze, the words triggering an alarm in his mind. *Chubby Senior.*

That was the code. His memory snapped into sharp focus. He recalled the moment vividly, on the ride from Box Gallery to Lenscape Photography Rentals, he had typed the code, *S3P16C105B,* into the Lyt Meeter. That was when he saw the phrase for the first time: *"Sawyer must die. PPI will be clean. Operatives in place. Plans in motion. Kessler is the disguise. P4M code: 'Chubby Senior.'"* The seemingly innocent title on Pro4uM hadn't been advice, it was a veiled directive, buried in plain sight.

"'Chubby Senior,'" he muttered. "Could be code for something bloated or overextended."

"PPI itself?" Kranch suggested, his voice low and skeptical.

"Possibly," Reed said, his thoughts exploding. "'Make your subject look the best they can look'... It's about appearances. Misdirection. Hiding flaws."

"Fabricating reality," Carter added grimly, sitting back.

Kranch's frown deepened. "So, Grimes is posting this, why? To warn someone? To reinforce protocol?"

"Or to give instructions," Reed said, his voice hardening. He tapped the edge of his seat, piecing the clues together. "If this is code, it's about keeping PPI's facade intact, ensuring no one sees the cracks."

Carter shook his head. "Still doesn't explain why Grimes is in play. He's not high-ranking. At least, not enough to be running a show this big."

"Maybe he's another fall guy," Kranch offered, his tone edged with cynicism. "Someone Barry's using to take the heat, like they're trying to do with you."

"Or worse." Reed said, leaning forward. "What if Grimes is Barry's right hand, the one doing the dirty work and covering his tracks?"

Reed's eyes flicked between Carter and Kranch, gauging their reactions. Both men looked uneasy, their earlier focus now replaced with wariness.

"We need to know more," Reed said finally, his voice steady. "If

Grimes is connected to this, if he's posting coded messages like this, he's a thread we can't ignore. We dig into his connections, his role in Barry's plans, and figure out how to use it against him. So, for now, we just gather intel. Watch his posts. See if the name comes up again."

The van fell into a heavy silence, the city lights of Vienna flickering outside as they neared the hotel. In the quiet, Reed's thoughts churned, the name Marty Grimes echoing like a distant drumbeat. He didn't know who this man was yet, but he could be the key to unraveling Barry Cox's plan.

But if he wasn't careful, he might also be the key to their downfall as well.

Reed let his expression go thoughtful. "Doesn't Marty Grimes put on some kind of photography convention? Seems like I remember going to one of those events he organizes."

Carter nodded quickly, snapping his fingers. "Yeah, SYNC! Synchronized Network of Creative Photographers. It's a big deal, tons of professionals, workshops, gear expos, the works."

Kranch tilted his head, intrigued. "What's the angle here? Just another front for PPI?"

"Possibly," Reed replied, his tone sharpening. "But if Grimes is involved and SYNC's tied to PPI, it could be more than that. A convention that big, packed with professionals from all over? And let's not forget how much Barry loves basking in the photography world's spotlight."

Carter brought his arms together in front of him, frowning. "Okay, but how's that useful to us?"

Reed's smirk was subtle but calculating. "Think about it, a massive event with Grimes at the center. If there's a thread worth pulling, SYNC could lead us to it. We'd have access to people and intel that's usually out of reach. And it just might be the kind of event that could lure Barry out of the shadows. The question is, when's the next one?"

Kranch pulled out his phone and scrolled quickly. "Looks like it's just over a month away. Big conference center in Las Vegas."

"Perfect," Reed muttered. "Let's keep this in our back pocket. If this thing ties back to Barry or PPI's inner circle, it could be the crack we need to blow this whole thing open."

Reed pressed forward, his voice dropping as the van jolted over uneven pavement. "We've got a serious problem," he said, holding their attention. "Kessler's movements, his locations, his vulnerabilities, are being mapped out in real time on Pro4uM. It's all there for anyone who knows where to look. Every PPI operative, anyone familiar with Pro4uM, PPI, or Kessler's connection to it, has access to this data. This isn't just intel, it's a roadmap for anyone looking to take him down."

Kranch frowned. "What's PPI's angle? Decoy or...?"

Reed nodded grimly. "Collateral damage is my guess. Kessler's a high-profile target. If he gets taken out, it'll send shockwaves, and PPI can sweep in and clean up however they see fit, reputation intact, no questions asked."

Carter exhaled sharply. "So, they're willing to sacrifice a Secretary to cover their tracks? That's cold, even for them."

"It gets worse." Reed's tone darkened. "The coded message I'm supposed to deliver to Kessler, it'll be sent to me seconds before I photograph him. I won't even have time to process what it says before I'm supposed to hand it off."

Kranch cursed under his breath. "That's not a setup. That's a death warrant, for him or you."

Reed straightened, his expression hard. "That's why we can't let it play out. Kessler's safety has to be priority one. If we lose him, we lose any chance of exposing the Architect."

Carter leaned back, his brow furrowed. "Alright, so how do we protect him without tipping off every PPI operative in the room?"

Reed gestured to the pile of equipment stacked beside them. "We use this. Cameras, lighting rigs, audio setups, they're not just for the shoot anymore. Every piece will be wired to record interactions, capture conversations, and monitor Kessler's surroundings. If anything goes sideways, we'll have it on tape."

Kranch rubbed his chin, his military background clicking into gear. "Alright. So, we split responsibilities, divide the room and cover every angle."

"Exactly," Reed said, his voice steady as he looked between the two men. "Here's how we do this. I'll handle Kessler directly. My job is to keep him calm and cooperative, gain his trust so he doesn't suspect anything is wrong. At the same time, I'll be coordinating the setup for all the covert recordings. Cameras, lighting rigs, audio mics, they'll all be wired to capture every detail. If anything slips through the cracks, the gear won't miss it."

He shifted his focus to Carter. "Carter, you're the eyes in the room. Your job is to watch the players, every PPI operative, every hotel staffer, and every so-called security guard. Document anything suspicious. If someone looks out of place, acts jittery, or moves toward Kessler, you'll be our first line of defense."

Carter nodded, his expression sharpening as the weight of his role settled in. "Got it. I'll work the edges, blend in, and keep tabs on anyone who looks like a threat. To PPI, it'll still look like I'm keeping you under surveillance."

Reed turned to Kranch, who sat silently but alert, waiting for his orders. "Kranch, you're on shadow duty. Stay glued to Kessler. If someone gets too close, you intercept them. If you sense a threat, you neutralize it, quietly and fast. Your only priority is his physical safety. If anything feels off, you call it immediately. Since I'll be sticking close to Kessler, PPI will assume you're shadowing me."

Kranch cracked his knuckles as he gave a short nod. "Understood. I'll keep him breathing."

Reed leaned back, his eyes flicking between them. "Let's get one thing straight: this isn't about PPI protocols anymore. We're not following their playbook. From this point forward, we're working as a team, no divisions, no secrets. The goal is simple, keep Kessler alive and expose Barry Cox. If we get one shot at taking down the Architect, we make it count."

The tension in the van was thick, the air heavy with unspoken fears. But each man carried a spark of determination, a shared understanding that this mission was about more than survival, it was about taking control of a game they'd been forced to play.

Reed broke the silence. "Remember, we protect Kessler above all else. Losing him would be catastrophic, not just for this mission, but for everything we're trying to expose. Agreed?"

Carter and Kranch exchanged a glance before nodding in unison. "Agreed," they said.

Reed's voice softened, though his resolve didn't waver. "Good. Let's move fast, stay sharp, and stay one step ahead of PPI. The second we get complacent, they'll bury us."

The three men sat in silence for a moment, the sound of the van's engine filling the void. Each of them was lost in their own thoughts, bracing for what lay ahead.

The stakes had never been higher, but for the first time, they weren't operating in the dark. With their roles defined and their alliance solidified, they were no longer pawns, they were players, ready to flip the board.

Carter's laptop pinged with a sharp, familiar sound, drawing the attention of everyone in the van. Reed and Kranch exchanged a quick glance, both recognizing the unmistakable chime of a private message on Pro4uM.com. Carter furrowed his brow, clicking to open the notification.

"What is it?" Reed asked, his voice low but tense.

Carter's lips pressed into a thin line as he stared at the screen. "It's... odd," he muttered. "The message is from 'unknown.'" He glanced up, his unease plain. "No one uses aliases on Pro4uM. Everyone uses their real names; it's protocol."

"What does it say?" Kranch pressed.

Carter hesitated, then read the message aloud. "'New Objective: Monitor Marty Grimes.'" He sat back, the weight of the words settling over him. "Well," he added dryly, "I guess we don't have to wonder what 'Realign objectives to accommodate operational flexibility' means anymore."

Reed's mind was already moving, the implications spinning out like threads in a web. "They're shifting focus," he said, almost to himself. "Why Marty Grimes? What's his role in all this?"

Carter leaned forward, his tone sharper now. "My original orders were to monitor you, Reed. That's what they wanted, keep an eye on you for any 'suspicious behavior.' Now they're throwing Grimes into the mix? Feels like they're scrambling."

"They are," Kranch interjected, pulling out his phone. "This isn't just a coincidence. If Grimes is their new target, there's something they're not telling us. Let's dig." His fingers moved quickly across the screen as he searched for intel on Marty Grimes.

Except for the sound of the van's engine, minutes passed in tense silence. Finally, Kranch let out a low whistle, his eyes fixed on the screen. "Got something," he said, his voice grim. "Grimes isn't high-level, barely a blip on their radar until now. But here's the kicker: they're positioning him as the scapegoat."

Reed's brow furrowed. "Scapegoat? How do you know?"

Kranch didn't look up, his expression hardening as he scrolled through Pro4uM. "There's a post today by Barry. He titled it 'Pet Photography: Goats.' Seems harmless, but..." Kranch clicked into the post, reading aloud with deliberate care. "'Had a buddy ask me to photograph his goat, thought I'd share some tips. Funny name for a goat, though, Darty.'"

Carter leaned forward, confusion evident. "Darty? What's that supposed to mean?"

Kranch's jaw clenched as he turned the screen toward them. "Look at the timestamp. It went live this morning, right after Carter got his objective realignment update. And we all know Barry doesn't post anything without a reason."

Reed's eyes sharpened as he pieced it together. "Darty... it's an anagram for Marty. He's not even trying to hide it. That's his way of marking Grimes, he's the fall guy, plain and simple."

"And the goat reference?" Carter asked, still trying to wrap his head around it.

Reed's tone turned grim. "A goat isn't just a cute animal. In Barry's world, it's a 'scapegoat.' He's signaling that if anything blows up, the blame lands squarely on Grimes.

Reed leaned back. "But I think he's setting Grimes up so that we are all looking the wrong way while Barry orchestrates the real play. And if this goes sideways, Grimes, Kessler, and probably us are expendable."

Reed's face hardened as he tapped the side of the van. "Oh Barry, you are good." He cut himself off, a sharp grin forming. "But you slipped. This post connects the dots. We've got proof of his plan, and now, we have leverage."

Kranch sat back, his expression dark but resolute. "We need to move carefully. Barry will come down hard if he even suspects we're onto him. If the mission fails, Grimes takes the fall. PPI gets to keep its hands clean, Barry included."

Reed nodded, gripping the edge of his seat. "Then we use this. Let's make him think his plan is working, until we can turn it against him."

Reed's computer pinged. He recognized the sound instantly, the photo files were now digitized and ready for a search. It was now time to take a step toward building trust.

"I was able to take a plane to Vienna," Reed began. "Had at least an hour's jump on y'all. So, I went to Box Galleries, found a bunch of files, and copied them. It's in my computer now, digitized, searchable." He paused, letting the weight of his words settle. Then, with a faint grin, he asked, "What do you think, boys? Should we search 'Marty Grimes'?"

Kranch leaned forward. "Grimes? Alright, let's see what your fancy setup digs up. If this guy's the thread, maybe it's time we start pulling."

Carter grinned, the tension easing slightly. "Finally, some action. Let's see if Grimes is the golden ticket or a dead end. Either way, I'm betting this search gets interesting."

Reed's fingers flew over the keyboard, the search processing with quiet precision. The results populated in seconds, and his eyes locked onto a file labeled *"Directive: Grimes Liability."* He opened it, his breath catching as the words glared back at him:

"If operation fails, assign full liability to M. Grimes. Sawyer classified expendable. Kessler marked as acceptable collateral. Authorized: B. Cox."

Reed leaned back, a sharp grin forming. "Got ya, Barry!" he muttered under his breath. Then, louder, to Kranch and Carter, he said, "Boys, we've got him. This is the proof we need to set the trap. Grimes is the scapegoat, and Barry's the one pulling the strings. And now we can prove it."

The weight of the revelation settled over the van. They had what they needed to start dismantling the Architect's operation, piece by calculated piece.

Carter's face hardened, his earlier unease morphing into anger. "So that's the play. If something goes wrong, they burn Grimes and move on. It's classic Barry, stay in the shadows, let someone else take the fall."

Reed's voice was sharp with conviction. "Then we stop it. If we take down Barry, we don't just save Grimes, we expose the entire PPI underbelly. Every secret, every operation. It all unravels."

Kranch nodded, his expression resolute. "But we have to be smart about it. If Barry catches wind of what we're doing, he'll bury us all before we get close."

Reed's gaze swept over the group, his tone steady but fierce. "So we don't give him the chance. This photo shoot isn't just a job, it's our battlefield. We'll use it to gather more intel, bait Barry into exposing himself, and plant evidence that ties him to this entire operation."

Carter twitched in his seat. "You know they'll be watching, right?

Not just Barry, PPI as a whole. If we slip, even once, they'll know we're not following protocol."

Reed nodded. "That's the risk we take. But this is our best shot. Everything about this shoot, the cameras, the setups, even our proximity to Kessler, gives us a chance to flip the script."

Kranch's jaw tightened and clenched, his expression hardening. "Understood. But what about the bait? How do we draw Barry out without him realizing it's a trap?"

Reed was gripping the edge of his seat in the van as he glanced between Kranch and Carter. "Alright," he began, his tone steady but weighted. "Have either of you ever heard of a Light Meter, spelled L-Y-T M-E-E-T-E-R?"

Both men exchanged puzzled looks, shaking their heads. "Sounds like something out of a cheap photography gimmick ad." Carter responded.

Reed exhaled deeply, his confidence bolstered by their genuine confusion. He reached into his bag and carefully pulled out the Lyt Meeter, holding it in his hand as if it carried the weight of a loaded gun. "This," he said, his voice low, "is our key. Our edge. And maybe, just maybe, our way to control Barry Cox without him even realizing it."

Kranch's eyes narrowed as he studied the device. "That little thing? What is it, exactly?"

Reed began to explain, turning the device in his hand to show them its sleek, run-of-the-mill design. "On the surface, it's disguised as a light meter, something every professional photographer would carry. But beneath the casing? It's a code generator, hardwired into Pro4uM's most secure channels. I've been using it to decrypt messages, including Carter's 'realign objectives' update. But it's more than that."

Reed tapped the device lightly. "It doesn't just receive information. It can manipulate what gets sent through PPI's system. Think of it as a Trojan horse, we can feed Barry's network only what we want them to see."

Carter let out a low whistle. "You're saying we can use it to… what? Rewrite PPI's orders?"

"Not quite," Reed replied. "Barry's too smart to fall for outright changes to his commands. But we can use the Lyt Meeter to subtly adjust the narrative, redirect his focus, plant seeds of doubt. We don't need to control him outright. We just need to make him believe that he's still the one pulling the strings."

Kranch his skepticism giving way to cautious interest asked. "And how does this help us bait him into the open?"

"That's the beauty of it," Reed said, his voice sharpening with determination. "Barry thrives on control to keep himself untouchable. He orchestrates everything, down to the smallest detail. So, we give him something to 'fix.' Something he thinks he can manipulate, like Marty Grimes."

Carter frowned, leaning forward. "Grimes? How?"

Reed said with confidence, "The evidence is clear: Grimes is the perfect scapegoat. Barry's setting him up to take the fall for whatever happens to Kessler. With the Lyt Meeter, we can make sure Barry believes Grimes is following orders, right up until the moment we turn the tables on him. Let Barry think he's got full control of the operation. And when the time's right, we'll have everything we need to take him down, evidence, witnesses, and the one thing he can't manipulate: the truth."

As the van approached the hotel, the grandeur of Vienna's cityscape gave way to the sleek, modern facade of the building. Reed's eyes swept the scene instinctively, cataloging every detail. Consciously, a black SUV idling near the curb, its tinted windows concealing whoever was inside. A subtle turn of his head revealed two figures, just near enough to watch the hotel entrance with unnerving focus.

Reed thought to himself, *They're already here.* PPI's shadow loomed large, its operatives blending into the bustling scene like predators waiting to strike.

Reed turned towards the driver, his voice calm but laced with urgency. "Change of plans. "These two need to grab some supplies from a grocery store a couple of blocks over. Drop me off first."

The driver glanced back in the mirror, but Reed's tone left no room for questions. "Got it," the man said with a shrug, pulling to the curb near the hotel.

Reed kept his gaze forward, his voice low but steady, speaking to his allies. "Stick to protocol. Get dropped at the grocery store and come back separately. Staggered arrivals keep us clean. We need to appear we are playing by their rules."

Carter nodded, agreeing. "Last thing we need is to raise flags."

The bellman greeted him with a polished yet somewhat artificial smile. After he handed over all the camera gear from Lenscape the automatic doors swept open. Cool air brushed his face as a man near the concierge desk fidgeted, adjusting his tie twice in thirty seconds. Reed's instincts prickled.

This hotel wasn't a safe haven. It was a stage, and everyone had a role to play.

As the van eased into traffic behind him Reed didn't glance back. His focus was forward, on Kessler, the mission, and dismantling the machine PPI had spent years building.

But first, he had to survive the night. Reed checked into his room, a generic suite that felt more like a waiting room than a sanctuary. After a quick sweep for listening devices, he threw his bag on the chair and collapsed onto the bed. The digital clock on the nightstand glowed 10:45 PM. The pieces were set. The game would truly begin in the morning. He closed his eyes, forcing his mind to quiet down.

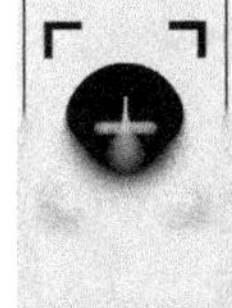

8

CRITICAL FOCUS

Reed woke up before dawn, the gray light of Vienna seeping through the thin hotel curtains. His laptop glowed on the desk, his screen full of notes and plans. The day was pressing in on him and he decided coffee was necessary. He checked his watch: 5:47 AM. The early hour gave them an advantage, as the hotel staff wouldn't be in for another hour.

He ran through his mental checklist, inventorying his equipment bag. Three Canon R5 bodies, a bunch of prime lenses and his trusty 70-200mm zoom. Each piece of gear had been modified to house tiny recorders, a delicate operation that had taken lots of prep. The cameras weren't just cameras anymore; they were weapons in a war without bullets.

Reed got to the hotel meeting room early, armed with coffee and donuts. The staff greeted him with smiles, none the wiser to the operation that was unfolding around them. The smell of fresh coffee filled the air, making it seem like business as usual. Reed knew it was anything but.

"Nothing like coffee to start the day," he said, setting the box down on a side table. The casualness belied his high alertness, scanning every person that entered the room, every shadow on the wall.

As he unpacked his gear, Reed chatted with Kessler's assistants, asking about their lives, their routines. It wasn't small talk. It was reconnaissance. Each question was calculated, each answer filed away for later.

"This setup looks good," one of the assistants said, nodding at Reed's gear. The assistant lingered a beat too long, his eyes scanning the equipment with an intensity that set off alarms in Reed's head.

"Thanks," Reed said, smiling. "Just trying to make you guys look good. Speaking of which, can I tweak the lighting a bit?" He headed for the softboxes, adjusting them with precision. Each move was choreographed, a dance of deception.

Under the guise of adjustments, Reed planted hidden recorders: in a light stand, under a table, even in a decorative plant. Each move was evidence of a pro doing his job. The recorders were tiny, about the size of a coin, and could pick up conversation from across the room. He'd placed them strategically: one by the water cooler where people congregated, another by the window where private conversations would happen. While Reed worked the room, Carter walked the hotel, his camera slung around his neck. His Canon R3 looked legit, enough to justify his presence but modified with surveillance gear. He stopped to chat with the security team, feigning interest in their protocols, his face calm and professional.

"Just want to make sure everything's smooth for the Secretary," he said, easy. "You know how these high-profile shoots can get." Every word was deliberate, every interaction designed to seem natural while gathering intel.

As they talked, Carter's eyes scanned. A man dressed as hotel staff hung around the service entrance, fiddling with an earpiece. A van parked in the loading dock. Carter's gut told him these weren't coincidences. The van was in perfect position to see both the main entrance and the service area. It was too perfect to be random.

As he snapped photos discreetly, uploading them to the team's shared drive, it was clear PPI was here and they weren't being subtle about their interest in the Secretary. The photos weren't just documentation; they were digital breadcrumbs, archived in case every-thing went sideways.

Kranch moved through the hotel with quiet purpose, his military training evident in every step. His camera bag was bigger than just photography gear: backup weapons, comms devices and extraction gear were hidden among the lenses and filters. He placed a stack of luggage carts near a stairwell, blocking access if needed. A mainte-nance sign in front of a service door. Furniture in a lounge area was rearranged, creating obstacles to slow down an exit.

To anyone watching, Kranch's actions looked normal, just hotel staff doing their job. But they were defensive traps, carefully laid to give the team an edge if things went bad. Each move was meticulous, measured against scenarios.

When Secretary Kessler arrived, the atmosphere changed. His entourage moved with precision, their suits crisp, their faces unread-able. The air seemed to vibrate with tension as they swept through the lobby. Reed greeted him with professional courtesy, guiding him through the setup, all while watching the reactions of those around them.

"We've got everything ready for you, Mr. Secretary. Tonight, will be smooth," Reed said, calm. He watched Kessler's face for any sign the Secretary understood the subtext of his words. Kessler nodded, his face a mix of command and concern. As his team went over the schedule, Reed noticed a flicker of exchange between two aides: a glance too quick, a gesture too stiff. They moved too synced, too premeditated. The realization hit him like a shot, PPI operatives. They carried themselves differently from regular security; they were more aware, more controlled, more deadly.

Reed chatted with Kessler's team, throwing in purposeful misdi-rection. He adjusted his camera settings as he spoke, each movement precise and professional, hiding the fact he was reading their reactions.

"I might need to step out for a few minutes during the shoot tonight," he mentioned casually, knowing PPI's operatives would latch onto the detail. "Probably around 8:30 PM, is that okay?" The time was chosen carefully: far enough away to seem plausible, close enough to keep them focused.

Kessler nodded in approval, but Reed saw the faint tightening around his eyes. The Secretary was trapped and couldn't escape alone.

It was a calculated risk, a red herring to distract them. Meanwhile, the hidden recording devices captured every word, every glance, every nuance. The data streamed silently to secure servers, building a digital evidentiary record.

Reed, Carter, and Kranch met mid-morning in a quiet corner of the hotel. The location wasn't random; it had clear sightlines to both exits and enough background noise to cover their conversation. Carter pulled up the photos he'd taken, pointing to the man with the earpiece and the van near the loading dock.

"These guys aren't hotel staff," Carter said, his voice low and intense. "They're too polished. Too aware. Look at their posture, their positioning. Classic PPI formation patterns." He swiped through more photos, each one revealing another layer of surveillance around them.

Reed nodded, studying the images. "The two aides with Kessler… they're PPI. They're not here to help him, they're here to control him. Look how they bracket him, never letting anyone get too close." He paused, thinking. "They're good, but they're not subtle. They're showing force, trying to intimidate." Kranch's face hardened as he watched the security footage on his tablet. "Traps are set. If they move, we'll have time to react. I've got emergency exits covered, and the hotel's security cameras are feeding us real-time updates."

Reed placed one final recording device in Kessler's briefing folder, his hands steady despite the knot in his gut. This one was the most important; it was smaller than the others, almost undetectable, but capable of picking up everything within a ten-foot radius. As he walked back into the meeting room, one of Kessler's aides, hand on his hidden microphone, whispered, "We're in position. Waiting for the word."

This was it. The plan was in place, the stage set. Now, all that was left was to see who would make the first move. Reed glanced at his watch again: 11:23 AM. Hours until the event, but seconds could be the difference between success and failure.

Tonight, this ends here, Reed thought. *One way or another*. The weight of his camera felt good against his chest, a reminder some-times the best weapon wasn't a gun, but the truth through a lens.

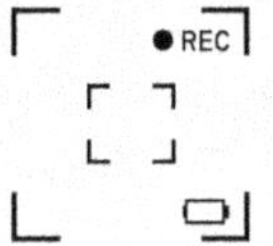

9

THE VIEWFINDER

Reed leaned against the marble counter of the hotel lobby, his fingers drumming a rhythm as he waited for the concierge's attention. His thoughts spun out of control, going through the team's assignments. PPI was watching their every move, waiting to pounce on any deviation from protocol.

The clerk came over with a fake smile. "Can I help you?"

Reed nodded, keeping his voice calm and professional. "Just looking for one of my team members. Has Marty Grimes checked in yet?"

The clerk typed on the computer, eyes flicking over the screen. "Yes, sir. Mr. Grimes checked in this morning. Room 912."

Reed's muscles tightened but his face remained expressionless. Grimes was already here. Either Barry was moving ahead of schedule or the team was behind. "Thanks," Reed said with a practiced smile, stepping back from the counter. He adjusted his camera bag, the weight of it grounding him as he headed towards the revolving doors.

Outside the humid air of Vienna hit him like a wall. The noise of tourists mixed with the clinking of glasses from the bar next door. Reed didn't know who "Mike" was but everyone in the bar loved him. He caught snippets of conversation, "...another round for all my friends!", followed by a loud "Miiiiiike!" The bar was loud and chaotic and perfect cover: a quiet patio where the noise and normalcy could hide a clandestine meeting. With PPI watching their every move, appearances had to be airtight. To the casual observer Kranch was tailing Reed and Carter was tailing Grimes. A public meetup like this could pass as coincidence so long as they followed PPI protocol.

Reed slipped into the shadows of the side street and pulled out his phone. A quick text went out to Kranch and Carter:

"Meet: next door. Outdoor seating. Cafe Merlot. Follow PPI protocol."

Reed knew the drill. He'd sit first, look casual, maybe order a drink. Kranch would show up a few minutes later, position himself near enough to hear but not at the same table. Carter would come last, blend in as a tourist or businessman grabbing a bite between errands. The goal was clear: coordination without exposure. The outdoor patio of *Cafe Merlot* was hopping, glasses clinking, laughter, waitstaff darting between tables. Reed sat in the corner, choosing a spot with a clear view of the entrance and the street. The noise around him was perfect cover for whispers.

A waiter approached and Reed ordered a coffee and said, "My associate will be joining me, Mr. Grimes. Can you send him to my table when he arrives?" Playing his part to the hilt: just another photographer taking a break before a busy day. He pretended to scroll through his phone but his eyes were locked on the activity around him.

Reed decided to take a chance and send a Private Message on Pro4uM to Marty Grimes. *"Mission critical, meet me at Café Merlot immediately. Mention my name and the waiter will direct you."* Reed's thumb hovered over the send button for a second before he tapped it. The risk was high, Pro4uM was PPI's domain and every message was logged and analyzed. But without Grimes the puzzle would remain incomplete.

A few minutes later, right on cue, Kranch showed up. True to form he didn't acknowledge Reed, instead he chose a table a few seats away. His posture was casual, but Reed caught the flick of his eyes scanning the patio for threats. Kranch ordered a soda and leaned back in his chair as if he were on a break from tailing his "target."

Carter was next, slipping into a seat near the far end of the patio, closer to the street. He was dressed in a blazer and holding a tablet and blended in with the lunch crowd. His eyes met Reed's for a second and a subtle nod passed between them.

Reed waited until the waiter walked away before speaking in a low voice, loud enough for Kranch to hear. "Grimes is here. Checked in this morning."

Kranch didn't look up from his drink, his lips barely moving. "Room?"

"Nine twelve," Reed replied, pretending to sip his coffee.

Grimes was not subtle. Reed watched him closely, noting the conversation with the waiter. Heads nodded, a few awkward laughs were exchanged and then a quick gesture in Reed's direction. Together they started walking towards him. Marty Grimes trailed behind the waiter, his movements hesitant, shifting his weight with every step as if unsure of each step. He was a small man in his late 40s with the kind of face that blended into a crowd. Thinning hair was combed neatly but his glasses sat slightly askew on his nose giving him a frazzled look. Grimes was dressed in a slightly rumpled blazer over a button-up shirt and jeans. It was the kind of outfit that could pass for either casual professionalism or someone barely holding it together.

But it wasn't his clothes that caught Reed's attention: it was his eyes. Wide and darting like a cornered animal they scanned the patio with nervous precision, pausing briefly on each patron before landing on Reed. A flicker of recognition crossed his face followed by a brief hesitation. He looked like a man who knew he was walking into a trap but had no choice but to see it through.

"Mr. Grimes?" the waiter asked with a nod towards Reed's table, his voice cutting through the buzz of the bar and the street. A few heads turned sensing a shift in the atmosphere.

Grimes nodded quickly, too quickly, his hand fussing with his glasses in a vain attempt to compose himself. "That's me," he said, his voice tight and strained. He followed the waiter towards Reed's table his movements a mix of reluctance and determination.

Reed stood up his expression calm and professional though his mind was calculating. "Mr. Grimes" he said warmly extending a hand as if this were just another meeting. "Glad you could join me."

Grimes shook his hand his grip damp and shaky. "Mr. Sawyer" he said his voice faltering as he glanced over his shoulder clearly uneasy. "I got your message. I'm here. Now what?"

Reed gestured for him to sit his smile unwavering. "Let's talk," he said, his tone measured and deliberate. "You have more eyes on you than you think; and if we don't act fast, you're going to take the fall for something you didn't start."

Reed leaned in his tone sharp but low. "We don't have much time so I'm going to skip the small talk. What's your role with PPI?" Grimes winced his eyes narrowing. "You know I can't answer that. Protocol, "

Reed waved his hand dismissively. "I know the protocol, Grimes. No talking, no questions, no breaking the chain. But if you want to get through this in one piece, you're going to break it right now. Things aren't always what they seem, Marty. Sometimes the picture isn't as clear as you think."

Grimes opened his mouth to protest but Reed cut him off. He pulled out his phone and placed it on the table between them and tapped the screen to bring up the message he'd found. The file labeled *"Directive: Grimes Liability."* glowed brightly in the dim light: He opened it, *"If operation fails, assign full liability to M. Grimes. Sawyer classified expendable. Kessler marked as acceptable collateral. Authorized: B. Cox."*

Grimes froze his breath catching audibly. He stared at the screen his face going white as the message sank in. "What... what is this?" he whispered.

"It's your future" Reed said bluntly. "That's what Barry has lined up for you. When everything goes sideways, and it *will*, you're the one they're going to hang out to dry."

Grimes's hands trembled as he reached for the phone his fingers hovering over the screen as if he needed to feel it was real. "This can't be right" he muttered. "I've followed every order done every-thing by the book...""

"That's exactly why you're the perfect scapegoat" Reed said leaning back slightly. "Barry is counting on you to follow orders blindly. And when the dust settles, he'll have the perfect fall guy to keep his hands clean."

Grimes's gaze snapped up to Reed's his eyes wild. "Why are you showing me this? What do you want from me?"

"Trust" Reed said simply sliding the phone back into his pocket. "I don't need you to explain yourself and I don't have time to spell this out. You're in grave danger Grimes. Your only way out is to trust me and help me take Barry down." Grimes hesitated his shoulders sagging under the weight of what he'd just seen. His voice was shaking but had a hint of hope. "What do I do?"

Reed leaned in again his voice urgent. "First you listen. Then you follow me. If we're going to get through this, we need to work together; we need to move fast."

Reed's tone softened just enough to sound less aggressive. "So, can we at least start with why you're here? Just the highlights."

Marty hesitated his gaze darting around the crowded restaurant before settling back on Reed. He shrugged trying to play it cool. "It's nothing big. Routine stuff. I'm supposed to shadow Secretary Kessler's team during the shoot; I need to make sure all the optics are in line. Barry said the press would be watching and it's critical we get everything looking polished."

Reed raised an eyebrow for Marty to continue.

"I mean it's babysitting work" Marty added quickly. "Smile

adjustments, positioning the Secretary just right; you know the little things that make the big picture work. They've got me double-checking the media angles and making sure no one says anything they shouldn't. It's nothing glamorous and definitely nothing worth raising eyebrows over."

Reed nodded slowly his face neutral. "Nothing glamorous. Right."

Marty leaned back in his chair suddenly defensive. "That's it. I swear. If it were something more, I wouldn't be the one doing it. Barry's got people way higher up for that kind of thing."

Reed smiled faintly but his eyes stayed sharp. "Right, the little things. Funny how it's always the little things that end up mattering most."

Marty shifted uncomfortably but Reed didn't press further. The trap was already set.

Reed gestured to the far side of the tables where Kranch and Carter sat silently their eyes fixed on Marty. "Marty" Reed said calmly, "meet the team." He nodded towards them. "This is Kranch and Carter. They're already up to speed."

Marty nodded at them cautiously his fingers fidgeting with the edge of the chair. Kranch nodded curtly his jaw tight while Carter leaned back in his chair his posture relaxed but his eyes sharp. "For now, Marty" Reed said "you just do your job. Nothing more, nothing less. Carter here will be sticking close to you. So don't get nervous when you see him around every corner."

Marty looked at Carter his eyebrows raising slightly. "I won't be nervous when I see him at every corner. I'll know it's normal."

"Carter is your contact to the team. If you have questions or notice anything off you go to him. Not me, not Kranch. Him. Understood?"

Marty nodded slowly. "Understood."

Reed leaned in speaking low so the conversation wouldn't carry. "We have a plan in place but it's critical that PPI feels everything is tracking normally. No surprises, no slip-ups. You follow Carter's lead and we'll get through this."

Marty exhaled looking slightly relieved but the tension in his shoulders remained. "Alright. Got it."

Reed straightened up. "Now about your convention. SYNC, right?"

Marty's expression shifted slightly the tension replaced by mild confusion. "Yeah, what about it?"

"Will Barry be a speaker?" Reed asked pointedly.

Marty shook his head quickly. "No, he doesn't usually show up to these things. Too high-profile, I guess. But I know he loves the photography world's spotlight."

Reed nodded thoughtfully then leaned in again his tone decisive. "But if he needs to be it can be arranged, right?"

Marty hesitated. "I mean... yeah, probably. If I pitch it right. Why?"

"Because we need him to be the keynote speaker" Reed said firmly holding Marty's gaze. "And not just any speaker, we need him front and center with the entire attendance watching."

Marty blinked his jaw dropping slightly. "You're serious?"

"Dead serious" Reed said. "Call Barry make it casual and tell him like it's something you forgot to mention until now. 'Oh, by the way Barry you will be the keynote speaker.' That kind of casual. Can you make that happen?"

Marty ran a hand over his face exhaled slowly. "It won't be easy but yeah... I think I can make it happen. The current Keynote speaker will not be happy, but I think I can make him happy." "Good" Reed said leaning back with a small smile. "Because that's how we'll set the stage. Literally."

The meeting was short, as planned. As Reed stood to leave, he thought to himself *So many moving parts. I've got to get Kessler on our side and then we can really begin.*

Back at the hotel Reed's mind was calm but alert. Grimes was on board now. The lines were beginning to connect.

Reed checked his watch: six hours to showtime. Time was ticking and every second counted. He slipped into the hotel's business center and looked around to confirm what he already knew, he was alone. Perfect. The sterile hum of the computer stations and the faint buzz of the fluorescent lights made the room feel almost peaceful. For now, it was his command center.

He sat down at a corner workstation and booted up the computer. Glancing around to make sure he was still alone he logged into Pro4uM.com. With a few keystrokes lines of code and hidden memos scrolled across the screen each one a piece of a much larger puzzle. Reed's focus sharpened as patterns began to emerge. Phrases like "Strategic alignment confirmed" and "Asset integration under-way" indicated a level of planning. And then there it was, Kessler's name. Not just once but again and again his name tied to keywords: "Fulcrum", "Keystone", "Architect's Directive".

He leaned back and exhaled slowly. This wasn't speculation anymore. Kessler wasn't a target of opportunity, he was the target. PPI's plans revolved around him using his influence to legitimize a global agenda that Reed was only starting to understand. He pulled out the Lyt Meeter and ran a cross-check against the data on Pro4uM.com. The device hummed faintly processing the input before confirming what Reed dreaded most. This wasn't coincidence. It was fact. Reed went back to the screen and dug deeper. Cross-referencing Pro4uM's encrypted chat with the files from the Box Gallery revealed even more. PPI wasn't just manipulating Kessler, it was controlling entire countries. Each new discovery exposed another layer of Barry Cox's shadow empire: coups disguised as democratic transitions, economic crashes masquerading as market corrections, and puppet leaders installed through supposedly free and fair elections. Behind every major global upheaval Reed found PPI's fingerprints, hidden in innocent photography assignments and equipment purchases.

The pattern was both brilliant and sick. Every real photography event was a cover for something darker and Barry's influence was missing from the official records. Kessler wasn't just another target;

he was the unwitting centerpiece of an operation that spanned the globe. Reed's hand hovered over the keyboard the weight of this reality settling on his shoulders. It was worse than he had thought.

Time was running out. Reed closed the files and shut down the computer. As the screen went dark Reed hesitated. His finger hovered over the power button. Something nagged at him, a feeling there was more he hadn't found. He leaned forward and tapped the keyboard and the screen flickered back to life.

Reed typed in a new query and focused on PPI's operations in New York. His fingers moved with precision skimming through encrypted chat and internal memos until he found a glaring vulnerability. PPI's servers thought to be impenetrable could be compromised by a physically implanted device; *'This will be useful later,'* Reed thought. It was a crack in their armor hidden in plain sight.

Reed's lips curled into a cold smile. This was their weakness.

The photo shoot wasn't just about protecting Kessler, it was about trapping Barry. Get him talking. The Secretary wasn't just a target; he was an ally in taking down Barry Cox.

The covert recording devices Reed had planted earlier now meant even more. They would capture every word, every interaction, irrefutable proof Reed and his team could use to take down Barry Cox. But one thing was clear: without Kessler's trust none of it would matter. The computer went dark and its hum died away. Reed sat back and ran his hand through his hair. He knew convincing Secretary Kessler wasn't just about showing him evidence like cryptic codes on a fake website and a silly gadget, it was about changing his perspective on this situation. The Secretary had to see how Barry had manipulated him used his influence and positioned him as the unwitting cornerstone of PPI's operations. Without Kessler's complete understanding and cooperation, the whole thing would fall apart before it even started. The recording devices weren't enough Reed needed concrete proof that even a seasoned politician couldn't deny.

Reed sent a text to Carter and Kranch laying out the grim reality of what he'd found. He kept it short concise and encrypted, every word chosen carefully to avoid detection. He thought about bringing Grimes in but the risk was too great. For now, Grimes needed to keep doing what he was doing. The less he knew the safer he'd be.

Reed went back to his room and sat on the bed his mind racing. Anxious but resolute. Dismantle Barry and PPI falls like a house of cards. The thought of killing him flickered briefly, a dark impulse born of desperation. He dismissed it immediately. This wasn't a spy novel and he wasn't James Bond. You only kill people in stories like those. In the real world the truth was the weapon that brought men like Barry to their knees.

He looked at his watch. Five hours to showtime. The shoot would be the tipping point, the moment of no return. No second chances.

Reed's thoughts turned to the scope of what he'd found. The scale of Barry's corruption and PPI's manipulation was global. He couldn't just expose a piece of it; he needed the whole picture. It was the only way to make sure the lies weren't just revealed but destroyed.

Everything was in place and the photo shoot was hours away.

10
FOCAL POINT

Reed opened his eyes, his pulse climbed. He never napped, especially not during an op. But there it was, 20 minutes gone, the faint impression of his watch against his temple where he'd leaned back on the bed. What time is it? His mind spun until he focused on the clock; there was still time. His head felt clearer than it had in days, but clarity came with a sobering thought. They had no backup plan. Every part of this op hinged on Secretary Kessler. If Kessler didn't play along what then? Reed swung his legs off the bed and stood up. No margin for error. No Plan B. His hand brushed against the camera bag as he moved a gentle reminder of the tools he'd prepared, but even flawless execution wouldn't matter if Kessler refused to join them.

Shoving the nagging doubt to the side Reed opened the door and stepped out into the hallway. As he made his way to the meeting room his eyes took in everything. A bellhop lingering near the elevators polishing the same brass panel too many times. A housekeeper's cart just ahead parked at an angle that partially blocked the hallway. Reed's heart rate picked up. Coincidence? Maybe. But in PPI's world coincidences didn't exist. He tightened his grip on his gear. This was a chessboard, every move calculated, every piece strategically placed. And somewhere Barry Cox was moving those pieces.

Reed got to the meeting room early glad for the calm before the storm. He set his bag down and checked out the equipment one piece at a time. Cameras, light stands, microphones, each tool serving a dual purpose. The shoot required precision and professionalism, but the covert op required something more: subtlety. Every stand, every lens, every cable was examined. He adjusted the hidden microphones in the light stands testing their placement to make sure they covered the room maximally. He repositioned the cameras to make sure they'd capture more than Kessler's best angles. This wasn't just a shoot; it was a surveillance op wrapped in artistic disguise. In the lobby Carter blended in like a chameleon, chatting up a security staff member. His easy smile and relaxed demeanor hid the fact that he was taking in every person in his line of sight. He made mental notes: the man in the concierge uniform with the earpiece, the service van parked too close to the loading dock. Nothing overt, but nothing ordinary either. A quick click on his phone and photos of the anomalies went to their shared drive. If Reed had missed anything Carter wasn't going to let it slip through the cracks.

Kranch moved through the hotel like a ghost. He wasn't following Kessler yet but his eyes flicked to exits, bottlenecks and the hidden traps he'd set earlier. The luggage carts were still in the stairwell, and the maintenance sign was still in place near the service door. Small obstacles, barely noticeable but enough to buy seconds if things went sideways.

Reed's mental gears turned faster than he could follow as he finished setting up the room. One critical piece was missing: isolating Kessler. Without that they had no op. He rehearsed his approach silently. He'd play the professional, concerned about lighting, angles and aesthetics. That's how he'd get Kessler away from everyone else. But once they were alone everything would shift. Reed would show his hand, reveal the conspiracy and force

Kessler to see the truth. The risk was huge but there was no other way.

The room was set, the gear was laid out, every microphone and camera in place. Reed allowed himself a rare moment of satisfaction. The shoot was a powder keg, but the pieces were in place. Then the door opened and the calm was shattered.

Grimes walked in, his eyes wide and nervous. He looked out of place, shaky, out of breath as if he'd seen too much but understood too little. He passed Reed quickly and quietly. "Barry is here," he whispered, the words cutting through Reed's focus. Reed stopped dead, his mind spinning. It was odd. Barry Cox didn't show up in person, he thrived in the shadows, orchestrating chaos from afar. But on the other hand, it made perfect sense. Given what Reed now knew about how crucial Kessler was to Barry's plans there was no way Cox would let this play out without him here in person.

Reed adjusted his stance, his face neutral as Grimes moved further into the room. Inside his mind he clicked frame by frame. Barry's presence changed everything. The stakes were huge and the danger was unmistakable. But there was a silver lining. If Barry Cox was here that meant they had the chance to get him on tape linking him to the whole operation. The Architect was stepping into frame.

He glanced at the hidden cameras, each one a silent witness waiting to record the truth. For the first time Barry's control played to their advantage. Reed had to fight the urge to smirk. "Alright Barry, let's see how perfect your plan looks on tape."

Reed turned to Grimes. "Where is he?"

Grimes gestured vaguely toward the hallway. "Near the lobby, I think. He's keeping low, just observing for now. But... he's here."

Reed's body tensed. The game was on and the board had changed. He pulled out his phone and sent a quick text to Carter and Kranch: *Barry in the building; all eyes open.* Then he put the phone back in his pocket and knew it wasn't just about prep anymore. It was about execution.

As Reed moved across the room, his resolve hardened. This was their moment, the moment of truth where everything came together or fell apart. Barry Cox was on stage and Reed was going to make him the star of the show. Reed's heart beat faster as he approached Kessler's entourage. The Secretary sat alone, his chief aide standing nearby, watching him. Kessler was deep in thought, a notebook open in his hands. Reed caught a snippet of his mumbled words: "Section 3 needs revisiting. Something about Keystone feels off." He adjusted his camera strap, taking a deep breath. This had to go smoothly.

He walked forward with confidence. "Secretary Kessler, I hope I'm not interrupting but I wanted to run something by you about the lighting for the shoot."

Kessler looked up, his face neutral. "Is there a problem?"

"No sir," Reed said, his voice calm. "But the lighting in the briefing room can be tricky with the window glare. I just wanted to do a quick walkthrough to finalize the angles. It'll only take a minute and will get the best shot."

Kessler hesitated, looked at his chief aide who shrugged. It was a small ask to fit into his busy schedule. After a moment he sighed and nodded. "Alright, let's get it over with."

Reed smothered a sigh of relief as he gestured for Kessler to follow. He led the way down the hallway, moving casually, unremarkably. They entered a small side room Reed had scouted earlier, a private space that passed as a prep area.

Once Kessler was inside Reed closed the door and locked it. The Secretary raised an eyebrow but didn't speak, his face unreadable. "Alright Mr. Sawyer, what's this really about?"

Reed turned to face him, his face hardening. "I need your full attention, sir. What I'm going to show you isn't part of the shoot, it's something you need to see."

Kessler's body stiffened, his instincts on high alert. "What is this, some kind of stunt?"

"Not a stunt," Reed replied, his voice firm as he pulled out his tablet. "It's your life, and the truth about who's running it." Reed took a deep breath, calming himself as he turned on the tablet. The room felt smaller now, the weight of what he was about to show pressing down like a physical fog. "Stay calm, Secretary Kessler. This is going to be tough to hear but it's important."

Kessler folded his arms, his expression skeptical but watchful. "You've got my attention. Start talking."

Reed tapped the screen, brought up images. "Let's start here." He swiped through photos he'd taken during his prep, the bellhop lingering by the lobby, the cleaner's cart near the exits, the earpiece visible on a supposed hotel staff member. "These aren't accidents or coincidences. They're PPI operatives and they've been following you."

Kessler leaned in, his eyes narrowing as he looked at the images. "Why would they be following me?"

"That's what I'm about to explain." Reed swiped again, brought up screenshots of encrypted messages from Pro4uM. "These are coded messages tied to your office. The language looks harmless, meetings, travel itineraries, but I've decrypted the subtext. They're coordinating actions, steering decisions that all lead back to PPI."

Kessler's face twisted. "And you're telling me this is happening under my nose?"

Reed nodded. "It gets worse." He brought up another file, personnel profile. "Recognize these names?" he asked, pointing to two entries.

Kessler's eyes scanned the profiles, his face hardening. "They're my aides. Trusted staff. What are you saying?"

"I'm not saying anything. I'm showing you the evidence." Reed zoomed in on a report that revealed the operatives' true identity. "These two have been on PPI's payroll for years. They've manipulated your schedule, intercepted your communications and positioned you exactly where The Architect wants you."

Kessler's hands clenched into fists. "The Architect? Who the hell is that?"

Reed's voice low and deliberate. "Barry Cox. He's the man behind PPI's global plan and you're a key piece of it. You've been turned into a pawn, Secretary. But it's not too late to fight back." Kessler's skepticism began to crack but the doubt remained in his eyes. Reed had to deliver the knockout punch. He swiped to an audio file, reordered from his hidden mics and hit play. The room was filled with the cold, calculating voices discussing Kessler like a pawn on a chessboard.

"...if Kessler doesn't play along, we have contingencies. The man's a figurehead, nothing more. His removal would serve the same purpose and Barry's plan would move forward without a hitch."

Reed stopped the recording and looked at Kessler. "Barry Cox is here. Right now. He's not leaving this to chance. He's making sure his plan goes off without a hitch."

Kessler sat down hard, his face pale but set. "You're telling me I'm surrounded. My own people, my own aides, part of this... conspiracy?"

"Yes," Reed said flatly. "But this is also your chance to expose it. You're the key, sir. If you help us, we can take down Barry and dismantle PPI's entire operation."

Kessler looked at the tablet then back at Reed, the weight of the decision settling in his eyes. "What do you want from me?"

Reed leaned in, his voice firm. "Your trust. Your cooperation. And your willingness to take a risk. If we do this right, we won't just save your career. We'll stop PPI for good."

Reed barely had time to breathe before Kessler was on him, his tone sharp, his words precise. "Mr. Sawyer, do you realize what you're saying here? That a small photography institute, a little club with a side gig in security, is somehow controlling me? Controlling the U.S. government?" He laughed, though his eyes flashed with anger. "I don't know whether to call this ridiculous or insulting."

Reed stood his ground, his hands steady despite the surge of irritation. "I'm not here to insult you, Secretary. I'm here to warn you." Kessler waved the tablet away, leaning back with a look of incredulity. "And betray me? My staff? These are vetted professionals, Mr. Sawyer. Background checks so thorough they make the CIA blush. You think two operatives slipped through because your 'Picture Protection Institute' decided to play James Bond? Come on."

Reed bit back the urge to roll his eyes at the condescension. "They're not playing James Bond. They've been getting embedded in positions of power for years using Pro4uM as their primary way to stay hidden. It's not just you, sir. It's global. This is bigger than..."

"Save the drama," Kessler cut in, his voice rising. "We're the government. We don't get outsmarted by a group of photographers playing spies. The idea you've uncovered something we haven't is ridiculous. You have pictures and some suspicious messages. Show me something real or let me get back to work."

Reed held his breath, reining in his temper. "You want real? Fine." He tapped the tablet again and pulled up a shaky, grainy video. "This is from this morning. The quality isn't great, I wasn't set up right yet, but watch."

Kessler leaned forward reluctantly as the video started to play. It was a wide shot, taken from an unstable angle, of two of Kessler's aides near the lobby corner.

"Can't hear a thing," Kessler muttered.

"Just wait," Reed said softly.

The audio crackled and several words cut through the static: "Kessler... eliminated... expendable... personally."

Kessler's face went white and he sat back slowly, his earlier bravado slipping away. "What... what is this?"

Reed pounced. "Your trusted aides plotting against you. Now, I can't say exactly what they're planning but I don't think 'eliminated' or 'expendable' sounds good for you. Especially not when The Architect is involved."

Kessler's eyes were glued to the screen, his mind racing. "How... how did you get this?" "Don't matter," Reed said flatly. "What matters is this is just the beginning. You're wondering how you didn't see this coming? PPI is a machine built for this kind of infiltration. They don't just manipulate individuals, they manipulate the narrative. They make sure you don't see what's happening until it's too late."

Kessler rubbed his face, visibly shaken but still hesitant. "If this is true, then why tell me now? What do you want me to do about it?"

Reed leaned in, his tone urgent but controlled. "I don't want you to act impulsively. I want you to listen. To work with me. Because if you don't, Barry Cox wins. You become a pawn in his game or worse, another casualty."

Kessler sat silently for a moment, his face expressionless. Then finally he spoke, his voice firm. "I'll cooperate. But I have conditions. Strict ones."

Kessler began, "First, this stays between us. Absolute discretion."

A knock sounded at the door. Both men froze, looking at each other. Kessler raised a hand, signaling wait. "One minute!" he said, his voice steady. He leaned towards Reed, lowering his voice. "We need to move this along."

Reed nodded and then whispered. "Second condition?"

Kessler continued. "Next, anything involving my staff goes through me first. No exceptions."

Reed hesitated, knowing how much this would slow them down. "That'll complicate things, but I get it. We need a way to signal if we think you're in personal danger. A code phrase."

Kessler's skepticism relaxed. "What do you have in mind?"

Reed whispered. "Two phrases. First, if we get everything we need and your involvement is over the phrase will be: 'Great shot, you're all done.' The second, if you need to get out immediately because the danger is imminent then I'll say: 'This shoot is over. Get out from in front of my camera.'" Reed paused, letting the words sink in. He looked at Kessler. "One last thing. This whole operation hinges on a mission code I need to give to you. I don't have it yet, it'll come as the shoot begins. My instructions are simple: I'll ask for your phone, input my contact info and embed the code there. It's seamless, untraceable."

Kessler nodded curtly, his face expressionless. He didn't elaborate on what the mission code was for and Reed didn't press. Some things were better left unknown.

Reed's pulse steadied, his resolve solidifying. This was their shot, and now as Kessler left the room the Secretary was finally in the game.

Reed sat back down and typed out a quick text: *Kessler in.*

He retrieved the Lyt Meeter, tapped a few buttons and the screen lit up with an interface that looked mundane but held the power to send covert messages.

"This is where we get creative," Reed said to himself.

"Phase Two greenlit. Architect oversight required. Key asset in position for final evaluation."

Reed thought, *"That should get him."*

"Barry won't ignore it," Reed said under his breath. "He's too arrogant to sit on the sidelines. He'll either show up himself or send one of his top operatives to make sure nothing messes up his plan."

He set the Lyt Meeter down and stood up.

What's Barry's endgame, Reed thought. *Kill Kessler? Frame him?*

Whatever it was, the shoot was the perfect bait. Barry wouldn't leave Kessler to chance.

Reed spoke into his earpiece to Kranch and Carter. "Kessler has conditions, absolute discretion and total control over anything involving his staff. It'll slow us down but keeps him in the game."

He paused and then added, "If Barry moves during the shoot we pounce. No hesitation. Don't let Kessler's conditions hold you back."

"Confirmed," Kranch said.

"Confirmed," Carter echoed. Reed walked outside the ballroom, his mind running through scenarios like a photographer examining negatives for flaws. Everything was in place, or so it seemed. Kessler was briefed and on board, Carter and Kranch were in position, and the surveillance was as tight as could be. If Barry Cox was going to move, this was the moment.

Reed looked at his watch. Less than two hours to go.

His phone buzzed and he hesitated before flipping the screen. A text from Kessler. His gut dropped as he read the words:

"Meeting moved up. I've been summoned to Suite 918. Immediate attendance required. Shoot canceled."

Reed's throat closed as the weight of the message hit him. Suite 918 wasn't on the schedule. In fact, it wasn't even in the hotel's directory of meeting rooms. He ran a hand through his hair, his stomach twisting. This wasn't a hiccup, this was a seismic shift. The shoot wasn't just delayed, it was over.

He shouted into his earpiece to Carter and Kranch. "Kessler's been pulled. Suite 918. And he canceled the shoot!"

Kessler was walking into the lion's den. Suite 918. Reed knew it, Barry was there.

The thought electrified Reed's gut. Barry doesn't just run operations, he makes them personal. Kessler isn't a pawn to him, he's a liability. And Barry Cox doesn't leave liabilities to chance.

They needed Barry, not just in the shadows but out in the open.

To do that, Reed had to get the photoshoot back on. They needed the photoshoot. They needed Barry to be exposed.

Carter's voice came back in his earpiece. "What do we do? If Barry's there Kessler's as good as dead. I say we pull Kessler!"

Reed's response was low and steady though the tension crackled beneath his words. "No. Not yet." He breathed slowly, forcing calm into his voice. "We don't intervene yet. I think I have a way to get this back on track."

"But Kessler..."

"I know," Reed said, more sharply this time, his tone final. "We'll pull him at the last second. Trust me, Carter. Just stick to the plan."

Stick to the plan. The phrase echoed in Reed's mind as he walked into the hallway and headed to the elevators. He was a photographer, he would use what he had, his camera slung over his shoulder as he moved with purpose. Every step felt heavy with meaning; his senses were on high alert.

Suite 918 loomed ahead, on the opposite side of the hotel, a long walk. As Reed approached the hotel room he could hear muffled voices, rising and falling in a staccato rhythm. One of them was definitely Kessler's.

Barry's voice cut through the air, smooth and measured, the voice of a man who never raised his voice because he never needed to. The Architect. Reed's heart raced.

His mind was running scenarios, each one a tightrope of survival and exposure. *If I go in too soon, we lose everything. If I wait too long Kessler's dead. Barry's not here to intimidate, he's here to finish this himself. That's how he operates. That's how he's always operated.*

Reed stood up straight, forcing his pulse to calm down as his photographer persona slid into place. Adjusting the strap of his camera, he walked towards the door of Suite 918. The door was slightly ajar. Then he pushed it open and walked in and shut it behind him.

"Barry!" Reed called out, a perfect blend of surprise and warmth, honed to disarm. "Well, I'll be. You didn't tell me you'd be here. How long has it been, two years? Three?"

Barry turned, his face expressionless but his body language controlled, his dark eyes calculating. He didn't smile but there was a flicker of recognition on his face. "Reed Sawyer," he said smoothly, his tone dripping with fake brotherhood. "The man who always gets the perfect shot." Reed walked in, calm as could be, his camera bouncing lightly against his chest. He glanced at Kessler, seated stiffly at the small conference table, his face pale but composed. Barry stood behind him, his hand resting almost casually on the back of Kessler's chair, a predator with his prey.

Reed, still in photographer mode, said, "Now that's a picture!"

"I didn't know you were involved in this shoot," Reed said, his tone light, almost conversational, while his mind spun. *Keep him talking. Make him feel in control. Don't let him see the trap closing.* "What brings you out of the shadows, Barry? This isn't usually your style."

Barry's smile was thin, his eyes sharp, his tone smooth as silk.

"Sometimes, Reed, you have to handle things personally. You know how it is, details matter."

Reed nodded, his mind cataloging every movement, every word. *Details matter. Yes, Barry, they do, and soon every one of yours will be recorded,* Reed thought. He slung his camera into his hand and raised the lens. "Mind if I get a few shots? Always nice to have a behind-the-scenes for the archives."

Barry tilted his head slightly, a calculated gesture. "Go ahead."

The clicks of the shutter filled the room, hiding the tension. Reed lowered the camera slightly, his voice casual and light. "You know, Barry, it's funny, I was just thinking about that shoot we did in D.C. Remember? You were so hands-on back then, too. Always right in the middle of it. Always making sure everything went exactly your way. We could really use your expertise today, your experience would be invaluable."

Barry's eyes flickered, the smallest crack in his mask of calm. He looked at Kessler, whose stiff body seemed to be searching for an escape. "Well, sure, I guess I could make an appearance. I'm always detail-oriented. That's what makes me good at what I do."

Reed smiled faintly, his voice dropping just low enough for Barry to hear. "Funny thing about details, though. They always leave a trail." Barry didn't change expression but Reed saw the flicker of understanding in his eyes, the realization that this wasn't a coincidence. But his ego wouldn't let it end here. Things had to play out.

Reed straightened, backing away from the door with a smile. "Well, I won't keep you, Barry. You and the Secretary have a lot to talk about. See you downstairs in an hour." He glanced at Kessler, his eyes locking with the Secretary's for a beat. The relief on the Secretary's face was obvious, but so was the tension simmering beneath it.

As Reed stepped into the hallway, his pulse thrummed in his fingertips, pushing him forward.

A soft chime from the elevator at the far end of the hallway caught Reed's attention. A woman with a clipboard emerged, her heels clicking against the floor. Two men flanked her, their move-ments precise. Reed's gut twisted with fear. *Was this Barry's inner circle? His hit team?*

Reed nodded as he passed them. He wondered if they were there to kill the Secretary. But Reed had changed things and plans had changed. Having a photo of Barry and the Secretary together undoubtedly saved the Secretary's life. But time was running out and Kessler's life was still on the line. Hopefully now the original plan was back in motion.

As Reed walked out of the elevator, the Lyt Meeter vibrated softly. He pulled it out of his bag and the screen flashed a coded confirmation message: *Architect oversight confirmed, Barry.*

Reed tapped his earpiece as he walked away from the elevator, his voice low and urgent. "Carter, Kranch, we're live. Everything's back on track. One hour. Be ready."

11

DEPTH OF FIELD

Barry closed the door behind Reed, his face a mask. He turned back to Secretary Kessler who had stood up but still looked unsure. "Secretary Kessler," Barry said smoothly, "thank you so much for coming up here. Unfortunately, we have to postpone. I'll see you downstairs for the photoshoot in about an hour."

Kessler hesitated for a moment, clearly not sure to trust Barry's last-minute change of plans but nodded and left the room without a word. The sound of the door closing was followed by the click of the lock.

Barry paced the suite. His mind moved in all directions, but it always came back to one thought: *What in the world is Reed up to?* Of all the agents in PPI, Reed was the most reliable. Not just reliable, perfect. Years of grooming had led to this moment and now of all times Barry felt something slipping out of place. That was not acceptable.

He stopped at the window, his eyes wandered over the city below, but his mind was a thousand miles away. Memories of working with Reed surfaced, fleeting moments of camaraderie. They had had some great times behind the lens together. Barry had always admired Reed's precision and ability to capture the moment others missed. It was like him. In those moments Reed had seemed like a protégé, a younger version of Barry before the stakes got high.

A small smile crossed his face as he thought about some of his greatest images of all times. Like the time he caught a world leader mid-smile, a shot that ran on every front page. Or the award-winning series of portraits of children in remote parts of the world that made him a darling of the press. Those were the images that defined him publicly, the charming, successful Barry Cox. The man people trusted, admired, even envied.

But the smile didn't last. Barry's thoughts snapped into the darker corners of his mind like a camera shutter. Control. That was the word that defined him privately. His all-consuming need for it, his ruthless tactics to maintain it and his cold indifference to anything or anyone that got in his way. The charm that won him accolades in the photography world was just a veneer, carefully applied and polished to hide the operator beneath. As Barry walked back to the table, he thought to himself: *This is what a leader does. It's no different than a king ruling a country. A king makes decisions for the greater good even if a few citizens have to suffer along the way. Sacrifices have to be made for the bigger picture. Always.*

He thought of Secretary Kessler. Barry hated it had to be this way but there was no other. If Kessler gets that code, he will truly be a liability, and liabilities had to be eliminated. He couldn't risk the code falling into Kessler's hands. It would open too many doors. The code wasn't just a threat; it was a catastrophe for everything Barry had built. And Barry prevented catastrophes.

Barry's fingers drummed against the table as he thought about the photoshoot. He curled his lip in disdain. *I should be the one taking that photograph anyway. I'm better than Sawyer.* The thought fed his ego, his disdain for weak links almost palpable. Kessler was weak. Sawyer was weak. They were all pawns, pieces to be moved or sacrificed as needed. But Barry Cox, *The Architect*, was the one who controlled the game.

A cold grin spread across Barry's face. He picked up his phone and typed a quick message. His thumb didn't hesitate as he hit send.

"Architect oversight confirmed, Barry."

The message sent. The plan was in motion. And Barry Cox was going to make sure nothing, no one, not even Reed Sawyer would stop it.

Barry's early days were marked by relentless drive and crushing disappointment. His living room was a makeshift studio, a mess of secondhand backdrops and cheap lighting equipment. Clients were few and far between and even when they did show up Barry often gave them free sessions just to build his portfolio. But the cost of his generosity quickly became unsustainable. Meals were skipped, bills went unpaid and Barry's hunger, both physical and emotional, grew sharper. At night Barry would sit in the dim light of his desk lamp and scroll through the portfolios of successful photographers on his old laptop. Their perfect websites, busy studios and glowing reviews were a far cry from his quiet existence. He craved recognition, a validation of his talent and the respect he felt he deserved. But the market was overcrowded and Barry for all his drive was just another name in the sea of others.

Desperation breeds cunning. Barry started staking out the parking lot of a well-known photography studio in town, a local favorite with a steady stream of clients. He parked his beat-up sedan across the street and watched as families, couples and high school seniors filed in for their sessions. At first, he just observed, taking mental notes of the flow of clients and the subtle charm of the studio. But soon he was taking bolder steps. Approaching potential clients before they reached the studio doors, Barry armed himself with charm and a portfolio of his best work. Promising quicker turnarounds and lower prices he was able to convince a few, and he even stole some away from his competition. It, sorta worked, temporarily. But even that small victory wasn't enough for him.

Then inspiration struck. Why compete for clients when he could eliminate the competition entirely? Barry's plan was bold, dangerous and meticulously thought out. His first move was to befriend the rival photographer, a jovial man who mistook Barry's interest as genuine friendship. Barry made himself indispensable, offering to assist with shoots, share equipment and swap trade stories. Behind this facade of friendship Barry was studying the studio, its layout, its vulnerabilities and its routines. Every detail was a puzzle piece and Barry was assembling the picture of its downfall.

After months of earning trust Barry made his move. During what seemed like a harmless visit to the rival studio he tampered with one of the lights, replacing a functioning part with a faulty one designed to overheat and spark. He left without a thought, confident in his plan. A week later in the dead of night the studio was consumed by flames, the fire devouring everything in its path. Investigators chalked it up to faulty wiring, a tragic accident that no one could have seen coming. Barry played the role of the grieving friend to perfection attending the rival's benefit fundraiser with tears in his eyes and words of condolence on his lips. His performance was flawless, a masterclass in deception.

The aftermath played out exactly as Barry had planned. With the rival photographer left with nothing, no equipment, no studio and no clients, it was exactly as Barry predicted. That photographer's clients were desperate to reschedule their shoots, so they turned to Barry. Conveniently he had availability and a small studio to accommodate them. Within days his empty calendar was full, his reputation soared and his small business boomed.

Barry never looked back. To him it wasn't a crime but a calculated sacrifice for success. He justified it with the same logic that had driven his rise: kings don't build empires by playing fair. And in his mind Barry wasn't just a photographer anymore, he was a king, shaping his own destiny one move at a time.

Barry's rise in the photography industry was like a rocket to the moon. His charm and talent behind the lens made him a sought-after speaker at photography conventions and schools. He became the golden boy of the industry, mesmerizing audiences with his lectures on lighting, studio management and most intriguingly his ability to "read the room", a subtle nod to his skill of manipulation. Every smile every anecdote was perfectly crafted to hide the darkness beneath his polished exterior.

It was at one of these conventions, a big event with the cream of the photography world in attendance, that Barry caught the eye of Luc Hudson. Hudson a prominent figure in PPI's public facing operation recognized in Barry what others had missed. Beyond his technical skill and charm Barry exuded control, a calculated precision in his interactions that Hudson found fascinating. To Hudson Barry wasn't just a good photographer; he was a strategist, someone who could command attention and manipulate those around him. Hudson saw potential, not just in Barry's work but in his ability to influence. Quietly he began to cultivate a relationship, framing it as mentorship. He introduced Barry to the surface benefits of PPI membership: a big professional network, exclusive training sessions and access to high profile opportunities. For Barry it was an open door to grow his small business. He joined as a regular member and used PPI's resources to solidify his reputation. Exclusive galleries showed his work, cutting edge technology streamlined his craft and private client lists expanded his reach. To Barry PPI was a means to an end, a tool to further his ambitions.

But Luc Hudson had bigger plans. He made sure PPI's hidden leadership took notice of Barry, not just his skills with a camera but his ability to manipulate people and situations. Barry was no ordinary talent, he was a strategist, someone who could be molded into an asset. It wasn't long before his skills were deemed too valuable for PPI's surface level operations.

The moment of truth came at a gallery in New York. Barry had been invited by Hudson under the guise of a networking event, a glamorous evening with elite photographers, art collectors and critics. The air was thick with talk of composition, technique and artistry but Barry's mind was elsewhere, scanning the walls for inspiration.

It was then, as he stood near a dramatic black and white portrait, that he overheard snippets of a conversation. Two men, standing just out of earshot, spoke in hushed tones. Their words were cryptic, phrases that didn't quite fit the polished world of art and photography. Barry's instincts pricked up. These weren't art enthusiasts discussing apertures or lighting techniques, this was something else. Something hidden.

His curiosity piqued Barry edged closer, catching snippets of their conversation. Phrases like "Keystone initiative" and "contingencies in play" stood out in his mind. This wasn't a typical gallery event, it was a front, a cover for something much bigger. Before he could piece more together a hand clapped firmly on his shoulder.

"Barry," Hudson's voice cut through his thoughts, smooth and deliberate. His smile was practiced and polished, but his eyes had an edge. "It's time I showed you the real power of PPI." Barry followed Hudson into a private room at the back of the gallery. The atmosphere changed instantly. The refined sophistication of the gallery disappeared and was replaced by something colder, harder. The room was bland but the energy in the room was anything but. Hudson motioned for Barry to sit, his tone all business now.

"This," he said, "is the PPI you don't read about in the membership brochures."

What followed dispelled any doubts Barry may have had. Hudson explained the true purpose of PPI, the surveillance, the covert operations, the influence they had over governments, industries and even media. As he spoke Barry's world opened up. This wasn't just a professional network; it was an invisible empire. A machine that operated in the shadows, manipulating global events with precision. It was everything Barry didn't know he wanted but instantly desired.

By the time Hudson finished Barry wasn't just interested, he was hooked. The world of photography conventions and galleries now felt like a stepping stone, a mere precursor to the power that lay before him. Barry saw the opportunity for what it was, an invitation to leave behind the ordinary and step into a world where he could be unstoppable.

Barry didn't hesitate. When Hudson asked him to join PPI's covert operations Barry volunteered. To him this was more than an opportunity, it was a doorway to real power. No longer confined to the world of portraits and shutter speeds his camera became a tool of influence, manipulation and control. In Barry's eyes he hadn't just found his true calling, he had found a throne. And nothing, absolutely nothing, was going to get in his way.

Barry's rise through PPI's covert ranks was lightning fast, surgical. Every move was deliberate, every action designed to eliminate obstacles and consolidate power. Leaning back in the leather chair of Suite 918 a rare smile spread across his face. His journey replayed in his mind like a perfectly composed series of photographs, each frame capturing another victory, another conquest. It all started with Luc Hudson, the man who had pulled him from nowhere and given him the keys to the PPI underground. Hudson had believed in him, championed him. But that belief had been Hudson's downfall. Barry couldn't stomach Hudson's idealism, his naive idea of the greater good. Worse Hudson had started to question Barry's methods, the very methods Barry knew were necessary in their world of shadows and secrets.

So, Barry did what he did best: he eliminated the problem. Planting false evidence wasn't just easy, it was poetic. A few doctored documents, a few whispers in the right ears and Hudson was gone. Banished from PPI without even a chance to plead his case. Barry still remembered the look of shock on Hudson's face when it hit him. That memory made Barry's lips curl into a dark smile. By the time Hudson was out Barry had already taken his influence, his projects, his network, Reed Sawyer included.

Barry's grin faltered as he thought of Sawyer. Reliable, meticulous, sharp, but lately something was off. Reed had been distant, his moves harder to read. Loose ends weren't just inconvenient, they were dangerous. And Reed was starting to look like a loose end. After today's events in the Suite, it was confirmed what Barry had already set in motion: Sawyer would be taken care of. Soon.

His thoughts turned to other rivals within PPI who had dared to challenge him, their ambitions snuffed out with surgical precision. Barry's favorite tactic was blackmail, a well-placed photograph, an incriminating whisper and their resolve crumbled like sandcastles under the tide. There was something very satisfying about it, the way a single image could destroy a life, end a career or tip the balance of power. It was the perfect weapon, silent but deadly.

But Barry's biggest realization was far more profound. His photography assignments weren't just jobs, they were opportunities. A chance to collect secrets, to listen in on whispers not meant for his ears. His lens was a window into the vulnerabilities of the powerful. Over time Barry had mastered the art of turning his photographs into leverage, his camera into a scalpel. He didn't just take pictures, he took influence. And with that influence came control. For Barry, there was no greater thrill than knowing that behind every composed frame, every carefully captured moment, lay the threads of a web only he could weave. It was his kingdom and he was the architect.

Barry's path was growing darker. The assignments were riskier, the stakes higher, the consequences more deadly. He remembered the first time someone had to die because they threatened his plans. The weight of the decision was lighter than he'd thought. Easier. Now the bodies in his wake barely registered, a mere calculation, a necessary cost of leadership. Collateral damage. The price of ambition.

Barry adjusted his cufflink, his thoughts snapping back to the present. Vienna. Today. Secretary Kessler. It had all been leading to this, the culmination of years of planning, manipulation and elimination. How many bodies had he had to step over to get here? Too many to count. But Barry didn't waste time on regrets. Regret was for the weak. Leaders had no room for such indulgences. They did what had to be done.

Kessler wouldn't see it coming. Neither would Sawyer. By the end of the day Barry would have everything he needed, and anyone foolish enough to get in his way would be an afterthought.

Barry's thoughts spun deeper into the empire he'd created. He'd turned PPI into something far more sinister. It wasn't just covert anymore; it was a precision engineered machine for control, manipulation and dominance. And Barry, *The Architect*, was the master.

His rise to full power had been inevitable. With Hudson gone and a few other high ranking PPI members eliminated or neutralized Barry had taken control. He'd reshaped the covert division into his own image, a shadow empire that could bend governments, leaders and corporations to his will. Destabilize regimes? Manipulate elections? Collapse economies? It was all part of the game. The beauty of it? Every move was made under the guise of a global photography network. Who would suspect the man behind the lens?

Barry smiled, the amusement flickering to life as he thought of the last fool who'd dared to challenge him. What was his name? Bill? Bob? Jerry? Didn't matter, he was irrelevant now. What mattered was the plan. That little worm had thought he could blow the whistle, as if Barry wouldn't see it coming a mile away. "Amateur," Barry said, his voice dripping with contempt.

The plan was laughable. The guy, whatever his name was, thought he could leak sensitive information about PPI's shadow network: Barry's manipulation of foreign leaders, his orchestration of covert ops. He'd even reached out to a journalist, convinced he could expose Barry's empire. But Barry knew everything. Always.

The whistleblower's "accident" was tragically poetic. A car crash on a rainy night, caused by faulty brakes. No one questioned it. Why would they? Barry had made sure the narrative was seamless, the evidence untraceable. The little worm and his secrets were buried together, his brief rebellion reduced to a footnote.

Barry chuckled, a cold, low sound that filled the quiet room. "So predictable."

And that was the beauty of Barry's world. His plans didn't just succeed, they strangled resistance before it could get started. Every loose end tied up. Every potential threat eliminated. The Architect left nothing to chance.

He chuckled, a rare genuine laugh. It wasn't just about the win, it was about the message it sent. The entire network knew the stakes after that. Cross Barry Cox and you disappeared. His reputation as a man who left no loose ends had become a legend. Fear wasn't just a tool; it was a work of art and Barry was the master.

His philosophy was unyielding: *Power is everything. Trust is weakness.* Trust was a liability, a crack in the foundation of control. That's why Barry trusted no one. Not his operatives, not his allies, not even the few people he considered friends. Everyone was expendable. Everyone was a means to an end. And Barry controlled every end.

He grinned. "The Architect" wasn't just his title; it was his name. Every move, every decision, every life taken or spared was a deliberate stroke in the grand design he'd been perfecting for years. He didn't just play the game. He owned it.

As he prepared for the op ahead, he thought about how far he'd come. From a struggling photographer desperate for recognition to the most powerful man no one even knew existed. Barry gazed at his reflection in the window, a cold, calculated smile stared back at him. "Power is everything," he said, the words cutting the air. "And I don't lose."

His eyes dropped to his bare hand, where a wedding band had once been. How many times had he been married? He wasn't even sure. More than four, anyway. The number had blended into the noise of his chaotic life, a detail too trivial for someone of his ambitions to remember. The irony wasn't lost on him. The Architect, master of precision and control, couldn't even keep track of his own failed marriages.

He chuckled, shaking his head. He never loved any of them, not really. Love required vulnerability and vulnerability was a crack in the foundation. Relationships were tools: alliances for appearances, fleeting companionship or leverage when needed. Every one of them had eventually crumbled under the weight of his need for dominance.

Control was his currency. There was no partnership, no compromise, only Barry's way. And when that became clear, they always left. Or he pushed them out. Some quietly, others in drama. Didn't matter. Emotions were a distraction and Barry had no patience for distractions.

He thought of his father, a man weighed down by sentiment and family obligations, watching helplessly as his business went under. Barry had sworn he'd never fall into that trap. Weakness. That's what it was.

He frowned as a name flickered in his mind. **Marcus.**

"No," he muttered, shaking his head sharply as if to banish the thought. "Not now."

But it was already there, lurking. His younger brother. The last time they'd spoken, they'd ended in anger. Barry had built walls so high, so impenetrable, that even the memory of his own brother felt like an intrusion. He wasn't moved by guilt or regret; Marcus was just another piece in a game too big for sentimentality.

"Think of legacy," he whispered, the word tasting bitter, metallic, like blood on his tongue. Legacy. The thing that drove him forward, even as it consumed everything in its path. His failed marriages. His estranged family. They were small sacrifices for the empire he was building. Relationships were messy, unpredictable, uncontrollable. Sacrifices were necessary. He justified it all with the same reasoning he always did: *The world doesn't need bleeding hearts. It needs visionaries.*

Barry's mouth curved into a thin smile as he turned back to the window, the Vienna skyline glinting in the afternoon sun. Love, family, those were crutches for the weak. They were casualties of his relentless pursuit of power.

"The weak cling to connection," he said, his voice cold. "The strong forge their own path."

The knock at the door snapped Barry out of his thoughts. His expression hardened as he walked towards it, pausing just long enough to clear all expression from his face. When he opened the door, the woman and her 2 companions entered without a word. Their movements were deliberate, their presence suffocating the room like a storm cloud.

"Change of plans," Barry said, pacing before them like a predator sizing up its prey. "We hold until after the photoshoot. Be ready." He stopped mid-step, turned to meet their blank stares and spoke in a voice that froze the air. "See you in 10 minutes at the stairwell. I'll brief you there."

They nodded in unison, their obedience mechanical. Without a word, they exited, their precision mirroring the stakes. Barry locked the door behind them, the soft click of the latch echoing in the silent suite. Alone again, he took a moment to mentally run through every detail of his plan. Years of manipulation, ambition, and ruthlessness had led to this moment.

There could be no mistakes.

Barry went to the desk, his laptop glowing faintly as he opened it. Pro4uM.com, the PPI forum set as his home page, flashed across the screen. He navigated to the "Chubby Senior" thread and started typing a message to Marty Grimes. Every word was calculated, every phrase precise. Innocent to anyone outside their network. But beneath the surface, the message was a deadly command. Barry leaned back and studied his work, a small smile on his lips. He was the Architect, the puppet master. Every string pulled by his hand, and no one else saw the big picture except him.

Yes, Sawyer had to go.

Barry closed the laptop and stood up, his movement fluid despite the tension coiled inside him. He crossed the room, his fists clenched as he turned his mind to Secretary Kessler. Another loose end, another liability. The code would never reach Kessler's hands, not now, not ever. Kessler wasn't a person anymore; he was a problem. A threat.

And threats didn't survive in Barry's world.

Barry winked at himself as he adjusted his tie, squared his shoulders. His empire would endure. His name, The Architect, would be whispered in the shadows long after he was gone.

Barry stared at his reflection in the window for a long moment, a cold smile forming. He then turned his gaze to the camera bag in the corner, just another tool of his trade. But Barry knew better, this bag held more than just equipment; it held the key to the next part of his plan.

He unzipped the bag and his fingers brushed against the lens with a red cap. He lifted it out and felt the weight in his hands, the cool metal surface grounding him in its deadliness. It was a marvel of engineering. A gun modified to conceal a single-shot, a silenced weapon behind its fake pristine glass. To anyone else, it was just another lens.

A small smile played on his lips as he turned the lens in his hands, admiring its simplicity. The irony wasn't lost on him. When the moment came and someone said, "Let the shoot begin." it would be Barry's shot that would end it all.

He slid the lens back into the bag and zipped it shut. His mind, always ten steps ahead, was already running through the next phase. Everything was in place, Kessler, Grimes, Sawyer, the board was set, and Barry Cox, The Architect, was the only one who knew how the game would end. He pulled out his phone and opened the encrypted app reserved for his inner circle. Each key pressed purposefully, the message crafted with precision:

"Shoot is a go. Finalize setup. Kessler removal follows. No deviations."

He sent. Seconds later, the confirmations rolled in:

"Confirmed."

"Understood."

"Ready."

Barry's lips spread into a slow smile. Everything was on schedule.

He slung the camera bag over his shoulder and the weight of the red-capped lens against his side was a constant reminder of his control. Each step toward the elevator was deliberate. He replayed the sequence in his head: the shoot, the diversion, the elimination. Nothing had been left out.

The elevator doors opened with a soft ding and Barry stepped inside. He straightened his posture as he looked at his reflection in the steel walls. His confidence was evident, each movement precise, each thought sharp. He pressed the button for the floor where the secret meeting at the stairwell would take place and watched the numbers descend as he calculated his next move.

The elevator slowed to a stop and the doors opened with a whisper. *"There's only one Architect in this world,"* Barry thought as he stepped out. *"And I don't leave things unfinished."*

The elevator doors closed behind him.

12

EXPOSURE TIME

arty was already logged in to Pro4uM.com when Barry sent him the message in the Chubby Senior thread. Its casual tone was a thin veil over its deadly intent:

"I had a Chubby Senior to photograph this week. His name was Tom. I told him he had to go, he needed to lose weight. I ended the session. Under no circumstances was I going to allow him in my studio. I recommend you do the same with any of your observations."

Marty's heart sank. The meaning was unmistakable. "Tom" was Reed Sawyer and he wasn't just being observed, he was the target. Barry's message left no room for misinterpretation. He wanted Marty to kill Sawyer today.

Marty sat back in his chair, his pulse pounding. This wasn't what he signed up for. He'd always known PPI operated in the shadows but this? This was something else. His mind was spinning with excuses, but each one was being crushed by Barry's implied threat. Failure wasn't an option, especially not when it came to Barry Cox.

Marty closed his laptop and stared at the innocent camera bag on his bed. He reached for it instinctively, his hands shaking as he opened the compartment. His fingers brushed against the cold metal of the concealed weapon Barry had made him carry, a "just in case" precaution that now felt like a setup, a ticking time bomb.

His mind spun. *What if I don't do it? What if I miss? What if Barry finds out?* He tried to calm his breathing but the knot in his chest tightened. Barry always found out.

Marty replayed the message in his head, clinging to the absurdity of it. Marty knew what it meant. Kill Sawyer.

It wasn't the first time he'd followed orders that walked the line but this? This was different. This was kill or be killed.

Marty's mind went back to memories he'd tried to forget, operatives who had failed Barry. Their excuses had seemed reasonable at the time: hesitation, uncertainty or inability to deliver. But Barry had no tolerance for failure.

Marty remembered when Barry had casually mentioned a previous operative who "lacked loyalty". The story had been told with a detachment, but the message was clear: obedience was survival. Barry's words echoed in Marty's head: *"Disloyalty isn't a mistake. It's a choice. And choices have consequences."*

Marty had always been loyal, or at least compliant. But he'd never been asked to kill someone before, let alone someone like Reed Sawyer.

Marty's hand hovered over the weapon, his mind flicking back to Reed. He remembered their brief conversation at the café that morning. Reed had been calm, almost casual but there was something in his tone, a hint of knowing.

"Things aren't always what they seem, Marty," Reed had said, his eyes piercing. *"Sometimes, the picture isn't as clear as you think."*

Marty had brushed it off at the time, attributing it to Reed's cryptic nature. But now the words gnawed at him. What if Reed wasn't just another cog in Barry's machine? What if Reed knew something, something Barry didn't want him to know?

The idea was ridiculous. Barry was The Architect. He saw everything, controlled everything. The notion that someone could outsmart him was laughable.

And yet...

Marty shook his head, trying to silence the flicker of doubt.

He reasoned with himself, trying to push away the growing unease. *Barry knows what's best. He's always known what's best. If he says Reed has to go, then Reed has to go. It's not my job to question it. It's my job to follow orders.*

But what if Barry was wrong?

Marty stood up, pacing the room. He muttered to himself, "Barry doesn't make mistakes. Barry doesn't make mistakes. Barry doesn't, "

But the doubt lingered, faint but persistent.

What if Reed really is onto something? And what if Barry knows it too?

Marty paced again, then sat on the edge of his hotel bed, staring at his phone as Barry's message replayed in his head.

He gripped the bedframe, his knuckles white. *Reed was right. Barry's making me the fall guy. If anything goes wrong, it's my name that'll be in the reports, not his.*

Reed had hinted at secrets, about Barry, about PPI. Secrets Marty had been too scared or too loyal to consider. But now? Now the pieces were falling into place and the picture wasn't one he wanted to be a part of.

Marty rubbed his temples, his mind a blur. Telling Reed the truth wasn't just dangerous, it was treason. But what choice did he have?

He looked at the schedule for the photoshoot, the tight timeline leaving no room for deviation.

Marty's gaze flicked to his camera bag, reasoning kicking in. *If I follow Barry's orders, I'm complicit in this. If I tell Reed, I'm dead. Either way, I lose.*

But a spark of determination emerged from the fear. *Maybe, just maybe, Reed has a plan. And if he doesn't, he needs to know what he's walking into.*

The shoot was soon, very soon, and Marty might have a very small window of opportunity!

Five minutes. Maybe less. It's not much, but it's all I've got.

Marty went through the possibilities in his head. *What if Barry's watching? What if someone else sees me talking to Reed? What if this is already a setup, and Barry's testing my loyalty?*

But the alternative was worse. If he stayed silent, Reed would walk into the shoot blind and Marty would be the one holding the gun, literally and figuratively.

Marty pulled out his phone and texted Reed:

"Prep area. NOW."

He hit send and shoved the phone into his pocket, his hands shaking. He couldn't back out now. Whatever happened next, he was in.

With that, Marty headed to the prep area, his resolve solidifying with every step.

Down in the ballroom, Reed adjusted the settings on his main camera, the lens glinting under the fluorescent lights. Every angle, every shadow was perfect, not for the photos, but for the hidden cameras. With Barry coming, the stakes had gone through the roof. The cameras weren't just tools anymore; they were weapons. He reviewed the layout in his mind. One device embedded in a light stand, another in the decorative molding near the entrance. His most critical piece, a pinhole microphone with camera, was nestled near the main stairwell. This would be a perfect meeting spot to talk "business" if he were Barry. Every device was positioned to capture Barry's every word and movement.

Just then his phone buzzed in his pocket. He pulled it out, his heart skipping when he saw the sender: **Marty Grimes.**

The message was short and to the point: *"Prep area. NOW."*

Reed checked his watch. Less than an hour to the photoshoot. He hesitated, his instincts flaring. Marty was a wild card, someone caught between loyalty to Barry and his own survival. But he couldn't ignore the message.

He typed a quick reply: *"On my way. Has to be quick."*

As he hit send, the Lyt Meeter vibrated in his pocket. He pulled it out, the message glaring up at him in bold text:

"The shoot is a go. Finalize setup. Removal of Kessler follows immediately. No deviations."

A shiver ran down his spine. This wasn't a vague hint or coded phrase, it was as plain as day, Secretary Kessler had less than an hour left.

Reed's voice remained steady as he spoke into his earpiece, masking the panic beneath. "Carter, Kranch. Prep room. Now."

Moments earlier, while Grimes was figuring out what to do, Barry strode into the dimly lit stairwell, a light flickering above. His execution team, a woman and two men, was already assembled, their black suits blending into the shadows. They stood at attention as Barry approached, his presence commanding and deliberate.

He didn't waste time, speaking in a low, measured tone. "The photoshoot goes as scheduled. No deviations. The Secretary will be eliminated on my signal. I'll handle it personally." Barry's hand touched the camera bag on his shoulder, where the modified gun/lens with the hidden silenced weapon lay waiting. "It must look clean, unavoidable. A tragic, unforeseeable accident. No loose ends. Do you understand me? I'll make sure it's done right, and then we move forward, unshaken, untouchable. There will be no mistakes." The operatives nodded in unison, their faces expressionless. Barry's gaze landed on the tallest of them, a big man with a scar along his cheek. Antonio Dovere was one of Barry's most trusted operatives. Only Seth Gauthier, Barry's number one, was closer to him.

"Sawyer," Barry said to Dovere. "He's next. Marty Grimes will take care of him, as ordered. But we can't leave this to chance."

Barry's eyes bored into Dovere. "You'll tail Grimes. Stay close, but not so close he notices. If he hesitates, or worse, if he betrays us, you take out Reed. And you do it in a way that everyone thinks Grimes pulled the trigger, but make it messy. A struggle, something that fits the narrative. In the mess, take out Grimes too. Got it?"

Dovere smiled faintly, confidence oozing from him. "Got it, sir."

Barry nodded, still calculating. He didn't trust Marty, not completely. Grimes had always been competent, but soft, a man who followed orders but lacked the killer instinct. Barry had seen the hesitation in his eyes during past assignments, the flicker of doubt that could blow everything.

"The timing is critical." Barry said. "The photoshoot goes as planned. Kessler is first, personally, by me. Sawyer's next, courtesy of Grimes. And Grimes? He won't leave the building either. This ends today." Barry chuckled humorlessly, "We'll be the heroes, making sure no one else gets hurt. I want it airtight, clean, precise, and above all, believable."

Barry continued, "The world will see what I want them to see. Nothing more. Nothing less. And if anyone tries to screw up, well... accidents happen all the time in this business."

Barry paused, scanning the team for any sign of panic. There was none. These were pros, loyal to him and his vision. He allowed himself a small, pleased smile. "Any questions?"

"No questions, sir." Dovere replied, his voice flat. The others just shook their heads. Barry turned, his mind working with precision and control. Every piece was in place. The Secretary, Sawyer, Grimes, they were all pawns in his game, pieces to be sacrificed for the greater good. As he descended the stairwell, a dark thought flickered through his mind: *This is why I'm the Architect. No loose ends, no liabilities, only results.*

Unbeknownst to him, every word, every calculated instruction had been recorded, captured by Reed's hidden devices. The trap was closing, though Barry, ever the puppet master, thought he was the one pulling the strings.

Reed headed toward the prep room, and his moves didn't go unnoticed by one of Barry's operatives, who watched him with narrowed eyes. Reed was moving with that same easy confidence he always had. Sawyer had a way of blending in, of becoming invisible, but the operative had been trained to notice even the smallest deviations. And this? This wasn't routine.

He had just seen Carter, pacing just outside the door, and Kranch, leaning against the frame. Strange.

Those two had gone in the room and now here comes Reed Sawyer. They weren't supposed to be gathering like this.

Should he report this? The instructions he had received earlier couldn't have been clearer: *No deviations.*

He hesitated, his hand hovering over his encrypted communicator. Doubt crept in, was this a real opportunity to act or another one of Barry's famous loyalty tests? Barry had a rep for setting traps, for sending false directives to flush out operatives with divided loyalties. But this was just a photoshoot. It was about to start, and they had to be ready. His heart raced as he weighed the risk of delaying against the fallout of reporting too soon. He set a mental timer, two minutes. That's it. Less than two minutes would be normal for last minute prep at an important shoot. Anything more, just a second over, and he would report it as suspicious.

Just then Reed walked into the prep room, with Grimes right behind him.

The room was already hopping when Reed arrived. Carter was against the wall, his face tight with tension. Kranch was peering through the crack in the door, scanning every shadow like a hawk on the hunt.

Grimes burst in last, his face white as he clutched his phone. Grimes spoke first, his voice shaky. "Did you read the 'Chubby Senior' thread? Barry's ordered me to kill you, Reed. At the shoot. Today."

Carter's shoulders shot up as he cut in, "Operatives are swarming this place. They're everywhere, watching us right now, bellhops, waiters, you name it."

Kranch added grimly, "Barry's on the move. I saw him with three operatives near the stairwell, looks like his execution team."

Reed held up his hand, silencing the group. His voice was calm but his eyes blazed. "Team, this is what we train for. Remember, to them we're just a photography team getting ready for a normal photoshoot. Nothing suspicious about that. But let me show you something."

He tapped into the surveillance feed on his phone, pulling up the footage from the hidden camera in the stairwell. The grainy screen flickered to life and there was Barry, right out in the open, with his operatives flanking him. His voice, smooth and deliberate, filled the room:

"The photoshoot goes as planned. Kessler is first, personally, by me. Sawyer's next, courtesy of Grimes. And Grimes? He won't leave the building either. This ends today."

The room was silent, the weight of Barry's words crushing them. Reed looked around at the team. Grimes looked like he was going to puke. Carter's fists were clenched, his knuckles white. Even Kranch, usually unflappable, looked shaken.

Reed pocketed his phone and stood up, his voice firm. "Mission is scrubbed. We're not playing Barry's game anymore. We've got the intel we need. Only thing left to do is get the mission code to the Secretary."

He looked at Kranch. "You've got defensive maneuvers in place, right?"

Kranch nodded. "Kessler will be safe. I'll get him out." Reed's voice dropped slightly. "As soon as the shoot starts, I'm sure the mission code will come in and I'll give it to the Secretary. Then I'll give the Secretary a secret phrase signaling danger. Kranch, as soon as I say, 'Great shot, you're all done. This shoot is over. Get out from in front of my camera.' move Kessler. Get him out of here immediately. Don't stop for anything."

Kranch nodded. "Understood."

"Good." Reed's eyes fell on Carter and Grimes. "You two are on the execution team. Do not let them execute Barry's plan. Stick to them like glue. Barry has backups, he always does. Make sure they don't get near Kessler."

Reed's gaze shifted to Grimes. "Marty, you're part of this team now. Take this earpiece and stick close to Carter, and do not let Barry's team take control. Got it?"

Grimes nodded. "Got it."

They had Barry on tape. They had him dead to rights. But now they had to get that mission code to the Secretary. Then get out alive.

Outside the room the Operative hesitated, uncertainty crossing his face. Just as he was about to report this strange meeting. The Prep Room door opened.

Sawyer stepped out first, looking calm as if he hadn't just been in a secret meeting. The others followed, equally expressionless. Each went in a different direction, a coordinated dispersal that drew no attention.

The Operative was still questioning this unusual meeting. The instinct to report rising. But just as he was about to report this, from down the hall a familiar voice called out.

"Reed!"

Barry Cox walked towards the ballroom, his voice warm and friendly, his face relaxed. Reed turned and smiled at Barry like an old friend. They exchanged a few words and Barry's body language was so relaxed he could have been on a Sunday stroll.

The Operative froze, his hand dropping away from his communicator, sliding back into his pocket. If Barry was this casual, if he was talking to Sawyer like they were buddies, then surely... this was all part of the plan. He hesitated for only a moment before logic and loyalty took over. The Architect didn't make mistakes.

The operative stood up straight, his body relaxing. Whatever had just happened in the Prep Room didn't matter. The photoshoot was about to start, and the plan would go off without a hitch.

Barry's smile was disarming, his face bland. Barry's voice boomed warmly, his hand out for a handshake. "It's been too long, my friend. I really enjoy working with you. We always have so much fun, don't we?"

Reed clasped Barry's hand, matching the friendly energy though his guts twisted with unease. "Always a pleasure, Barry," he said, keeping his tone light.

Barry leaned in slightly, his grin growing wider as if they were sharing a joke. "I brought all my special equipment. You know how I am, I like to do things my way. Can I borrow your tripod? I'll save some time."

The request was harmless enough, but he knew its true meaning. Barry wasn't here to help; he was here to control.

So this is how it's going to go down, Reed thought, his mind calculating. If Barry used his tripod it would give him a direct line of execution, whatever that was. And Reed couldn't let that happen.

Maintaining his façade, Reed chuckled. "Barry, you always make my gear work overtime." He looked at his watch then back at Barry. "Tell you what, let's set up side by side. We'll make it a team effort. You take point and I'll do backups. That way we've got all angles covered."

Barry's smile faltered for a second before he recovered. "Sounds good," he said, his tone friendly but calculated.

Reed nodded and stepped past Barry with his camera bag slung over his shoulder. His thoughts were ten steps ahead. He had to stop whatever Barry was planning but he couldn't tip his hand, yet. In the ballroom the time had come. The air was heavy with an invisible energy that made every movement feel weighted. Reed stood behind his camera, adjusting the focus ring with precision. His hands were steady, but his eyes flicked briefly to his phone. Still no codes for Kessler. His brain was screaming at him. *Come on. Come on. This is too close.*

The room was spotless. The floor reflected the lights, their stands casting long shadows on the walls. Every piece of equipment was in place, but the room felt anything but orderly. Tension simmered beneath the surface, certain and electric. Reed could feel it in the tiny movements of the other players in the room.

Kessler walked in, his shoes clicking on the floor like a countdown. His face was blank, years of political training had carved his mask of calm, but Reed saw the tiny twitch of his fingers as he clasped them together. *He knows something's off*, Reed thought.

"Right this way, Mr. Secretary," Reed said, his tone professional. He led Kessler to the small stage-like area where the lights and camera were set up. The backdrop, a Denny Mfg. OM-2542, a gradient of blues and grays, was meant to be soothing. Reed moved with purpose, positioning the Secretary under the lights. "This will only take a few minutes."

Kessler nodded curtly, his lips pressed together. *Stay calm. Trust the plan.* But his eyes darted to the edges of the room as if the walls could betray him.

Barry's voice boomed out. "Everyone and everything in place? Let's get rolling."

Reed turned to Barry who was standing a few feet away, leaning against the table. His posture was relaxed but his eyes were anything but. They were sharp, hungry, scanning the room with a precision that sent a shiver down Reed's spine. Barry bent to pick up his camera, his hand brushing over the lens with the red cap in a ritualistic gesture. His face tightened for a second, almost imperceptible, but Reed saw it. *This is it. This is how he's going to do it.* Reed turned back to the Secretary, his nerves on edge. His camera felt heavy, the weight of the moment pressing down on him. He adjusted the angle, framing Kessler in his viewfinder. Sweat prickled at the back of his neck but his hands were steady.

His eyes flicked to his phone. *Still no mission code. Come on! This is too close.*

Behind him Kranch moved, his massive presence a shadow at the edge of the room. His eyes narrowed as he watched Barry, his stance ready, waiting for the phrase cue. Carter stood near the far corner, his back to the wall, looking like a tourist to anyone who didn't know better. His fingers tapped against his side, but his eyes were on the Secretary, then Barry, then back again.

The room felt stopped, every movement slow and deliberate like a scene stretched to the breaking point. Barry stepped forward, his camera ready, the red lens cap off but dangling on a string. "Alright, ready Secretary? Smile for the camera," Barry said, his voice smooth, almost sneering. His finger hovered over the shutter release.

The Secretary adjusted his tie, completely oblivious to the storm around him. The lights hummed in Reed's ears, amplified by the tension in the air. Barry's camera about to click, and it would all be over for the Secretary.

Reed's chest tightened. *No. No way. Not this time Barry!*

Instead, Reed stepped in front of Barry, blocking his camera and more importantly the red-capped gun disguised as a lens. With his own camera on a tripod, effectively blocking Barry's line of sight to the Secretary, Reed took one shot.

Reed breathed out sharply. "Great shot, you're all done."

Kessler's eyes went wide for a second, but Reed didn't falter. His voice rose, firm and commanding, his eyes on the Secretary.

"This shoot is over. Get out from in front of my camera." Kranch moved fast, stepping forward with precision. His big hand wrapped around the Secretary's arm. "Come on, Secretary," he said, his voice low and command.

Kessler hesitated for a second, his eyes flicking to Reed. Confusion crossed his face.

Reed looked at the Secretary and nodded sharply. *Yes, this is part of the plan.*

Kranch's grip didn't relax, his movements purposeful and calculated. The Secretary nodded and allowed himself to be led out, his steps smooth and composed like a man used to following orders when the stakes were high.

Barry's smile fell, his eyes narrowing. "What's going on here?" he said, his voice sharp. The mask of friendliness slipped. His hand clenched on his camera. "We're not done."

"Oh, we're done," Reed said. His tone was cool, confident and sarcastic but his heart was wired. "That's a wrap."

Barry's eyes darted between Reed and the Secretary, calculating.

Suspicion clouded his face but he didn't move, his control slipping by degrees.

Reed's phone buzzed finally, the notification vibrating on his palm. He looked down, the code on the screen: *Section 3. Page: 16. Code: 105-B*. Reed's eyes went wide. He couldn't believe what he was seeing. He had the mission code all along? *What is going on? What does this mean?* His mouth compressed into a hard line. What exactly does this mean?

As Kessler and Kranch reached the door the room seemed to cool. Reed met Barry's gaze, unflinching. "So, Barry," he said evenly. "What's next?"

Reed kept one hand on his camera, the other on the table as he scanned the room. His eyes flicked to Kessler's security team, three big agents near the exits. They were moving now, their eyes on the Secretary like they sensed the storm.

"Stand down," Kessler said, his voice calm but firm. He raised his hand, halting them. "It's all going according to plan. I'm fine." Reed thought *Good cover, Secretary. Now let's hope that's true.* But Kessler's words did nothing to calm the growing storm in the room. Reed's focus shifted back to Barry who now stood still, his hand on the red-capped gun disguised as a lens, his face a blank mask.

Barry signaled to his number one, Seth Gauthier, near the hallway. Reed caught it. *Not good*, he thought.

Gauthier left the ballroom and headed for the hotel's electrical room, moving swiftly but smoothly, blending into the background noise. Carter's voice crackled in Reed's earpiece, low and urgent. "Heads up, one of Barry's guys is going to the electrical room. My guess? They're going to shut off the power."

Reed's heart raced but his voice was calm. "Stay with him, Carter. We can't let them cut this room dark."

Carter's response was short and tense. "On it."

Barry shifted slightly, raised his camera, the gun/lens with the red cap now pointed at Reed. His movements were deliberate, each step a calculated move. He was calm, but too calm. The kind of calm that sent shivers down Reed's spine like the silence before a storm. Barry's finger rested on the shutter release, but his grip tightened ever so slightly. His eyes were on Reed, piercing and unblinking, a predator sizing up his prey.

Reed's hands were on his own camera, still on the tripod but now pointed at Barry. Every muscle protested to move, to react, but he held firm, waiting, calculating. The room seemed to freeze, the tension coiling like a spring about to snap.

Barry spoke, his voice soft and conversational, a knife wrapped in velvet. "Sometimes," he said, tilting his head. "The best shots are the ones you don't take."

The words hung in the air, cold and unfathomable. Reed's mind raced to interpret the layers of meaning. Barry's small smirk grew, a hunter savoring the final seconds before the pounce.

Then it happened. A soft pop. A silenced shot muffled and fatal. The sound sliced through the heavy atmosphere like a scalpel. At that same instant, Reed pressed the shutter release. The camera clicked as the bullet fired. Reed's eyes widened as the realization struck him like a physical blow. Barry had fired his lens gun. And Reed's camera had captured it all.

13
NEGATIVE SPACE

Reed ducked and his camera hit the floor. The muffled crack of the shot was so quiet it barely registered over the hum of the lights, but Reed knew what it meant. He hit the ground and rolled behind the table for cover his thoughts scattered.

The room erupted into chaos. Kessler's security detail sprang into action. They had been trained to know what a gunshot sounded like even a silenced one. Their commands and movements sliced through the room. "Code Black! Secure the Secretary!" one of the agents barked. The lights overhead flickered once then stabilized casting long shifting shadows across the walls.

Reed stayed low his pulse pounding in his ears. He clenched his teeth trying to get his composure back, but his mind wouldn't stop replaying the sound of the silenced shot. His body trembled as he crouched behind the table.

Then he felt it, a tiny pinch on his right earlobe. He reached up and brushed against it. When he pulled his hand back his fingers were smeared with blood. Reed's breath caught. The shot had grazed him. If he hadn't ducked it would've been a clean kill.

So close. Too close.

His camera lay beside him, the tripod collapsed. He grabbed it and held it like a lifeline his fingers shaking. He looked towards the center of the room where Barry Cox was standing unflinching. The red capped lens was still attached to the camera with a hole down the middle of the front glass its deadly secret hidden behind the shiny exterior. Barry lowered the camera slowly his smirk growing wider as if savoring the moment. His composure was unnerving a stark contrast to the chaos around him.

Reed's earpiece crackled to life. Kranch's voice came through sharp and urgent. "Reed status?"

Reed forced himself to breathe to push through the fear haze in his mind. "Barry took the shot. Barely missed me. Protect Kessler. Get him out and to safety now!"

"Got it. Extracting him now" Kranch replied, his voice steady but tense.

Through the earpiece Carter's voice came through. "Reed, you good? Do you need help?" "No" Reed replied, his voice steady now the adrenaline kicking in. "Protect the Secretary at all costs!"

Barry turned slightly, his eyes narrowing as he caught Reed looking at him. His smirk faltered for a second, a flicker of doubt crossed his face, then it was gone, replaced by his usual cool arrogance. He tilted his head as if to say *Let's see what you'll do next.*

Reed disconnected his camera from the tripod and slipped it into his bag and secured it tightly. His thoughts ticked through the next steps, each one calculated deliberate. Barry had made his move and barely missed. Now it was time for Reed to counter.

The room suddenly got thicker. Kessler's security team surged forward their movements precise but frantic a well-rehearsed choreography of protection. Kessler's team fanned out their hands hovering near concealed weapons scanning the room for secondary threats.

Kessler and Kranch had left the ballroom just before Barry took the shot. They were on the move, their strides quick but measured. Moving further away from danger now.

Reed stayed low his body pressed against the floor as he crawled towards better cover. He risked a glance towards the door Kessler and Kranch were long gone hopefully safe. The security detail followed moments later. But by then it was as if the Secretary had disappeared into thin air. They reached the hallway only to find... nothing.

"What?" one of the Secretary's men muttered his head snapping left and right scanning the corridor for any sign of Kessler. His comms crackled but no one responded. The hallway stretched out empty and eerily quiet.

"Where's the Secretary?" another of the Secretary's men demanded his voice rising with tension. He pressed his earpiece harder against his ear. "Anyone report! Do you have eyes on the Secretary?"

But there was no reply. The hallway cameras placed for extra security were suddenly offline their screens showing nothing but static. The team's confusion turned to frustration their training barely holding their panic at bay.

Barry watched the disorder unfold with calm detachment. His eyes searched for Reed, who was still crouched behind the table. For a brief second, their gazes locked. Barry offered a slight, mocking tilt of his head.

Reed's earpiece crackled to life. Kranch's voice came through low and steady. "I've got the Secretary. He's safe."

Reed breathed out slowly relief washing over him. Of course, Kranch had pulled it off, silent and seamless the extraction executed with precision. Kessler wasn't just gone. He had disappeared a ghost slipping through Barry's web of control.

Then the room went black. The lights flickered and died and the room was plunged into total darkness. Reed froze his breath catching in his throat. He couldn't even see his hand in front of his face. The weight of the darkness all around him amplifying every sound, the scrape of a chair a distant murmur the faint shuffle of feet.

Through the earpiece Carter's voice came through tense but

steady. "I couldn't stop it. Lights are down. Barry's backup plan. We need eyes on him."

Barry didn't run, he didn't need to. This wasn't panic, it was control. His contingencies were layered and redundant. This was how Barry operated. While this scenario had been a long shot in his playbook it was still accounted for. He grabbed his camera bag his smirk faint but visible in the occasional flicker of light from frantic flashlights slicing through the darkness.

Kessler's security was trained but clearly unprepared for this level of disruption and chaos. They scrambled to get it back together. Voices shouted over each other. Orders barked through comms were met with confused replies. The faint wail of an alarm somewhere in the hotel added to the pandemonium.

In the middle of all this Reed stayed calm his voice steady and sharp as he directed his team through their earpieces.

"Kranch get the Secretary to the fallback location."

"On it" came Kranch's response the sound of movement faintly audible in Reed's ear.

"Carter, see if you can't get those lights back on."

"Already moving" Carter replied his voice a steady presence in the storm.

"Grimes" Reed commanded his tone carrying weight and urgency. "Eyes open for Barry. Grab him if you can. Keep him in the hotel." Grimes hesitated for a second before responding his voice firm. "Understood. I'm on it."

Barry took a slow step back he was enjoying the mayhem. To him this wasn't an escape; it was an exit. His eyes closed shut for a second as he mentally visualized the room. He knew every inch of it, the positions of the furniture the exits the likely blind spots. He moved with precision slipping past flustered security and panicked operatives with the ease of a ghost.

Flashlights swept the space briefly illuminating Barry's form before he vanished into the shadows. Barry's operatives moved seamlessly through the crowd, their distractions subtle but devastating. Fire alarms began to wail triggered by smoke from tampered light fixtures. Power surges rippled through the hotel's electrical system sending bursts of static through comms and dimming lights further. Smoke seeped into the hallway from a sabotaged air vent adding to the confusion.

Reed tracked the anarchy his mind working faster than ever. *Barry is staging his victory. He's making this look like a mess we can't clean up.*

Barry's smirk never faltered as he slipped into the stairwell disappearing into the mayhem he had orchestrated. In his mind the pieces were still on the board, but the game was already his. Barry had time resources and layers of deception. As the door to the stairwell swung shut behind him Barry whispered to himself his voice carrying a quiet menace.

"Checkmate Sawyer. You just don't know it yet."

Barry's far-flung contingency plan was executed flawlessly by Seth Gauthier his number one operative. Barry had anticipated their attempts to stop Seth from killing the lights, so he had a kill switch installed, a tap on his phone and the room was plunged into darkness.

Gauthier wasted no time moving to the next phase of the plan. He headed directly to the private airstrip where he began preparing the jet for Barry's escape from Vienna. Meanwhile a black SUV with an operative behind the wheel waited idly a short distance from the hotel ready to spirit Barry away the moment he slipped outside. Inside the hotel disorder erupted as people scrambled to make sense of the sudden blackout and the carefully orchestrated distractions that had thrown everything into disarray. Gauthier didn't fully agree with Barry's methods, but he couldn't deny the man's ability to plan prepare and execute contingencies with precision.

It felt like only minutes had passed when the SUV pulled up to the private airstrip. Barry stepped out his face lit with a triumphant smile radiating the confidence of a man who believed he was untouchable. He knew his gun/lens had missed its mark but the look on Reed Sawyer's face, stunned and pinned behind that table, had made it all worthwhile. The consequences of his actions would follow him back to the U.S., but Barry was unfazed. As always, he had a plan. He would clear his name and ensure his survival, just as he always did.

Barry's polished shoes clicked against the smooth concrete of the private jet hangar the sound echoing faintly in the cavernous space. He ascended the steps to the jet his confidence unshaken despite the turmoil left behind at the hotel. The Architect never faltered. He adjusted his cufflinks with precision his thoughts already focused on the next steps in his plan.

As he reached the top of the stairs his encrypted cellphone buzzed in his pocket. He paused pulling it out the soft glow of the screen illuminating his sharp features. The sender was unknown. The message brief and jarring:

"Your time is up, Architect."

Barry's eyes narrowed scanning the hangar reflexively. No one was there, just his operatives stationed dutifully around the perimeter. Deleting the message with a flick of his thumb he slipped the device back into his pocket brushing off the warning like a gnat.

He stepped onto the plane the soft hum of the engines masking his growing suspicion. But doubt fleeting as it was gnawed at the edges of his certainty. Who had sent that message? Minutes earlier back at the hotel Reed's mind was on overdrive even as his breathing slowed. *Barry doesn't just escape, he orchestrates every step. He's always ten moves ahead.* The room still buzzed with mayhem, but Reed's thoughts were fixed on the one thing he couldn't shake: *"Section 3. Page: 16. Code: 105-B."* What does it mean? Why would Barry risk everything to keep Kessler from it? The code nagged at him like an itch he couldn't scratch a piece of the puzzle just out of reach.

Over the earpiece Reed's voice came through steady and resolute. "As soon as possible regroup, service corridor beneath the hotel."

The team began moving. Reed stayed low using the shadows and the cover of panic to slip through the confusion. He glanced toward the stairwell door Barry had exited through his nerves on edge. *This doesn't end here, Barry.*

It didn't take long for the lights to flicker back on and the havoc to subside. In the dimly lit service corridor, the team regrouped each member looking battered but resolute. Grimes arrived last his face pale and drawn though his jaw was set with determination. "I've got something" he said his voice unsteady as he held up his phone. "Barry's Pro4uM messages," he said, his voice unsteady. "He was going to pin all of this madness on you, Reed. Kessler, you, me. We were all going down."

Reed locked eyes with Grimes nodding. "Of course, classic Barry. What else?"

Grimes scrolled through the messages his finger trembling slightly. "This thread, it's filled with coded instructions to his team, but the language is unmistakable. He was going to set himself up as the hero. He was going to create the narrative where you're the scapegoat, I'm collateral damage and Kessler's death was an 'unfortunate consequence'. If this had gone down according to Barry's plan, he gets away clean with more power than before." Kranch stepped forward. "I've got something too. During the photoshoot I slipped trackers on Barry's team. Most of them got shaken off but one still seems to be active." He pulled up a map on his device showing a blinking dot moving through the city. "It's heading toward a private hangar near the edge of town."

Reed studied the screen his mind already working through the possibilities. "A private hangar..." He trailed off his thoughts turning darker. *Of course, Barry would have an escape plan.*

Carter, standing next to Grimes, frowned. "Do we call this in? Let the authorities handle it?"

Reed shook his head his expression hardening. "Not yet. This doesn't end with Barry running, it ends with him exposed. We have evidence but it's not enough to topple him. We need to show the world who he really is not just catch him in the act." Reed continued. "We follow the tracker, but we do it smart. Barry thinks he's untouchable and we need to let him keep thinking that. When we take him down it has to be final. No loose ends no spin."

They had evidence, a plan and a trail to follow, but they were up against The Architect a man who had built an empire on deception and control.

Grimes asked. "Did the code ever come in?"

Reed's expression twisted in frustration. "Yeah, it came in but it was too late to get it to Kessler. Kranch had already helped him get out."

Reed's eyes narrowed. "That code has to be something big. The way Barry reacted, it was unbelievable. And the lengths he went to just to keep Kessler from seeing it, tells me it's more than just numbers. Whatever it is it's tied to everything. We'll figure it out."

Grimes shifted uncomfortably leaning against the wall of the dimly lit service corridor. His voice was low heavy with regret. "I hesitated back there. When I got Barry's orders, I should've come to you immediately. If I had, " He stopped his words catching. "If I had maybe some of this could've been avoided." Reed turned to him his expression firm and understanding. "You're here now. That's what matters. We're going to expose him, my friend. Every part of him. You've got my word."

Grimes met Reed's gaze a flicker of resolve breaking through his guilt. "No more hesitation. Whatever it takes I'm in. Barry's going down."

Carter caught Reed's eye and motioned for him to step aside for a moment. His voice was low but urgent. "Look we've got more than enough to take this to the Embassy. Audio video eyewitnesses, it's airtight. Why not call it in now? Let them handle it?"

Reed let his eyes go distant for a moment before locking onto Carter's. "Because Barry doesn't just need to be stopped, he needs to be seen. Embarrassed exposed and forever remembered as the monster he is."

Carter frowned shaking his head. "We can't risk him slipping away while we wait for the perfect moment Reed. You know what he's capable of."

"I do" Reed said his voice steady but laced with fire. "And that's why this has to be done the right way. If we just stop him quietly, he'll find a way to spin it. Barry's built his entire empire on controlling the narrative. This isn't just about stopping him Carter, it's about making sure everyone sees who he really is. No more shadows. No more facades."

Carter studied Reed's face the conviction etched into every line. Slowly he nodded. "Alright. But we're walking a fine line here."

Reed placed a hand on Carter's shoulder. "That's why we're a team. Barry's made mistakes tonight, big ones. Now it's our turn to make sure he pays for them."

Grimes overhearing their conversation stepped closer. "We'll make it happen Reed. Whatever it takes."

Reed nodded a faint but determined smile tugging at his lips. "Then let's get to work controlling this mess before Barry can spin it his way." Reed's team worked with quiet precision in the service corridor the tension between them unspoken but detectable. Carter was working on digitally forged documents, a mix of fabricated witness statements, falsified security logs and doctored correspondence that would lay the groundwork for their plan. Each piece was crafted to do two things: clear Barry of direct involvement in the chaos while simultaneously exonerating Reed and his team from any suspicion.

"This has to be airtight" Reed said his tone clipped but focused. "Barry can't suspect we're the ones creating this narrative. If he smells even a hint of what we are doing here he'll disappear before we can expose him properly."

Kranch nodded receiving various documents being airdropped to his phone. "The narrative has to look clean, Barry's plan backfired but not because of us. Just another chaotic event gone sideways."

Grimes spoke up "I'll admit this doesn't seem to be what we

should be doing. Seems opposite. Won't this just give him another chance to regroup? Feels like we're letting him off the hook."

Reed shook his head his expression firm and resolute. "We're not letting him off the hook" he said with a faint smile. "We're just letting him run with it." Reed's smile deepened as he added "Once he feels safe free of all this 'Kessler' mess we'll yank that hook back so hard he won't know what hit him. We're tightening the leash. The more comfortable he feels the more mistakes he'll make. He's a control freak, he can't resist meddling. And when he does, we'll be ready."

Carter shared a small map of the hotel to everyone's devices pointing to the exit routes. "Kranch and I will handle the 'accidental' discovery of these documents. Security will eat it up especially with the turmoil upstairs. Grimes you stay low start leaking what we have here to the press. Reed, keep refining the timeline. Let the authorities think what we are feeding them is their idea. Everything needs to line up."

Reed glanced at the forged papers on his phone a grim determination in his eyes. "This isn't about clearing our names, it's about setting the stage. We make it look like Barry was never involved but we also make him complacent. Let him think he's won. And then we strike." The team moved with precision each member executing their role with efficiency. Splitting up across the hotel they worked quickly to plant the evidence and shape the narrative. Using key Wi-Fi connections compromised computer terminals and security server logs they carefully released every piece of fabricated data. Each file each log entry was meticulously crafted to weave a story of mistaken identities and unfortunate coincidences. By the time they regrouped the false trail would be seamlessly in place leaving anyone following it chasing shadows.

Reed surveyed their work. "Barry thinks he's untouchable. Let's make sure he keeps thinking that just long enough for us to burn it all down."

With everything accomplished the team regrouped their

breaths still heavy from the bedlam of the past few hours. Grimes leaned against the wall his expression thoughtful. "Reed earlier today you asked me about SYNC. Is that part of your master plan? I've been thinking, once things settle down for a day or two, I'll send a formal invitation to Barry to be the keynote speaker. It could play perfectly into the 'Barry is innocent' narrative. Feeding his ego like that? He won't be able to resist showing his face. He'll think it's all about him, his spotlight his moment. There's no way he'd skip it."

The idea of Barry showing up at SYNC had already crossed Reed's mind. "A public stage" he murmured to himself. "It's a bold move, risky, but if he's looking for a way to make an impact that's how he'd do it."

Grimes straightened a spark of hope in his eyes. "I can set it up. Make him the center of attention. Use the platform to show everyone exactly who he is."

Carter clasped his hands over his chest his expression skeptical. "You're talking about putting the Architect in front of thousands of people and hoping we can control the narrative? If we screw this up, we'll be the ones exposed. And Barry? He'll spin it faster than we can recover."

Reed nodded his eyes squinting. "Carter's right. Barry will be expecting us. He's paranoid by nature." Kranch spoke up his voice calm and deliberate. "We can't do this alone. We'll need people on the inside, staff security and especially tech support. Barry's too good at covering his tracks. We'll need allies to keep him in the spotlight long enough to take him down."

"This is all true." Reed said "But, I have some intel I haven't shared with y'all yet. PPI has a vulnerability in their servers in New York. There's a chance they could be compromised by a physically implanted device."

Reed continued "Combine these devices with a staged presence at SYNC and it could be lights out for Barry Cox. We could tell the story we have collected here to the world."

Turning to Carter. "Do you know how we could make that happen?"

Carter nodded slowly his mind was trying to process a hundred things at once. "It's possible but we'd need highly specialized equipment, small discreet and easy to hide. And then there's the real challenge: getting something like that into a building as secure as PPI headquarters. That's no small feat."

Kranch interrupted. "Leave the sneaking to me. I have a knack for making the impossible happen. It's not gonna be easy, but it can be done."

Reed again directed his thoughts to Carter. "As soon as we get back to the States, we'll have you focus on designing the devices."

Carter smirked a glint of determination in his eyes. "Got it. I'll make it work."

Grimes raised his hand slightly stepping forward. "SYNC is my turf, those people are my people, I know them well. I'll reach out to them carefully. No one knows Barry's true side better than I do. I'll make sure we have the support we need."

Carter looked at Kranch who nodded in agreement. "This could work. Barry thrives on control. If we make him believe he's still the puppet master, he'll walk right into it."

Reed's mind was going a hundred miles an hour now, as the pieces of the plan began to take shape. He turned to Grimes. "Make the connections. Get us access to the SYNC stage and the staff. We need Barry to feel like it's his show his moment. And when the time comes, we'll flip the script."

Grimes nodded. "Consider it done." The room's tension shifted as the uncertainty gave way to resolve. They had a plan a glimmer of hope. SYNC would be the stage, and Barry Cox wouldn't see it coming.

Reed leaned against the cold tile wall of the service corridor. He pulled out his camera and cradled it in his hands. It felt heavier than usual as if the events of the last few hours had seeped into its frame.

He took a deep breath and turned it on and scrolled through the recent shots stopping on the one that mattered most.

Barry Cox was poised like a predator, his fingers still wrapped around the weaponized lens. The faint glint of the dangling red cap was unmistakable. The hole down the middle of the glass and a slight wisp of smoke were visual confirmation of Barry's intent. The image was sharp, perfectly captured. It was just like the old cliché: "A picture is worth a thousand words." And this image was not only worth words, it told a thousand stories. Stories that could dismantle Barry's empire in an instant.

But Reed thought *a single photograph no matter how bad it made Barry look wasn't enough.* The world wouldn't just believe an image. Not when Barry's entire existence had been built on deception manipulation and carefully curated lies.

Kranch's voice pulled him from his thoughts. "Reed you good? Barry's private jet took off a while ago." Something everyone already knew.

Reed nodded but didn't take his eyes off the screen. "Just a second."

His thumb hovered over the playback button replaying the events in his mind: Barry's calm smirk the silenced gunshot the confusion that followed. The image wasn't just evidence, it was a piece of the puzzle. And puzzles only made sense when you had all the pieces.

Carter looked over his shoulder catching a glimpse of the photo. "That's the money shot huh?"

Reed turned off the camera and slung it back over his shoulder. "It's a start" he said. "But it's not enough. If we want the world to believe it, if we want them to see Barry for what he really is, we need the whole picture."

Grimes nodded in agreement his resolve growing. "And that's what SYNC is for."

Reed looked at his teammates all of them focused. "Negative

space isn't empty, it's where the truth hides. And we're going to show the world. Let's go," he said and pushed off the wall. "We've got a lot of work to do."

14
CONTRAST

Barry sat in the corner of a dim office in Tulsa, the hum of the overhead lights and the soft rustle of papers on his desk blended together. The glow of one monitor cast long shadows on his face as he scrolled through the latest reports from his assets. He leaned back in his chair, the leather creaking under him, a hint of a smile on his lips.

The situation at the photoshoot was under control. The reports were clean, efficient and tidied up, exactly how Barry liked it. The chaos had played right into his hands and any evidence of his involvement had been expertly hidden. While the Secretary's sudden disappearance had raised eyebrows, the authorities, the press, everyone, saw Reed Sawyer and his team as nothing more than clumsy photographers caught in the crossfire, not as operatives working against Barry.

"Talented," Barry murmured, thinking of Reed, his voice low and dismissive. "But naive." His fingers tapped on the edge of the desk. "A pawn in a game he doesn't even know he's playing."

Barry's phone buzzed on his desk, the ID flashing *Marty Grimes*. He picked up, his tone smooth and confident. "Marty, what can I do for you?"

Grimes's voice on the other end was warm, almost reverent. "Mr. Cox, I just wanted to personally congratulate you on Vienna. Those accolades you're getting are well earned. For a moment I thought things might've gone sideways but it's clear you had it all under control. Getting the Secretary to safety? That's no small trick. Well done."

Barry leaned back in his chair, a small smile on his mouth. He knew there was more to this call but he wasn't going to let Grimes rush him. "Thanks, Marty. Not every day you get to play hero for someone like Secretary Kessler. But let's not waste our time, or mine. What can I do for you? I'm busy." Grimes chuckled. "Of course, Mr. Cox, I'll get right to it. Here's the thing: SYNC needs you. Badly. The buzz around you is crazy. Since Vienna my phone hasn't stopped ringing, texts, calls, messages, all with the same demand: 'Barry Cox has to be the Keynote Speaker'. Even the current Keynote has expressed interest in stepping aside, saying you're the only one who can fill the role."

Grimes's voice went soft and pleading. "Mr. Cox, this is your moment. The community is calling for you and frankly I can't think of anyone better to keynote SYNC. You've been the architect of so much. This is your chance to be in the spotlight, not just behind the scenes."

Barry smiled, the flattery washing over him like a warm wave. He leaned forward, his hands gripping the edge of his desk as the idea settled in. This was what it meant to be the Architect, when one plan failed, another succeeded. "Marty," Barry said, his voice measured but full of confidence, "I'd be honored. I have some ideas already. Trust me, it'll be the best Keynote speech anyone's ever heard."

Grimes let out a relieved laugh. "Thank you, Mr. Cox. SYNC is in good hands. I'll have my team coordinate with yours."

The call ended and Barry still held the phone, a big smile on his face. His ego puffed up with pride. Who else but him could turn turmoil into triumph? Barry Cox, the Architect, was back in the game and the world was watching.

Across the country in New Orleans, Reed's office was bathed in light and purpose. Sunlight streamed through the blinds and scattered across the desk where photographs and documents were spread out like puzzle pieces. Reed flipped through his notebook, each page filled with the frantic scribble of a man desperate for answers. A tablet sat beside him, displaying a timeline of Barry's movements pieced together from memory.

Reed's elbows were on the desk, his fingers massaging his temples. Every detail mattered. Every scrap of information brought him closer to the truth. Barry's plans were deliberate, calculated, yes, but patterns were emerging. Patterns Barry thought no one would see.

Reed's phone buzzed on the table. He looked down at the screen. *Marty Grimes*. He swiped it open and read the text: *Barry is in as Keynote.*

A slow smile spread across his face. He typed a quick reply: *Well done, my friend. That's perfect.*

Before putting the phone away, he stared at the screen for a moment. Barry taking the bait meant the SYNC stage was set. The pieces were falling into place and soon the Architect would be in the spotlight of his own making, one he wouldn't escape.

He pocketed his phone and was ready for the next move.

Back in Tulsa, Barry's eyes narrowed as he brought up Pro4u-M.com on his encrypted device. A new thread caught his eye, nothing too obvious but a glimmer of activity from Reed Sawyer. He chuckled to himself. "Reed, Reed, Reed," he said. "You're clever, I'll give you that. But clever only takes you so far."

Shadows danced on the walls of Barry's office as he stood and surveyed the room like a king admiring his kingdom. To him this wasn't a game, it was a work of art and Reed was just a pesky smudge he'd soon wipe away.

Reed was oblivious to Barry's smug thoughts as he sat back in his chair and stared at the photo he had taken of Barry shooting the red capped gun/lens at him. The image was clear, sharp and inescapable.

Barry was careful, a master of covering his tracks. But Reed would make sure the world saw this image, and the whole story it told.

In the dim light of his office, Barry pulled up a file on Reed Sawyer, his mind already calculating the next elimination. Across the country in New Orleans, Reed stared at the pinned photo of Barry on his board, his fists clenched.

Reed slowly leaned back in his chair. The plan forming in his mind was delicate and complex, it had to be. Barry couldn't just feel safe; he had to feel unbeatable. Invincible. Reed typed deliberately on the keyboard under the John Smith alias on Pro4uM. The title was vague, meant to only catch the eye of one person: **"A Rogue Factor?"**

The post read:

"I've been going over the Vienna footage. Something doesn't add up. The authorities are saying the Secretary's team was jumpy that day, over-prepared, almost like they expected trouble. One of the agents might have misjudged. Looks like it could be an accidental discharge of one of their weapons? Stranger things have happened. I think we're all just chasing ghosts here."

Reed hit **Post** and sat back for a moment. To add further credence to the narrative he logged out of Pro4uM under John Smith and then logged back in under his real name. Then he added a reply to his own post:

"Good point. Those guys are trained to react fast. Split-second decisions don't always go right. But which agent fired the shot and why hasn't anyone come forward? Must be trying to cover their tracks. I was there, front row seat. Could have been any one of them."

Reed read the reply over carefully. It was ambiguous enough to make it seem like he was confused but detailed enough for Barry to interpret as confirmation: Reed Sawyer wasn't onto him. Instead, the post made Reed seem like he was chasing shadows, focused on Kessler's team rather than Barry himself.

Perfect.

Halfway across the country Barry sat in his dim office reading the latest posts on Pro4uM. His eyes landed on the thread title **"A Rogue**

Factor?" and his eyes widened with satisfaction. A slow smile spread across his face, sharp and mean.

"Well, well," Barry said. "I knew Sawyer was good but naive? I didn't realize how naive." He sat back and the leather of his chair creaked under his weight, and he chuckled low in his throat. To Barry this post was proof of everything he thought about Reed Sawyer: clever maybe, but out of his depth. The fool didn't even suspect him. If anything, this rogue agent theory was the perfect distraction to keep Reed occupied. SYNC would be his grand stage, a perfect opportunity to solidify his control and finalize his plans, free from any interference from the likes of Reed Sawyer.

Back in New Orleans Reed refreshed the thread and watched as the replies started to roll in, each one pushing the narrative further away from Barry. Satisfaction spread across his face.

Reed said to himself "Barry is moving exactly where we want him. The King is getting more and more exposed with every move. He is walking right into the light."

Reed scanned the sprawling notes and documents in front of him. Each file, each photo was a piece of Barry's twisted empire. It was like trying to assemble a puzzle with half the pieces burned. But as Reed went through the timeline of PPI's most notorious ops a pattern started to emerge, a faint but undeniable thread running through Barry's most brutal moves.

In all the notes, the Pro4uM messages and even the files digitized from Box Gallery a name began to appear. The name stood out like a beacon of light in the darkness. Marcus Cox. He was Barry's younger brother; a name Reed had come across before in unrelated contexts. Marcus had been a promising government official, well-respected for his work in foreign policy. But years ago, he had vanished without a trace after a PPI-linked op overseas. Official records said "unresolved circumstances" but whispers in the back channels said betrayal and blackmail.

Reed sat back and his mind started to spin. Could Barry really have done this? Marcus was his brother for goodness's sake. Barry was ruthless, yes, manipulative, cunning and devoid of a moral compass, but would he really eat his own family? Reed's gut said no but the doubts refused to go away. The more he thought about Marcus's story the more uneasy he became. Marcus had been close to Barry, closer than anyone, knew the details of Barry's rise to power and his twisted moves. If anyone knew the secrets of how Barry became The Architect, it was Marcus. And that was the problem. Barry didn't just discard people when they became problematic, he erased them. Friends, allies, even family, they were all expendable if they threatened his empire.

But Marcus? The Marcus he'd heard about didn't fit the profile of someone who just vanished without a trace. If Barry had really eliminated him why were so many questions still unanswered? The thought haunted him. What if Marcus wasn't dead? What if the files and whispers were part of a cover-up? What if Barry had locked him away, hidden him as a loosed end too dangerous to cut off completely?

The idea sent a shiver down his spine. Marcus might hold the truth, the kind of truth that could tear Barry's empire apart at the seams. Reed didn't dare hope, not fully, but the thought wouldn't leave him. If Marcus was alive, he wasn't just a key, he was *the* key. And if he wasn't? Well, maybe the ghost of Marcus was still enough to unravel Barry's web of lies.

Reed went through Pro4uM posts, cross referencing cryptic messages he'd intercepted over the years. One thread in particular caught his eye: a seemingly innocuous post about landscape photography tips from an account named *Pinnacle View*. The tone was too precise, too clinical and one reply mentioned the "fragility of foreign landscapes", a phrase Marcus had used in a now deleted article from Box Gallery before he disappeared.

If Marcus was alive and leaving breadcrumbs, it would take precision and subtlety to track him without alerting Barry.

The stakes were high. If Barry found out about this Marcus would almost certainly vanish again, permanently this time. But if

Reed could reach Marcus first, he might have the leverage to finally expose Barry. It was a dangerous gamble but one he had to take. Miles away Barry was reading Pro4uM and the **"A Rogue Factor?"** posts. Barry's lips curled into a satisfied smile. "Perfect," he said to himself, leaning back in his chair. "Reed's as blind as the rest of them." The post was developing exactly as Barry wanted.

But Barry's confidence flickered briefly as he read another message, a innocent reply on a landscape photography thread. Something about the wording felt familiar, like a ghost tapping on his shoulder. He waved his hand dismissively. His plans for SYNC would fix any doubts.

Back in New Orleans, Reed looked at the pinned photo of Barry on his board, his face hardening. Marcus was ticking in his mind. He could be the first crack in Barry's armor. Reed wrote a single note under Marcus's name: *The past never stays buried.*

Reed adjusted the angle of his laptop screen, the glow of the display lighting up the documents on his desk. The room felt heavier now as the pieces started to fall into place. The code, *Section 3. Page: 16. Code: 105-B*, had been haunting him since Vienna and finally its meaning was starting to become clear.

As he read through the materials Reed continued to sift through Pro4uM's encrypted messages and cross reference them with the scanned documents from Box Gallery. His hands hovered over a worn notebook where he'd logged every lead. The picture it painted was interesting.

The code was possibly tied to a classified operation, Barry Cox had orchestrated to infiltrate and manipulate a major international trade agreement. On the surface it was just minor trade concessions. But beneath the surface it was a complex web of blackmail, coercion and sabotage designed to control global supply chains. Barry's fingerprints were all over it.

These classified documents weren't just bureaucratic noise; they were the threads that could unravel PPI. Reed's pulse hammered as the pieces fell into place:

- **Doc 3449** - It implicated PPI as the hidden hand behind political leaders and trade agreements globally.
- **Doc 898** - It had direct evidence of Barry's involvement in covert operations, irrefutably proving he was The Architect.
- **Doc 99312** - The most unsettling of all. It wasn't just another piece of the puzzle, it was the anchor and it tied back to Marcus Cox, Barry's younger brother. Doc 99312 had a full account of Marcus Cox's role as a government liaison to ensure the integrity of international trade negotiations. His task was to prevent corporate interests from exploiting and maintain transparency across multiple countries.

Reed stopped, his eyes fixed on Marcus's name in bold at the top of Doc 99312. Marcus's disappearance had been a mystery for so long but now the dots connected with terrifying clarity. Marcus had been a government official tasked with safeguarding a crucial trade deal that Barry had sabotaged for his own gain. When the operation fell apart Marcus vanished to protect PPI's darkest secrets.

Reed saw it all now. If Kessler had received that code in time, it would have exposed Barry's shadow ops, toppled PPI's influence and revealed the truth about Marcus's disappearance.

As Reed scrolled through the Box Gallery documents he stopped on a personnel file. **Marcus Cox**. Almost the whole file was redacted but one line stood out: Marcus was working for Secretary Kessler when he disappeared. Reed's heart rate quickened as the pieces fell into place.

If Marcus was working for Kessler, then that code was meant to expose PPI's global manipulation. Whatever Barry did to Marcus the code would have unlocked the truth.

Reed looked at the file in his hand, his brain trying to process everything at once. The code, it could unravel everything. But as he thought back to the mayhem of the photoshoot a wave of frustration washed over him. Thirty seconds. If that code had come just thirty seconds earlier, he could have handed it to Kessler right there. Everything could have been exposed in real-time, Barry's plans, PPI's shadow ops and even the truth about Marcus.

He replayed the moment over and over in his head. If only. The ache of how close they had come made the weight of their failure feel crushing. And worst of all he had the code all along and didn't know what it was. Reed shook his head, forcing himself to focus. Wishing for what might have been wouldn't stop Barry now. A new thought hit him: *Why not just call Secretary Kessler now? Give him the code.* It would be so simple. Reed reached for his phone, then froze. **Wait.** His mind churned as he began to reason, weighing the risks involved.

Calling Kessler wasn't just risky, it would expose them all. If Barry even suspected Kessler had the code it would be game over. Barry's reach was vast, his ability to eliminate threats unmatched. He would have taken Kessler out in Vienna to prevent him from getting the code. There was no telling what he would do if he thought Kessler actually had it.

The stakes were too high. Reed gripped the edge of the desk as the weight of it all hit him. Marcus's connection. Marcus's disappearance. Barry's willingness to erase his own brother. Nothing was sacred. Not blood. Not trust. Not loyalty.

Reed took a deep breath, his resolve firming. The code wasn't just something to be filed away, it was a weapon. A weapon that could shatter Barry's carefully constructed image and expose the rot within PPI. But using it wouldn't be easy. Barry wouldn't stop hunting anyone who dared to use it against him.

Reed closed the notebook and reached for his phone. He texted Carter and Kranch: *"Regroup tomorrow, encrypted ZOOM Meeting. We need to discuss Marcus and the code. It's bigger than we thought."*

He put the phone back on the desk, his mind already moving faster and faster. The SYNC convention would be the perfect stage to set the final trap, but Barry was unpredictable.

Reed, ever planning, began to study the SYNC convention floor plan spread out before him. The enormity of what they were about to attempt weighed on him. This wasn't just about exposing Barry, it was about making sure there was no escape, no deniability.

Grimes had said he had secured Barry's keynote spot. *Barry will love it,* Reed thought. The spotlight, the applause, it's his fuel. But Reed knew better than anyone: Barry's ego would be his downfall.

Reed picked up his phone and dialed Marty Grimes. Two rings later Marty answered, his tone brisk. "Hey, Reed, what's up?" Reed kept his tone cheerful, almost congratulatory. "Marty, the team is getting together on Zoom tomorrow. Can you join us and talk about SYNC? There are some details we need to hash out."

Grimes sighed heavily, his schedule weighing on him. "No, sorry. Too much to do for the convention. The logistics alone are killing me. Plus, with Barry now confirmed as keynote..." He trailed off, lost in thought.

"About that," Reed said gently. "Everything set with Barry? No chance he'll back out?"

"Oh, he's in," Grimes replied, his voice perking up. "Actually, he seemed excited about it. Said something about 'being honored, having ideas,' and 'it being the best Keynote ever.' You should have seen how quickly he jumped at the chance."

Reed's grip on the phone tightened. "Tell me about the setup. How exposed will he be?"

"Completely," Grimes said, his voice dropping. "He'll be alone on stage, spotlight on him, in front of the whole convention. Thousands of photographers in the room, potentially tens of thousands more live streaming, including the Secretary. No security detail allowed near the podium, it would ruin the optics. It's... it's perfect for whatever you're planning."

Reed's mouth curved into a small smile. "And the timing? How long will he be up there?"

"Forty-five minutes minimum. Could go longer, Barry loves an audience. Once he starts talking about his vision for photography's future..." Grimes paused. "Reed, whatever you're planning... it's going to work, isn't it?"

"It has to," Reed said firmly. "You've done good, Marty. Really good. Keep me posted if anything changes."

"Will do," Grimes said, his voice steady now. "And Reed? Be careful. Barry's been... different lately. More intense. Like he knows something big is coming."

"That's exactly what we're counting on," Reed said, ending the call.

He put the phone down slowly, feeling satisfied. The pieces weren't just falling into place, they were locked in, ready to go. The plan was unfolding like a Swiss Army Knife. The image of Barry with the red-capped gun/lens was the centerpiece. Add to that Barry's incriminating words at the stairwell and the newly discovered documents tied to the code and they had a solid case. SYNC was going to be a show to remember, a perfect storm of evidence to take down Barry's empire. SYNC wasn't just an opportunity, it was the ultimate stage to deliver the knockout punch.

Reed's phone buzzed with a group text from Kranch. "Keynote audio setup is almost complete."

"Good," Reed replied, his eyes on the photo of Barry with the red-capped lens. The image felt heavier now, a grim reminder of the stakes. "This isn't just for us, it's for everyone watching. When this hits, it'll hit the world like a freight train."

Kranch replied quickly. "This will be airtight. The audio will speak louder than any denial Barry can offer. No wiggle room."

Reed nodded to himself, feeling a small sense of calm amidst the confusion. Everything hinged on the Keynote being the moment they exposed Barry.

Carter texted in next. "Barry's overconfident. He thinks the photoshoot mess was a fluke. Your posts on Pro4uM are keeping him focused on minor players. He has operatives running around trying to plug leaks that don't exist."

Reed smiled to himself. The misdirection was working better than he'd hoped. Barry still thought he was the master of the universe, totally unaware every move he made was bringing him closer to his downfall.

Reed knew the risks. Barry didn't go down without a fight. He'd seen firsthand what Barry would do to eliminate a threat.

The next day, the team joined via Zoom, their faces glowing in the dim light of their screens. Each person reviewed their tasks, the tension evident as they coordinated for SYNC. Kranch walked through the final steps for the audio integration. Carter outlined the security measures to keep Barry unaware but ensure nothing was missed. Carter also said he thought he had found the perfect devices for PPI's Servers. Reed was silent, his eyes locked on the picture on the wall behind him, Barry in the middle of it all. He thought to himself, *Barry, I know your secret. And I'm going to make sure everyone knows it.*

Across the country in his private office, Barry sat in his high-backed chair, reading a report from one of his operatives. "SYNC preparations are complete. Your keynote is ready." Barry's eyes lit up as he leaned back, a tiny smile.

"SYNC will be my triumph," he thought, his ego inflating. Everything was going according to plan. To him, it was all perfect.

15
FLASH POINT

Reed sat in his office, the blue glow of his laptop casting sharp shadows across the cluttered desk. The room hummed with tension as he worked his next move, he needed a cryptic message to get inside Barry's head and manipulate his ego. Maybe something through the Lyt Meeter would do the trick. He knew Barry's type: a man who loved control and thought himself untouchable. If Reed played this right, the message wouldn't just get Barry's attention, it would consume him.

The draft on the screen was simple, too simple: *Seems like someone at PPI is playing a dangerous game. Maybe it's time for the professionals to clean house. Thoughts?*

Reed's finger hovered over the "Send" button. Something was off. The words were too direct, too easy. Barry needed more than just bait, he needed a riddle, a mirror to reflect his own arrogance back at him. The message had to be cryptic, ambiguous, personal enough to make Barry think he'd found a hidden meaning but vague enough to keep him guessing.

Reed leaned back in his chair. His heart thudded once, a tiny reminder of the stakes, but he pushed the feeling aside. This had to be just right. Barry needed to feel like he was still in control, the smartest man in the room. The message had to challenge him subtly, without tipping his hand.

"Too obvious," Reed muttered to himself. He highlighted the text, his cursor paused for a moment before he hit "delete."

The blank screen stared back at him, mocking. But then, he had it. Reed's fingers flew across the keys, typing a new message. This one was sharper, more ambiguous but with just enough venom to get Barry's attention.

Reed's next move was crucial. The message needed to get more private, more covert. He needed Barry to feel like the walls were closing in, to question everyone around him.

Reed read through the final draft. This was it, the flash point. A small spark, in just the right place.

The cryptic leak through the Lyt Meeter read: *A light to guide the path, but it cuts two ways. Psalms 3+16+100:105B*

Reed smiled to himself as he thought about Barry's reaction. The numbers were ambiguous. Was it a reference to the Bible? A hidden message? The Code? Reed knew Barry's calculating mind would spin wheels over the connections and get paranoid.

Barry's response was almost immediate. His hand tightened around the tablet as he reread the post for the fifth time. The room went dim around him as he focused on the screen. "Who's leaking this?" Barry muttered, his calm facade cracking ever so slightly.

"Section... Psalms... 119?" he whispered, piecing it together. His jaw clenched as he opened an online Bible and read the verse aloud, "Your word is a lamp for my feet, a light on my path." Barry rolled his eyes, thinking to himself, *what does the B mean?* The Bible wasn't his strong suit. Was this a reference to guidance or judgment? The words "lamp" and "light" hit a nerve. Barry had always seen himself as the one who lit the path for others but now it felt like a spotlight was shining on him.

Barry threw his operatives into a frenzy. He needed to know who was behind the leak. Meetings were held at odd hours. Operatives scoured Pro4uM for any clues. Phone logs were examined with a fine-tooth comb.

Barry slammed his fist on the desk, the sound echoing through the room. "Find them!" he snapped, his voice rising with barely controlled anger as he glared at Seth Gauthier, his second-in-command.

Back in New Orleans, Reed sat at his desk, watching the chaos unfold. His trap was working. Barry wasn't entirely shaken, but not yet. But the cracks were forming and soon they would widen into a chasm Barry couldn't escape.

Barry stared at the message, re-reading it for the sixth, maybe seventh, time. It was too close to the secret code Marcus had created. Too dang close. Could someone else know The Code? The thought sent a shiver through him, but he kept his face neutral. His jaw clenched, his fingers dug into the edge of his desk. The Code, that pesky, nagging code, never really went away. Every time it resurfaced, it dragged Marcus's shadow along with it. Marcus was gone. Barry had made sure of that. And as far as he knew, that meant *nobody* else in the world could possibly know the code. But now someone had sent it to Reed in Vienna. Someone was putting pieces of it into scripture on Pro4uM. This should be over. Barry thought he'd buried all of this when he took care of Marcus.

Even thinking Marcus's name made his stomach twist. He hated the vulnerability it exposed in him, the crack in his otherwise impenetrable mask. He avoided saying the name out loud as if speaking it might summon ghosts better left in the ground. He leaned back in his chair, the dim light of the office throwing long shadows across his face.

That code. It would have been Kessler's key to everything, his entire empire. It would have connected all the dots Barry had worked so hard to hide: Marcus's disappearance, PPI's silent control of governments and his elimination of threats to his power. If Kessler had gotten his hands on that code everything would have fallen apart.

Barry swallowed hard, trying to push the memories back. Marcus had been working for Kessler when he started to suspect something deeper, something darker, about PPI's operations. That was when he became a liability. The decision had been easy in theory: Marcus had to go. But the way he had to accomplish it? That was something Barry rarely allowed himself to think about.

The Code pointed to the document that would ruin everything. If it ever got out it wouldn't just dismantle PPI's carefully constructed facade as a legitimate organization. It would expose Barry as a criminal mastermind, the puppeteer behind the curtain of global economies. Worst of all it would reveal his ultimate betrayal, eliminating Marcus to protect his own identity as The Architect.

Barry's breath caught as he pushed the thoughts away. He looked at the message again, trying to decipher its meaning. Was someone onto him? Could Reed or someone else have connected the dots? The ambiguity of the words bothered at him, and he felt a flicker of doubt.

No. He shook his head, forcing a cold smile to his lips. He hadn't come this far by being uncertain. The Code would stay buried. It had to. Barry sat in the dark room, his encrypted tablet emitting an eerie glow on his face. He read the leaks again, one eyebrow raised. The posts were vague, but the intent was clear. Someone was threading a needle, weaving together pieces of information to take him down. The coded reference to "Section 3. Page: 16. Code: 105-B" bit deeper than he let on, tormenting him at the edges of his composure.

Barry sat back in his chair, his fingers drumming on the armrest as he thought. He replayed the message he'd received in Vienna: *"Your time is up, Architect."* The phrase echoed in his mind like a taunt. It wasn't just a message, it was a challenge. Nobody was deeper in PPI than he was. Nobody. The idea that someone had both the guts and the access to send that message made his stomach turn.

He glanced at the reports from his operatives, who had been working around the clock to trace the source of the leaks. But the trail was faint, layered with misdirection and he hated how well done it was. Whoever was behind this knew him. They knew how he operated.

He spoke into his secure comms, his voice low and commanding. "Deploy Surveillance Deployment Alpha. I want every potential leaker tracked, tagged and eliminated. No exceptions."

"What about the threads?" one of his operatives asked.

Barry's smile returned. "We flood Pro4uM. Create dozens of threads. Mimic the leaks, scatter them across the forum and drown out the real ones. Nobody will know what's real and what's false."

He leaned forward, his eyes glinting. "And make sure the misinformation is convincing. Use just enough truth to bait anyone watching. I want them spinning in circles."

The operative hesitated. "And if we find the source of the real leaks?"

Barry's smile turned cold. "Eliminate them. Fast." He ended the comm link and sat back in his chair. But despite the confidence in his voice, the message lingered in his mind. His instincts, honed from years of manipulation and power plays, told him something was off. *Someone* was watching him, someone who knew too much.

Barry picked up his phone and stared at the screen, the words *"Your time is up, Architect."* burning in his mind.

He thought the impossible. Could there really be someone deeper in PPI than him? The thought sent a shiver down his spine, but he pushed it away. No. That wasn't possible. He was the top dog, the king of this carefully constructed kingdom. Nobody was above him.

But the leaks. The message. The code.

They all said otherwise.

Back in New Orleans, Reed scanned the Pro4uM boards. Barry's operatives were flooding them with fake threads. He saw the play at once. They weren't aimed at him; they were bait for anyone else who might be watching. Threads vanished as fast as they appeared, replaced by vague, misleading posts that mimicked the leaks Reed had planted.

He couldn't help the smile that creased his lips. Barry was spooked, his empire showing its cracks. That was the plan, to spook Barry, make him react and force him into a mistake. But as Reed watched the commotion unfold his satisfaction was laced with something else, something weird.

He swiveled his chair slightly, staring at the photograph on the wall in front of him. Barry with the weaponized lens, the image sharp and framed to perfection. Next to it, another photo he found deep in the Pro4uM archives, a much younger Barry standing beside Marcus. Reed's gaze lingered on Marcus. *Who are you, Marcus?* he thought. And why did Barry erase you?

His hand drifted to the edge of his desk, his fingers brushing against the notebook filled with notes and theories. The code, Section 3. Page: 16. Code: 105-B, was the thread that connected everything, but it still didn't make sense. The code wasn't just Barry's secret; it was Barry's nightmare. But that begged the question Reed couldn't shake: *Why would Barry give me the very thing that could destroy him?* Reed was stumped, his elbows on the desk. *From the beginning*, he thought. *From New Orleans to Vienna, every step I've taken has been planned. Barry manipulated me, sure. But someone else has been guiding me too, pushing me to find this. To expose him.*

His hand clenched around the pen. The code wasn't something Barry would ever let someone else get their hands on, not even by accident. It was too dangerous, too revealing. Barry had built an empire of control and that code was the one thing that could unravel it. So why had Reed been given it?

He breathed out slowly, his eyes narrowing. *Whoever gave me that code wanted me to take down Barry. But who can be above Barry?* The question hung in the air, unanswered. Barry was The Architect, the mastermind. There's no one above him. And yet...

He wasn't just up against Barry. He was a pawn in someone else's game, a game he hadn't even realized he was playing. *Who are you?* Reed thought. *And what do you want?*

The uncertainty ate at him, but one thing was clear: if Barry was spooked, then he was doing his job!

Barry sat in his office staring at the list of names on his encrypted tablet, his inner circle, the most trusted members of his operation. Trust. It's a fragile illusion, isn't it? Barry knew loyalty could be bought, manipulated or enforced through fear. And now someone in his circle was betraying him. Someone was feeding the flames of these leaks and burning everything he built.

His mind churned as he thought about the Pro4uM madness, the leaks slipping into the cracks faster than his operatives could plug them. False threads, misinformation, counter-leaks, none of it was working. The leaks kept coming, precise and deliberate, like a scalpel cutting through his defenses. It had to be an inside job. There's no other explanation.

Barry called in his senior operatives, his voice cold and clipped as he issued the summons. When they gathered in the dimly lit conference room at his Tulsa base the air was thick with tension. Barry stood at the head of the table, his gaze sweeping the room. "We have a problem," Barry said, his voice calm but deadly. "Someone in this room is feeding the enemy. Someone here is a traitor."

The operatives murmured, their eyes skipping to one another. Barry slammed his fists down hard on the table and the room fell silent.

"I don't need excuses," he growled. "I need results. And I need loyalty."

Barry stepped closer to the table, his presence suffocating as he leaned over the nearest operative, Lou Witzel. "Lou," he whispered. "Do you know what happens to traitors?"

Lou shook his head. "No, sir."

Barry smiled faintly. "Good. Let's keep it that way."

Over the next few hours Barry questioned each of his team members. His methods were calculated and quiet, probing questions with veiled threats, silence to amplify the pressure. He watched their body language, their micro expressions, looking for a hint of guilt or deception.

But that wasn't enough. Barry needed more than words. He needed proof.

After the meeting Barry planted false information among his operatives, each piece tailored to the individual. Each snippet of misinformation was plausible but distinct, a breadcrumb trail to the traitor if it showed up online. He sat back and waited for the trap to spring.

Days passed. The leaks continued. And then one of the false threads appeared on Pro4uM.

Barry was furious. He summoned the operative who received that particular piece of misinformation, a senior member of his team, Victor Lane. Victor was experienced, trusted, someone Barry had relied on for years. And yet the evidence was clear.

Victor stood in Barry's office, his hands shaking as he tried to explain. "I don't know how it happened, sir. I didn't leak anything. You have to believe me."

Barry's face was cold as ice. "Believe you? Victor, belief is for the weak. I deal in facts. And the facts don't look good for you."

Victor's protests fell on deaf ears. Barry waved his hand and dismissed him. "You're done here." That night Victor vanished. His name was deleted from the system, as if he'd never been part of PPI. Barry didn't tolerate hesitation or betrayal.

Barry sat in his office alone, the weight of his paranoia crushing him. The thoughts in his head kept repeating over and over. He couldn't shake the feeling the leaks weren't coming from one source. *What if it wasn't just Victor? What if the rot went deeper?*

He massaged his temples, exhaustion creeping in. His mind wandered back to the message he received in Vienna: *"Your time is up, Architect."* Who had the power, the audacity to challenge him?

Barry's eyes narrowed. If there was one thing he knew, it was this: No one was untouchable. Not even him. God forbid someone would bring him down. Not without a fight.

A few days later, though it felt like weeks, Reed stood in his office, leaning against the desk. His eyes stayed fixed on the screen as Pro4uM threads exploded. He exhaled sharply, and he sent a message to the team, *Can we have a Zoom meeting now, Urgent!*

Amazingly the whole team was available. Within minutes they were all gathered and at full attention. Reed locked in on the Pro4uM thread and then shared his screen to the whole team. "Look at this," he said. "He's panicking."

The team gazed at the madness on the forum: threads being deleted and reposted, new threads mimicking the leaks but with bizarre, off-topic twists. Carter narrowed his eyes. "Which ones are ours and which are Barry's?"

Reed smirked. "Those three," he said, highlighting specific threads. "Those are us. The rest? That's him trying to muddy the water."

Kranch unmuted himself and interrupted Reed, his voice skeptical. "Barry's spreading himself too thin. But the more erratic he gets, the more dangerous he becomes. You sure this is the right play?"

Reed quickly responded, edging into the screen. "This is what we need. He's paranoid, he's distracted and he's looking over his shoulder. That's when he makes mistakes." Reed sighed, feeling every emotion. "Carter, Kranch, I need both of you to start preparing for the next posts. Use the data we got from Vienna. Cryptic, ambiguous but specific enough to keep him guessing."

Carter frowned. "What if he figures out it's us? What if one of his people tracks these back to us?" Reed turned to him. His voice was even. "He won't. Not yet. Barry's looking inward right now. He thinks the leaks are coming from within his team. The more desperate he gets the more he'll burn through his own resources looking for a mole that isn't there."

Grimes spoke next. "And what happens when he figures out there's no mole?"

Reed's gaze didn't waver. "By then it'll be too late for him. We just need to keep the pressure on. Make him sweat."

Kranch tapped his fingers. "What's the next move?"

Reed nodded at the screen. "The next phase starts now. Barry thinks he's playing chess but he doesn't realize we're flipping the board."

The team went silent as each member absorbed the weight of it all. Reed took a deep breath. "Let's make this count."

Back in Barry's dim office he sat back in his chair, the glow of his encrypted messaging app making eerie shadows on his face. His eyes were fixed on the words:

"The Architect's mask is slipping."

The message was short, cryptic and unnerving. Barry muttered under his breath, "Who is doing this?" His mind raced through every possible source. It couldn't be one of his operatives, he'd rooted out every weak link. Could it be someone outside? Or worse, someone closer than he dared to imagine?

He clenched his fists, breathing deeply to calm himself. Barry Cox, *The Architect*, didn't lose control. Not ever. He prided himself on being untouchable. But this, these leaks, these whispers in the dark, felt like a shadow creeping closer. He shook his head. No. This wouldn't stand. He'd crush whoever was behind this.

Then a thought occurred to him. SYNC. The photography convention was three weeks away. A stage where he could control the narrative, solidify his power and silence the doubters. The spotlight would be his, and no one would dare challenge him once he delivered the keynote of his career. SYNC wasn't just a platform; it was his redemption.

Barry smirked, his confidence growing again. "Let them try to unseat me," he muttered. "They'll regret it." He opened the *SYNC Keynote* folder on his desk. Dozens of slides and talking points were waiting for him. Barry loved presentations. His ability to mesmerize and manipulate audiences was unmatched. This one though, had to be different. Bigger. Better. It would be his magnum opus.

He leaned forward, his fingers flying over the keyboard. The theme would be unity and excellence in the photography industry, a thinly veiled metaphor for his own power. He'd show them his achievements in front of and behind the camera and subtly take shots at anyone who dared to question him.

"Let's remind them," Barry said to himself, a smile creeping up the sides of his face, "why I'm the one they all look up to."

As he worked, his ego grew with every passing minute. SYNC wasn't just an opportunity, it was his stage to regain total control. The leaks, the paranoia, the shadow of doubt, they'd all be erased under the brilliance of his performance. He'd emerge from SYNC not just a leader but a legend.

Barry clicked to the final slide, the words bold and unapologetic: *The Future of Photography Belongs to Visionaries.*

He sat back, staring at the screen. SYNC would be his masterpiece.

16

SILENT EXPOSURE

B arry sat at his desk, refreshing Pro4uM. The screen blinked back at him: no new posts, no messages, no updates. For days, the cryptic threads had gone quiet. No leaks. No chatter. Just silence.

He frowned, his finger tapping against the mouse. Silence wasn't normal, not here, not now. Silence was strategy.

"They're either scared, or planning something," Barry muttered. His words carried weight in the stillness of the room.

He hit the intercom. "Seth, ramp up surveillance. Full spectrum. I want alerts on every flagged account, every encrypted ping."

Seth appeared moments later, a tablet in hand, his expression cool. "I've already doubled the algorithms and swept for any backdoor activity. Nothing's coming through."

Barry didn't look up. "Do it again. This time, widen the parameters. Assume they've found a workaround."

Seth hesitated, the briefest flicker of doubt crossing his face. "We're running everything we've got. If there's something out there, we'll find it."

"It's too clean," Barry said, his voice sharper now. "Too quiet. It's never this quiet on Pro4uM, not this group."

Seth shifted but said nothing. He'd worked under Barry long enough to know when to push back, and when to stay quiet. Barry didn't trust silence. Silence was camouflage. A weapon. A warning.

By the second day, Barry was pacing the office, his confidence unraveling at the edges. He barked orders, scrutinized every minor detail, and cross-checked the intel himself. By the third, he hadn't slept. The silence wasn't just suspicious; it was personal. It felt directed, deliberate.

"They're playing with us," he muttered under his breath, staring at the dark monitors. "They want us to blink first."

Seth entered, his tablet still in hand, his tone steady. "Barry, you've got the best surveillance team in the game working this. Maybe it's nothing. Maybe the silence is just...silence."

"No," Barry snapped, his gaze fixed on the screen. "It's never just silence. Not with them."

Seth nodded and left, but Barry could feel the unspoken doubts hanging in the air. For now, Barry held his ground, but the seeds of doubt were there, growing in the quiet spaces.

Back in New Orleans, Reed was sitting at his desk, the glow of his laptop reflecting off the window. He'd been reviewing plans for hours, each line more critical than the last. SYNC was just weeks away, and every decision from here on out mattered.

He exhaled sharply, closing the laptop. SYNC wasn't a secret, not to PPI, not to anyone in the industry. It was the biggest international photography convention of the year, drawing professionals, hobbyists, and every sort of vendor imaginable. Its scale made it the perfect cover, but it also made it dangerous. The more public the event, the harder it was to stay unseen.

Reed stood, pacing the length of the room. "We can't leave this to chance," he muttered, grabbing the burner phone from the desk. Online coordination had worked so far, but the next stage of planning required precision, and trust. Both were best handled in person.

He typed the message to his team: *Secure passports. Meet in Cabo. Two days.*

Cabo wasn't just a getaway, it was a calculated move. Its distance from SYNC's host city, Las Vegas, kept them off PPI's immediate radar. The tourist-heavy atmosphere made it easy to blend in, a place where strangers came and went without scrutiny. But the real advantage? Cabo was a blind spot. One of the only places where PPI had no official operational presence, a dead zone for their surveillance.

At least, that's what the records said. And if there was one thing Reed had learned, it was that Barry Cox never left anything *truly* unchecked. Even in the shadows, they had to stay sharp.

The replies came in quickly: a mix of confirmations and one-word acknowledgments. Each one felt like a piece of the puzzle falling into place. Reed double-checked the details in his head: their cover stories, the route to Cabo, the contingency plans if anything went sideways.

He slipped the phone into a drawer and turned back to the window, the city lights twinkling in the distance. Cabo was a way for the team to make sure everything was working in their favor. Everything had to be airtight before they walked into SYNC. If PPI got even the slightest whiff of their real agenda, they'd be finished before the event even began.

Each team member made their way to Cabo, following carefully staggered schedules designed to avoid suspicion. The routes were deliberate, the cover stories seamless.

Carter was the first to move, booking his flight under the guise of an official PPI assignment. As a mid-level coordinator, he had just enough visibility to make the cover plausible without drawing undue attention. His supposed task? Scouting potential locations for PPI's expansion efforts in Mexico. If anyone checked his itinerary, it would appear routine, a company man on a routine trip.

Kranch took a different approach, arriving a day early. His cover was tied to a local photography workshop, a believable fit given his reputation as a mentor in the industry. He checked into a modest hotel near the waterfront and immediately made appearances at a few tourist-heavy spots, snapping photos and engaging with locals. If anyone was watching, he looked like exactly what he claimed to be: an enthusiastic instructor soaking up Cabo's scenic backdrops.

Grimes was extremely busy with last minute SYNC duties, but he made the time for the sake of the team. He followed shortly after Carter. Leveraging his well-known role as an event coordinator for SYNC, he arranged meetings with local venues under the pretense of exploring options for "future SYNC-related events." His inquiries about lighting setups, catering packages, and breakout spaces were so mundane they bordered on boring, exactly as he intended.

Reed was the last to arrive, slipping into Cabo with little fanfare. His persona was that of a tourist photographer, someone looking to build a portfolio of vibrant street scenes and striking landscapes. He traveled light, carrying only a single bag and a vintage camera hung casually around his neck. To anyone paying attention, he was just another traveler chasing inspiration in Mexico's golden light.

The team had arranged to meet at a local golf course, Puerto Los Cabos. Just four strangers sharing a round of golf was hardly note-worthy, even to the most watchful eyes.

Puerto Los Cabos was perfect for this type of meeting. Its design was both luxurious and strategic: every third hole circled back to a comfort station offering food, drinks, and, most importantly, privacy. The layout was ideal for discretion; no one could keep track of what hole you were on, and the team could vanish into the course for hours without raising suspicion. Play three holes, strategize at the comfort station, then finish the round. Clarity and cover in equal measure.

Each team member had booked the 9:13 tee time, ensuring they'd be paired together seamlessly. They arrived with the calm demeanor of men out to enjoy a leisurely round, blending effortlessly into the sunny, tourist-filled atmosphere. Golf bags slung over their shoul-ders, they played the first three holes with practiced ease, their silence broken only by casual chatter.

Carter, ever the smooth talker, made light jokes about his errant shots. "Guess I'll need a better caddie next time," he quipped as his ball veered into the rough. Kranch played his role as the gruff instructor, muttering complaints about the heat and glaring at his golf glove as if it were to blame for his poor grip. Grimes took on his usual role as the perfect organizer, fussing over their pace and offering tips on reading the greens. Reed, quiet as always, blended into the group like a shadow, listening intently to every word and watching for anything out of place.

The weight of their real purpose loomed beneath the surface. To any onlookers, they were just another group of golfers enjoying a round under the Mexican sun. But the tension was discernible, simmering beneath their calm exteriors.

By the time they reached the comfort station, the transition was seamless. They ordered cold drinks and snacks, staking out a shaded corner where they could talk without being overheard. The comfort station was small but well-stocked, its rustic charm adding to the illusion of an ordinary outing.

Reed in a hushed tone, keeping his voice low. "Alright, let's keep this in code. Carter, start us off."

Carter nodded, adjusting his cap. "We'll take the shot on the 16th hole," he said, his tone measured. The phrase was loaded with meaning: the planned moment during SYNC when Reed would expose Barry's crimes.

"Watch for the wind," Grimes added, using the code they'd agreed upon for monitoring Barry's operatives during the event. "There's a strong chance they'll adjust their approach."

Reed listened carefully, then glanced at Kranch. "Your read?"

Kranch leaned back in his chair, his voice gruff but steady. "If we stick to the plan, Barry won't even see us lining up. But if there's any shift, any shift, I'm calling for a mulligan." Mulligan: code for pulling the plug and initiating an immediate escape.

Reed nodded, his face impassive. He unfolded a course map, a practical stand-in for SYNC's floor plan, and began outlining the broad strokes of their strategy. "The key is to keep Barry overconfident. He has to believe he's untouchable. That's our window. If we press too soon, he'll see it coming. Too late, and we lose the edge."

The discussion carried on for hours, moving in careful, measured steps. Each member played their part, asking questions, proposing adjustments, and refining details. The coded language flowed effortlessly, sounding to anyone nearby like nothing more than a passionate debate about golf strategy.

By the time they left the comfort station and returned to the course, the sun had shifted lower in the sky. The final three holes passed in deliberate calm, their focus shifting back to their covers. Each step and swing appeared routine, but the weight of their plans pressed invisibly on their shoulders.

In the golf cart, Carter sat beside Reed, his posture tense. The hum of the cart was the only sound for a moment before Carter broke the silence. "Reed," he said, his tone edged with frustration, "why not just call Kessler and give him the code? It's the same as if you'd handed it to him that night. It'd be over."

Reed's gaze snapped to Carter, sharp and unyielding. "You think this ends with a phone call?" His voice was low, deliberate. "If I call him, it doesn't just blow back on me, it paints a target on Kessler's back. Barry's eyes are everywhere. If he catches even a whisper that Kessler has the code, he'll bury him, and us, before we can take our next breath."

Reed was gripping the wheel of the cart, his words weighted with urgency. "And let's say Kessler gets the code. What then? On its own, it doesn't mean anything without the evidence we've gathered, images of Barry with that weaponized lens, the audio from the stairwell where he outlined the assassination plan, every single piece of proof tying him to the attempt on Kessler's life. The code alone doesn't expose Barry; it's just the key. Without everything we've compiled, it's useless."

Carter rested his hands on his biceps, his gaze steady but laced with skepticism. "So, we just hold onto it? Hope for the best?"

"No," Reed said, his voice firm and unflinching. "We deliver it all.

Together. Strategically. When it hits, it has to hit so hard that Barry has no way out. This isn't just about the code, it's about tying his hands so tightly that nobody can cover for him."

Carter exhaled sharply, the weight of Reed's words sinking in. He sat back, his expression unreadable, the tension in the cart thick enough to cut. Finally, he nodded, though reluctance lingered in his posture. "Okay, Reed. But this better work."

Reed adjusted his cap, his tone unwavering. "It has to."

As the cart slowed to a stop near the 18th hole, Reed stepped out, glancing toward the others who waited at the green. His voice dropped to a quiet but commanding tone. "Stay sharp. This game isn't over until the final putt."

The others nodded, their expressions unreadable, their roles intact. Together, they walked off the green with unhurried strides, blending seamlessly into the relaxed atmosphere of the course. But as they left, the tension lingered, as heavy as the heat rising off the manicured grass.

Back in Tulsa, Barry leaned back in his leather chair, a satisfied smirk playing on his lips as he reviewed the report. "Threats neutralized." The words were simple, definitive, the kind of message he liked to see. His operatives believed they'd handled the situation, contained whatever had been brewing. And Barry believed them, mostly.

He set the tablet down, steepling his fingers as he let the feeling of control wash over him. They thought they could play against him, but he'd outmaneuvered them, just as he always did. SYNC was only weeks away, and with no more distractions, Barry could focus on his keynote. He could already hear the applause, see the admiration in the faces of attendees as he took the stage. SYNC would cement his place, not just as a leader in the photography world, but as untouchable.

Yet, as he spun his chair toward the wide windows of his office, something nagged at the edge of his thoughts. A faint unease he couldn't quite pin down. The silence on Pro4uM.

Barry reached for his phone, opening the forum out of habit. Nothing. No cryptic messages, no hidden codes. The threads were active, but only with the usual chatter, camera specs, editing software, upcoming contests.

"What's going on?" he muttered under his breath, the smirk fading from his face. The silence had stretched on too long. It was unnatural. He had expected more, panic, retaliation, something to signal his opponents' next move. But the quiet unnerved him far more than any noise ever could.

His finger hovered over the refresh button one last time before he closed the app. They were planning something. They had to be. And if they weren't, then he had won. Barry leaned back in his chair, forcing his smirk to return. He'd already won. This was just paranoia.

At least, that's what he told himself.

Back at the clubhouse, Reed was just slinging his bag over his shoulder when a voice called out behind him. "Excuse me, señor, are you Señor Sawyer?"

Reed froze mid-step. This didn't compute. His thoughts jammed like traffic in a tunnel. Slowly, he turned to face the man, keeping his expression blank while his pulse picked up speed. "Yes, I'm Reed Sawyer."

The speaker, one of the club's professionals, approached with a small envelope in hand. "Message for you, señor."

Reed's eyes narrowed slightly. His voice was calm, measured. "Where did you get this message?"

The man shrugged, his tone casual. "A boy from the village brought it by. I do not know who he was."

Reed reached for the envelope, his fingers brushing the crinkled paper. The club professional nodded and stepped back, busying himself with a cart of clubs as if the exchange was nothing out of the ordinary. But Reed knew better.

He tore the envelope open with deliberate precision, unfolding the single sheet inside. Five words, hastily scrawled, stared back at him:

Keep moving to the light.

Reed stared at the note, his eyes narrowing. Cryptic. Too cryptic. He turned the paper over, searching for more, but it was blank on the back.

He glanced around, scanning the clubhouse and the surrounding grounds for anything, or anyone, out of place. Nothing. Just tourists laughing at the bar, caddies wiping down carts, and players coming off the course.

Reed slipped the message into his pocket, his stern expression masking the unease settling in his chest. The phrase wasn't familiar, but it had the unmistakable fingerprints of someone in the network. Someone who knew where to find him. Someone who wanted him to know they were watching.

He adjusted his cap and stepped toward the parking lot, his stride unhurried. Outwardly, nothing had changed. But inside, his thoughts churned.

Was this a warning? A signal? Or something worse?

Reed reached his rental car, pausing just long enough to glance back at the clubhouse. He saw the club professional walking away, chatting with another golfer. No sign of the boy who'd delivered the message.

Sliding into the driver's seat, Reed pulled the note from his pocket again, reading it once more. "Keep moving to the light." The words felt more like a riddle than an answer.

He started the car and drove off, his instincts kicking into high gear. Whoever had sent the message, they'd just added another variable to an already dangerous game.

17

OUT OF FOCUS

Kessler paced the length of his secure office, the sharp click of his polished shoes cutting through the low hum of the ventilation system. The blinds were drawn, casting the room in muted light. Near the desk stood Petersen, his wiry frame rigid, a tablet in hand. He watched Kessler carefully, saying nothing as the tension in the air thickened.

"I've attended hundreds of diplomatic events," Kessler said, his voice taut with anger. "Thousands of mundane obligations, banquets, ribbon-cuttings, goodwill tours. Never once did I think posing for a photograph could get me killed!" He stopped abruptly, slamming his hand against the desk. "A photoshoot, Petersen. A simple photoshoot!"

Petersen remained silent, letting the storm pass.

Kessler turned sharply, pointing a finger at him as if he alone were responsible for the fiasco. "Do you know how close they got? Inches, Petersen. Inches away from ending my career, and my life, in one calculated stroke."

He resumed pacing, each step sharper than the last. "And it wasn't just about my safety. That shoot was supposed to secure critical intel. Intel we've now lost because someone turned diplomacy into a trap." He stopped again, his eyes narrowing. "Do you know what's worse than a failed mission? A failed mission that *they* will spin as our incompetence. 'Oh, poor Kessler,' they'll say. 'Can't even handle a routine press event.'" His tone dripped with disdain.

Petersen shifted slightly, finally speaking in a steady voice. "Sir, we're working to recover what was lost. Reed Sawyer is still in play. If anyone can help us piece this back together, it's him."

Kessler scoffed, waving a hand dismissively. "Reed Sawyer. The man who vanished into thin air. Do you know how that looks, Petersen? Where is he? Why hasn't he called me with the codes? I'm left here cleaning up this disaster with no proof, no leverage, and no plan."

Petersen hesitated but pressed on. "Sawyer's methods are unconventional, no doubt. But we still have assets in motion, and he's the key to making this work."

Kessler fixed him with a hard stare before running a hand through his hair. His anger softened, shifting into tightly controlled exasperation. "We don't have time, Petersen. Every hour that passes gives them more room to maneuver. If we don't strike soon, clear, precise, and devastating, they'll bury us before we can react."

Petersen nodded, his expression resolute. "Then we double down. Use every resource we have to pull Sawyer back in and finalize the plan."

Kessler sighed, leaning heavily against the desk. His shoulders slumped, but the fire in his voice remained. "Make it happen. And tell Mr. Sawyer, wherever he is, that if he doesn't pull this off, I'll deal with him personally."

He pushed off the desk and strode to the far side of the room. His gaze grew distant, his voice quieter, though still edged with tension. "This entire disaster," he murmured, "reminds me of Marcus."

Petersen looked up, uncertain. "Marcus, sir?"

"Yes," Kessler said, turning back, his expression grim. "Marcus was my trusted aide years ago. He had a knack for uncovering what others couldn't, or wouldn't. One day, he came to me with whispers of a shadow operation, global in scope. He said they were influencing events, manipulating outcomes, all under the guise of photography."

"Photography?" Petersen asked, his brow furrowing.

Kessler nodded, letting a wisp of air escape between his teeth. "At first, I thought it was absurd. Photography, something so mundane, so safe. But Marcus wasn't one to chase shadows. He had fragments of data, intercepted communications, just enough to show he was onto something. He never named names outright, but he hinted at someone at the top. Someone orchestrating it all."

"The leader," Petersen said, leaning forward.

"Exactly," Kessler replied, his voice softening. "Marcus never said who. Maybe he didn't know. But he was certain of one thing: this wasn't a rogue group or a one-off operation. It was an entrenched network. And untouchable."

Petersen hesitated. "Who?"

"That's the question, isn't it?" Kessler's tone grew clipped. "Marcus never had the full picture. Just fragments. But over months, he pieced together enough, a trail of encrypted files, coded notes, scattered clues. Bit by bit, he was unraveling them."

Kessler's expression hardened. "And then, just as he was about to hand me the most critical piece of evidence, he disappeared. No warning. No trace. One day, he was arranging a meeting to deliver everything. The next... gone."

Petersen frowned. "And you think, "

"I don't think," Kessler cut in, his voice sharp. "They silenced him. He got too close, and they made sure he wouldn't get closer. Everything he worked for disappeared with him."

Petersen spoke cautiously. "But why now? Why does this remind you of Marcus?"

"Because Reed Sawyer is walking the same path," Kessler said, his voice low and deliberate. "At the photoshoot in Vienna, Sawyer came to me with some wild story about PPI, that so-called 'club' with its little side gig in security, claiming they were the ones behind it all. He's following the same threads, chasing the same shadows.

And just like before, time is running out. They don't leave loose ends, Petersen. Not then. Not now."

Petersen's expression tightened. "But Reed's still out there. That's more than we had with Marcus."

"For now," Kessler said, the weight of his words settling heavily. "But if we're not careful, this time it will all end the same way."

He moved to the corner of his office, his hand brushing the polished wood of a locked cabinet. His gaze turned distant, as though he were seeing something far beyond the room. Marcus's disappearance lingered in his thoughts, a shadow of a moment when the truth had been within reach, only to slip away.

Marcus had been more than an aide; he had been a confidant, a strategist, someone Kessler could trust in a world where trust was a luxury. Losing him wasn't just personal, it had left Kessler without the ally he needed to uncover the truth. Without Marcus, the pieces had scattered, and the trail had gone cold.

Kessler sighed, his hand resting on the cabinet's edge. It wasn't just about trust anymore. It was about precision. About systems. He had developed a multi-layered method for organizing classified information, a way to protect the truth.

He glanced at his desk, where a sleek black laptop sat closed. It connected to a secure server housing meticulously organized files, grouped into high-level categories: *International Trade Agreements. Covert Operations. National Security Threats.* Within each category, files were further subdivided, a labyrinth of data waiting to be unlocked.

The true brilliance of the system, Kessler reflected, was its reliance on codes, a precise sequence of numbers and letters. These codes didn't just label documents; they acted as keys, unlocking encrypted sub-documents buried deep within the files. Without the correct code, even the most carefully curated data remained untouchable, its secrets hidden behind layers of digital security.

It wasn't an easy system to navigate, not even for him, but it was necessary. For national security. For accountability. For survival in a world where information was power, and power was the ultimate weapon.

Yet, as meticulous as the system was, it was also fragile. Kessler knew that better than anyone. Without the right code, a critical document was little more than an unreadable cascade of ones and zeroes. All the truths it contained, buried. All the decisions it could inform, delayed. Every detail, no matter how vital, locked away, useless without access.

He opened the laptop, scrolling through the familiar array of files, their categories as clear and ordered as his thoughts. But the weight of memory clung to him. The day Marcus had vanished, he'd promised Kessler the key to everything, one final code to unravel the shadow network.

And then, he was gone. No delivery. No explanation. Just silence.

Kessler snapped the laptop shut, the echo cutting through the room. The system he'd built was a testament to that loss, a way to ensure that even if he couldn't trust people, he could trust the order he'd created. But now, as Reed Sawyer followed in Marcus's footsteps, Kessler felt the old doubts creeping in.

Without the code, even the best intentions amounted to whispers on a locked page.

His thoughts circled back to the maddening conclusion he couldn't escape: he had been so close. So painfully close. "It was right there, so close," he muttered under his breath, his voice barely audible in the stillness.

His hand clenched into a fist. The memory gnawed at him, a constant reminder of how the truth had slipped through his fingers. Despite his position as one of the most informed figures in national security, he felt outmaneuvered. And by whom? A shadowy network disguised as photographers? *NO!* The idea seemed absurd. *No way this was reality.*

The thought burned like acid. Kessler was used to being in control, always two steps ahead. He represented the U.S. Government for crying out loud. But this time was different. The deeper he dug, the clearer it became, this photography club, this organization didn't just cover its tracks; it thrived on misdirection. Every move, every breadcrumb, seemed designed to lead investigators into an endless maze.

"The key," he muttered again, his tone hardening. "It's the one piece I need." He didn't need to finish the thought. The absence of the missing code hung over him like a weight, stalling everything.

Kessler turned back to the black laptop, the unsolved puzzle pressing heavily on him. For years, he had mastered the art of strategy, outmaneuvering some of the most dangerous figures in global politics. But now the rules of the game had shifted, and he was playing catch-up.

His frustration ran deeper than the immediate crisis. It was rooted in who he was: a principled public servant who had dedicated his life to transparency and justice. For decades, he had fought corruption and manipulation, refusing to compromise even at great personal cost. Estranged from his family, he had sacrificed his private life for the ideals he believed in.

Among his staff, Kessler was both feared and respected. His uncompromising integrity inspired loyalty, not out of obligation, but belief. They followed him because they trusted his mission. Even now, as they faced shadowy forces operating beyond their reach, their resolve to uncover the truth and dismantle the network remained steadfast.

Kessler sat at his desk, staring at his reflection in the darkened laptop screen. Anger burned in his eyes, but it was matched by determination. This wasn't just about finding answers, it was about dismantling the invisible machine pulling the strings behind the scenes.

Leaning forward, his voice dropped to a low, firm whisper. "No more shadows. This has to end."

The words hung in the air, a quiet promise to himself and the team that stood beside him. This wasn't just another mission. It was personal.

18

SHUTTER SPEED

Reed sat alone in his studio, the light of the desk lamp casting shadows over the scraps of paper scattered in front of him. Each note was written in his own hand, the words blunt and cryptic, like fragments of a puzzle just out of reach:

- *Reed, we need to talk. Now.*
- *Look closer, Reed. You're in the frame.*
- *Section: 3. Page: 16. Code: 105-B.*
- *Someone's watching. Play your part.*
- *If Kessler falls, it's failure. Watch the shadows, but move only in the light.*
- *Keep moving to the light.*

Reed leaned back, the fingers of both of his hands dragging through his hair as he stared at the messages. What did it all mean? Individually, they were vague, almost meaningless. But together, they screamed something louder, a pattern. A deliberate hand guiding him.

Someone was steering him.

The pen in his hand tapped against the desk, a steady rhythm as his mind turned. Whoever was sending these notes knew too much, where he'd be, what he needed, and when. The messages always arrived at critical moments, pushing him just far enough to avoid disaster. Or to be manipulated.

Ally or enemy?

The question clawed at him. Was this some invisible savior or a masterful trap, a way to use him as a pawn? He turned his attention to the third message: *Section: 3. Page: 16. Code: 105-B.* That note had saved his life in Vienna, helping him unlock the escape route he hadn't even known existed. But the others,

Play your part.

Move only in the light.

The words looped in his head, taunting him with their precision. Reed stood abruptly, the chair scraping across the floor as he began to pace. Every instinct screamed that the sender was always one step ahead. Watching. Controlling. It gnawed at him, this sense of being outplayed in a game he barely understood.

He stopped at the window, his reflection faint against the night outside. The city stretched into the distance, the flicker of lights blurring into a thousand moving parts. Each one a shadow. Each one a question.

Friend or foe?

Reed's fists clenched at his sides, the tension coiling in his chest. Whatever game was being played, standing still wasn't an option. He turned back to the desk, his eyes narrowing on the last message: *Keep moving to the light.*

The phrase haunted him. It wasn't just cryptic, it was a challenge.

He remembered the flight to Vienna, the cryptic message: *Move only in the light.* But in a world where every shadow hid a secret and every truth was wrapped in lies, what did the light even look like? And now, he was being told to *Keep moving in the light.*

"Who are you?" Reed muttered, his voice low and tight, as

though speaking the words might summon an answer. Silence pressed back at him.

"Keep moving to the light." He repeated, testing the words, as if they might unlock something more concrete. A clue. A direction. Anything?

His fingers strummed against the desk. "Let's see what the light reveals." Reed started reasoning the situation. He wasn't alone in this. Maybe the team could help, after all, they knew nothing about the secret message he'd received at the golf course in Cabo. *It was time they figured all of this out,* he thought to himself.

Reed opened a secure connection on Zoom and sent a message to the team. His face appeared on the screen, eyes burning with focus. It was their first coordinated meeting since leaving Cabo, Mexico. Each member dialed in from their own corner of the world, their screens arranged in a grid, different places, same purpose. Behind Reed, a map of Manhattan and a schematic of *The Darkroom*, PPI's impenetrable fortress, were pinned to the wall.

"This is it. We've been playing defense long enough." Reed's voice was steady, deliberate. He let the weight of the moment settle before continuing. "As I was leaving Cabo, I was handed a message by one of the locals. Just five words. The message said, 'Keep moving to the light'."

Kranch frowned and spoke up first. "What does that mean?"

Carter came next, "Better question, how many of these cryptic messages are you gonna get?"

Finally, Grimes leaned into the screen, his voice quieter, more cautious. "And how did they even know you were there? That's what's got me."

Reed began to explain in his normal, controlled and calming voice. "Kranch, 'moving to the light' means we keep pushing. We don't back off, we drag the truth into the open, where Barry can't hide. Carter, I've gotten at least six of these messages now, and every single one has put us a step closer to Barry and exposing PPI. Grimes..." He hesitated for a second, then shook his head. "I don't know. I was careful. We were all careful. No one should've known we were there. And yet... someone did."

He let that hang for a moment before pressing on. "Look, weird or not, this message is telling us to move forward. So that's exactly what we're gonna do. We infiltrate PPI. We plant those streaming server devices. And we bring Barry into the light."

Reed directed his next comments to Carter, "Did you get the server devices in and ready?"

Carter's screen lit up, his voice steady and firm. He leaned back in his chair, the faint glow of framed photography awards reflecting in the background. "Yes, of course, I have them. A live broadcast of incriminating evidence from inside The Darkroom during Barry's SYNC presentation, I can picture it now. Beautiful! But I'll say it again: it's ambitious, even for us."

"Ambitious," Reed agreed. "But necessary. Barry's empire is built on secrecy and manipulation. If we hit him live, in front of the world, it won't just strip away his armor; it'll bury him. It's the *perfect* stage."

Kranch's feed flickered on as he began to talk, his cluttered workshop framed by scattered tools and rolled-up blueprints. He tapped a stylus against his tablet and said, "You guys know I have a knack for making the impossible happen. I've been planning exactly how we could plant streaming devices in PPI's servers. I mean, it isn't just risky, it's borderline suicide. Facial recognition, heat sensors, full surveillance grids. If we so much as breathe wrong, they'll know we're there."

Grimes, surrounded by the soft glow of blinking monitors in his garage, smirked faintly. "Once the devices are in place at PPI, I'll take it from there. The stream can be discreetly inserted directly into SYNC's central systems. When Barry takes the stage, we'll activate the feed whenever we're ready. We'll broadcast every single piece of evidence from PPI to SYNC's audience, and beyond. Trust me, no one's coming back from this."

Carter began to speak, his skepticism clear. "And the evidence? What exactly are we showing?"

Reed picked up a folder from the edge of his desk, holding it briefly before setting it back down. "We've got enough to start: the images of Barry with the weaponized lens, the audio recording of his assassination plan, and the files tying him to the hit on Kessler. But we're not stopping there." He leaned closer to the camera, his voice dropping slightly. "The Darkroom isn't just PPI's nerve center. It's their graveyard. Hidden archives, sealed records, things Barry's buried so deep, no one's supposed to find them. We take everything we can."

Kranch frowned, his face set. "Breaking in is one thing. Getting out alive? That's another story. We're walking into the lion's den, Reed."

Reed met Kranch's gaze through the screen, unflinching. "That's why we plan it perfectly. Barry will be in Las Vegas for SYNC, along with half of his key personnel. Security will still be tight, but it's the best window we'll ever get."

Carter leaned forward, his expression grim. "And if something goes sideways?"

Reed's mind doubled down. "Then we adapt. But we don't back down. Not now. Not ever."

For a second, the line went silent, the weight of the plan settling over them like a thick fog.

Grimes broke it first, a small grin tugging at his lips. "Infiltrating PPI headquarters? Let's get it done. Sounds like a normal Tuesday."

Kranch exhaled, nodding reluctantly. "If we pull this off, Barry won't know what hit him for sure."

Reed's gaze moved across the grid of faces, lingering on each of them. "We're not just doing this for Kessler, or for ourselves. We're doing this to end Barry's empire, once and for all."

He paused. "We move in 12 hours. Kranch meet me in New York. Carter stay put in front of your computer, we'll need to confirm these devices will work in real time. Grimes, get SYNC ready, you know what to do. Team, be ready."

The screens blinked to black as the call ended. Reed leaned back in his chair, the hum of the quiet room pressing in around him. His gaze shifted to the map of The Darkroom pinned on the wall. He traced a finger over its edges, his thoughts running over the plan again, testing every angle.

12 hours later in New York, Reed adjusted the brim of his cap, the gray uniform of a maintenance worker doing little to ease the knot in his chest as he and Kranch entered *The Darkroom's* lobby. The building was all sharp lines and reflective surfaces, a fortress disguised as modern architecture. They carried toolkits, moving with deliberate ease, blending into the hum of early-morning routine.

"Remember," Kranch muttered under his breath, voice low. "We're invisible. Maintenance gets overlooked. Stick to the script, and let me talk."

Reed nodded, shifting his grip on the toolkit. To anyone watching, it held nothing but wrenches and screwdrivers. Hidden inside, though, were streaming devices capable of pulling PPI's empire apart.

The first checkpoint loomed, a pair of security guards scanning IDs and bags.

"Morning," Kranch said casually, handing over their fabricated credentials.

One guard took the IDs, barely glancing before scanning them into the system. Reed shifted, feigning the disinterest of someone bored with manual labor as Kranch filled the silence.

"Big glitch in the sub-basement," Kranch said. "Power's acting up. You know how it is, everything works fine until it doesn't."

The guard smirked, handing back the IDs. "Ain't that the truth. Go ahead."

Reed exhaled quietly as they passed, but halfway to the elevators, his pulse spiked. Ahead, at the next checkpoint, a familiar face stood waiting.

"Duenkel," Reed murmured, his voice tight. "Barry's enforcer. Right side. He'll know me."

Kranch didn't glance over, didn't slow. Instead, he adjusted his pace, sliding just enough between Reed and Duenkel to shield him. "Follow my lead."

The second checkpoint. Duenkel's gaze snapped onto them immediately, suspicion sharpening the lines of his face.

"Morning," Kranch said briskly, flashing the ID again. "Sub-basement. Power issues."

Duenkel's eyes lingered on Reed, narrowing. "What's his name?"

Reed froze.

Kranch shrugged, unbothered. "He's my helper. New guy. Doesn't talk much. I told him to let me handle the chatter." He lowered his voice conspiratorially. "Not much of a people person, if you know what I mean."

"Helper, huh?" Duenkel's tone dripped skepticism.

Kranch flashed the ID again, his voice sharpening. "Look, we're just trying to fix your systems before you've got a blackout on your hands. You wanna call this in, or can we do our job?"

The pause was ice-cold. Reed's heart hammered in his chest. Finally, Duenkel waved them through, though his eyes followed them all the way to the elevator bank.

Inside the elevator, Reed jabbed the button for the lower levels. His voice was low and sharp. "That was too close."

Kranch grinned faintly, unshaken. "Nah. People love a good excuse to stop caring."

Reed smirked despite himself. "I'll give you that one. But Duenkel's not forgetting this."

"Doesn't matter." Kranch adjusted the strap on his toolkit. "By the time he figures out who we are, it'll be too late."

The elevator dinged, the doors sliding open. As they stepped into the narrow, humming server room, Reed's focus sharpened.

The first streaming device was small and unassuming, disguised as a maintenance component. Kneeling beside the panel, Reed worked quickly, his hands steady. He slid the device into place, its magnetic clasp locking tight.

"Done," he whispered.

Kranch scanned their handheld monitor. "It's live. Signal's clean."

A sharp *beep* from the server froze them both.

Reed's stomach dropped. The monitor flashed: **Anomaly detected: Server 3A.**

"Silent alert," Kranch muttered, his voice dark. "We've got maybe sixty seconds."

"Move. Now."

Reed shoved the tools into his bag, and they slipped out the door just as approaching footsteps echoed down the hall. Ducking into a maintenance shaft, they crouched in the shadows as two PPI officers passed, flashlights sweeping.

"That was close," Kranch whispered.

"Too close," Reed agreed, voice tight. "But it's done. Let's move."

The halls were dim, labyrinthine, every sound amplified. Their footsteps were soft but deliberate as they approached the encrypted communications server.

Reed reached it first, kneeling to expose the core. The second device, a transmitter capable of bypassing PPI's encryption, slid into place.

"Thirty seconds," Kranch warned, his eyes scanning the corridor.

"Got it," Reed said, locking the transmitter into place. The green light blinked to life. "Done."

Their final target was the central monitoring station. Cameras lined the corridor, and two guards blocked the door.

"We need a diversion," Kranch whispered.

Reed pointed upward to a maintenance shaft. "Give me a minute."

He climbed silently, maneuvering through the shaft until he reached a utility panel. With one flick of the switch, the lights in a nearby corridor began to flicker, and the cameras lining the hallway went dark. In the distance, a faint alarm beeped, barely audible over the hum of the building.

"Disturbance in Corridor 5C," a guard muttered into his radio. "Checking it out."

The moment they moved, Kranch gave Reed a thumbs-up. Together, they slipped into the monitoring station.

Reed worked fast, planting the final device on the monitoring hub. This was the anchor, the connection linking all the others to Grimes's secure server at SYNC.

Kranch stood by the door, a stun baton hidden in his grip. "You good?"

"Almost." Reed snapped the device into place. The blinking stabilized. "We're live."

Footsteps approached. Reed grabbed his bag, his voice tight. "Go."

They slipped out the back exit just as the guards returned, unaware of the breach.

Once they were clear, Kranch let out a quiet laugh. "Three devices. Zero alarms, sorta. We might just survive this."

Reed's expression stayed serious, his voice low. "If we keep this up, we'll do more than survive. We'll finish this."

Reed and Kranch waited patiently to see if all their hard work inside the Darkroom would pay off. The server devices were in place, but were they working? Would Carter gain access to the supercomputers? Would the vulnerabilities they installed work, or had all of this been a waste of time? Reed and Kranch could only hope.

While waiting for the streaming devices to fully integrate with PPI's servers, Carter's fingers flew across the keyboard of his computer back at his office, the glow of his monitors reflecting in his focused eyes. Lines of code streamed across one screen while fragments of Barry's SYNC presentation flickered on the other. The trigger devices Reed and Kranch had planted had begun punching through deeper layers of PPI's encryption, peeling back Barry's meticulous plans one file at a time.

"What have you got?" Reed's voice crackled through the secure channel.

Carter paused, stroking his chin with his hand as he scanned the screens. "Barry's not just delivering a keynote. He's orchestrating a power play. The slides are layered, on the surface, it's corporate buzz: growth, innovation, global reach. But dig deeper, and you see the real message."

"What message?" Kranch's voice cut in, sharp.

Carter clicked through several slides, highlighting specific sections. "Subtle blackmail. Each story is just personal enough to remind key PPI members who holds the reins. Barry isn't persuading them, he's controlling them."

Reed leaned toward his own monitor, his expression hardening. "And his contingencies?"

Carter hesitated, his voice grim. "That's where it gets worse. Barry's prepped false narratives to deploy if there's any disruption, leaks, doctored data, accusations of rogue sabotage. Guess who the scapegoats are?"

"Us," Kranch said flatly.

"Correct. He's also planted operatives at SYNC to intercept suspicious activity. Everything points to us as rogue agents."

Reed sat back, thoughts snapping into place like puzzle pieces. Barry wasn't just expecting resistance, he was exploiting it, weaving it deeper into his web.

"We won't outpace all of this," Carter added, typing furiously. "The trigger devices bought us access, but they also bought Barry time. Two minutes, maybe less, that's our window to block whatever he's planning at SYNC. After that..."

"After that, we lose," Reed finished. "Barry's playing a long game, but he doesn't know we're already inside. Those two minutes are our chance. We take it, or we walk away with nothing."

Kranch frowned. "And what exactly do we do in two minutes? Pull the plug on his whole presentation?"

"No," Reed replied, his gaze sharpening. "We let him play his hand. Then we show the cards he doesn't want anyone to see. If we shut him down too early, he'll spin it as sabotage. If we time it right, we'll expose him before he can react."

Carter nodded, his hands still flying. "I'll keep digging. The trigger devices let me pull data, but the deeper I go, the harder it gets. Barry has got the worst of it locked up tight. If I can crack it…"

"Do what you can," Reed said. "But if you can't crack it in time, we move with what we have. No second chances."

Kranch's usual smirk was gone, replaced by something darker. "Barry's got operatives watching every angle. If they spot us, "

"They won't," Reed interrupted. "We'll stay in the light, just like the message said. If Barry wants to hide in the shadows, fine. We'll shine a light so bright he won't escape it."

Carter paused, his eyes flicking toward the camera. "Reed, this is a long shot. Even for us."

With his voice steady Reed said: "It's the only shot we've got."

The line fell silent, the weight of the mission pressing heavy on all of them. Finally, Carter's voice broke through. "All right. Let's make it count."

Reed exhaled, nodding to himself. "Now we just have to get out of here."

Ahead, the final turn loomed, the loading dock doors and freedom just beyond.

"Almost there," Kranch murmured.

But Reed's neck prickled. He glanced back and froze. A PPI operative had stopped mid-step, his gaze locked on them. Reed's stomach dropped as the man's hand moved to his radio.

"He's made us," Reed hissed.

"Keep moving," Kranch replied, sharply.

"Hey!" the operative barked, his suspicion hardening into certainty.

Before Reed could respond, the fire door slammed open. An alarm blared as sunlight spilled into the hallway, cutting through the silence.

"Go!" Kranch shouted.

They bolted for the alley. Behind them, shouts echoed as more operatives spilled out from side entrances.

"We're pinned," Reed said, glancing left and right.

"Not yet," Kranch shot back.

Their earpieces crackled to life. Carter's voice cut through the chaos, steady and controlled. "I've got you. Hold tight."

Reed didn't have time to ask what that meant. As they sprinted toward the street, every traffic light in a five-block radius blinked green at once.

It was as if the entire city surged forward. Horns blared. Engines roared. Traffic gridlocked in seconds as cars flooded the intersections.

Reed and Kranch ducked through the gridlock, weaving between stalled vehicles. Operatives scrambled, shouting into radios, but the mess Carter had orchestrated bought Reed and Kranch the precious seconds they needed.

They slipped into an alley, out of sight. Kranch leaned against the wall, catching his breath. "Carter, remind me to buy you dinner."

Carter's voice came through, smug. "You'll owe me more than dinner when this is done."

Reed stood at the alley's edge, watching operatives struggle through gridlocked streets. His shoulders relaxed, but only slightly.

"The Architect doesn't just build plans," he muttered, his voice low. "He builds traps."

Kranch looked over. "What was that?"

Reed shook his head, his gaze still fixed on the chaos. Barry's hand was everywhere, every move planned to the letter.

"Come on," Reed said finally, adjusting the strap of his bag. "We're not out yet."

Kranch pushed off the wall. "Where to?"

Reed's gaze hardened. "First, somewhere safe. Then we dismantle Barry, one piece at a time."

They slipped into the labyrinth of city streets, leaving the chaos behind.

While Reed and Kranch were escaping PPI headquarters, back in Tulsa Barry stood in the center of a cavernous studio, conference table tucked into a corner, arms crossed, as a fancy Hollywood director paced in front of him. Massive screens lined the walls, test footage and animations flickering across them. The air buzzed with energy, technicians adjusting lights, sound engineers testing levels, and the barely audible hum of orchestral music playing from a speaker overhead.

"Mr. Cox," the director said, his hands gesturing theatrically as he spoke. "This isn't just a keynote. It's a *production*. The audience needs to feel like they're witnessing history."

Barry's lips curled into a satisfied smile. "That's exactly what they'll be witnessing."

The director nodded eagerly, flipping through his notes. "I'm thinking dramatic lighting to set the tone, sharp beams, controlled shadows. We'll use cinematic visuals, slow pans, sweeping shots, to showcase your achievements. And the music? Something grand, orchestral. Subtle at first, then building to a crescendo when you take the stage. It'll be unforgettable."

Barry raised an eyebrow. "And the transitions?"

"Seamless," the director assured him. "Each segment will flow perfectly into the next, milestones, triumphs, the future. It will be a story that cements your leadership, when you speak, everyone will listen. The narrative is designed to make you undeniable. You'll command the room."

Barry turned toward the massive screen, where an early mockup of the presentation played, a sequence of glowing words spelling out *Leadership. Vision. Influence.* before fading into shots of sleek, state-of-the-art photography gear and globe-spanning maps. Barry's voice, pre-recorded, boomed across the room, delivering carefully curated soundbites:

"PPI doesn't just set the standard. We *are* the standard."

Barry's smile widened as the director paused the playback, turning expectantly toward him.

"It's good," Barry said, his tone sharp. "But not good enough. The lighting needs to hit harder. I want shadows that make me the center of focus. Make it dramatic, cinematic. Every single frame needs to remind them who I am. When they walk out of SYNC, I want my name on everyone's lips."

The director scribbled notes, nodding furiously. "Understood. Perfection, no exceptions."

Barry's gaze hardened. "There's no room for anything less. SYNC will be the moment that solidifies everything we've built, PPI's absolute public dominance."

He took a step closer to the director, his voice dropping to a quiet, intense whisper.

"This isn't just a photography show. It's about total influence. When I step on that stage, they need to believe in me. And more importantly, they need to fear what happens to their careers if they cross me. Do you understand?"

The director swallowed, sensing the weight of Barry's words. "We'll get it right. Trust me."

Barry gave a curt nod, but his attention was already drifting back to the massive screens. *Trust.* It was a word he seldom used, and rarely meant.

For Barry, SYNC wasn't just another event, it was his empire's crowning jewel. Every pixel, note, and pause had to be flawless.

But as the technicians adjusted spotlights and the director barked orders to his team, Barry's overconfidence began to show. He waved off an assistant wanting to talk about operational updates. When a security report came through his phone, routine surveillance alerts, he barely glanced at it before silencing the notification.

"These details can wait," Barry muttered, eyes fixed on the dazzling test visuals of his entrance. "Nothing matters more than this presentation."

Around him, the studio buzzed with activity, but cracks were beginning to form in Barry's armor of control. His focus had narrowed, his vision consumed by the grandeur of SYNC. Barry wasn't watching the shadows.

He sat back in his seat at the studio, the hissing of studio lights in the background as he scrolled through presentation notes on his tablet. The grand SYNC production was coming together perfectly, no detail overlooked, no frame out of place. He allowed himself a small smile, the satisfaction of a man in complete control.

Just then, his phone buzzed, the screen lighting up with a new message. No sender, no subject, just a single line:

"Even stars burn out and become dark."

Barry's brow furrowed as he read it. He turned the phone in his hand, as if a different angle might reveal more. The words were again cryptic, vaguely threatening, but more than that, *unnecessary.* Barry had no patience for games.

"Another troll," he muttered, swiping the screen to lock the phone. "Or someone trying too hard to be clever."

He tossed the phone onto the table in front of him and returned his attention to the tablet, his mind already moving past the message. His fingers swiped through slide transitions and lighting notes, every detail of the SYNC presentation a carefully calibrated step toward his domination of the room, and beyond.

But for a split second, the words lingered. *Even stars burn out.*

Barry's lips pressed. It wasn't that he feared the message; he simply found it *annoying.* Distractions like this had no place in his world. If his opponents thought they could rattle him with ominous one-liners, they were more desperate than he'd realized.

"They're grasping," he muttered, brushing the thought aside. If anything, the message only solidified his belief, he'd already won. His opponents were scrambling in the dark. Let them send riddles and warnings; he had the spotlight.

Barry stood at the head of the conference table surrounded by the SYNC planning team. Mockups of his keynote presentation flickered on the oversized screen. His gaze lingered on the visuals, tweaked cinematic transitions, adjusted bold graphics, and carefully scripted soundbites showcasing his achievements. Every frame dripped with even more authority, his authority.

"Seamless," Barry said finally, his tone louder than normal. "But it needs to hit harder. Stronger visuals on PPI's global reach. Show dominance, not complacency."

The Hollywood director cleared his throat, flipping through his notes. "We've added a proposed emotional segment, a series of testimonials from key PPI leaders. Personal stories, gratitude for your leadership. It'll humanize the moment, it will add weight to, "

Barry held up a hand, silencing him. "No." His voice was calm, but the room stiffened. "I control the message. Every word, every image. I don't need others speaking for me." He tapped the table for emphasis. "This isn't a charity dinner. It's a statement."

The director nodded quickly, scribbling notes. "Of course. Your voice will carry the moment."

Barry sat back down, his focus shifting to the presentation slides once more. It was flawless, exactly as he'd envisioned. Any deviation from his narrative would only muddy the impact. And Barry wasn't one for compromise.

A junior operative stepped inside hesitantly, clutching a tablet to his chest. His shoes barely made a sound as he approached, his gaze flicking nervously to Barry.

"Sir," the operative began, his voice careful. "I have the latest encrypted security update for SYNC."

Barry didn't look up from his tablet. "Go on."

The operative cleared his throat. "There are... a few flagged anomalies. Small ones, but worth a closer look."

Barry's gaze finally lifted, sharp and impatient. "So, what's the problem?"

The operative hesitated, glancing down at his screen. "One of the anomalies is a flagged entry earlier today at PPI headquarters. Two men posing as maintenance workers entered the building. Credentials checked out, and nothing appears to be out of place..." He paused, his voice lowering. "But security hasn't verified their purpose. It's unusual, "

Barry's brow twitched, a flicker of irritation crossing his face. "Unusual?"

"Yes, sir," the operative pressed. "Given the scale of SYNC, it might be prudent to heighten precautions, review entry logs, double-check clearance levels, ensure, "

Barry cut him off with a sharp wave of his hand. "Heighten precautions? For what?" He leaned back in his chair, exhaling in faint amusement. "Two men with toolkits? *Maintenance workers?* And what, now you think they're spies? Saboteurs?"

The operative shifted awkwardly. "I'm not suggesting that, sir, but, "

Barry let out a humorless chuckle, his voice laced with condescension. "Listen carefully. I've accounted for everything. Every variable. Every possibility. We're operating a fortress here, not a neighborhood coffee shop. This isn't *amateur hour.*"

The operative looked as if he wanted to press the issue, but Barry's gaze froze him in place. After a long silence, Barry extended a hand. "The report."

The operative handed over the tablet and, with a stiff nod, retreated quickly from the room. The door clicked shut behind him, leaving Barry with just his thoughts.

He scrolled through the report lazily, the flagged anomalies barely warranting a glance. The maintenance worker entry was a blip, noise against the backdrop of a flawless operation. He locked the tablet and tossed it onto the table with a dull thud.

"Routine noise," Barry muttered. "Nothing more."

The director looked up from his notes, his expression uncertain. "Sir, after this last set of tweaks, what do you think of the presentation, lighting, transitions...?"

Barry held up his hand and halted the director in mid-sentence. He buttoned his jacket and said: "It's perfect!"

He crossed the room to where a lectern had been set up for

rehearsal. Sliding his notes onto the podium, Barry surveyed the space as if it were already filled with SYNC's elite attendees. This was his moment, his triumph, and nothing, not whispers of anomalies, not panicked junior operatives, would tarnish it.

The lights dimmed. Music swelled softly in the background, an orchestral rise that matched Barry's practiced timing. He gripped the edges of the lectern, his posture exuding authority as he began.

"Leadership is not given; it is earned."

His voice carried through the large studio room, steady and commanding. Each line of his keynote landed perfectly, rehearsed to the point of perfection.

But beyond the brilliance of the production, faint cracks lurked. A monitor flickered briefly in the far corner, and a slight distortion ran through the sound system, imperceptible to anyone not looking for it. Barry didn't notice. He was focused on his performance, his vision, his rise.

As he delivered the final line, Barry's smile returned, smooth and self-assured. "SYNC isn't the future. It's *my* future."

The music peaked, then faded to silence.

For a long moment, Barry stood at the lectern, soaking in the imagined applause, the triumphant energy of his own making. To him, everything was perfect.

But behind the polished veneer of control, unseen chaos stirred. The cracks in his empire were spreading, quiet and deliberate, and the storm gathering just beyond his reach was ready to consume everything he'd built.

19
PRE-
VISUALIZATION

The sprawling lights of the Las Vegas Strip stretched out below as Reed's plane descended into McCarran International Airport. Even from the air, the city pulsed with energy, neon signs flickering, traffic snaking through the arteries of the desert metropolis.

Reed stepped off the jetway into the terminal, a carry-on slung over his shoulder. His baseball cap was pulled low, shielding his face from the endless stream of security cameras. He moved with purpose but without haste, blending into the sea of arriving passengers.

Kranch was already waiting near the baggage claim, leaning casually against a pillar, his phone in hand. A worn leather jacket hung from his broad shoulders, and he looked every bit the tired traveler.

"Smooth flight?" Kranch asked as Reed approached.

"Uneventful," Reed replied, his eyes scanning the crowd.

"Good. Carter's landing in forty minutes. Grimes is already on-site."

They moved together toward the airport exit, navigating through the controlled chaos of SYNC attendees arriving from every corner of the world, photographers lugging camera bags, crew members in branded polos, influencers vlogging their way through the terminal.

SYNC wasn't just a convention, it was *the* convention. The place where deals were made, careers launched, and reputations cemented.

Outside, the air buzzed with taxi horns and shuttle engines. They slipped into a black SUV waiting at the curb.

As the vehicle pulled away, Kranch adjusted his earpiece. "Grimes says the main floor is already buzzing. Barry's crew is everywhere. We will be watched the moment we step into the venue."

Reed's eyes flicked to the passing skyline. "Good. Let them look. We'll give them exactly what they expect to see."

The SYNC convention floor at the Las Vegas Convention Center was a controlled frenzy, setup crews darting between booths, banners hoisted skyward, and high-tech displays blinking to life.

Grimes stood near the main stage, clipboard in hand, headset on, blending perfectly with the chaos.

When Reed and Kranch slipped through one of the side entrances, Grimes didn't look up immediately. He finished giving orders to a lighting technician before walking toward them.

"Welcome to the circus," Grimes said, his tone dry.

Reed smirked faintly. "You seem at home."

Grimes gestured toward the massive stage looming behind him. "This place is Barry's cathedral. Every camera, every light, every cable, it all runs back to him. He's not just hosting this; he's *owning* it."

Kranch scanned the floor, his gaze sharp as he noted clusters of security personnel and the way their eyes lingered a beat too long on certain individuals. "And us?"

Grimes' expression hardened. "We're ghosts right now. But once this thing kicks off, we'll have maybe two minutes to do what we need to do before someone realizes the system's been compromised."

Reed felt sick to his stomach at the reminder. *Two minutes. That was all they'd have to turn the tide, or lose everything.*

"Then let's make every second count," Reed said firmly.

Grimes led them away from the chaotic stage floor, weaving through rows of equipment crates and half-finished setups until they reached a quieter corner, a temporary operations booth humming with quiet urgency. Screens displayed live security feeds, floor schematics, and logistics schedules.

"We've got backend access thanks to Carter's devices," Grimes said, his voice low, eyes scanning the monitors in front of him. "Barry's rehearsals are locked down tight, full security detail, closed-loop surveillance. Nobody gets in or out without clearance."

Reed crossed his arms, his focus sharp. "And Barry himself?"

"Arriving later today. Private jet. The director's already here, fine-tuning every second of his keynote."

Kranch stepped closer to the monitors, his jaw tight. "Anything on Duenkel?"

Grimes' expression darkened, his voice dipping lower. "He's here. Barry brought him in early. If Duenkel sees us, it has to be as photographers, not operatives. He's naturally suspicious, so it's best we stay off his radar."

Reed nodded. "Then we stay invisible. We play our part. Barry wants a show, and we'll give him one, but on our terms."

Grimes nodded. "Every piece is in motion."

"All right," Reed said, his tone firm but quiet. "We split up. Kranch, secure our access points. Grimes, keep monitoring the feeds. Carter will be here soon. I'll start mapping our routes."

Kranch adjusted the strap on his toolkit, his usual smirk absent, replaced by something colder. "Clock's ticking."

"It's always ticking," Reed replied.

Without another word, they dispersed into the chaotic heartbeat of the convention floor. The symphony of noise, crew members barking orders, forklifts whining as they maneuvered crates, distant bursts of feedback from sound tests, wrapped around them like static.

Above, enormous banners stretched across the cavernous ceiling:

SYNC: A New Vision. They fluttered faintly in the sterile breeze of industrial air conditioning, a manufactured wind in a manufactured reality.

Reed moved with purpose, weaving through clusters of setup crews and tech personnel. His steps were measured, his gaze sharp, but the weight of the days ahead pressed against him like an anchor.

Every plan was set. Every risk calculated. But Barry was a master at flipping traps against their makers. And Reed knew they were dancing on borrowed time.

His phone buzzed in his pocket.

Reed slipped it out carefully, shielding the screen from any wandering eyes. The message was plain, untraceable:

"2 Corinthians 6:14B."

He froze for a beat, the verse hanging in his mind like a riddle suspended in midair. Quickly, he typed it into a search bar and whispered the passage under his breath:

"Or what fellowship has light with darkness?"

The words settled heavy in his chest. Reed's gaze flicked over the crowd, his breath steady but sharp, half-expecting someone to step from the shadows, eyes waiting and knowing.

Minutes later, in a quieter corner near a service entrance, Reed regrouped with Kranch and Grimes. The noise of the convention floor faded to a distant hum as he held up his phone for them to see.

"2 Corinthians 6:14B," Reed said, his voice clipped. "It says: 'Or what fellowship has light with darkness?' Any guesses?"

Grimes frowned, arms crossing tightly over his chest. "What? Are we getting scriptures now?"

Kranch ran a hand over the back of his neck, his brows knitted together. "I don't like it. Who sends something like this in the middle of an op? Are they trying to warn us... or mess with us?"

Reed pocketed the phone, his jaw flexing with tension. "I don't know. But someone's been steering us from the start, and they're still watching. Every message comes when we need it, but never enough to give us answers."

For a moment, silence settled between them, heavy and thick, broken only by the ticking of distant ventilation fans.

"Add it to the list," Kranch said finally, his voice tight.

Reed nodded, the verse embedding itself into the growing puzzle in his mind. But unlike the other cryptic phrases, this one lingered. It felt... *heavier.*

As they moved back into the swirling current of the crowd, Reed couldn't shake the feeling that the verse wasn't just a message, it was a warning.

The stakes couldn't be higher now. Barry's operatives were everywhere, men and women in plain clothes but with sharp eyes, scanning faces and watching patterns. Every casual glance, every half-step out of place, felt like it could unravel the entire operation.

Twice, Reed caught a security agent lingering on him a second too long. Once, Kranch doubled back behind a set of stage curtains to avoid crossing paths with a guard whose gaze lingered a beat too long. And Grimes narrowly sidestepped a technician whose interest in his clipboard seemed far from casual.

Every corner they turned, every movement they made, it all felt like walking a tightrope above an open flame.

But the team pressed on, each member vanishing into their respective tasks with disciplined focus.

Reed's hand brushed against the phone in his pocket. *Or what fellowship has light with darkness?*

It wasn't just a verse, it was a question.

And Reed wasn't sure if he wanted to know the answer.

Carter arrived at the Las Vegas Convention Center just after noon, blending effortlessly into the flood of attendees pouring through the grand entrance. He wore a pressed polo shirt with a fake event coordinator badge clipped to his belt. With his camera bag slung across his shoulder and a confident stride, he looked like every other tech-savvy professional walking the SYNC setup.

Reed spotted him from across the main floor. Their eyes met

briefly, and Reed gave a subtle nod before turning away, disappearing into the maze of booths and banners.

Minutes later, the four regrouped in a cramped utility corridor off the main exhibition hall. The hum of HVAC systems filled the space, fluorescent lights flickering weakly above them.

Carter dropped his camera bag onto an overturned crate and unzipped it, revealing a sleek tablet and a tangle of cables and devices. "Alright, status update," he said, keeping his voice low.

"Grimes has control over the live-feed monitoring," Reed began. "Kranch secured access points for the streaming devices, server room, encrypted comms, and the surveillance hub."

"And Barry?" Carter asked without looking up, his fingers already flying across the tablet.

"Arriving soon," Grimes replied, glancing over his shoulder. "The director's locked down his rehearsal space. Security's airtight."

Carter nodded, scrolling through a schematic map of the convention center displayed on his screen. "First things first: I need to make sure the devices Reed and Kranch planted at The Darkroom are connecting properly. Without those streams, this whole operation is dead in the water."

His fingers moved with precision, opening connection logs and encrypted pathways. Green indicators blinked on the screen as the devices began reporting back.

"Connection's live. Signal strength is stable." Carter squinted at one section of the display. "But there's intermittent lag on the third device. Could be environmental interference, could be someone poking around where they shouldn't be."

Kranch's brow furrowed. "Can you fix it?"

"I can stabilize it for now, but if someone starts sniffing around the system, we'll lose that feed. And if we lose one, we lose redundancy. Barry's security systems are too tight for half-measures." Carter's voice was steady, but an edge of tension sharpened his tone.

Reed leaned against the wall. "Do what you can. We can't afford even one weak link."

Carter's fingers flew across the tablet again. After a tense moment, the flickering green indicator stabilized.

"Alright. That should hold. Now let's talk about the security vulnerabilities here at SYNC."

He swiped across his screen, bringing up a schematic of the venue. Red outlines highlighted weak points: secondary exits, blind spots in surveillance, and inconsistencies in guard patrol routes.

"This is where Barry gets sloppy," Carter said, pointing to a poorly monitored hallway near the back of the keynote stage. "It's an old service corridor. Cameras are outdated, blind spots everywhere. If we need to slip backstage without being noticed, that's our route."

Kranch leaned closer, studying the map. "What about the main presentation feed? How do we patch our stream into Barry's keynote without tipping anyone off?"

Carter tapped the screen again, highlighting a small control room tucked behind the main stage. "That's our insertion point. It's where all the live feeds merge before hitting the main projection system. We get into that room, plug in a hardline connection, and our stream overrides whatever Barry's showing on stage."

Grimes allowed himself a faint smile. "Leave that to me. After all, I'm the *'Event Organizer.'*"

Carter smirked but continued. "Good. Now, they rely on rotating personnel for that room, and the handoff times are sloppy. If we time it right, we'll have about ninety seconds to patch in before anyone realizes something's wrong."

Reed's eyes narrowed as he studied the schematic. Ninety seconds. Barely enough time to tie a shoelace, let alone hijack a live broadcast in front of an international audience. But it was the only window they had.

"Kranch," Reed said, his voice firm. "You make sure the hardline connections are perfect. I'm betting they're located above the stage in the lighting rig. Grimes, keep eyes on security patrols, cameras, and anything out of place. Carter, stay on the backend and keep those devices stable. I'll run interference if anyone gets too close."

Kranch smirked faintly. "And if something goes wrong?"

"It won't," Reed said. But the edge in his voice betrayed the uncertainty gnawing at him.

Carter glanced up from his tablet, his brow furrowed. "One more thing, you all need to know something about Barry's backup plans."

Reed's attention snapped to him. "Go on."

"I've been digging through the encrypted files from *The Darkroom*. Barry's contingency layers have contingency layers. If something goes wrong during his keynote, if anything feels even slightly off, he's got trigger protocols in place. We're talking venue lockdowns, scrambled feeds, and enough false evidence to frame us as rogue operatives in real-time."

Grimes exhaled sharply. "So, in short, we've got one shot."

"One shot," Carter confirmed. "If we miss it, Barry flips the narrative, and we become the villains."

Reed's jaw tightened. "Then we don't miss."

The four men stood in silence, the weight of the mission pressing down like an anvil.

Finally, Carter shut his tablet with a sharp snap and tucked it back into his bag. "Alright, gentlemen. We're officially out of prep time. It's go-time."

Reed looked at each of them, seriously. "Stay sharp. Stay invisible. We move when the light hits."

They nodded in unison before dispersing into the labyrinth of the convention center, each man vanishing into the bustling crowd.

Above them, **SYNC: A New Vision** banners fluttered under the hum of air conditioning.

Grimes moved through the backstage corridors with the casual confidence of someone who belonged there. His *Event Organizer* badge hung prominently from his neck, and a tablet was tucked under his arm. Every step, every glance, every conversation was calculated.

He stopped frequently, chatting briefly with technicians,

nodding at security guards, blending seamlessly into the organized chaos.

At the main control booth overlooking the auditorium, Grimes leaned over a technician's shoulder, pointing at a screen. "Barry wants those transitions flawless. Double-check the timings on all slides. If anything stutters, it's your job on the line."

The technician nodded, oblivious to Grimes discreetly slipping a small, inconspicuous device onto one of the primary control routers.

A **SIGINT (Signal Intelligence)** transmitter.

It would give Carter remote access to Barry's terminal during the presentation, funneling every keystroke, every action, straight into their system.

Grimes straightened, his eyes briefly scanning the screens before moving on. Barry's rehearsal was locked in today from **2:00 PM to 4:00 PM**, and the keynote was set for tomorrow at **8:00 PM sharp**.

"Schedule's tight," Grimes muttered into his earpiece. "Barry's keeping a close leash on rehearsals. We have no room for error."

Kranch moved like a shadow high above the stage, crouched low in the tangled metal framework of the lighting rig. Dust hung heavy in the air, and the faint smell of ozone from recently tested stage lights clung to every surface.

Below him stretched the vast auditorium, rows of empty seats, the gleaming LED backdrop glowing faintly, and the podium standing at the center like an altar waiting for its sermon.

It was perfect. From here, Kranch could see everything without being seen.

Then, movement.

Barry entered below, flanked by the Hollywood director and a small entourage of aides. The director gestured wildly toward the LED screens, his voice carrying faintly but incomprehensibly in the cavernous space.

Kranch froze, pressing himself flat against the rigging as Barry paused near the podium.

Barry's sharp gaze swept the stage, pausing on a stack of crates near the lighting controls. Then, his eyes caught something.

A wrench. Carelessly left behind on the stage floor.

Kranch's heart pounded.

Barry stepped closer, picked up the tool, and inspected it briefly. His brow furrowed, and his lips pressed into a thin line.

"Get this cleaned up," Barry said sharply, tossing the wrench onto a crate. "This is supposed to be perfect."

One of the aides nodded, scurrying to obey.

Barry lingered a moment longer, his gaze sweeping upward toward the rigging. His eyes narrowed briefly before turning back to the director.

"Let's run it again. From the top."

Kranch remained frozen in place until Barry and his team moved further downstage. His heartbeat thundered in his ears as he whispered into his earpiece, "That was too close. I'm staying put for now. Barry's paranoid, but he didn't see me."

"Stay sharp," Reed's voice crackled in response. "We're too far in to slip now."

Down on the stage floor, Reed crouched behind a curtain stage-left. In front of him lay an open black equipment case, revealing sleek connectors and a tablet interface.

This was the link, the critical hardline connection between the devices planted at *The Darkroom* and the live broadcast feeds being prepped for Barry's keynote.

Reed worked quickly, snapping cables into place with precise clicks. Each sound felt amplified, each second stretched thin.

The auditorium was mostly empty now, save for a handful of technicians running final checks and *one man* pacing near the podium.

A tall figure in a sharp suit.

Reed froze. The man wasn't a technician.

He was one of Barry's operatives.

The operative's gaze swept the stage, landing on Reed. Their eyes locked, just for a second.

Reed ducked his head, pretending to fumble with one of the connectors.

The operative's brow furrowed, suspicion flickering in his eyes. He took a step forward, his hand brushing the earpiece tucked discreetly in his ear.

Reed's pulse roared in his ears. *Move. Think. Now.*

But before the operative could advance, his radio crackled sharply.

"Unit Six, report to the southeast entrance immediately. We've got an issue with the VIP logistics."

The operative hesitated, eyes still on Reed. But duty pulled louder than suspicion. He turned and strode offstage, disappearing through a side door.

Reed exhaled slowly, his breath measured as he pulled out his phone.

Text to Carter: *That was too close. Stick to the plan.*

The reply came almost instantly: **Always.**

Reed tucked the phone away, his hands returning to the cables. Every movement felt heavier now, every moment tighter.

Above him, Kranch was still in position. Grimes was watching the feeds. Carter was stabilizing the backend.

They were in place. But the clock was ticking.

Barry's operatives were everywhere, and every second felt like borrowed time.

Reed finished the final connection and zipped the equipment case shut. He melted back into the shadows, slipping away from the stage just as two more security agents entered the space.

For now, they were still invisible.

But invisibility wouldn't last forever.

The auditorium stood as the epicenter of an empire. Towering video walls showcased PPI branding and polished statistics, painting Barry's organization as an unstoppable force.

Strategic beams of light carved sharp patterns across the stage, converging on the podium at center, a pulpit from which Barry would deliver his carefully crafted sermon. Overhead, hidden speakers pulsed with the glory of an orchestral soundtrack, crescendos swelling and falling with cinematic precision.

Barry stood at the podium, one hand gripping its edge, scanning the rows of empty chairs stretching into the dim shadows. His sharp suit caught the glow of the stage lights, casting faint shadows behind him.

Offstage, the Hollywood director paced nervously, tablet in hand, frustration etched into his furrowed brow.

"Mr. Cox, I'm telling you, if we don't smooth out the pacing in the third transition, it's going to feel rushed. The emotional weight, "

Barry cut him off with a sharp wave of his hand. "No. The pacing is exactly right. The audience doesn't need to dwell; they need to be moved. They'll feel what I want them to feel."

The director hesitated, but Barry's icy glare kept him silent.

Barry stepped out from behind the podium, walking the length of the stage with the measured confidence of a man who owned the air he breathed.

"This isn't just a speech," Barry said, his voice calm, assured. "This is the moment they see me as the only leader. Every light, every sound, every pixel delivers one message: without me, there is no PPI."

The director nodded stiffly, scribbling notes onto his tablet.

Barry paused, squinting into the sea of empty chairs. For a moment, his sharp eyes scanned the upper rigging of the auditorium, the shadows where Kranch had been just minutes before.

"Security protocols," Barry said suddenly, his voice dropping an octave. "Bring them up."

A junior aide scrambled forward, tablet in hand. "Yes, sir. All entry points are sealed. Keynote access is restricted to credentialed personnel only. Surveillance feeds are running constant sweeps."

Barry snatched the tablet, his eyes flicking across the data points.

The security map displayed grids of camera coverage, patrol routes, and restricted zones.

"There's an anomaly logged here." He jabbed a finger at a high-lighted sector near the side entrance.

"It was a maintenance error, sir," the aide stammered. "Technicians reported a minor equipment malfunction earlier. It's been resolved."

Barry's lips pressed into a thin line as he stared at the report. Then, just as quickly as the tension rose, it deflated.

"Minor equipment malfunctions," Barry muttered, tossing the tablet back to the aide. "We're surrounded by incompetence. If I want something done right, I'll have to do it myself."

The aide flinched as Barry turned sharply back to the director. "Start the sequence again. From the top. I want every cue hit perfectly this time."

"Yes, Mr. Cox," the director said, his voice tight with forced compliance.

The stage lights dimmed, casting Barry's figure in stark silhou-ette. The massive screens behind him erupted with dazzling visuals, PPI's sleek logo followed by inspirational imagery of sprawling cityscapes and dignitaries shaking hands in photo-perfect compo-sitions.

Barry closed his eyes for a brief moment, inhaling deeply as the soundtrack swelled around him. When he spoke again, his voice carried through the empty hall like a monologue rehearsed a thou-sand times.

"Leadership isn't claimed. It's earned. It's forged in the fires of challenge, sharpened by adversity, and wielded with vision. Tonight, the world will see the light, and they'll know who holds it."

The final note of the soundtrack lingered, hanging in the silence that followed.

Barry exhaled slowly, his confidence absolute.

"Lock it in," he said, turning away from the stage. "Tomorrow, we own the world."

The director and aides scrambled to follow him as Barry strode offstage, his shadow stretching long across the polished floor.

High above in the rigging, Kranch remained motionless as Barry exited below. Even from this distance, he could feel the force of Barry's confidence, his absolute certainty that every detail was under control.

But Kranch knew something Barry didn't: cracks had already formed in the façade.

In the dim corridors beneath the stage, Reed moved with careful precision, double-checking the connections at the feed junction.

Backstage, Grimes monitored live surveillance feeds from his tablet, fingers moving across the screen as he adjusted camera angles and flagged blind spots.

And somewhere, Carter worked silently from his remote station, the glow of his screens reflecting in his focused eyes.

They were already inside.

Barry might have controlled the stage, the lights, and the music, but in the shadows, Reed and his team were setting their own traps.

The team regrouped in a dimly lit service corridor, huddled around Reed as he spread a detailed map of the auditorium across an overturned crate. The rustling of the convention floor buzzed through the walls, distant but ever-present.

Reed's voice was low, steady, carrying the weight of the moment. "Barry set the stage," Reed said quietly. "All we have to do is hit the switch."

Kranch let out a slow breath, his chest tightening slightly. "And what if those lights shine on us too, Reed? What if these messages you've been getting are leading us into a trap?"

Grimes glanced between them, tension etched into his expression. "He's got a point. We've been following breadcrumbs from someone we can't see, can't name, and definitely can't trust."

Reed's gaze lingered on the map before him, his brow furrowed in thought. "Whoever's been sending these messages, they've kept us alive. They've gotten us this far. But you're right... we have no idea what their endgame is."

He hesitated, his voice lowering. "We could be walking into something worse than Barry."

Silence hung heavy in the air, broken only by the faint drip of a leaky pipe somewhere down the corridor.

Kranch spoke first, his voice quieter now. "So, what do we do?"

Reed looked up, meeting their eyes one by one. "We stick to the plan. If someone's playing us, they'll have to work harder to stop us. Tomorrow, the truth goes public. Barry's empire crumbles. And if someone else is waiting in the wings..." His jaw tightened. "...then we deal with them next."

No one spoke, but the weight of their unspoken agreement settled over them like a final seal on their fate.

In the dim control room, Reed's gaze locked onto a monitor showing Barry pacing the stage. His voice echoed through the cavernous hall, amplified by the empty silence.

"PPI is more than a network, it's a force that shapes the world."

Reed's knuckles whitened against the edge of the console. His voice was low, resolute. "Not after tomorrow, Barry. Not after tomorrow."

The monitor flickered briefly, static crackling along the edges before stabilizing again.

Tomorrow, Barry's empire would rise.

Or it would fall.

Reed turned away, his figure dissolving into the shadows.

On the stage, Barry remained under the lights, confident, composed, and blind to the storm about to consume him.

20
BACKLIGHT

The convention was today.

In the predawn silence of the control room, Reed sat alone, bathed in the cold glow of monitors flickering with security feeds and system diagnostics. A single desk lamp cast a tight circle of light over the sprawling map of photographs, notes, and diagrams pinned across the wall. Lines of red string stitched connections between faces, places, and motives, a spider's web spun by Barry Cox.

At the center of it all, pinned like the heart of the labyrinth, was a single photograph: Barry Cox. His face stared back at Reed, frozen in time, a constant reminder of the stakes.

Reed leaned back in his chair, his eyes drifting over the map. The operation he and his team had built reminded him of a backlight in photography, a single, precise source of illumination positioned behind the subject. When done right, it created clarity, sharpness, and focus. But the smallest misstep, a light angled just slightly wrong, a shadow cast where it shouldn't be, and the entire image was ruined.

This operation was their backlight. Every piece, every player, every second had to align perfectly, or the truth they were trying to expose would remain buried in darkness.

He leaned forward again, scanning the plan laid out before him. Every access point, every device, every contingency, checked, double-checked, and then checked again. There was no room for improvisation now. Timing was everything.

The difference between success and failure wasn't hours anymore, it was seconds.

Reed's gaze settled on the stack of cryptic messages scattered across the desk: *Look closer, Reed. You're in the frame. Move only in the light. 2 Corinthians 6:14B.* Each phrase sat heavy in his mind, their meaning still elusive, their timing too precise to be coincidence.

Were they guidance or manipulation? Warnings or something else entirely?

The thought gnawed at him as he glanced at his watch. Fifteen hours. That's all that separated them from either victory or catastrophe.

In fifteen hours, Barry would step onto that stage, lights flaring, music swelling, the world watching. And in those same fifteen hours, Reed would have to pull every string, execute every maneuver, and pray that nothing, *nothing*, was out of place.

In fifteen hours, the world would know the truth.

Or it would know nothing at all.

Reed pored over the intricate web of evidence, each clue a fragment of a larger, elusive puzzle. The relentless pressure of the past few days bore down on him, a heavy reminder that even a few stolen hours of sleep were desperately needed. With time slowly shifting into an ally, he resolved to slip away to his hotel, a quiet haven where he could sharpen his focus and brace himself for the inevitable storm ahead.

Several hours later, across the city another web was being woven. One of contingencies, of backup plans, of carefully constructed lies. While Reed worked to expose the truth, Barry Cox was ensuring that truth would never see the light of day.

Barry's private suite exuded quiet opulence, a far cry from the spectacle of the SYNC convention floor. Floor-to-ceiling windows overlooked the neon sprawl of Las Vegas, the city that never slept was fully coming to life. The curtains were partially drawn, casting angular shadows across the plush carpet and polished mahogany conference table.

Five figures sat around the table, each one handpicked, trusted, and loyal, at least as far as Barry believed loyalty could stretch. Seth Gauthier, Barry's second-in-command, occupied the seat closest to him, his expression sharp and attentive, every muscle poised like a coiled spring. The others, field operatives, logistics specialists, watched Barry with varying degrees of wariness.

And then there was Dovere, Antonio Dovere.

He sat slightly back from the table, his silhouette draped in shadows despite the soft overhead light. His custom-made charcoal suit carried an effortless elegance, every line precise, every fold intentional. Dark hair, slicked back with an almost mirror-like shine, framed a face carved from marble, sharp jaw, straight nose, and eyes so deep-set they seemed to pull the light inward. A faint scar traced along his cheekbone, nearly disappearing into the creases of a subtle, knowing smile. His hands, gloved in supple black leather, rested lightly on the edge of the table, fingertips barely touching the polished surface.

Dovere exuded a stillness that carried weight, a presence that made the air feel thinner, the shadows deeper. He said nothing, but his silence spoke volumes, pressing against the room like an unspoken threat.

Barry stood at the head of the table, sleeves rolled up, a tumbler of expensive whiskey untouched in front of him. His posture was relaxed, confident, yet his sharp eyes scanned the faces before him with the precision of a stalker sizing up its prey.

"Gentlemen," Barry began, his voice smooth but carrying an edge, "SYNC isn't just another event. It's *the* event. For me, for us, and for PPI as a whole. Tonight, when I take that stage, the world will see not just a leader, but *the* leader. A visionary. A king."

The men exchanged brief glances. Seth remained stone-faced; his focus locked on Barry.

"This keynote isn't just about PPI's future," Barry continued, pacing slightly. "It's about *my* future. Everything we've built, all the groundwork, all the smoke and mirrors, it culminates in this one moment. And when the final words leave my mouth, no one will question who holds the strings. No one will question where the light shines brightest."

Barry stopped pacing and placed both hands on the table, leaning in slightly. His voice dropped, quieter but colder. "But power always invites a challenge, doesn't it?"

No one spoke. The silence hung heavy, weighted and ear piercing.

"That's why we have contingencies," Barry said, straightening up. "If something, *anything*, goes wrong tonight, we'll pivot. I've constructed a narrative, an ironclad narrative that transforms me from the architect of this empire... into its savior."

He gestured to Seth, who slid a slim tablet across the table. The screen flickered to life, showing a prepared media presentation, graphics already polished, key phrases bold and attention-grabbing.

Barry continued; his voice steady. "If an attack happens, if an exposure threatens us, this narrative goes live. The presentation transforms. I'll stand on that stage and deliver not a keynote, but a revelation. The story will change, and the world will see me as the man who exposed a deep, festering conspiracy within PPI."

The tablet displayed fabricated screenshots, emails, transaction logs, out-of-context surveillance photos, all painted with a manipulative brush. The names attached to them belonged to high-ranking members of PPI: rivals, skeptics, and even a few key allies Barry could afford to sacrifice.

Dovere spoke up, his voice measured. "You'll be the hero. The whistleblower who tore down a corrupt faction within your own empire."

"Exactly," Barry said, his voice ice-cold. "By the time the dust settles, those who oppose me will be gone, the loyal will be rewarded, and the world will beg me to rebuild PPI in *my* image."

One of the operatives cleared his throat cautiously. "And... what about Sawyer? He's still in play."

Barry's smile faded. "Sawyer is a loose thread. He thinks he's in control, but he's walking exactly where I want him to walk. If he surfaces tonight, he'll fit perfectly into the final act, whether he realizes it or not. If he interferes, he becomes part of the conspiracy I'll expose. If he runs... well, let's just say I have contingencies for that, too."

The operatives nodded, satisfied, or at least quieted.

Barry's gaze swept the room once more. "Each of you has a role to play tonight. Seth, you'll handle any unforeseen disruptions backstage. Dovere, your team will monitor the floor, eyes open for Sawyer, eyes on anyone who doesn't belong. The rest of you... stay ready. If I give the signal, we pivot to the secondary plan without hesitation."

He stepped back from the table, his voice growing quieter but heavier with meaning. "This isn't just business. This is legacy. My legacy. And if anyone threatens that, *anyone*, I want them erased before the applause even starts."

The men nodded, a ripple of agreement passing through the group. Seth closed the tablet with a decisive snap, his expression unreadable.

Barry turned away from the table, walking toward the window. The sprawling lights of Las Vegas reflected faintly in the glass, twin images of the city stretching into infinity.

"Tonight," Barry said softly, almost to himself, "they'll see the light. And they'll know whose hand holds it."

Barry turned back towards his operatives, his sharp silhouette framed against the glow of the Vegas skyline. His voice carried a dangerous calm, each word deliberate.

"If this backup plan goes into effect, Reed, Kessler and a bunch more will become the faces of betrayal, with Reed being the face of a rogue faction within PPI." Barry's smile was cold, calculated. "They may have slipped through our fingers in Vienna, but tonight, they'll have nowhere to hide."

He took a step closer to the operatives gathered before him, his eyes locking onto each of them in turn. "If I'm in charge, they burn. If something goes wrong, they burn. Either way... *we* win."

The operatives exchanged uneasy glances. The plan was audacious, even by Barry's standards. But Barry didn't tolerate doubt.

"Everything is in place," he said, his voice lowering to a razor-edged whisper. "The narrative, the contingencies, the failsafes, it's all been accounted for. By the time the dust settles, every eye will be on me."

One of the operatives hesitated, their voice barely above a murmur. "Sir, with respect, it's... a complex execution. A lot of moving parts."

Barry's gaze snapped to him, silencing the air around him. He took two steps forward, stopping just inches away.

"Do you doubt me?"

The operative froze.

"Do you doubt *this*?" Barry gestured broadly, his voice rising with a mix of anger and theatrical flair. "Every detail, everything has been accounted for. Nothing can stop what's coming."

Silence hung heavy in the suite.

Barry took a step back, straightening his jacket as he exhaled slowly. His smile returned, a thin blade of confidence slicing through the tension.

"Just a few more hours," he said softly. "And then, it's done."

The operatives nodded, any remaining hesitance buried under the weight of Barry's dominance.

Barry reached into his pocket and retrieved a small, unmarked thumb drive. Its matte surface gleamed faintly under the suite's overhead lights as he held it between his fingers, turning it slowly, deliberately.

"This," Barry said, his voice dropping into a low, measured tone, "is our failsafe. Should anything, *anything*, go wrong tonight, this little piece of plastic will ensure our story remains intact."

He crossed the room, the quiet horns of the city outside barely audible through the thick glass windows. The shadowy figure, Dovere, stepped forward from the edge of the light. His presence was a quiet storm, an unspoken force in the room.

Barry extended the drive toward him. Dovere took it without hesitation, slipping it into the pocket of his sleek black jacket.

"Stay near a terminal with a secure internet connection," Barry instructed, his words sharp and clipped. "If I give the signal, or if things unravel beyond repair, you plug it in. One click. That's all it takes. The drive will connect to PPI's servers and initiate the failsafe protocol."

Barry's voice softened slightly, but the cold certainty remained. "We'll walk away untouched. Heroes. Untarnished by the chaos we left behind."

For a moment, no one spoke. The weight of the thumb drive in Dovere's pocket felt heavier than it should have. The operatives exchanged quick, sidelong glances, but no one dared question Barry's command.

"Understood?" Barry asked, though it wasn't a question, it was a warning.

Dovere nodded once. "Understood."

Barry smiled, his confidence impenetrable. "Good. Now, let's make history."

The operatives began to disperse, leaving Dovere standing in the shadows, thumb drive secure in his jacket, while Barry turned back to the massive floor-to-ceiling windows overlooking the glittering Las Vegas skyline.

But then his phone buzzed.

Barry glanced at the screen, his smile faltering. The message was simple, yet it hit with the precision of a sniper's bullet:

"The light reveals all, Architect. Even the cracks."

For a brief moment, Barry's mask slipped. His grip on the phone tightened, and his sharp eyes scanned the empty suite as if the sender might be lurking in the shadows. The words gnawed at him, *light reveals cracks.* Was this a bluff? A warning? A taunt?

His paranoia flared, but his pride smothered it. No one knew his plan. No one could touch him.

With a sharp exhale, Barry locked his phone and shoved it into his pocket. "Bluff," he muttered under his breath. "It's just noise."

But it wasn't just noise, not to Barry. The message clung to the edges of his mind like a stain he couldn't scrub away.

He turned sharply back to Dovere, his voice cutting through the heavy silence. "Increase surveillance on every angle of the convention. Every booth, every crew member, every backstage pass, I want eyes on everything and everyone. No anomalies. No surprises."

Dovere nodded again and slipped out the door, disappearing into the shadows of the hallway.

Alone again, Barry straightened his suit and stared out at the skyline. The city sparkled below him, but his reflection in the glass stared back, sharp, shadowed, and subtly distorted.

He pulled out his phone, his fingers moving with controlled urgency as he typed a message to Seth: *"Get in here now. I need you to execute a reserve plan, immediately."*

Time was closing in. The curtain was about to rise.

And cracks or no cracks, Barry intended to hold the spotlight until the final bow.

A few hours later, the sun was getting low on the horizon, painting the Las Vegas skyline in streaks of molten gold and deep violet. From the rooftop of his hotel, Reed stood with his hands braced on the railing, his gaze fixed on the glittering sprawl below. The city was alive, pulsing, vibrant, unaware of the storm about to break over it.

The wind howled around him, carrying the distant murmur of traffic and the pulsing rhythm of music from the Strip. In that shifting interplay of neon and shadow, somewhere, Barry was busy orchestrating his elaborate performance, that thought unsettled Reed to his core. If only he could have stolen a few hours of sleep, maybe, just maybe the edge of anxiety would have dulled just a little. Yet, under the circumstances things were what they were, and soon, everything would fall into place, hopefully.

Footsteps approached from behind. Carter stepped up beside him, his expression tight with worry. He stared out at the same horizon, his voice low. "We're cutting it razor-thin, Reed. I know I said it before, but I've got to say it again. If even one thing goes wrong..."

Reed didn't look away from the view. His voice was steady, his resolve unshakable. "Barry built his empire on shadows and lies. All we have to do is turn on the light."

The city lights flickered to life below them, an ocean of stars against the encroaching night. Reed pulled out his phone, checking the time. In just a few hours, the convention center would fill with people, tech enthusiasts, industry leaders, press. None of them knowing they were about to witness either the greatest reveal in photography history or its greatest cover-up.

Carter shifted beside him. "The team's ready. Everyone knows their position."

Reed nodded, finally turning from the view to face his friend. The same determination he felt was mirrored in Carter's eyes. "Barry thinks he's directing this show," Reed said, his voice hardening. "But he forgot one thing about light."

"What's that?"

"Once it's on, you can't control where it shines."

The clock was ticking. Below them, Las Vegas continued its nightly dance of neon and shadow, oblivious to the forces gathering in its midst.

21

THE CAPTURE

Kranch was in place. Carter was in place. Reed was in place. Grimes, ever the chameleon, moved through the controlled chaos of the SYNC convention floor like smoke through cracks in a wall. He was everywhere, checking light cues, adjusting security placements, and coordinating last-minute logistics with a sharp eye and sharper tongue. His headset crackled with fragmented conversations, surveillance updates, and the faint murmur of excited pleasantries being exchanged backstage.

In the green room just offstage, Barry Cox paced like a caged animal in a glass cage. The muffled hum of the swelling crowd filtered through the heavy curtains, blending with the faint crescendos of an orchestral score being fine-tuned by unseen sound engineers. The digital clock above the doorway glowed red, ticking down the minutes.

Less than sixty minutes until showtime.

Barry adjusted his cufflinks, silver, polished, and catching the light like shards of ice. His suit fit him like a second skin, every line sharp, every angle deliberate. His gaze snapped to Seth Gauthier, his second-in-command, who stood silent and still as a statue, his phone clutched in one hand. Seth was Barry's counterweight, calm where Barry burned hot, measured where Barry accelerated, but no less dangerous.

Barry stopped pacing. His voice was low, sharp-edged, and final. "Execute."

Seth didn't blink. His fingers moved across his phone with mechanical precision, firing off encrypted messages to operatives embedded across the convention center.

On the floor, agents in plain clothes began to shift, subtle movements, easy to miss unless you knew exactly what to look for. They drifted into key positions, closing gaps, tightening invisible nooses.

At the security checkpoints, guards stiffened their posture, their eyes scanning faces with extra intensity. Entrances and exits began to lose their casual openness, transforming into narrow choke points.

In the rigging above the stage, Kranch watched as two guards subtly repositioned themselves near the technical booth. Their body language was wrong, too stiff, too alert. He gripped the metal beam beneath him, his knuckles turning white.

In the tech hub, Carter's tablet flickered, a sharp pulse in the firewall. Someone was probing their network, pressing against their digital defenses with methodical aggression. Carter's lips thinned as he typed a rapid series of commands, fighting to keep their backdoor connections alive.

Near a service entrance, Reed felt it, that prickle at the back of his neck, the phantom weight of unseen eyes following his every move. A janitor mopped the same patch of floor one too many times. A woman lingered near an emergency exit, her phone never quite pointed at her face. Every detail hummed with the electric charge of suspicion.

The net was tightening.

Backstage, Barry adjusted his tie with the satisfaction of a conductor lifting his baton. His smirk was faint, but it carried the weight of inevitability.

To the untrained eye, SYNC looked flawless, polished, refined, another glamorous keynote ready to unveil innovation and vision to the world. But beneath the surface, unseen gears were grinding, invisible wires were pulling, and every player was being maneuvered into position.

SYNC wasn't an event anymore, it had become a battleground. And Barry Cox had just given the order to fire the first shot.

Suddenly, the storm struck without warning.

Kranch was perched high above the stage in the rigging, a shadow among shadows, watching the floor below with hawk-like precision. His headset crackled with faint static, Grimes muttering updates into his ear. But then, a metallic *clank*. A sound out of place.

Before Kranch could turn, two figures in black tactical gear appeared on either side of him, moving with practiced silence. One of them lunged, grabbing Kranch by the collar of his jacket, while the other jammed a pistol into his ribcage.

"Don't fight. Don't speak. Move."

The command was delivered in a low, sharp whisper, but the cold steel pressed against Kranch's side made the order unnecessary. His mind raced, how had they gotten up here? But there was no time for answers. His headset was yanked off, the wire snapping, and he was dragged backward into the shadows, disappearing from his vantage point above the stage.

At almost the exact same moment, Carter sat hunched over his tablet in the tech hub, his fingers flying across the keyboard as he patched into another layer of Barry's firewalls. The flickering signals were stabilizing, the green indicators on his screen solidifying into steady lines.

"Gotcha," he muttered under his breath.

The door behind him creaked open. Carter froze, his hand hovering over the keyboard. Two men stepped inside, one blocking the exit, the other closing the door with deliberate slowness.

"Step away from the console," the taller of the two said, his voice low and deadly. A pistol, silencer attached, was aimed directly at Carter's chest.

Carter raised his hands slowly, palms up. "Listen, guys, I'm just running diagnostics. Tech stuff. You sure you've got the right guy?"

The second operative stepped forward, his glare cutting through Carter's weak attempt at an excuse. "Move. Now."

Carter was yanked from his chair, his tablet slipping from his hands and clattering onto the floor. One operative picked it up, tucking it under his arm as they marched Carter out the side door and into an unmarked hallway.

Meanwhile, in the back of the auditorium, Reed stood near the rear doors, his stance casual but his focus razor-sharp. The auditorium was filling up now, attendees filtering in and finding their seats, their faces glowing with excitement and anticipation.

Reed scanned the rows, his trained eyes picking out subtle anomalies, Barry's plainclothes operatives woven into the crowd like invisible threads in an intricate tapestry.

He felt them before he saw them.

Two men approached from the side aisles, cutting through the sea of chairs with extreme grace. Their suits were clean but ill-fitting, their shoulders too rigid for anyone attending a photography conference.

One of them stepped directly into Reed's path, his jacket parting just enough to reveal the black grip of a sidearm holstered under his arm. The other positioned himself slightly behind Reed, blocking any easy retreat.

"Mr. Sawyer," the first man said smoothly, his voice a polished blade. "We'd like to have a word with you. Now."

The second man's jacket shifted, flashing another weapon tucked against his ribs.

Reed's pulse quickened, but his expression remained carefully neutral. The weight of the crowd behind him pressed against his back, hundreds of people, oblivious to the thin line Reed was walking.

The lead operative leaned closer, his voice dropping to a growl. "Don't make this difficult."

For a brief, fleeting second, Reed considered his options, fight, run, disappear into the chaos. But he knew better. Not here. Not now.

He raised his hands slightly, palms out. "Alright, gentlemen. Lead the way."

The operatives flanked him, one on each side, and began guiding Reed out of the auditorium.

Reed didn't resist as the two operatives guided him out. The distant hum of chatter and excitement from the growing crowd faded behind them, swallowed by the sterile silence of the side hallway. Their footsteps echoed against the polished tile floor, the cold fluorescents casting sharp shadows along the walls.

They turned a corner, stepping into a narrow service corridor where the air was thick with the faint smell of industrial cleaner. A service door marked *Authorized Personnel Only* loomed at the end of the hall.

The lead operative stopped walking and turned to face Reed. His expression was blank, but his hand hovered near the pistol under his jacket.

"This is where we make things official, Mr. Sawyer," he said flatly.

The second operative reached into his jacket and pulled out a set of stainless-steel handcuffs. The metal caught the light, flashing briefly before they were snapped open with a sharp *click*.

"Hands in front," the lead operative ordered.

Reed hesitated for half a second. The hallway was empty, quiet, too quiet. A dozen escape scenarios flickered through his mind, but none ended without gunfire. He could almost feel the weight of the crowd in the auditorium behind him, each unsuspecting person a potential collateral casualty.

With a resigned breath, Reed extended his arms forward. The cuffs clicked shut around his wrists, biting into the skin just enough to remind him that his freedom was no longer his own.

The lead operative gave the cuffs a sharp tug, testing their security. Satisfied, he gave a curt nod to his partner.

"Let's move."

One operative gripped Reed's arm while the other positioned himself slightly behind, maintaining a hand near his weapon. Together, they steered Reed through the service door and into a dimly lit stairwell.

Above, the stage lights flared, a technician testing one final dramatic cue. The crowd continued to fill the seats, the murmurs and soft laughter masking the quiet, surgical extraction taking place right under their noses.

Three operatives down. Three pieces removed from the board.

Somewhere deep within the labyrinth of doors, hallways, and hidden rooms in the convention center, a door slammed shut behind Reed. The metallic *clang* reverberated through the sterile space, lingering in the cold, stale air. Overhead, fluorescent lights buzzed faintly, casting a harsh, clinical glow over the small, windowless room. The walls were bare concrete, and a single metal table stood in the center, surrounded by three mismatched chairs.

Kranch and Carter were already there, handcuffed to their chairs. Kranch's lip was split, a faint smear of blood trailing down his chin, while Carter's head hung low, his expression a mixture of frustration and simmering rage.

Reed stumbled slightly as he was shoved forward, his cuffed wrists throwing off his balance. The operative behind him caught his shoulder, not out of kindness, but to keep him from hitting the floor.

Kranch's sharp eyes locked onto Reed's, and in that brief exchange, an entire conversation passed between them, apology, anger, regret.

"Sit him down," came a calm but authoritative voice.

Seth Gauthier stepped out from the shadowed corner of the room, hands tucked neatly behind his back. His suit was immaculate, the sharp lines accentuating his rigid posture. His usually composed expression was marred by something else now, a flicker of disappointment, perhaps, or something colder.

The two operatives forced Reed into the remaining chair and secured his cuffs to a metal loop welded into the tabletop. The sound of metal on metal grated against the silence.

Seth stepped closer, his polished shoes clicking against the concrete floor. He didn't speak immediately, letting the silence stretch long enough for it to become suffocating. Finally, he turned his sharp gaze to the two operatives.

"I'll take it from here," he said evenly.

The operatives hesitated, exchanging glances. One of them shifted slightly, as if to object, but Seth's piercing stare froze him in place.

"You have your orders," Seth continued, his voice lowering slightly but losing none of its edge. "Guard this door. No one in, no one out. No exceptions. Do you understand me?"

"Yes, sir," one of them replied, his voice clipped and formal.

Seth stepped aside as the operatives left the room. The heavy door closed with a deep *thud*, the metallic lock clicking into place.

The silence that followed felt heavy, oppressive.

Seth took a slow, measured breath, his eyes sweeping over the three men in front of him, Kranch, bruised but determined; Carter, simmering with silent frustration; and Reed, steady and watchful, his sharp gaze locked onto Seth.

Seth began to pace, his hands still neatly clasped behind his back, the faint echo of his footsteps filling the sterile room.

He stopped abruptly, turning his head slightly toward Reed.

The silence that followed was sharp enough to cut glass.

The air hung heavy, charged with something unspoken, something dangerous.

Without breaking eye contact, Seth reached into his pocket and pulled out a small, black walkie-talkie.

No one spoke. No one dared breathe too loudly.

Seth raised the walkie-talkie to his lips, his voice low and sharp.

"Grimes, I have all three. Execute the plan."

A brief crackle of static was followed by a curt response from Grimes. Seth's expression didn't change.

Switching to his earpiece, Seth spoke again, this time with quiet intensity. "Barry, the plan has been executed perfectly. You'll be on stage in about fifteen minutes."

Satisfied, Seth lowered both devices.

At that moment, backstage, Barry Cox stood just behind the curtain, watching the empty podium with a sharp glint in his eyes. In his earpiece, he received Seth's message.

A thin smile curved across his lips as he slid the phone back into his jacket.

The net had closed.

SYNC was his stage now.

And Barry Cox intended to give the performance of his life.

Back in the windowless room, Seth stepped forward and unlocked Reed's handcuffs with a sharp *click*. The cuffs clattered onto the cold concrete floor. Seth repeated the process with Kranch and Carter, freeing them one by one.

He straightened, meeting Reed's steady gaze.

"Everything is in place," Seth said firmly. "You have around fifteen minutes."

For a moment, Reed studied Seth, the weight of unspoken understanding passing between them.

"Thank you," Reed said, his voice steady.

He turned to Kranch and Carter. The blood on Kranch's face had started to dry, flaking at the edges, but his expression was frozen, shock. Carter looked the same, his face white, the blood drained away. Confusion. A hint of something close to disbelief. A million emotions flashing across his face all at once.

What had just happened? Barry had won. The game was over. They had both accepted it. Their lives, over.

But no. The board had shifted. Again.

Could this really be happening?

"Follow me," Reed said. "I'll explain on the way."

Without waiting for a response, Reed moved swiftly toward a hidden back exit door, Kranch and Carter falling in behind him. The door clicked shut behind them. The corridor was dimly lit, the distant hum of the convention floor muffled by layers of concrete and insulation. They moved quickly, their footsteps sharp against the polished floor, the air thick with urgency.

They were on their way to where Grimes had set up a special control room deep within the convention center, a hidden nerve center shielded from Barry's operatives and surveillance grid. Reed led the way, whispering as they moved.

"When we were in Vienna," Reed began, glancing back at Kranch and Carter, "I received a message from Seth. He told me Barry was spiraling, that his grip on PPI was slipping and that a growing number of operatives were beginning to question his leadership. Seth said Barry's obsession with control was blinding him, making him reckless."

They rounded a corner, slipping through an unmarked door into the control room. Screens flickered across the walls, live feeds streaming from hidden cameras scattered throughout the convention center. The air buzzed with the hum of electronics and the faint chatter of distant voices through the speakers.

Grimes was already inside, his eyes darting between monitors, headset firmly in place, fingers tapping rapidly across a keyboard. When he noticed Reed, Kranch, and Carter entering, he stood, pulling off his headset with a smirk.

"Well, look who made it out from under Barry's thumb," Grimes said, his voice edged with relief. He winked as he passed them, pausing briefly at the door. "I've got SYNC duties to perform, gentlemen. Try not to burn the place down."

And with that, he slipped out of the room, leaving the trio surrounded by a wall of flickering screens and the weight of the moment hanging heavy in the air.

Reed turned back to his team, his voice edged with exhaustion.

"Seth was the one who suggested placing the recording device at the stairwell in Vienna. It was his idea to create a failsafe, to capture Barry's voice, his words, his intent. Almost every breadcrumb we followed, nearly every piece of intel we acted on, it all came from Seth."

Kranch frowned, tension visible in his squared shoulders. Carter's gaze stayed locked on Reed, suspicion and frustration flickering in his eyes.

"So, all those encrypted messages, the light and darkness stuff, the scriptures, that was Seth?" Carter asked, his voice sharp.

"No," Reed said firmly, shaking his head. "I don't think so. Whoever's behind those messages... they only seem to step in when we start veering off course. Like they're nudging us back into place."

Reed's eyes swept the room. "For now, we stick to the plan. Until we know more, it's all we've got."

"Why didn't you tell us sooner?" Carter asked, still confused.

"Because we couldn't take a chance on even the smallest crack in the plan," Reed said, his tone firm and apologetic at the same time. "Barry needed to believe he was untouchable. He had to feel invincible, like nothing could stop him. Seth also told me that Barry was receiving encrypted messages, those ones about light and shadows, he was getting them too. Those messages rattled him. They made him paranoid, and Seth used that paranoia to guide him right into this moment."

Reed stepped closer to his team, his voice dropping lower.

"I couldn't risk telling anyone. Not until now. Because if Barry suspected even a whisper of this alliance with Seth, it would have all come crashing down."

Silence hung in the air. Reed looked Kranch and Carter in the eyes, his expression raw.

"I'm asking you to trust me now. To forgive me for keeping you in the dark. But it was the only way to get us here, to this moment, with a real shot at bringing Barry down."

Kranch let out a slow breath, his shoulders relaxing slightly,

Carter hesitated, then gave a small nod, his frustration fading under the weight of Reed's words.

Reed broke the silence between them, "We've got less than ten minutes before Barry takes the stage." Reed's resolve as hard as ever. "So, let's finish this."

The cavernous auditorium of the SYNC convention hall buzzed with anticipation. Thousands of attendees sat shoulder-to-shoulder in the dim light, the massive LED screens casting a mysterious and elusive glow over the crowd. Both the six and seven blade PPI logos shimmered in brilliant white against a sleek black backdrop as a cinematic orchestral score thundered through the speakers, building to a crescendo.

Then silence.

A single spotlight illuminated the stage.

From the shadows, Barry Cox emerged.

He walked with purpose, his sharp suit catching every gleam of light, his expression one of confident authority. The applause erupted like a tidal wave, crashing over him in waves of admiration and respect. Barry paused at the podium, savoring the adulation, his smile spreading wide with an air of cunning.

He raised a hand, and the applause faded into a hushed stillness.

Barry leaned into the microphone, his voice smooth, magnetic, carrying the weight of a man in charge.

"What does it mean to control what others see? In this digital age, perception isn't just reality, it's power. At any given moment, billions of images are being shared, consumed, believed. But who decides which of those images matter? Who shapes the story they tell?"

He let the question hang in the air, the silence pregnant with expectation. The crowd was rapt, every face turned upward, every pair of eyes locked on Barry.

"At PPI, we don't just capture moments, we define them. We decide which stories get told, which truths get seen. And today..." His smile sharpened as he straightened his posture, hands gripping the edges of the podium. "...I'm going to show you exactly what that means."

At that exact moment, timed to the second, Reed's hand hovered over the keyboard, his jaw set in iron determination. He turned to Carter, who gave a single nod.

"Do it."

Reed hit 'Enter.'

In less than a second, chaos ignited across every screen in the SYNC auditorium, across laptops and smartphones, and on live broadcasts streamed to newsrooms around the world. A cascade of digital notifications flooded across the globe.

Photographic Evidence: Barry Cox with the weaponized lens, his face frozen in a moment of sinister intent.

Financial Records: Encrypted accounts showing billions funneled through shell corporations, hidden under PPI's glossy exterior.

Internal Memos: Documents signed by Barry himself, detailing cover-ups, coercion, and the dismantling of those who had opposed him.

The special encryption key, that haunting code, **Section: 3. Page: 16. Code: 105-B**, was transmitted directly to Secretary Kessler, who, true to his word, was waiting on standby. Within moments, Kessler's team activated secure channels, disseminating the evidence to global agencies, investigative journalists, and key governmental figures.

In return, Kessler's team sent Reed the contents of his classified file. The evidence was catastrophic: Barry had murdered his brother Marcus. Plans, maps, strategies, it was all there, laid out with chilling precision. Every detail of Barry's scheme to seize control of PPI and manipulate global affairs was exposed, a blueprint for power built on betrayal and blood.

Carter compiled the data into a concise, devastating presentation. The file was uploaded and streamed directly to the SYNC audience, every device now displaying the whole truth.

Inboxes pinged with a bulk email blast containing links to all of the evidence. Social media feeds exploded with the hashtag **#PPIExposed**, already trending worldwide.

Barry, still unaware of what was unfolding, continued speaking confidently at the podium, his voice smooth, his presence commanding. But beneath the stage lights, a ripple of unease began to spread through the audience.

It started with flickers of confusion, furrowed brows, sideways glances, the glow of screens illuminating stunned faces. Murmurs swelled into sharp whispers, whispers into shouts. Eyes darted between Barry and their devices, disbelief spreading like wildfire. Shock rippled through the crowd, followed by a wave of gasps as the truth hit. Barry had betrayed them. No denying it now. It was out there, raw and undeniable, for everyone to see.

Barry paused midsentence. His fake smile faltered, his rhythm broken. Cracks began to show in the Architect's façade.

From the stage, under the sharp glare of the lights, he could see it, the flicker of blue screens illuminating faces across the audience. The realization hit him like a punch to the chest.

He knew. In an instant, he knew.

His hand gripped the podium, his smile twitching as if trying to hold itself together.

But the damage was done.

Barry's carefully constructed empire was crumbling in real time, and the world was watching every piece fall.

In the hidden nerve center, Reed, Kranch, and Carter watched the storm unfold across dozens of monitors.

"Every feed is holding," Carter said, his voice steady. "The media's running with it."

Reed nodded, his chest rising and falling as adrenaline surged through his veins.

"It's happening," Kranch said, a mixture of disbelief and relief threading through his voice. "We actually did it."

But Reed wasn't smiling. His eyes stayed locked on Barry's frozen expression on one of the screens, his face illuminated by the glow of the monitors.

"It's not over yet," Reed said, his voice low and razor-sharp.

Back on stage, Barry forced himself to stand straighter, grasping the podium so tightly his knuckles turned white. His voice wavered, just slightly.

"Ladies and gentlemen, please, please remain calm."

But calm was impossible. The illusion had shattered, and panic was seeping through the cracks. Attendees stood, shouting questions, holding up their phones, their faces illuminated by damaging headlines and streams of evidence. Security teams hesitated, their eyes darting between Barry and the growing chaos in the crowd.

Backstage, Seth's earpiece crackled to life, operatives speaking over each other in fragmented bursts.

"Sir, the feeds, "

Seth silenced the voice with a sharp tap of his finger. His expression was an unreadable mix of pride and relief. He knew there was no salvaging this.

Barry's lips trembled as he fought to regain control, his sharp gaze sweeping across the restless auditorium.

But the light was shining too brightly now. Every flaw, every crack in his perfect veneer was exposed.

In a last-ditch effort to seize control back from the jaws of collapse, Barry triggered his grand slideshow. The auditorium lights dimmed slightly, and the speakers blared to life, drowning out the rising voices of the crowd.

In the dim glow of the control room, Reed turned to his team. His voice was low, steady, and sharp with urgency.

"Barry knows he's lost. But that doesn't mean he won't fight back. He's cornered now, and cornered animals are the most dangerous."

His eyes flicked to one of the monitors where Barry's slideshow was beginning, the polished visuals, the swelling orchestral music, the towering confidence of a man trying to reclaim control.

Reed's face was set in stone, his voice resolute. "It's time."

Carter's fingers flew across the keyboard, overriding Barry's control of the presentation feed. The slideshow froze mid-transition, the screen flickering before snapping to black. The music cut out, leaving an eerie silence hanging over the auditorium.

The house lights dimmed even more, and a single spotlight flared to life, bright and unforgiving, pinning Barry at the center of the stage. His microphone crackled once and then died, leaving him speechless under the harsh beam.

The silence was shattered by the unmistakable sound of Barry's own voice, crystal clear, broadcast across every speaker in the hall:

"The photoshoot goes as scheduled. No deviations. The Secretary will be eliminated on my signal. I'll handle it personally. It must look clean, unavoidable. A tragic, unforeseeable accident. No loose ends. Do you understand me? I'll make sure it's done right, and then we move forward, unshaken, untouchable. There will be no mistakes."

At that exact moment, every screen in the auditorium blinked to life, displaying a single frozen image: Barry Cox, standing, grinning with cold confidence, the weaponized gun-lens clutched in his hands, smoke still curling from its barrel.

The audience gasped, loud, collective, sharp.

The recording continued to play, Barry's voice unwavering in its ruthless clarity:

"The world will see what I want them to see. Nothing more. Nothing less. And if anyone tries to screw up, well... accidents happen all the time in this business."

The final syllable echoed through the cavernous hall, reverberating into stunned silence.

Barry stood frozen at the podium, his face pale, his eyes wide as he stared out into a sea of horrified faces.

Reed, watching from the control room, leaned closer to the monitor. His voice was a quiet razor.

"Checkmate."

Barry's eyes scanned the chaos of the auditorium, his carefully constructed empire unraveling right before his eyes. Faces lit by the disastrous image of him holding the weaponized lens, voices rising in confusion and anger, the crowd teetering on the edge of panic.

Then Barry saw him, Dovere, his most trusted operative, the man to whom he'd given the failsafe drive. The shadowy figure was stationed near one of the side exits, half-obscured by darkness, his leather-gloved hands resting easily at his sides, his stoic expression betraying nothing.

Barry's voice cut through the chaos, sharp and commanding.

"Engage!!" Barry's command crackled through every operative's earpiece, setting off a chain reaction.

The word cracked like a gunshot across the auditorium.

Dovere's subtle nod triggered a coordinated response. Like pieces on a chessboard, Barry's agents began moving into position, some melting into shadows, others drifting toward predetermined stations. Each had their role, their moment, their specific task in Barry's grand contingency.

But it was the smallest movement that caught Grimes's attention.

Near the edge of the auditorium, partially concealed behind a structural pole, a figure crouched low. The soft blue glow of a laptop screen illuminated Dovere's face from below. His fingers moved across the keyboard with urgency, eyes locked on the screen with laser focus.

Grimes moved quickly, weaving through the scattering crowd...

The moment he was close enough to see the screen, Grimes froze. It was Barry's failsafe protocol, a cascade of encrypted commands flowing across the display. His stomach dropped.

"Stop!" Grimes lunged forward, grabbing for the laptop.

Dovere reacted instantly, shoving Grimes backward with surprising strength. Grimes stumbled but recovered, lunging again. This time, he managed to knock the laptop sideways, but it was too late. A sharp, metallic *click* echoed as the man hit *Enter*.

Grimes's voice roared through the earpiece, panic and urgency mixing in a sharp edge.

"Barry's secondary plan has been executed! Less than two minutes!"

In the control room, Carter's tablet blared with flashing warnings. The cascading script told him everything he needed to know, Barry's failsafe protocol had been triggered.

A secondary network had come online, completely bypassing Carter's systems. Devices embedded deep within PPI's infrastructure, planted days ago by Reed and Kranch, had been compromised. Instead of delaying Barry's plan, they were now amplifying it, helping to deliver its devastating message.

Carter's voice was tight, focused, and loud as he screamed.

"No, no, no... not like this."

His fingers flew across the keyboard, every keystroke a battle against the countdown flashing in the corner of his screen. A red timer ticked down mercilessly.

1:54... 1:53... 1:52...

Reed leaned over Carter's shoulder; his voice low and intense. "Can you stop it?"

Carter's jaw clenched.

"I can try. But he's routed it through three layers of encryption. He's had this in place for a while. I can slow it, maybe. But stop it? Not with this little time."

Kranch stepped closer, his voice steady despite the rising tension.

"What happens if it goes through?"

Carter didn't look away from the screen.

"Barry's backup narrative activates. Every piece of evidence we've released gets buried under layers of disinformation. He'll make himself look like the hero who stopped *us*. The whole world will see us as traitors."

1:25... 1:24... 1:23...

Reed slammed his fist on the table, the sound echoing in the tight control room.

"Then buy us time. Whatever it takes."

Carter nodded, sweat beading on his forehead as he continued typing.

"Hold on. I might have a way to reroute his signal. It won't stop the upload, but it'll corrupt the data, make it unreadable."

Reed's eyes flicked to the monitor showing Barry still onstage, shouting to his operatives as the crowd surged around him.

"Do it!"

Reed turned back to Carter.

"You have less than ninety seconds. Make it count."

Carter didn't respond, his focus absolute. His fingers moved like lightning across the keys, fighting Barry's digital fortress with every ounce of skill he had.

1:00... 0:59... 0:58...

The countdown blazed on Carter's screen, every second a nail driven deeper into their fleeting chance at victory.

0:54... 0:53... 0:52...

Carter's hands flew across the keyboard, lines of code flashing as he hacked and re-routed Barry's failsafe systems. Sweat dripped from his brow, his breath shallow and sharp.

0:48... 0:47... 0:46...

"Come on, come on..." he muttered under his breath.

Reed and Kranch hovered behind him, every nerve taut as they watched the digital clock tick toward zero.

Then, Carter slammed the *Enter* key.

The clock froze at **0:42**. Relief washed over the team. A long silence hung heavy in the control room as everyone let out a collective breath. Carter had done it.

But the victory was short-lived. Alarms flashed red across Carter's monitors, cascading like digital blood stains.

His voice was tight, controlled. "We stopped it... but not all of it. Part of Barry's failsafe still activated."

Reed's head snapped toward the monitors. "What part?"

Before Carter could answer, the *entire convention center* plunged into darkness.

The auditorium erupted into chaos. Thousands of attendees screamed in the suffocating pitch black. Security personnel scrambled, barking orders into dead radios as communication channels failed. Emergency lights flickered sporadically but failed to stabilize.

Somewhere in the dark, someone shouted, **"Stay calm! Please, stay calm!"**

But calm was impossible.

Key access points to the building locked down with heavy metallic clunks. Backup power systems failed to initiate. Smoke began seeping from ventilation ducts, non-lethal, but thick and disorienting.

It was chaos by design.

Backstage, Seth appeared out of the shadows directing Barry, a flashlight cutting through the gloom.

Barry's voice was tight, every ounce of his charm stripped away. "We're leaving. Now."

Seth nodded, leading Barry down an emergency corridor lined with blinking red lights.

In the Control Room, Carter's screens were a mess of alerts and warnings.

"Security's down. Communications are jammed. And... oh no." His voice caught. "Key personnel, security leads, response teams, they're being neutralized one by one. Barry had sleeper agents ready for this exact scenario."

Reed slammed his hand against the desk. "Can you stop it?"

"I already have. Barry's final phase, the false narrative, never got out. But the damage was done just enough for him to escape. He had this planned from the start."

Reed turned to Kranch, his voice furious. "We have to stop him before he gets out."

On the far edge of the convention center, an unmarked black SUV waited with its engine running. Seth shoved open the side door, ushering Barry inside. The vehicle's tinted windows reflected the flickering red lights of the emergency systems.

As the SUV roared to life, tires screeching against the asphalt, Barry's phone buzzed.

A single message glowed on the screen:

"You cannot outrun the light, Architect."

Barry's fingers tightened around the device, his jaw clenched. But he said nothing.

The SUV sped away, disappearing into the vast expanse of the Las Vegas desert, taillights shrinking into the night.

Back in the Control Room, Carter slumped back into his chair, his chest rising and falling with exhaustion. The glow from the remaining monitors painted his face in sharp contrast.

Reed stared at the flickering security feeds showing empty corridors and abandoned checkpoints.

Kranch shook his head slowly. "He's gone."

Reed's fists tightened at his sides. "For now."

Carter looked up, his voice tired and resolute. "We stopped his story from going out. The truth is out there now. People know."

Reed nodded slowly. "But Barry isn't finished. He's still out there, and he's still dangerous."

Kranch smirked faintly, trying to lighten the tension. "Well, at least we ruined his big night."

Reed turned back to the monitors, his gaze fixed on the last blurry image of Barry disappearing into the night.

"This isn't over. Not yet."

22

THE PRINT

The evidence against Barry Cox spread like wildfire. What began as murmurs among SYNC attendees erupted into a global storm as media outlets seized the story. News anchors delivered urgent reports, headlines blared across screens, and social media buzzed with clips from Barry's keynote gone horribly wrong.

Reed's team had executed their plan flawlessly. Live streams, intercepted communications, and classified documents unveiled during Barry's presentation played on a continuous loop across international news networks. The now-iconic image of Barry, frozen mid-speech with the smoking gun-lens projected on the massive screens behind him, had become a global symbol of exposure and betrayal, an image seared into the public consciousness.

The fallout from Barry Cox's exposure wasn't confined to headlines and breaking news stories, it became fuel for an entire media machine. Investigative nighttime news magazines latched onto the story, their promotional teasers buzzing across social media platforms and television screens.

"Tonight, in an exclusive tell-all: Luc Hudson, the former PPI Director, banished and framed by Barry Cox, breaks his silence. For the first time, he

reveals the truth about PPI's covert world, Barry's rise to power, and the shadowy operations that kept him in control. Don't miss this exclusive interview that promises to shake the foundations of everything you thought you knew."

The footage accompanying the teaser was stark, Luc Hudson, a man once synonymous with authority and quiet strength, now looked older, wearier. He stared directly into the camera, his voice low and deliberate. *"Barry didn't just build an empire. He built a cage, and locked all of us inside it."*

Meanwhile, morning talk shows seized on a different angle, catering to the public's insatiable appetite for scandal. Glossy promos painted a tabloid-like picture of Barry's personal life unraveling under the spotlight.

"One man. Multiple marriages. Countless lies. For the first time ever, every one of Barry Cox's wives in one room, speaking out about betrayal, manipulation, and abuse. Secrets from behind closed doors, and stories the Architect never wanted you to hear. Coming this week, only here."

Bright studio sets and sharp graphics flashed across screens, featuring stylized silhouettes of multiple women, each representing a chapter of Barry's carefully compartmentalized personal life. The promise of intimate revelations and raw emotion crackled in every frame.

But it wasn't just the prime-time programs fueling the fire. True-crime podcasts launched emergency episodes dissecting Barry Cox's methods, his strategies, his psychology, his missteps. Analysts broke down his demeanor during the keynote address, body language experts debated his tells, and cybersecurity specialists went through his past with a fine-tooth comb.

Social media boiled over with hashtags: *#TheArchitectExposed, #PPIRevealed, #BarryCoxTruth.* Memes flooded timelines, Barry's frozen expression during the keynote became an internet punchline.

The carefully curated façade of PPI, the balance of power, the illusion of control, was crumbling. Governments, intelligence agencies, and global leaders were paying attention now. Every document, every photograph, every intercepted recording painted a clear picture: Barry Cox wasn't a leader, he was a manipulator operating from the shadows, building an empire on secrets and fear while breaking the law at every turn.

While the world fixated on Barry Cox's downfall, chaos erupted behind the fortified doors of PPI's global headquarters.

The sprawling glass-and-steel building, usually a symbol of innovation and professionalism, now thrummed with an undercurrent of panic. Inside, corridors buzzed with activity as key personnel darted between offices, clutching files and whispering in urgent tones. The dual-natured empire of the *Professional Photographers Institute* and the covert *Private Protection Initiative* was fracturing under the weight of exposure.

In one wing of the building, the *Professional Photographers Institute* issued a public-facing statement on their website:

"The Professional Photographers Institute operates solely as a global organization dedicated to advancing photographic excellence, providing training, and fostering community among photographers worldwide. We have no involvement in, nor any knowledge of, any alleged covert activities linked to former Director Barry Cox."

Their social media channels were flooded with polished PR posts, flooded with carefully worded reassurances. But beneath the façade of confidence, panic festered.

Meanwhile, in the more shadowed corners of the building, the *Private Protection Initiative*, the clandestine arm of PPI, was crumbling under its own weight.

In a secure basement office, three industrial shredders ran non-stop, their motors growling as sensitive documents vanished into confetti. Black-suited operatives, faces pale and eyes wide, carried box after box of files into the shredding room. Digital security teams worked feverishly, fingers flying over keyboards as they deleted encrypted archives and rerouted server pathways.

"Wipe everything from Server Node 5," one technician barked, sweat beading on his forehead. "I don't care if it locks out half the building, just do it!"

In the executive boardroom on the 12th floor, chaos played out on a different scale. A panel of high-powered lawyers, hastily assembled, argued over legal protections, jurisdiction boundaries, and plausible deniability.

"We deny everything," one attorney snapped, pounding a fist on the table. "The *Private Protection Initiative* does not exist, and even if it did, Barry Cox acted as a rogue operative without oversight or approval."

"But the paper trail," another lawyer began.

"Will cease to exist by the end of the day," the first one interrupted, adjusting his designer glasses.

Phones buzzed incessantly with calls from government agencies, federal investigators, and international intelligence operatives demanding answers. Subpoenas began rolling in like tidal waves, each one a harbinger of deeper scrutiny and potential prosecution.

Agents from federal bureaus began arriving at PPI headquarters, their dark SUVs lined up outside like silent sentinels. Teams in dark suits and earpieces moved through hallways, accessing servers and requesting hard drives.

In the chaos, loyalties frayed. Junior operatives whispered about immunity deals. Senior executives quietly started contacting their personal lawyers. Some staff members simply disappeared, walking out the front doors with resignation letters scrawled on notepads.

At the heart of it all was a gaping vacuum of leadership. Barry Cox, the Architect himself, was gone.

No one was steering the ship, and the entire organization was adrift.

While the world absorbed the news of Barry Cox and the fall of PPI, one figure moved with purpose: Secretary Kessler. His involvement in the takedown of Barry Cox wasn't just political, it was personal.

From the moment Reed had sent him the final code, Kessler

knew the weight of what was about to unfold and the consequences of failure. The encrypted files Reed's team had uncovered weren't just pieces of Barry's operation, they were smoking guns, tying Barry directly to covert operations, illegal arms deals, and political manipulation on a global scale.

Kessler moved swiftly. He had already reached out to key allies across international intelligence agencies. Within minutes of the broadcast, an APB was issued, directives were sent, warrants were prepared, and diplomatic channels buzzed with urgent communication. Barry wasn't just a rogue businessman, he was now a high-priority target.

But Kessler's role went deeper than logistics. The Secretary had been the one to ensure Barry's name couldn't simply disappear into bureaucratic shadows. His team pushed the evidence into the hands of trusted journalists, safeguarding it from being buried or spun into obscurity.

The morning sun clawed its way over the Las Vegas skyline, casting long golden streaks through the glass facade of the convention center. What had once been a hub of energy and anticipation now sat draped in an eerie stillness. Banners fluttered weakly in the morning breeze; discarded flyers and promotional materials littered the floor, scattered like the remnants of a fallen empire.

In a secure control room, Reed stood with his hands deep in his pocket, eyes fixed on a wall of monitors displaying the aftermath of Barry Cox's exposure. Every screen flickered with news anchors delivering breaking updates, dissecting the evidence, and live feeds of the chaos unfolding at PPI headquarters. Footage from the keynote dominated every cycle, Barry's smug confidence frozen in time, the shocking revelations laid bare, and the undeniable ripple effect of truth detonating across the global news stage:

"Federal Agents Descend on PPI Headquarters Amid Growing Scandal."

"Barry Cox: Architect of a Double Life Exposed."

"Did the Photography Industry's Most Respected Institution Hide a Covert Spy Network?"

Carter sat at a table nearby, his tablet balanced on one knee, streams of encrypted communications flickering across its surface. "It's everywhere," he said, exhaustion heavy in his voice. "Every major network. Every social platform. Governments are scrambling, and PPI is fractured. They're turning on each other in there. Everyone's scrambling for cover, and no one's got a parachute. They're calling it the biggest corporate scandal in decades."

Kranch leaned back in a chair with his feet propped up on the table, a deep scowl carved into his bruised face. "That's a whole lot of suits swarming PPI headquarters," he said, his voice edged with frustration. "And yet, Barry's still out there. All that evidence, broadcast worldwide, and he's not under arrest, not in custody. How is that even possible?"

That was the unspoken truth hanging heavy over the team. The trap had been sprung, and the world had seen Barry's empire for what it truly was, but The Architect had escaped. Somewhere amid the chaos of the previous night, Barry had vanished into the shadows of Las Vegas.

"PPI's tearing itself apart," Reed said, his voice low. "But Barry? He doesn't vanish unless he has somewhere to go. He's out there, regrouping. And he's not going to let this empire fall without trying to take us all down with it."

Grimes entered, pulling off his headset, dark circles etched beneath his eyes. "We traced Barry as far as the perimeter cameras. He slipped into a black SUV right after the lights went out. No plates, no tracking signal. The vehicle swapped routes twice before disappearing from traffic cams. Whoever's driving him knows how to stay hidden."

Reed exhaled slowly. "He's still trying to win, still clawing for control. If he's hiding, it's not to escape, it's to regroup."

Kranch pushed off the table, his boots thudding against the tiled floor. "Then we stop him. We figure out his next move and cut him off before he makes it."

Grimes glanced between them; his expression tight with tension. "We're combing through leads, but this city's built for disappearing acts. Too many hotels, too many back rooms. He could be anywhere."

Reed shook his head firmly. "No. He'll go somewhere he can still pull strings and manipulate the fallout."

"Where?" Kranch asked.

Reed shrugged and pushed off the desk, rolling his shoulders back as if shedding the weight of the sleepless night behind him.

His phone buzzed in his pocket. He pulled it out, and his body went still.

A single message lit up the screen:

"The light bends before it breaks."

Kranch leaned over Reed's shoulder. "Another one?"

Reed's eyes bulged. These cryptic messages had been threading their way through this operation from the beginning, guiding, warning, and sometimes manipulating. But this one felt... different. It wasn't a clue. It wasn't even a warning.

It was a promise.

Reed read the message aloud, his voice tight.

Carter frowned. "Have you heard from Seth? Could that message be from him?"

"No," Reed said sharply, sliding the phone back into his pocket. "Seth's messages are different, more direct, more focused. This one... this one feels deliberate, intentional." Reed let his guard down a bit. "I'm worried about Seth. He's walking a razor-thin line, and Barry is just too smart."

At a small, nondescript hotel tucked away from the flashing lights and thundering energy of the Las Vegas Strip, Barry Cox sat at a modest desk in a dimly lit room. The suite was far from his usual standard of opulence, but it served its purpose, privacy, anonymity, control.

Outside, the distant glow of neon streaked across the drawn

curtains. Inside, the air felt still, with the weight of unraveling plans and dwindling options.

Barry's fury simmered just below the surface, his movements sharp but controlled as he arranged a set of documents in front of him. Screens displayed news feeds looping footage from the SYNC keynote disaster. Every headline screamed the same narrative: *Barry Cox Exposed, Global Scandal Unfolds.*

He rolled his eyes as he muted one of the feeds.

They had humiliated him. Stripped him bare in front of the world. But Barry Cox wasn't finished, not yet. His ego was itching to regroup.

He pressed a button on his phone. A secure line crackled to life.

"Seth," Barry said, his voice like sharpened glass, "We need damage control. Lock down every remaining asset, silence any loose ends, and focus on Sawyer. I want him erased from this story entirely."

On the other end, Seth's voice crackled through the speaker. "Understood. I'll handle it personally."

Barry's lips twitched into a faint smile. "See that you do."

But Seth was already moving in another direction. Across encrypted channels, Seth was about to start feeding intel to Reed, coordinates, operational status, key personnel still loyal to Barry. Each piece of information was going to tighten the noose around Barry's neck.

Seth typed swiftly; his face impassive as he sent the first post keynote message to Reed:

"Situation shifting. Stay ready."

Barry, pacing in his room now, let his gaze settle on Seth's latest report displayed on his laptop. His eyes narrowed.

Something wasn't adding up.

Seth was good, efficient, sharp, precise. But this? The timing, the tone, the vague updates... they were all off. Too polished in some places, too rushed in others.

Barry's mind began methodically dissecting every conversation, every instruction Seth had given him since Vienna. Patterns emerged; inconsistencies surfaced.

The gears in Barry's mind turned relentlessly, clicking into place with cold precision.

His eyes flicked to the encrypted chat on his screen. Seth's last update sat innocently in the text log, but now it glared back at him like an accusation.

Barry stood still in the center of the room; his sharp silhouette outlined by the faint glow of the monitors.

Seth?!

The realization hit Barry like ice water poured down his spine. It had been Seth all along. The delays. The disruptions. The intel that had mysteriously slipped through cracks that shouldn't have existed.

Every move, every misstep, it wasn't coincidence. It was choreography.

Barry's teeth grinding as his eyes darkened. His hand drifted to his phone.

He typed out a single message to Seth:

"Seth, it's reward time. Join me for a glass of whisky."

Minutes later, Seth sat across from Barry in the dim confines of the hotel suite. A faint light cast an eerie glow over the polished whiskey glasses between them. Barry lounged with one leg crossed over the other, one hand resting casually on the arm of his chair while the other swirled the golden liquid in his glass.

"Strange thing, loyalty," Barry said, his voice smooth and almost contemplative. "It's the most valuable currency in our world. More than money, more than secrets. And yet..." He paused, letting the silence hang heavy between them. "...it's also the easiest thing to fake."

Seth offered a tight nod, his glass poised just below his lips. His posture was composed, but his eyes, sharp, calculating, stayed fixed on Barry. "Loyalty's earned, not bought. You've always known that."

Barry chuckled softly, taking a slow sip from his glass. "That's the difference between us, Seth. I don't *earn* loyalty, I design it."

For a moment, the only sound was the faint clink of ice in his glass as he set his tumbler down. Seth hesitated, then took a sip of his own drink. The whiskey burned pleasantly on the way down, but almost immediately, something felt... strange.

His throat tightened. A bead of sweat formed at his temple.

Barry kept talking, his voice like velvet draped over steel. "You know, Seth, you've been a remarkable second-in-command. Methodical. Calm. Always where I needed you to be. But even the best tools wear out eventually. And when they do..."

Seth's glass slipped slightly in his hand, his fingers trembling against the smooth surface. His vision began to swim, the edges of Barry's form blurring.

"...you don't keep them around. You replace them."

Barry leaned forward, his sharp eyes locking onto Seth's. "You were never supposed to make it this far, Seth. But loyalty, oh, it's such an intoxicating thing, isn't it? It makes men like you think they're irreplaceable."

Seth's breath grew shallow, his chest rising and falling rapidly. His fingers twitched as he tried to set the glass down, but it slipped, tumbling onto the carpet and spilling whiskey across his polished shoes.

Barry remained still, watching Seth with a faint smile that never reached his eyes.

"Poison?" Seth rasped, his voice a broken whisper.

Barry raised his own glass in a mock toast. "Just a little insurance policy. You understand."

Seth's body slumped back against the chair, his muscles losing their strength. His vision dimmed, his head rolling slightly to the side. But as the world slipped out of focus, a faint flicker of satisfaction sparked in his fading consciousness.

Barry was running. The empire he'd built was burning. And Seth had played his part.

Barry paced the narrow hotel room, his face hot with anger. Seth's empty glass of whiskey still on the floor, untouched by Barry, though his own tumbler remained in hand. His shoulders were squared, his jaw set, but beneath the façade of control, there was a tremor in his fingers.

He pulled out his phone, swiping through encrypted contacts before landing on a name: Dovere.

The call connected instantly.

"Mr. Cox," Dovere's smooth, measured voice came through. It was as unshakable as stone, a stark contrast to Barry's sharp edges.

"Seth is no longer with us," Barry said coldly, his words like steel. "Congratulations, Dovere. You're my new second-in-command."

There was a brief pause, followed by Dovere's calm response. "Understood."

Barry exhaled, setting the glass down. "I need you to clean up every loose end. Seth's body, any trace of our involvement here, it all disappears. I want Reed and his team neutralized, no matter the cost. And Dovere..."

"Yes, sir?"

"Make sure there's nothing left for them to follow. No crumbs, no shadows. Nothing."

"It will be done," Dovere replied without hesitation.

The call ended with a sharp click, and Barry let the phone slip from his ear. For a fleeting moment, he closed his eyes, his breath slow and measured. The shimmering lights of Las Vegas stretched out below, golden and relentless.

He opened his eyes and stared at the city sprawling beneath him. Once, it had felt like his playground, his empire. Now, it was just another place to escape from.

Dovere moved with the precision of a surgeon and the cold detachment of a guillotine. His orders, sharp and direct, sliced through the chaos left in Barry's wake. Seth's body was removed quietly, any trace of Barry's presence in the suite erased with methodical care. Yet, beneath Dovere's polished exterior, the cracks in Barry's crumbling empire were impossible to ignore. Operatives were resigning in waves, their loyalty dissolving under the floodlights of international scrutiny.

In a dimly lit bar nearby, a newscast flickered on a dusty TV. Barry Cox's face filled the screen, frozen mid-sentence behind a bold headline: "Global Fugitive: Architect of PPI's Shadow Empire Exposed." A man hunched over his phone, knuckles white as he thumbed a message into an encrypted chat app.

'I have information. Barry Cox. His location. You need to move fast.'

The message had barely sent before Dovere's men found him. A brief scuffle in the alley, a muffled plea, then silence. Dovere adjusted his cufflinks as he stepped away from the scene, his face showing no emotion. Another loose end tied up.

But even Dovere's efficiency couldn't stem the tide. Federal agents swarmed the convention center, while investigators and auditors poured over records. His every move was met with resistance, not from Reed's team, but from the overwhelming volume of law enforcement descending on Las Vegas.

Back in the control room, Reed's gaze remained locked on the monitor displaying a map of the city. After the short text from Seth, nothing.

"Barry's replaced Seth," Reed said grimly. "And now they're both gone."

Where could Barry be at this point? Seth was the inside man, and the silence was deafening.

Meanwhile, on a private airstrip outside the city limits, Barry stepped out of a black SUV into the desert night. He was on the move again. A sleek, unmarked jet waited on the tarmac, its engines humming. Without looking back, Barry climbed aboard.

The cabin was dark as he settled into a leather seat. Through the window, Las Vegas sparkled like a fading mirage. As the jet lifted off, climbing into the night sky, Barry Cox disappeared into the clouds, leaving behind a smoldering empire, a fractured legacy, and enemies still hunting him.

The hunt wasn't over.

Not yet.

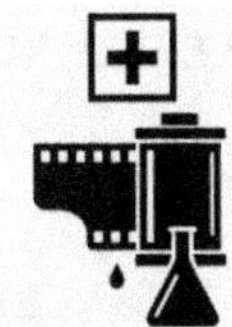

23
CROSS-PROCESS

Reed and his team were gathered in their temporary control room in Las Vegas. The air smelled faintly of stale coffee and electrical ozone, and the soft hum of computers filled the silence. Four monitors flickered in unison, each displaying fragmented security footage from Harry Reid International Airport.

Reed stood, eyes locked on one particular screen, the grainy clip showing Barry Cox stepping onto the tarmac, the faint silhouette of a sleek private jet in the floodlight haze.

"There he is," Reed said evenly, breaking the silence. "We've got him boarding, but that's where the trail ends."

Grimes, sitting at the main terminal, pinched the bridge of his nose. "Flight logs are either altered or gone. Someone erased this perfectly. No transponder codes, no tail numbers, no flight path."

Carter leaned against the table, tablet in hand, frustration evident in every line of his face. "So what now? We know Barry's airborne. Great. That narrows it down to *everywhere.*"

Kranch, with his arms always crossed and his jaw tight, spoke up from his corner. "Barry doesn't run without a purpose. He's got a destination, a plan, and probably a head start."

Reed nodded, eyes wide as he studied the footage. "He's not running scared, he's regrouping. And we're wasting time."

The tension hung thick in the room as the monitors switched to news feeds. Global headlines screamed across every screen:

"PPI EXPOSED: GLOBAL CORRUPTION SCANDAL ROCKS INTERNATIONAL TRUST."

"BARRY COX, THE ARCHITECT OF DECEPTION."

"FBI AND INTERPOL RAID PPI HEADQUARTERS: A FALLEN EMPIRE."

Video loops showed law enforcement raiding PPI headquarters, agents storming boardrooms, executives being escorted out in handcuffs, shredders practically overworking themselves into plumes of smoke.

Grimes scanned the news feeds, shaking his head. "It's a feeding frenzy. Every government agency, financial watchdog, and freelance hacker on the planet is clawing at whatever scraps of Barry's empire are left."

"Headquarters is locked down," Carter added grimly. "Operatives are resigning. Lawyers are billing overtime. The entire infrastructure is collapsing, and yet..." He trailed off, locking eyes with Reed.

Reed finished the thought. "Barry's still out there. Still pulling strings."

Kranch stepped forward. "He's not hiding in plain sight anymore, he's gone dark. And dark means isolation. He's pulling himself as far from this mess as possible."

Reed turned to Grimes. "Can you track high-value transactions? Anything out of place, yachts, compounds, offshore accounts?"

Grimes was already typing, lines of code scrolling down his screen. "I'm on it. But if Barry's using shell corporations, cryptocurrency, or offshore proxies, it's going to take time."

Reed checked his watch. "Time, we don't have."

Far away from the Vegas strip, a hot breeze swept through the balcony of a remote, high-security compound perched on the edge of jagged cliffs overlooking the Caribbean Sea. The sky was overcast, the waves below crashing violently against the rocks.

Barry Cox stood at the edge of the balcony, staring out into the endless gray horizon. His tailored suit was slightly wrinkled, his usually sharp features drawn with fatigue. Behind him, the glow of computer monitors cast faint shadows against the marble floors.

He turned away from the view and walked back into the compound's central control room. A lone operative, a nervous young man with slicked-back hair, stood by the desk.

"Status?" Barry asked, his voice cold and sharp.

"We sent out the signal, sir. The meeting point was established. But..." The operative hesitated.

"But what?" Barry's tone turned lethal.

"No one showed up, sir. Not one. We monitored every access point. No operatives arrived."

Barry tilted his head, and he turned away, his fists clenched at his sides. His empire was gone, abandoned, betrayed, and dismantled in real time.

After a long moment of silence, Barry muttered, almost to himself, "Loyalty is currency. And mine has been spent."

A flicker of movement below caught Barry's eye, a police boat patrolling too close, its spotlight cutting across the water. A second vessel followed in its wake.

Barry's paranoia flared to life.

"Too much activity. Too many eyes," Barry said. His voice was calm, but the edge of fear cut through.

The operative swallowed hard. "Sir, what are your orders?"

Barry turned sharply, already calculating his next move.

"Purchase something they can't follow," Barry said, a glint of manic calculation in his eyes. "Something mobile. Something that cuts us off entirely."

Hours later, in a dimly lit back room of a broker's office, Barry signed the final digital documents on a secure tablet.

The *Hampshire Feadship Yacht* was his now.

92 million dollars, wired in full. Overpaid, but immediate.

Barry stared at the photos of his new acquisition on the screen, a gleaming marvel of nautical engineering. A helicopter perched on the rear deck, a glass-enclosed lounge overlooking endless ocean horizons, and state-of-the-art security systems woven into every inch of its luxurious structure.

He turned to the broker. "Hire the best crew money can buy, pilots, cooks, deckhands. Pay them all upfront. One year of service."

"Yes, Mr. Cox," the broker replied, his voice trembling slightly.

"Make sure there's no paper trail," Barry added. "No lingering signatures, no breadcrumbs."

Forty-eight hours after Barry's yacht purchase, back in the temporary control center, Grimes' monitor flickered with fresh intel.

He called the team together. They rushed from their hotel rooms. "Got something," Grimes said, voice tight with excitement. "Someone just bought a luxury yacht, a Hampshire Feadship, for ninety-two million. Paid in cash, no financing. Immediate ownership."

Kranch straightened. "Barry!?"

Reed stepped closer, studying the data on the screen. The yacht had already been flagged on maritime records, a massive vessel anchored far from standard shipping lanes, somewhere near Puerto Rico.

Reed's eyes narrowed. "He's running to the sea. Isolated, mobile, untouchable."

Grimes leaned back. "A yacht like that doesn't move without leaving ripples. If we track those, we'll find him."

Carter cracked his knuckles, a rare grin tugging at the corner of his face. "Then let's make sure he doesn't get too comfortable out there."

Reed looked at each member of his team. "Kranch, Carter, we need a strategy session in New Orleans. Grimes, stay here in Las Vegas and keep your eyes on the digital feeds. We need someone with your expertise watching every angle."

Later, in the Big Easy, tucked away just beyond the loud chaos of Bourbon Street, the bar felt like a relic, dimly lit, its faded wallpaper peeling at the corners, a sticky sheen of time-worn residue clinging to the wooden tables. Overhead, a ceiling fan spun lazily, stirring the thick scent of bourbon, aged wood, and fried oysters.

Reed, Kranch, and Carter occupied a corner booth, their faces half-hidden in the shadows cast by a flickering neon sign buzzing faintly from the window. Outside, faint jazz notes floated in from the street, blending with the distant chatter of tourists and the occasional burst of laughter from passing crowds.

Carter scrolled through a tablet in front of him, his brow furrowed as he scanned maritime records and offshore financial transactions. Kranch, stared into his whiskey glass like it might offer him answers. Reed sat across from them, hands clasped, his sharp eyes bouncing between the two men.

A tired waitress placed three drinks on the table, two whiskeys, one black coffee, and disappeared without a word.

Reed broke the silence. "Barry isn't just running, he's *rebuilding*. He's out there somewhere with just enough resources to make this a long, drawn-out chase. If we don't cut him off now, he'll regroup. He'll rise again."

Carter set his tablet down with a sigh. "We know he's on that yacht. We know he's isolated. But he's got cash reserves, encrypted accounts, and connections in places we probably haven't even thought of yet. Guys like Barry? They don't run out of favors overnight."

Kranch took a sip of his whiskey, and said, "Then we starve him. Cut him off at every point, money, fuel, food, supplies. The yacht's big, but it's not self-sustaining. Sooner or later, he'll need to resupply. That's when we catch him."

Reed nodded. "Agreed. But supplies aren't the only thing keeping him afloat. He's got people, loyalists. And Dovere is at the top of that list."

Kranch snorted. "Dovere's not loyal. He's... *useful*. There's a difference."

Carter leaned forward. "Dovere's not stupid, either. He knows Barry's empire is crumbling, and he's sharp enough to see which way the wind's blowing. We just need to push him over the edge."

Reed tapped a finger against the table thoughtfully. "Barry's not subtle. Seth didn't see it coming, but Dovere? He's too careful to miss the signs. If Barry's even *thinking* about cutting him loose, Dovere could smell it."

The faint creak of the bar door opening caught Reed's attention, but it was just a lone figure shuffling in, head down, shoulders hunched. The bartender didn't even glance up as he poured another drink. However, Reed stopped tapping his finger and lowered his voice cautiously.

"Barry's got himself cornered, which means he'll start leaning harder on Dovere. Trust, loyalty, it's all transactional to guys like Barry. And Dovere? He's no fool. He'll notice when the balance starts tipping out of his favor."

Carter raised an eyebrow. "You're thinking we can use that?"

Reed's lips pressed into a thin line. "I'm thinking... if we plant the right seed, in the right way, Dovere will start asking himself some dangerous questions. About Barry. About survival. We don't need him to switch sides outright, we just need him to hesitate when it counts."

Kranch asked, "And what's the 'right seed,' Reed? You're dancing around it."

Reed exhaled slowly, his eyes narrowing in thought. "Let's just say... Barry has a pattern. A way of cleaning up loose ends when the walls start closing in. Dovere's sharp enough to recognize it if he sees it. We just need to make sure he gets the right glimpse, at the right time."

The silence stretched between them as the faint sound of jazz drifted in from outside. Carter broke it first. "That's a thin wire to walk, Reed."

Reed nodded. "Thin, yeah. But Barry's running out of shadows, and Dovere's smart enough to know he's standing in one."

The three men sat in silence for a moment, each weighing the risks, the possibilities, and the razor's edge they were about to walk.

In Washington DC, in an office bathed in fluorescent light and buried beneath layers of bureaucracy, Secretary Kessler worked tirelessly. The weight of international cooperation pressed on his shoulders as phone calls rattled through encrypted lines and diplomatic documents piled high on his desk.

Kessler leveraged every resource, every connection, every ounce of authority to clamp down on Barry Cox's offshore assets. The U.S. Coast Guard intensified maritime patrols, while financial watchdogs combed through offshore accounts with surgical precision.

Amid the chaos, Kessler uncovered something chilling: a folder Marcus had been working on before his death. The documents inside painted Barry not just as a corrupt manipulator, but as a key architect of a far-reaching conspiracy. The evidence pointed to financial crimes, espionage, and most incriminating, a clear motive and timeline for Marcus's murder.

Barry Cox wouldn't face mere charges of fraud or conspiracy, he would stand trial for murder.

While Kessler tightened the net, back in the bar in New Orleans, Reed's team had unknowingly walked straight into a trap.

Up to this point, nothing seemed out of place in their clandestine meeting, the bar was dim, worn, unassuming. Shadows danced across the peeling wallpaper, cast by the slow-turning ceiling fan. The jukebox was silent, and the bartender wiped an already-clean glass.

Reed had spent years reading rooms, attuned to the smallest inconsistencies. But this one had too many.

Kranch took a slow sip, eyes scanning the room over the rim of his glass. "Place feels wrong, Reed. Like someone's waiting for us to make the first move."

Carter sat kind of sideways in his chair, his casual posture betrayed by the sharpness in his eyes. "Not enough noise. Not enough movement. People are here, but no one's really *here*."

Reed's gaze flicked to the far end of the bar. Two men sat apart but carried the same stillness, their drinks untouched, their attention subtly shifting toward Reed's team. At the back corner, a woman sat at a table, her gaze dipping to her phone but rising just often enough to watch them.

The bartender disappeared through a door marked PRIVATE, the faint glow of a phone screen flashing briefly before the door clicked shut behind him.

Reed set his drink down with deliberate care. His voice was low, steady, but sharp as glass. "We've been burned. Dovere's got eyes on us."

Carter's jaw tightened. "You sure?"

Reed gave the faintest nod toward the two men at the bar. "Watch their hands. Watch their eyes. They're waiting for a signal."

Kranch's voice rumbled from deep in his chest. "We're sitting ducks, boss. What's the move?"

The jukebox let out a sharp *crack* of static, loud enough to make heads turn. One of the men at the bar slid off his stool, his hand lingering near his jacket pocket as he moved into a nearby booth.

The second man moved almost in tandem, slipping toward and into the same booth, his movements too casual to be natural.

Reed's voice was tight, controlled. "We're not staying to see how this ends. Move. Now. Regroup, Pirates Alley behind the Church."

Reed signaled with his eyes. Kranch shifted first, his large frame moving deliberately toward the back exit, shoulders squared. Carter tucked a slim tablet under his arm and angled toward the side door, his steps precise and quick.

Reed stood last. He pulled a few bills from his pocket, dropped them onto the table, and walked calmly toward the front door. His pulse drummed in his ears, but his expression betrayed nothing.

Just then, the bartender reappeared from the PRIVATE door, a phone clutched tightly in his hand, his gaze locking directly onto Reed.

A faint vibration, a phone buzzing, cut through the low hum of the bar. One of the men stiffened, his hand twitching slightly near his pocket.

Reed stepped through the front door just as the woman at the table raised her phone to her ear, whispering urgently into it.

Everyone took a different route to Pirates Alley. In what only seemed like seconds, the entire team had regrouped in the narrow alleyway. The damp air was heavy with the smell of fried food and stale beer, but it felt clearer than the stifling tension inside the bar. Reed knew this spot well, it was one of his favorite places to take portraits. The lighting was always impeccable, day or night.

Kranch spoke first, breathing heavy from the run to the alley.

"They weren't amateurs, Reed. Those guys were waiting for us. Dovere's people?"

Reed gave a sharp nod, his jaw tight.

"Yeah. And they weren't there to intimidate us, they were there to box us in."

Carter breathed heavily, barely catching his breath, his eyes darting down both ends of the alley. "Dovere's good, Reed. He's cutting off our routes, our resources, pushing us exactly where he wants us to go."

Reed's gaze swept the darkened alley, his mind buzzing. "Barry's mobility at sea is his biggest advantage. Dovere knows it. He's trying to keep us locked down here, spinning our wheels while Barry slips further out of reach."

Kranch stepped up on the sidewalk, his voice carrying a note of urgency.

"So what's the play? We can't stay here, Dovere's got this city mapped out."

Reed exhaled, trying to get the pieces of the puzzle to fall into place in his mind.

"We can't stay here. We have to move. But we don't just run, we use Dovere's tracking against him. He's watching us, which means he's revealing himself in the process."

Carter frowned slightly, processing Reed's plan.

"You want to let him track us... intentionally?"

Reed nodded, "Grimes is still monitoring digital movement back in Vegas. Every move Dovere makes, every order he gives, it leaves a trace. If we're careful, we can make Dovere lead us straight to Barry. Under the circumstances, that is the best plan I got for now guys."

Carter smirked, a faint spark of confidence returning to his eyes.

"Turn the predator into the prey. I like it."

Kranch cracked his knuckles, his scowl shifting into something closer to determination.

"Then let's give Dovere something worth chasing."

Reed's gaze flicked to the end of the alley, where the faint glow of streetlights painted lines of light across cracked pavement. "Let's move. Every second we waste here, Barry gets further away."

With that, the team melted into the night, slipping through the maze of alleys and neon-lit streets of the French Quarter.

Somewhere, Dovere's men were regrouping, recalibrating. Somewhere, Barry Cox was moving farther out to sea.

But Reed and his team were moving too, and they weren't chasing shadows.

As they moved silently through the streets, Reed's phone buzzed in his pocket. The team stopped as he answered.

"Reed, it's Kessler," came the sharp, direct voice on the other end. "We've got something, a lead. Maritime intelligence picked up irregular patterns in Barry's yacht movements. It's faint, but it's there. He's anchored somewhere remote, off the standard shipping lanes. I'm sending you the coordinates now."

Reed's eyes flicked to Kranch and Carter as a map loaded onto his phone, a blinking red dot marking the yacht's last known location. His voice was steady, but the sharp edge of determination was unmistakable.

"We've got him."

24

DYNAMIC RANGE

Reed and his team, armed with intel from Secretary Kessler and maritime intelligence, had tracked Barry Cox to open waters near Vieques, Puerto Rico. They secured a private villa in Pilón, a secluded neighborhood perched on the high hills of the island's southern coast. From their elevated vantage point, using a high-powered telescope set up on the terrace, they could see the Hampshire Feadship Yacht, a floating palace of glass, steel, and excess, anchored in an isolated pocket of the Caribbean Sea. The yacht drifted like a ghost ship under the pale light of the moon, silent and untouchable. Its position shifted frequently, forcing Reed and his team to constantly adjust their surveillance, but with the steady flow of maritime intelligence, they managed to keep their target in sight. Each glimpse of the distant yacht brought with it a heavy reminder: Barry was out there, still moving pieces on his invisible chessboard.

Inside, Barry Cox had attempted to seal himself off from the world. Surrounded by endless sea and just a few handpicked loyalists, his empire had shrunk to the length of a yacht deck. Dovere remained at his side, a cold, methodical enforcer who acted without hesitation and questioned nothing. But Reed knew something Barry had likely overlooked: isolation breeds vulnerability.

In Reed's Puerto Rico villa, a makeshift control center hummed with activity. He stood in front of a flickering bank of monitors, each displaying maps of shipping lanes, satellite images of the yacht, and maritime intelligence reports. Carter sat hunched over a tablet, his brow furrowed in concentration. Kranch leaned against a wall, arms crossed, his gaze sharp and alert.

Reed turned to face them, and said, "Barry's strength has always been his network. His ability to manipulate from the shadows, pull strings without being seen. But out there, he's alone. Dovere is the last pillar holding him up. If we break Dovere, the whole façade crumbles."

Carter looked up, skepticism etched across his face. "Reed, Dovere isn't Seth. Seth had cracks, you could see them in his eyes when Barry turned up the pressure. Dovere's different. He doesn't flinch, doesn't waver. You could put a gun to his head, and he'd still follow orders without blinking. The man is carved out of stone and programmed like a machine. I think if Barry told him to jump over-board with an anchor tied to his ankles, Dovere wouldn't hesitate, he'd just ask how deep the water is. Whatever loyalty looks like in Barry's world, Dovere embodies it. You're not going to shake that with a few clever words on a screen. If we're betting everything on Dovere second-guessing Barry, we'd better make sure that message doesn't just plant doubt, it needs to light a fuse."

Kranch grunted in agreement, his deep voice rumbling through the dimly lit room. "Reed, Carter's right. Dovere's not the kind of guy who loses sleep over moral dilemmas. He's not wired like that. You could show him Barry's entire empire crashing down in flames, and Dovere would still be there, holding the lighter and waiting for the next set of orders. But... everyone's got a line, even Dovere. Barry killed Seth. And Dovere's smart enough to know Barry doesn't keep loose ends alive for long. If we can make him feel that, make him believe he's not an exception to Barry's rule, then maybe, just maybe, we can crack him. But it's gotta be perfect. Dovere doesn't guess. He doesn't wonder. He only acts when he's sure. That message has to punch him in the gut, Reed. It has to make him feel like the knife is already at his back."

Reed nodded, "Which is why we won't ask him to turn. We'll make him think Barry already has. If we can plant a seed of doubt, Dovere's loyalty becomes a ticking clock. That's how we break him."

The room went quiet as the weight of the plan settled over them. It was audacious, reckless, even. Dovere wasn't just loyal; he was smart. Manipulating him would require precision, and even then, it was a gamble.

Carter's chair creaked as he ran a hand through his hair. It was obvious this whole thing made him nervous. "You're talking about baiting Dovere with a message he thinks he intercepted. But Barry's no fool, Reed. If Dovere brings that message to him, Barry will sniff out the setup. Guys like Barry don't survive this long without having an internal radar for manipulation. If he even suspects Dovere's loyalty is wavering, he'll turn the tables before we can blink. We're not just playing chess here, Reed, we're playing against someone who wrote the rulebook. One wrong move, one misplaced comma in that message, and Barry will smell the trap a mile away. Dovere might get spooked, or worse, he might double down on his loyalty. Either way, we lose."

Reed's gaze was unyielding. "That's why the message has to feel accidental, like Dovere stumbled onto something he wasn't meant to see. It needs to look like Barry let his guard slip."

Kranch pushed off the wall. "How do we even get a message like that to Dovere without raising red flags?"

Reed turned to Carter. "The Lyt Meeter."

The words hung in the air like a challenge. Carter's face went pale.

"No way, Reed. If we do this, if we strip it down, weaken the encryption, it's done. The Lyt Meeter's finished. We'll never get another use out of it. You're talking about burning one of our most valuable tools."

Reed stepped closer, "If this works, Carter, we won't need it again."

For a moment, Carter didn't move. Then he let out a long breath and nodded, rolling his chair over to the Lyt Meeter. The device sat on the desk, small and unassuming, but its value was immeasurable.

Carter began to work, his fingers flying over the controls as he stripped the device down to its bare digital bones. He moved relentlessly, bypassing failsafes and overriding security protocols. Each keystroke felt final, like chiseling away at a marble statue. Kranch hovered nearby, his broad shoulders tense. Reed paced, his mind running through every contingency, every potential failure point.

After what felt like an eternity, Carter leaned back, sweat dotting his brow. The Lyt Meeter was humming faintly, its light flickering erratically.

"It's ready," Carter said, his voice tight. "But this is a one-shot deal. Once we hit SEND, this thing's toast."

Reed nodded, stepping forward. "The message needs to be subtle. It can't scream setup. It has to feel like a glimpse behind the curtain, like Dovere caught something he wasn't supposed to see."

They crafted the message together, each word weighed carefully, balanced on a razor's edge.

"Seth served his purpose. Dovere will too. Loose ends get tied off eventually."

Carter's finger hovered over the **SEND** button. For a split second, hesitation flickered across his face. He looked to Reed, then Kranch. Their eyes held a clear message: *Push the button.* Taking a deep breath, he pressed it.

The Lyt Meeter shuddered. A wisp of smoke curled from its seams, and its faint hum died away. The small device slumped lifeless on the table; its final task complete.

Silence filled the room. All eyes turned to the monitor displaying a stream of digital signals. The bait was in the water, cast into the vast, endless sea of cyberspace.

Kranch broke the silence. "If Dovere bites, he'll second-guess every word out of Barry's mouth."

Reed said calmly, "And if he doesn't... we're dead in the water."

The team stood in silence, watching the screen like fishermen staring at a motionless line, waiting for the faintest tug, a ripple in the stillness.

Reed leaned against the table, his voice low. "Now we wait."

The camera feeds flickered. The static hum of electronics filled the air. Outside, the distant crash of waves against the shore echoed faintly. Somewhere, out in the vast emptiness of the ocean, Dovere's world was about to tilt, if they were lucky.

And if they weren't... they'd have to find another way.

The next seventy-two hours stretched like wire pulled taut over a pit of uncertainty.

In the cramped confines of their temporary command center, Reed, Carter, and Kranch existed in a haze of stale coffee, dim screens, and endless silence. The faint hum of servers and the occasional static crackle of a radio were the only sounds filling the void. Grimes, still stationed in Las Vegas, sent periodic updates, none of them offering any clarity.

Fatigue weighed heavy on all of them. Sleep came in scattered, restless shifts, twenty-minute naps stolen between data updates, heads slumped against the table or propped up against the wall. Someone was always awake, taking their turn monitoring screens, scanning for any flicker of movement, any hint of progress.

Meals were an afterthought. Protein bars and lukewarm coffee became a steady diet of caffeine and convenience. At one point, Carter had made a quick run down the hill to a roadside stand, returning with a grease-stained paper bag filled with empanadas. The smell alone had jolted them out of their haze, a fleeting reminder of the world beyond the four walls of their command center. They ate in silence, the warm, flaky pastry and savory filling a brief comfort before returning to the grind.

Carter paced like a caged animal, muttering under his breath about the odds of success. Kranch's attention shifted between the telescope and the monitors, eyes flicking between maritime traffic logs and communication intercepts, searching for even the faintest ripple in the digital ocean, and the actual ocean. Reed, seated at the head of the table, stared blankly at the dead Lyt Meeter, its charred components a painful reminder of their one-shot gamble.

It had been hours. Maybe days. The clock meant nothing anymore. The only rhythm they followed was the slow, grinding cycle of watching, waiting, and trying not to think about what would happen if they missed their window.

Each hour dragged on, every tick of the clock reverberating in their ears like a drumbeat of doubt. Messages poured in from Kessler, coded updates about maritime patrols, flagged signals, and uncon-firmed sightings. But none of it pointed to Dovere.

As the first day of waiting drew to a close, exhaustion began to set in.

On the second night, Carter broke the silence. "What if he's not biting, Reed? What if Dovere's already shown the message to Barry and they're laughing at us from the sundeck of that yacht right now?"

Reed didn't answer, his gaze still locked on the screens.

Kranch, ever stoic, grumbled, "It's Dovere. If he's thinking, he's not acting. If he's acting, he's not thinking. He's a slow burn, but if that seed took root, it'll grow. We just have to wait."

By the third day, exhaustion clung to them like a heavy fog. Eyes bloodshot, nerves frayed, they cycled through caffeine, cold water, and snacks, anything to stay sharp. Grimes pinged them once more, still nothing.

Hours dragged on under the weight of waiting, punctuated only by the hum of electronics and the occasional clink of coffee cups on the cluttered table. The sun dipped lower, painting the sky in molten gold and dusky lavender as shadows lengthened across the villa. Time was ticking away, but soon, they would know if it had all been worth it.

Miles away, across the vast ocean, Dovere had taken the bait, his doubt manifesting in subtle ways no one had noticed yet. For example, he lingered too long on his duties. He was seconds late to his assignments. The cracks were small, nearly imperceptible, but they were there. Even his responses to Barry were slower, not as crisp, laced with hesitation where there had once been certainty. He had started cross-checking intel he would have once accepted without question.

Even his movements had changed. His usual confident stride had stiffened, his steps more cautious, uncertain. He hadn't spoken his suspicions aloud, but the questions were forming, multiplying, pressing in on him with every passing hour.

Dovere needed to act. And he needed to act now.

Back in the villa, Kranch adjusted the focus ring of the telescope with deliberate care. The faint creak of the tripod echoed in the silence as he squinted into the eyepiece, tracking the glint of the Hampshire Feadship Yacht far out on the horizon. He let out a yawn, rubbing his eyes with one hand while keeping the other steady on the telescope.

And then he froze.

His posture straightened, and he leaned closer, his brow furrowing as he adjusted the focus one final time.

"Reed..." Kranch's voice was low, measured, but carrying a sharp edge. He turned slightly, eyes still locked on the telescope. "I think we've got something."

Carter took a look, typing rapidly on his laptop, translating the rhythmic morse code pattern of flashes into text.

.-.. . ... ..- .--. .-.. -.-- ..--- -.. .- -.-- ... -- . . - .--. ..- . .-. - --- .-. ..
-.-. ---

Carter glanced up, his face pale. "Resupply. Two days. Meet Puerto Rico."

The room went still.

Reed exhaled slowly, his eyes locked on the faint flicker of light seen through the telescope. "It's a signal. Dovere is doubting. And he's careful about it. That means he's not sold yet, but he's listening."

Carter, still thinking about the decoded message, muttered, "This isn't random chatter. He's creating a gap. He wants us to see it. The same message is being sent at intervals."

Reed nodded firmly; his voice low but resolute. "He's reaching out. It's subtle, cautious, but it's there. That's enough for me. We find him. We meet him in two days. Looks like our little message was received."

Meanwhile, back on the yacht, Barry walked the empty corridors of the Hampshire Feadship Yacht, his polished leather shoes echoing against the marble floors. The grandeur of the vessel, a floating palace of luxury, now felt more like a mausoleum.

Six staterooms, gleaming wood paneling, gold accents, and designer furnishings, yet only four were occupied: Barry, Dovere, and two of Dovere's most trusted men. The rest of the yacht, minus the staff was empty, hollow, a void where an empire had once been built and celebrated. Barry passed an ornate dining table set for twelve, untouched plates still sparkling under the soft glow of the crystal chandelier. The yacht had been built for celebration, for power, but now it felt like a stage set for failure.

He paused at one of the wide windows overlooking the endless ocean. The yacht was adrift in isolation, far from prying eyes, and yet Barry could feel them, eyes watching, shadows creeping in. His reflection stared back at him in the glass, a fine line of sweat clinging to his brow despite the air conditioning humming softly around him.

The crew avoided his gaze now, quick nods, hurried footsteps, and eyes cast downward whenever he passed. Even Dovere, the ever-reliable hammer in Barry's toolkit, had been quieter. Calculated, yes, but reserved. Dovere wasn't speaking as much, wasn't reporting every detail as he used to. And Barry noticed. He noticed everything.

Stopping near the grand staircase that spiraled down toward the lower decks, Barry gripped the polished wooden railing tightly. His knuckles went white as his mind raced. *Where had it gone wrong?* Vienna. Seth. SYNC. The escape from Las Vegas. All moments that had slipped, cracks forming in what he once thought was an unbreakable plan.

His empire had been vast, a network spanning continents, controlling information, people, and secrets. And now, piece by piece, it had crumbled.

Dovere was still loyal, Barry assured himself. He was a professional, and professionals don't let emotions cloud their judgment. But Dovere was no successor. No architect. He wasn't a man who could carry Barry's vision forward. Dovere was an enforcer, not a legacy.

Legacy. The word gnawed at Barry like rust on steel. That's what all of this had been about. Building something eternal, leaving his fingerprints on the world, ensuring his name wasn't forgotten. But now, the legacy felt brittle, ready to shatter with the faintest push.

Barry adjusted his posture, his breath steadying as he straightened his coat. He wasn't done. Not yet. There was still a path back, there always was.

He turned sharply, his eyes narrowing as he climbed the staircase to the control deck.

If he could eliminate Reed Sawyer, if he could regain control of the narrative, he could still twist the story to his advantage.

Barry Cox was not a man who faded into obscurity.

The air in Puerto Rico carried the sharp tang of salt and diesel fumes as Reed, Kranch, and Carter waited under the sweltering sun, spread across vantage points near *José Aponte de la Torre Airport.* The tropical humidity clung to them, beading on their foreheads and soaking into their clothes. Above them, the sky remained deceptively calm, an endless stretch of blue, a stark contrast to the tension simmering below.

Grimes' voice crackled through their earpieces from his remote station back in the U.S.

"Helicopter approaching. Same profile as the one on Barry's yacht. It's him."

Reed exhaled slowly, his gaze locked on the horizon. A distant, low thrum filled the air as the helicopter emerged, a sleek black silhouette slicing through the sky before touching down on the sunbaked tarmac of the small airstrip.

Kranch's voice came low and steady. "Eyes on Dovere. He's stepping out. Got two men with him. Both armed. Truck's waiting. Looks like they're heading out."

The trio exchanged quick glances, then split up, Kranch heading toward the far side of the airport, Carter blending into the traffic flow near the loading zone, and Reed trailing Dovere from a discreet distance.

Reed followed the supply truck into the parking lot of *Ralph's Food Warehouse*. The lights buzzed overhead, and the aisles smelled faintly of produce and industrial cleaner. Reed followed Dovere, keeping his distance as crates of bottled water, rice, canned goods, and other supply items were loaded onto carts.

Reed slipped into the produce section, maneuvering through stacks of cardboard boxes and crates of avocados. Dovere was examining a head of lettuce when Reed stepped into view, his hands raised, palms out.

"Dovere," Reed said, quietly.

Dovere's hand went immediately to his holstered pistol, his cold eyes locking onto Reed like a predator spotting prey.

"Easy," Reed said calmly. "You know how this ends if we go loud. I'm not here for that."

For a moment, the two men stood locked in a silent standoff, the hum of refrigeration units the only sound between them. Then, with a faint sigh, Dovere's hand moved away from his weapon.

"Talk fast, Sawyer," Dovere said, his voice sharp, his shoulders still tense.

Reed kept his voice low and measured. "You've been watching Barry, haven't you? You know he's unraveling. He's slipping, Dovere. And you know as well as I do, you're not Seth. You're not disposable. But Barry doesn't see it that way, does he?"

Dovere's eyes narrowed, his stoic face betraying just a flicker of doubt.

Reed continued. "Here's the truth, you can't win this on your own. But together, we can finish this. I have the Coast Guard standing by. One word from me, and they'll swarm that yacht."

Dovere's voice was low, almost a growl. "No, that is not going to work."

Dovere stepped slightly closer, his voice barely above a whisper. "First, I don't trust them. Second, Barry has a dead man's switch he carries in his pocket. The innocent crew and any coastguard aboard would be killed if he presses that button."

Dovere continued, "So, instead, how about I go back empty-handed. I'll tell Barry the area was crawling with suspicious activity, too hot to risk a resupply run. He's paranoid enough to believe it."

He glanced over his shoulder, scanning the aisle before continuing.

"I'll suggest shore leave for the crew next week. Barry will allow it. They have been acting funny and he knows they need a break. They'll head out, thinking it's just routine. But instead, they won't come back. You can make sure they're detained the moment they hit land."

Reed nodded slowly, processing the plan.

Dovere's voice dropped even lower. "That leaves Barry isolated. No crew. No supplies. No escape. He'll be desperate, and desperate men make mistakes. I'll dangle a lifeline, a contact, a dock, a fake escape route. And when he bites... you'll be waiting."

Reed studied Dovere carefully. There was no hesitation in his words, no flicker of doubt in his cold, professional demeanor. But beneath that icy exterior, Reed caught something else, a faint crack in the armor.

"What's stopping you from taking the yacht and disappearing yourself?" Reed asked bluntly.

Dovere smirked faintly. "Because, Sawyer, Barry Cox isn't just my employer. He's my unfinished business. And I don't leave loose ends."

Reed extended his hand. Dovere stared at it for a moment before clasping it briefly, an agreement forged in shadows and necessity.

"You know the stakes, Dovere. If this goes wrong, we all go down."

"It won't," Dovere said with steely certainty.

Dovere stepped back, his expression already shifting into the unreadable mask he wore around Barry. Without another word, he turned and disappeared into the warehouse, blending into the background like a phantom.

Reed regrouped with Kranch and Carter. The weight of the plan hung heavy in the air.

"He's going back," Reed said quietly. "Empty-handed. If Barry buys it, we'll have our opening."

Kranch rubbed his jaw. "It's a good plan, but it hinges on Dovere sticking to it. He could still sell us out."

Reed's eyes squinted in the bright sun, watching the helicopter fade into the distance.

"He won't," Reed said firmly. "Not this time."

The yacht drifted silently under a moonless sky, the soft lap of waves against the hull the only sound in the oppressive stillness. Dovere stepped onto the deck, his boots barely making a sound on the polished teak wood. His hands were empty, his face impassive, a mask carved from stone.

Barry stood near the bow, his silhouette sharp against the faint glow of distant starlight. The dead man's switch rested in his palm, his knuckles white from how tightly he gripped it. His gaze was locked on the horizon, where the sea stretched out into infinite darkness.

"No supplies?" Barry's voice was sharp, cutting through the night air.

Dovere shook his head slowly. "Too many eyes. Too many questions. I had to pull back."

Barry's eyes flickered with suspicion, but he said nothing. His fingers danced subtly along the dead man's switch, as though testing its weight, its power. For a moment, Dovere thought Barry might press it right then and there, just to remind himself he still held control.

Without another word, Dovere turned and walked away, disappearing into the labyrinthine corridors of the yacht. The flicker of doubt had been planted. The seed of paranoia, watered.

Somewhere in the shadows of the yacht, Dovere paused, exhaling slowly. Every move from here on out would need to be perfect, every word calculated, every glance controlled.

From the distant height of their villa's terrace in Pilón, Reed, Kranch, and Carter stood side by side, taking turns staring at the faint blinking lights of the yacht through the telescope.

"I sure hope this works."

Reed nodded slowly, his jaw set. "It has to work, so now we wait."

But the pieces were finally in place.

The next move belonged to Dovere.

25
RED-EYE

The yacht was no longer a refuge; it had become a gilded tomb.

Barry paced the hollow halls of the Hampshire Feadship Yacht, his reflection fractured across polished surfaces as he muttered fragmented sentences to himself. "Traitors everywhere... watching, always watching..." His fingers twitched unconsciously toward his pocket, where the dead man's switch resided like a cold comfort.

The luxury that had once symbolized his power now smothered him with its emptiness. Where nineteen souls once kept the vessel humming with life, only four remained, Barry, Dovere, and two increasingly restless men. The crew's absence after shore leave hung in the air like an accusation, their empty quarters a silent indictment of Barry's crumbling control.

Dovere's two remaining agents had taken to moving in pairs, their eyes constantly darting toward shadows and exits. During meals, their hands trembled slightly as they ate, watching Barry's every movement for signs of his growing instability. Just yesterday, Barry had thrown a crystal decanter against the wall, screaming about loyalty when one of them had accidentally interrupted his phone call.

Dovere observed it all with calculated patience. He'd begun positioning himself strategically, always within Barry's sight but just out of reach, feeding Barry's paranoia with subtle gestures. A whispered conversation that ended too quickly when Barry entered a room. A long stare at the horizon that suggested contemplation of escape. Each action was a carefully placed piece in Dovere's psychological chess game, pushing Barry closer to the edge while appearing to be the only one still standing firmly beside him.

The yacht's endless luxury, its gleaming marble floors, crystal chandeliers, and precious artworks, had transformed from symbols of success into mirrors reflecting Barry's descent. Each footstep echoed through the empty corridors like a countdown, each wave that slapped against the hull a reminder of their isolation.

Negative headlines and a storm of speculation looped endlessly on the yacht's muted screens, each broadcast a reminder of the chaos Barry could no longer control. His paranoia grew sharper with every step, suspicion clinging to him like a shadow. From the edges of the dimly lit corridors, Dovere observed him closely, his sharp eyes tracking the unraveling cracks in Barry's demeanor. The suffocating tension hung heavy over the vessel, infecting the air.

The Caribbean night pressed down on the yacht like a suffocating blanket, the air thick with salt and fear. A quarter moon cast weak silver light across the deck, its reflection fragmenting across the gentle swells below. The distance to shore, several miles of black water, seemed both impossibly far and tantalizingly close.

Rob Spiker, one of Dovere's men, had spent three years in Barry's service. Now, after watching Barry's spiral into paranoia, after seeing the coldness in his eyes grow darker each day, Spiker knew he had to act. His hands trembled as he worked the mechanisms of the small dinghy, each metallic click sending jolts of panic through his chest. The night wind carried the faint scent of land, trees, soil, freedom, mixing with the ever-present brine of the sea.

Every sound seemed magnified in the darkness. The gentle lap of waves against the hull. The distant cry of a seabird. The soft creak of the pulleys as he lowered the dinghy inch by careful inch. Spiker's breath came in sharp, controlled bursts, his heart hammering so loudly he was certain it would give him away. Just a few more minutes, he told himself. Just a few more minutes and he'd be free of this floating prison, free of Barry's increasingly unstable presence.

The shore beckoned, a darker line against the night sky. Spiker allowed himself to imagine reaching it, the scrape of the dinghy's bottom on sand, the splash of his feet in shallow water, the solid earth beneath him. His family would be waiting; he'd make his way to them, disappear into the world, start over...

The soft scuff of expensive leather on teak stopped his heart.

Barry Cox emerged from the shadows like a nightmare made flesh. His usual precise appearance had frayed at the edges, his pressed shirt was half tucked with the collar askew, the tie long since flung overboard in anger, but his movements carried an eerie, predatory grace. The dim light caught his eyes, reflecting something cold and reptilian. In his right hand, a pistol hung casually, as natural as a businessman's briefcase.

Spiker's muscles locked, his body caught between fight and flight. The blood roared in his ears as his mind raced through options, each one ending at the barrel of Barry's gun. He tried to speak, to explain, to beg, but his throat had closed, trapping the words.

Barry moved closer, each step deliberate. His face held an almost curious expression, like a scientist observing a specimen under glass. When he spoke, his voice was conversational, almost gentle. "You think there's a way out?"

The question hung in the air between them. Spiker saw his death in Barry's eyes before the gun even raised. In that final moment, time stretched like warm taffy. He thought of his family. He thought of his wife's smile, of promises he'd never keep now.

The gunshot cracked across the water like thunder, echoing off the waves. The impact spun Spiker, and as he fell, his last view was of the stars wheeling overhead, indifferent to the drama playing out beneath them. His body hit the deck with a dull thud, final and absolute.

Barry stood over the corpse, his expression unchanged. The acrid smell of gunpowder mixed with the salt air as he put the gun in his pocket. To him, this wasn't murder, it was maintenance, a loose thread snipped clean. With mechanical efficiency, he gripped Spiker's cooling body and heaved it overboard. The splash was swallowed by the darkness, leaving only ripples that quickly smoothed to nothing.

On deck, the other agent stood paralyzed, his wide-eyed gaze flicking between the dark water and Barry, breaths shallow and uneven, as if fearing he was next. From the shadows, Barry turned sharply, his movements mechanical, laced with barely restrained fury, then disappeared into the glowing corridors of the yacht, a storm brewing beneath his composed exterior. Behind him, the other agent remained motionless, the weight of what had just happened suffocating him as much as the endless ocean.

In the dimly lit bridge, Dovere stood in a spot where he had seen the whole thing unfold, his granite expression masking the calculations running through his mind. Spiker had been loyal, efficient, discreet, trustworthy. His death wasn't just an execution; it was a message. One Dovere had seen coming... but hoped to avoid.

As Barry walked on the bridge, you could cut the tension with a knife. Dovere's voice cut through the silence, measured and precise. "You just shot one of your own." The words carried the weight of accusation, though his face remained impassive. Years of training had taught him to hide his thoughts, but beneath that mask, fury simmered.

Barry waved him off, pacing again, his movements sharp and erratic. "You think I care? Loose ends get tied off."

The phrase hit Dovere like a physical blow. Those exact words, the same ones from the intercepted message he'd discovered. The same warning that had planted the first seed of doubt in his mind. He remembered staring at that message, weighing its truth against years of loyalty.

Time seemed to slow as memories cascaded through Dovere's mind: Seth's mysterious death, the growing list of disappeared operatives, the pattern he'd refused to acknowledge. Each death, each "loose end" tied off, had been a breadcrumb leading to this moment. Barry wasn't just eliminating threats, he was systematically erasing everyone who knew too much.

Dovere felt the weight of his sidearm against his ribs, suddenly very aware of its presence. His training screamed at him to maintain control, to wait for the perfect moment. But another voice, one that sounded surprisingly like conscience, whispered that waiting meant more deaths, more "loose ends" eliminated.

The realization hit him with brutal clarity: he wasn't looking at his employer anymore. He was looking at a rabid animal that needed to be put down. Barry had become exactly what the message had warned, a threat to everyone around him, including Dovere himself. The same paranoia that had served Barry so well in building his empire was now consuming it, piece by piece.

Every muscle in Dovere's body tensed as years of loyalty battled with survival instinct. He'd built his reputation on being the perfect soldier, the unwavering enforcer. But now, watching Barry's unraveling before him, he understood that true loyalty sometimes meant stopping the person you'd sworn to protect.

"You're done, Barry," Dovere growled, his voice carrying the weight of finality as he stepped forward. The decision, once made, felt like chains falling away. "This ends now."

Barry turned, eyes wide with paranoia. "You think you can touch me? I hold the switch!" He raised the dead man's switch like a trophy, daring Dovere to try.

But Dovere was done waiting. With a roar of fury, he lunged.

The bridge erupted into chaos. Dovere slammed into Barry, grappling for the switch. Glass shattered, controls sparked, and a gunshot rang out. The switch tumbled from Barry's hand, bouncing against the floor. Barry dove for it, his fingers clutching it just as Dovere grabbed his wrist. The struggle tipped over consoles and sent both men crashing into the metal railings.

Then it happened.

A piercing alarm shattered the night as the dead man's switch activated. Deep in the yacht's belly, the first explosion rocked the engine room, a precisely placed charge detonating near the main fuel lines. The blast shredded metal and ruptured hydraulic systems, sending superheated fluid spraying across exposed electrical panels. Sparks ignited the aerosol mist, creating a rolling fireball that roared through the narrow maintenance corridors.

The Hampshire Feadship's sophisticated fire suppression system activated, but it was overwhelmed within seconds. Emergency bulkheads slammed shut too late as the inferno reached the auxiliary fuel tanks. The secondary explosion was catastrophic, fourteen thousand gallons of marine diesel igniting in a chain reaction that split the yacht's hull like an aluminum can.

Flames climbed the service shafts, following paths of least resistance. The fire spread laterally through the lower decks, consuming the luxurious staterooms. Exotic hardwood panels fed the blaze, while Italian marble cracked and spalled in the intense heat. Crystal chandeliers melted, raining molten glass onto the burning carpets below.

The yacht's structure groaned under the thermal stress. Support beams warped and buckled as the fire reached the upper levels. Tempered glass windows exploded outward from the heat, letting in gusts of ocean air that only fed the flames. The once-pristine white hull began to glow orange from within, like some mythical beast awakening.

Seawater rushed in through the ruptured hull, creating a deadly dance between fire and flood. The competing elements tore the yacht apart, steam explosions adding to the chaos as cold water met superheated metal. The vessel began to list heavily to port as compartments flooded, its sophisticated stabilization systems long since destroyed.

The bridge, once a testament to modern marine technology, became an inferno. Digital displays melted, navigation equipment sparked and died, and the polished control panels warped beyond recognition. The fire's hunger seemed infinite, consuming everything in its path with indiscriminate fury.

From bow to stern, the Hampshire Feadship, a masterpiece of marine engineering worth just under a hundred million dollars, was being systematically destroyed. The precision of Barry's planted charges ensured no part of the yacht would survive. Every deck, every compartment, every escape route had been rigged to guarantee total destruction. This wasn't just an explosion; it was an orchestrated symphony of demolition.

Amid the chaos, the unmistakable thump of rotor blades began to cut through the cacophony of destruction. The yacht's helicopter, perched on the helipad, spun to life, its rhythmic pounding adding to the sense of impending doom. The glow of its navigation lights pierced the smoke-filled air, casting eerie, flickering shadows against the inferno.

Barry shoved Dovere against the railing and snapped a pair of handcuffs onto his wrist, locking him in place. The firelight danced across Barry's face, twisted into a crazed smirk. He leaned in close, his voice eerily calm amid the chaos.

"Every king needs a martyr, Dovere. Congratulations, you're mine. Enjoy the fire. You'll have the best seat in the house."

Barry stepped back, leaving Dovere trapped as the flames crawled closer. The bridge windows cracked under the heat, the roar of the inferno drowning out the alarms.

The flames climbed higher, licking at the walls of the upper decks, as the heat grew unbearable. Barry turned his back to the flames, stepping toward the helicopter with an unsettling calm. The sounds of chaos, alarms, roaring flames, and the guttural groans of the sinking yacht, seemed to fade around him, leaving only the relentless drone of the rotor blades as a dark symphony to his escape.

Barry disappeared into the smoke, his figure barely visible as he strode toward the helipad. The yacht groaned beneath his feet, its metallic frame twisting and shuddering as seawater rushed into its lower levels, feeding the chaos.

Dovere, bound to the railing and coughing violently through the thick smoke, strained against the cuffs cutting into his wrist. Flames crept closer, their searing heat biting at his legs as he twisted in a futile effort to free himself. He watched helplessly as Barry's silhouette disappeared onto the deck, illuminated for a moment by the flickering inferno.

Above, the helicopter's rotors spun faster, cutting through the chaos like a mechanical heartbeat. Barry climbed aboard with deliberate calm, his movements a chilling contrast to the chaos erupting around him. The helicopter began to rise, its searchlight sweeping across the deck, briefly illuminating Dovere amidst the flames.

As he lifted off, Barry glanced down and watched the inferno consume the yacht. The firelight swept over Dovere's defiant glare, flames licking closer to his trapped form. Smoke curled around him, choking the air, yet Dovere refused to look away, his stare locked on the shrinking helicopter as it rose into the night sky.

The yacht let out a final, tortured groan as explosions ripped through its remaining structure. Flames erupted from the bridge, sending debris cascading into the ocean below. The Hampshire Feadship Yacht tilted one last time before its fiery remains sank beneath the waves, leaving behind only the glow of embers and the distant, fading sound of the helicopter's blades cutting through the darkness.

From their high vantage point on the Puerto Rican coast, Reed and Kranch watched helplessly as the disaster unfolded. The moment the first explosion lit up the night, Reed had been on his satellite phone, desperately coordinating with the Coast Guard vessels stationed nearby. But the yacht's distance from shore and Barry's strategic positioning had made immediate intervention impossible.

"Coast Guard's moving in," Carter reported, his fingers flying across his tablet. "But their closest vessel is still fifteen minutes out. Two more are coming from San Juan, but..." He let the sentence hang, knowing they'd all done the math. Too far. Too slow. Too late.

The burning yacht cast a strange orange glow across the dark waves, turning the Caribbean Sea into a mirror of flame. Through the telescope, Reed watched the systematic destruction of their best chance to capture Barry. He tracked the helicopter's ascent from the burning deck, its sleek form briefly illuminated by the inferno below.

"We've got birds in the air," Kranch announced, one hand pressed to his earpiece. "Three Blackhawks scrambling, but, "

"But they won't make it in time," Reed finished, his voice tight with controlled fury. They had planned for everything, except Barry's willingness to destroy a hundred-million-dollar yacht just to escape.

Carter's tablet pinged with new data. "Helicopter's heading west-northwest. No flight plan filed. He could be heading anywhere. The Dominican Republic, Haiti, maybe even Cuba..."

"Or it's a maneuver," Reed cut in, his tactical mind already 5 steps ahead. "He knows we'll track the helicopter. This could be misdirection."

Kranch checked the telescope, his expression grim. "What's the play, Reed? We've got assets we can redirect, but we need a direction."

Reed's mind raced through the possibilities. Barry was wounded now, cornered, desperate, but still dangerous. Maybe more dangerous than ever. "He's not running blind," Reed said finally. "This was planned. The explosives, the helicopter, the timing, he had this fallback ready. Which means..."

"He's got somewhere to go," Carter finished, already pulling up maps on his tablet. "Somewhere we don't know about."

"He's gone, Reed. Again." Kranch's voice carried the weight of their collective frustration.

Reed didn't respond immediately, the flickering firelight catching the furrow in his brow as he processed their options. The helicopter's lights winked one final time before disappearing into the darkness, but Reed's expression had shifted from frustration to determination.

"Start running scenarios," he ordered, turning to his team. "Carter, I want every private airstrip within that helicopter's fuel range mapped. Kranch, get me everything we have on Barry's known properties and shell companies in the Caribbean."

As the Coast Guard vessels finally arrived, their searchlights cutting through the smoke of the burning wreckage, Reed had already turned away from the spectacle. Barry had orchestrated this escape with his usual theatrical flair, but he'd made one critical mistake: he was running out of shadows to hide in, out of allies to trust, out of places to disappear.

Reed stood on his villa's terrace, hands on hips, his posture rigid but his mind clearly calculating. The orange glow dimmed as the last remnants of the once-luxurious yacht disappeared beneath the waves, leaving only the reflection of the Coast Guard's searchlights dancing across the water.

"This doesn't feel like a win," Kranch muttered, kicking a loose stone from the ceramic tile floor of their balcony in frustration. "It's like we're always two steps behind."

Reed finally turned, his voice laced with determination. "He's still out there. But this time…" He paused, his gaze sweeping back to the smoldering wreckage below. "This time, there's no shadows left to hide in."

The words hung in the air as the distant roar of approaching helicopters and Coast Guard vessels filled the night. Kranch and Carter exchanged glances, their frustration momentarily replaced by a spark of hope in Reed's unyielding resolve.

In the distance, the ocean swallowed the last traces of the Hampshire Feadship Yacht. And above it all, the night sky remained dark and vast, a stark reminder of the hunt that was far from over. Reed stood firm, his figure silhouetted against the dim glow of the Coast Guard's lights, already thinking ahead to the next move.

26

BURNED IMAGE

In the early morning hours, the open sea stretched endlessly in every direction, an infinite expanse of restless gray waves beneath a pale, indifferent sky. The wreckage of the Hampshire Feadship Yacht had long sunk to the depths, leaving behind only a faint slick of oil and scattered fragments as its only trace. From the deck of a sleek maritime operations vessel, Reed gripped the cold metal railing, his knuckles white. His eyes scanned the horizon, sharp and unwavering, as salt spray clung to his skin and the wind tore at his jacket like invisible hands urging him forward.

Kranch stood nearby, his imposing frame motionless, arms crossed tightly across his chest, a sentinel of unyielding determination. Below deck, Carter's rapid keystrokes echoed faintly through the vessel, the terminal's screen illuminating his furrowed face as he sifted through fragmented data, maritime signals, helicopter flight paths, breadcrumbs scattered across the vast ocean. Above them, a Coast Guard helicopter hovered in restless vigilance, its searchlight slicing through the early dawn, chasing shadows that danced across the waves like ghosts refusing to rest.

Grimes's voice crackled through the earpieces, a lifeline connecting the team to his remote command center stateside. "Barry's escape chopper was on radar for a while, but it dipped low over the water and vanished off civilian systems. Listen, Reed, this wasn't a panicked move. That helicopter had a planned route. He's got another safe house, another contingency."

Reed tightened his grip on the railing and asked, "Can you tell where he's heading?"

Grimes hesitated, the pause heavy with calculation. "We're cross-referencing the helicopter's fuel range, weather conditions, and refueling points along the direction of the flight path. There's chatter about an isolated airstrip inland. It's remote, barely operational, but it could handle a chopper like his. If I had to bet, that's where he's going."

Kranch, standing firm beside Reed, added, his tone rough, "Barry's not built to keep running. He's too proud, too controlling. I think he will hunker down somewhere he can still pull strings and pretend he's in charge."

Reed's gaze remained fixed on the horizon, the faintest glint of determination in his eyes. "This time, we won't let him slip away. He's cornered, and we'll make sure he knows it. Let's finish this."

Inland, hidden deep within the rugged hills of Puerto Rico, an abandoned sugar plantation stood as a forgotten relic of another era. Overgrown vegetation swallowed the rusting machinery, and vines crept along the crumbling walls of what once had been a bustling estate. Now, it served as Barry Cox's last refuge. The makeshift landing zone, a barely cleared patch of uneven ground in the dense brush, had just managed to accommodate the escape helicopter. Its blades were still cooling, ticking faintly in the humid air.

Inside a decaying storage shed hastily repurposed into a command post, Barry sat hunched on a weathered crate, his shadow cast long and jagged by a dim, flickering lantern. His tailored suit, once a symbol of his dominance, was damp with sweat, streaked with dirt and salt, clinging to him like a shroud of defeat. His hair, always immaculate, now stuck out in wild, uneven tufts, and dark circles hung heavy beneath his eyes. But in those eyes, there was still fire. A flicker of the Barry Cox who had controlled an empire, now reduced to embers struggling to reignite.

On the crate beside him lay his phone, ominously silent. The screen stayed dark, no calls, no messages, no updates. It was as though the world he once commanded no longer existed. For the first time in years, Barry was truly, utterly alone.

He muttered to himself, his voice low and fractured, words spilling out as if he were trying to convince himself they made sense. In his trembling hand, a battered notepad bore frantic scrawls, lines of half-formed thoughts and disconnected phrases.

"Cut off the head... rebuild the body... time... I just need time," he whispered, the words trailing into a hoarse rasp. His pen dug deep into the paper as he underlined the word *time* repeatedly, the pressure tearing through the fragile pages.

His grip tightened on the pen as he calmed his mind, staring at the nonsensical patterns he'd drawn. For a moment, he admitted to himself what the rest of the world already knew, that his own thoughts were unraveling, slipping through the cracks of his once ironclad control. He exhaled sharply, shaking his head, before muttering again, this time more to the shadows around him than to himself.

"This isn't over. I'm not done."

But the hollowness in his voice betrayed the lie. Outside, the jungle stirred under the pale light of early morning, dew clinging to the dense foliage. The rustling leaves and the distant calls of awakening birds were a stark contrast to the suffocating silence within the shed, a reminder that, while Barry's empire crumbled, the world beyond continued to move forward, indifferent to his plight.

Later that day, back on the operations vessel, Carter slammed his hand on the table, making the surface tremble under the force. The sharp sound echoed through the vessel, drawing Reed and Kranch's attention from the upper deck. "Got him!" Carter's voice crackled with urgency. Reed and Kranch rushed to the lower deck, arriving just in time to hear Carter announce, "Barry's chopper refueled at a small private airstrip near the southeastern hills. No flight plan filed, no civilian oversight, it's a ghost location."

Reed leaned over the map Carter had pulled up on the screen, the faint glow of the monitor illuminating his focused expression. "How isolated?" Reed asked.

Carter zoomed in on the area, his fingers moving rapidly across the keyboard. "Very. There's a single dirt road cutting through the jungle to the airstrip, no backup routes, no exits. If we move fast, he's pinned."

Reed straightened, the determination in his eyes hardening into steel. "Let's move."

Kranch, standing nearby, cracked his knuckles, the sound echoing in the tense air. "Let's finish it," he muttered, his voice like gravel underfoot.

The faint crackle of Grimes's voice came through their earpieces, cutting into the moment. "Reed, heads up. I've been monitoring transmissions from Barry's emergency lines. He's been trying to reach contacts, every number he's got. But guess what? Nobody's answering. He's cut off. He's spiraling."

Reed's jaw tightened as he absorbed the information. He turned back to the map, his fingers gripping the edge of the table. "That means he's desperate," he said, sharply. "Desperate people make mistakes. We use that. But this time..." His voice dropped, the weight of his conviction unmistakable. "This time, we don't give him room to slip away."

A faint rumble of the ocean underscored the moment, the weight of the impending confrontation hanging heavy in the room as they prepared to make their move.

Later that night, using a Coast Guard helicopter, Reed, Kranch, Carter, and a top-tier team of Coast Guard, military, and police made their way to the remote location where Barry had been tracked. Opting for stealth over speed, they landed several miles out and commandeered a rugged truck to close the distance. The jungle was alive with sound, the whine of insects, the rustle of unseen creatures, but to the team, it felt oppressively silent. The thick air clung to their skin as they moved, the weight of the moment pressing down on every step.

They needed to make a decision, how would they approach Barry? Brute force, swift surprise, or something else? Reed took point and explained to the commanding officer that Barry was a loose cannon. Any attempt at surprise could result in someone getting hurt, or worse. Together, they decided the Coast Guard would cover the front and wait for Reed's signal. Military and police units would circle around to cover the back and sides, surrounding the building. Reed, Kranch, and Carter would enter carefully and disarm Barry.

Through the dense foliage, faint flickering lights glimmered from the plantation's makeshift hideout. Reed halted the team, crouching low. He whispered, "No mistakes. No second chances. Stay sharp."

Inside the shed, Barry paced like a caged animal, the space around him strewn with half-empty water bottles, crumpled papers, and hastily scribbled notes. The satellite phone in his hand trembled slightly as he stared at its blank screen. "Answer. Somebody answer," he muttered, his voice a blend of frustration and desperation. His sharp eyes darted to the cracked window, paranoia etched into his every movement.

Outside, Reed motioned to Carter and Kranch, pointing toward their positions. They moved in unison, a silent choreography honed by years of high-stakes operations. Carter flanked left, Kranch circled right, and Reed stepped toward the front, his heart pounding with each step.

Reed paused just outside the shed's doorway, the dim light from inside casting his shadow against the jungle floor. He steadied his breath, tightening his grip on his weapon. Then, with calm resolve, he stepped into the doorway, his voice cutting through the heavy air like a blade. "Barry."

Barry spun toward the sound, his bloodshot eyes widening. For a split second, the sharp, calculating architect of chaos seemed unrecognizable, just a man teetering on the edge. His tie hung loose, his shirt stained with sweat, and the weight of his collapse hung heavily on his hunched shoulders.

Reed's voice was sharp, unyielding. "It's over, Barry."

Barry's gaze flicked between Reed and the shadowed figures of Carter and Kranch through the window. His lips curled into a faint, bitter smile as his hands twitched toward the phone, his eyes blazing with a mix of defiance and fear.

"Over?" Barry said, his voice low, laced with mockery. "Reed, nothing is ever over."

The tension in the room was electric, every breath heavy with the anticipation of what would happen next. Reed's finger hovered over the trigger, his eyes locked on Barry's every move.

Barry's lip twitched, his jaw tightening as he forced a bitter smile. His hand clenched into a fist, the veins standing out starkly against his pale skin. "You think you've won?" he spat, his voice laced with venom. "You have no idea what you've undone, Reed. No idea *who* you've done it to."

Kranch stepped into view behind Reed, his weapon trained on Barry with unwavering precision. Carter appeared at the other side, his stance firm, eyes scanning every corner of the dimly lit shed for threats. Barry's gaze flicked between them, his breath hitching for just a moment before he masked it with a derisive chuckle.

"Your empire's gone, Barry," Reed said, his tone calm but edged with finality. "Your operatives are either dead, arrested, or turned. You're out of moves. This whole area is surrounded with military and police. There is no escape."

Barry's chest rose and fell as he took a shaky breath, his eyes darting erratically, to the cracked floorboards, to the peeling walls, to the jagged frame of the broken window, anywhere but to Reed's unflinching stare. The weight of his collapse was visible, etched into every twitch of his fingers and flicker of his gaze.

Reed stepped forward, closing the distance between them. His voice dropped to a measured, deliberate tone. "This doesn't have to end messy, Barry. But make no mistake, it *will* end."

Barry's laugh came suddenly, sharp and bitter, reverberating off the tin walls. "End? You think you've cornered me?" He took a half step back, his eyes narrowing. "You're a cog in a machine you can't even comprehend, Reed. Capture me, kill me, it won't change anything. You're a fool if you think I'm the architect of all this. I'm just, "

"Enough." Reed cut him off sharply, his eyes narrowing. "Every empire falls, Barry. This is yours."

Barry's defiance faltered, replaced by a flicker of fear as the room seemed to shrink around him. Reed's team stood poised, ready, and unrelenting. The endgame had arrived.

Barry's façade cracked like glass under pressure. His shoulders sagged, the tension leaking out of him in uneven breaths. For a fleeting moment, the fire in his eyes dimmed, replaced by something raw and unfamiliar, defeat. His hands, once animated with power and precision, now hung limply at his sides. Slowly, the proud, unyielding posture of *The Architect* gave way to the unmistakable slump of a man with no moves left. He was conceding. Yielding. Surrendering.

Kranch didn't wait. He moved in swiftly, his movements precise. Barry flinched as his arms were wrenched behind his back, the sharp *zip* of the ties echoing in the still air. Carter was already at his side, patting Barry down with quick efficiency, checking every pocket, every seam for concealed weapons or devices. He pulled a sleek knife from Barry's inner jacket pocket and tossed it to the floor with a metallic clatter.

Barry Cox looked *small*. The magnetic confidence, the carefully curated image of control and superiority, had evaporated like mist. What remained was a hollow shell of a man, stripped of the empire he had built, caught in the web of lies and power plays he had once commanded with ease.

Reed studied Barry, now restrained and diminished, and for a moment, the two men simply stared at each other, one steady, the other fractured. Barry's lips parted as if to speak, but no words came.

He looked down, his breathing ragged, and the silence that followed felt heavier than any words he could have uttered.

Barry was escorted out of the plantation hideout, his shoulders stooped under the weight of defeat. Reed walked directly behind him, weapon lowered but ready, while Carter and Kranch flanked him on either side, their vigilance unbroken. A faint glow of dawn crept over the horizon, casting long shadows through the dense jungle. Barry was in complete disarray, dirt streaked across his face, the tie he'd once worn like a badge of authority now dangling loosely around his neck.

Reed reached for his comm device, sending a sharp, succinct message. "This is Reed Sawyer. Barry Cox is in custody. Repeat, Barry Cox, The Architect, is secure."

Just then, all of the waiting authorities moved in quickly. Barry was loaded onto the commandeered truck. He was secured with three armed guards, including Reed, Kranch and Carter.

The dirt road ahead curved into view, and the faint sound of tires crunching over gravel was drowned out as the Coast Guard helicopter came into view. But Barry wasn't done yet.

As they neared the clearing, Barry's head snapped up to meet Reed's eyes. "You think this ends with me in cuffs?" he hissed, his former commanding voice returning. "You have no idea what's coming. I'm not the only player on this board, Reed. You've made enemies you can't even imagine."

Reed focused his stare into Barry's eyes. "Save it, Barry," he said coolly, his tone unyielding. "You're done. Your moves, your threats, your empire, it's all over."

Barry leaned in, his voice dropping to a conspiratorial whisper. "You think Kessler's clean? You think you've got it all figured out? The people I answer to, the strings I've pulled, they don't just disappear because I'm in handcuffs..."

Reed interrupted Barry. "You're right, Barry. Your mess doesn't disappear. But neither do we."

Kranch, growing impatient, said, "Shut up, Cox. Your soapbox time is over. No one wants to hear your crap anymore."

Barry smirked, a shadow of his former arrogance creeping into his expression. But the tension was broken as the hum of the helicopter grew louder. As they approached, their headlights cut through the thick jungle.

Reed watched silently as Barry was loaded onto the Coast Guard helicopter, his zip-tied wrists exchanged for reinforced cuffs. He was to be transferred from the jungle to the US Army Reserve Center. In an instant of clarity, his bravado wavered as the authorities tightened their grip on him.

The team watched as the helicopter lifted off. It was finally heading for the Reserve Center, Reed turned to Carter and Kranch. His voice was low, calm, and resolute. "He's in custody, but this isn't over. Not yet."

The jungle around them grew quiet again, save for the distant thump of helicopter blades fading into the distance. Reed knew that Barry's words, as venomous as they were, couldn't be ignored. The battle against The Architect might have reached a turning point, but the war for what he represented was far from finished.

Later, word of Barry Cox's capture spread like wildfire. An eager junior officer, unable to grasp the magnitude of the arrest, sent a single text to his brother at Reuters. That one message ignited a global media storm. News vans materialized seemingly out of thin air, their satellite dishes stretching skyward like metal flowers seeking the sun. The frenzy surrounding "The Architect" and his shadowy empire reached a fever pitch, transforming the once-quiet military base into a chaotic spectacle of flashing cameras and shouting reporters. Within hours, the narrow roads leading to the US Army Reserve Center were jammed with satellite trucks and journalists scrambling to capture the story of a lifetime.

The chaos outside was deafening, reporters shouting over one another, cameras clicking furiously, microphones thrust toward anyone in a uniform. Helicopter blades thundered overhead as aerial news teams vied for the best angle. The Reserve Center's gates were lined with spectators, conspiracy theorists, and protestors waving hastily scrawled signs, all vying for a glimpse of the man who had orchestrated one of the most elaborate deceptions in modern history.

From the helicopter, Barry was loaded into a secure Hummer. Inside the gates, federal agents poured into the compound, their presence a stark reminder of how high-profile this arrest had become. Barry's transport convoy rolled through the entrance, flanked by armored vehicles. Cameras zoomed in, capturing every detail as the world held its breath.

When Barry finally emerged, flanked by federal agents with his wrists secured in reinforced cuffs, the transformation was stark. The man who once commanded rooms with unshakable confidence now appeared haggard and broken. His once-pristine appearance was now stained, his hair disheveled, and his eyes hollow, lacking the fire that had once defined him. Camera feeds broadcast his image live to millions, a fallen figure, guilty, exposed, and utterly defeated.

As reporters narrated the spectacle, headlines flashed across screens: *"The Fall of The Architect"*, *"Barry Cox in Federal Custody"*, and *"PPI Spy Network Crumbles."*

Barry glanced toward the crowd, for a fleeting moment, the faintest flicker of defiance crossed his features. Then it was gone, replaced by the vacant look of a man whose empire had been reduced to ashes.

Reed stood at a secure observation point nearby, watching intently. The world saw a broken man, but he knew better. Barry Cox was a master of façades, and somewhere beneath the defeat, his mind was already calculating his next move.

Kranch and Carter stood nearby, their postures tense, the weight of the moment etched into their expressions. Grimes's voice crackled in Reed's earpiece, a reminder of the scale of their accomplishment.

"Barry's face is everywhere," Grimes reported. "Every major network. The media's in a frenzy. They're saying the international authorities are handling the transfer, but cameras haven't stopped rolling for a second. He's already front-page news."

The midday sun hung high, casting harsh light over the bustling scene. Tactical teams moved with practiced efficiency under the glare, their shadows sharp against the dusty ground. Armored vehicles stood as silent sentinels, forming an impenetrable perimeter, while military personnel coordinated with precision. Overhead, the steady thrum of helicopters filled the air, their rotors stirring the heat and creating fleeting ripples of shade across the makeshift staging area. The atmosphere crackled with urgency and tension, every detail a reminder of the magnitude of the moment.

In the center of it all, Barry Cox sat on a battered folding chair, his hands still bound. His head tilted slightly upward. Yet there it was, a faint smirk tugging at the corner of his mouth, defiant even in defeat.

Reed moved in as close as he could, his gaze fixed on Barry. The weight of the chase, the betrayals, the lives impacted, and the countless moments where victory had slipped through their fingers bore down on him. Every close call, every narrow escape replayed in his mind like a film he couldn't shut off.

And yet, here they were. The Architect, handcuffed and exposed to the world, surrounded by the very forces he once sought to manipulate. But as Reed watched Barry, he was still smirking, he couldn't shake a gnawing question. Was it truly over? Or was this just another move in Barry's endlessly tangled game?

A low, rhythmic thud-thud-thud filled the air, growing louder as a sleek black helicopter descended. Dust and debris swirled violently in its wake, forcing those nearby to shield their faces. The chopper was unmarked, no insignia, no identifiers. It exuded an air of ominous authority.

A team of high-profile international officials emerged, their dark suits pristine despite the confusion around them. Sunglasses obscured their eyes, and they moved with a deliberate, almost clinical precision. One of them strode toward the lead FBI agent, carrying a leather briefcase. The two engaged in a terse exchange, documents changing hands. After a quick scan, the agent nodded sharply and motioned to his team.

Barry was pulled from his chair. His cuffs remained on, but his posture was unnervingly casual, almost as if he were walking to a business meeting rather than being led toward an uncertain fate. The armed escort flanked him closely, but Barry seemed unfazed, his calm demeanor chilling against the backdrop of madness.

As Barry passed Reed, he slowed, his movements deliberate. Their eyes locked, and for a brief moment, the world seemed to narrow around them. Barry leaned in slightly, his voice low and measured. "Fine portraits require both light and shadow," he murmured, his tone almost conversational.

Reed froze, caught off guard by the cryptic statement. His mind churned, dissecting the meaning, but before he could respond, Barry had already moved on, his faint smirk still etched into his face.

Carter stepped up beside Reed, his expression tense. "What did he say?" he asked, his voice tight with curiosity. Reed hesitated, the words lingering like a riddle in his mind. "Nothing," he finally replied, the weight of uncertainty settling in his chest.

Barry was loaded onto the chopper, his movements deliberate, every step a controlled performance. As the door closed, Reed caught one last glimpse of him through the small window. Barry's face was eerily composed, his calm demeanor almost mocking.

The helicopter's blades roared to life, the craft tilting eastward as it rose into the sky. Dust billowed up once more, obscuring the view as the chopper disappeared over the eastern horizon. The scene felt definitive, like the final page of a story. But as Reed stood there, the unease in his chest refused to dissipate. It didn't feel like an ending, at least, not yet.

Reed's phone buzzed sharply in his pocket, jolting him from his thoughts. He pulled it out and answered.

"Reed," came Secretary Kessler's voice, steady but tinged with relief. "Congratulations on successfully capturing Barry. You've done the impossible. You're a hero. I guarantee we will not allow him to escape again."

Reed's gaze remained fixed on the helicopter, now just a dark speck against the pale sky. The rhythmic thrum of its rotors was fading, replaced by the distant hum of vehicles and the murmured chatter of agents. He replied evenly, "Thank you, sir. I'm watching his helicopter right now, being flown out by international authorities."

There was a pause on the line, long enough for Reed's unease to grow. When Kessler's voice returned, it was sharper, edged with confusion. "Helicopter?" he repeated, the word heavy with alarm. "They're supposed to be flying him out in a military transport plane! There's no helicopter authorized for this transfer."

Reed's stomach dropped, his grip tightening on the phone. "A transport plane?" he echoed.

"Yes," Kessler replied urgently. "Maybe they're rendezvousing at the Army Aviation Center first... I'll confirm that and handle it."

The line went dead, leaving Reed staring at his phone, a cold weight settling in his chest. The helicopter was now just a speck on the horizon, barely visible against the light-streaked sky. The nagging unease that had been with him all day now roared to life. Something wasn't right.

Reed lowered the phone slowly, his face pale, the media circus still a buzz around them. Carter noticed immediately. "What's wrong?" he asked, his voice edged with concern.

Reed turned to him, his eyes searching for answers in the commotion that suddenly felt too calculated. "What direction is the Army Aviation Center?"

Carter frowned, glancing down at his tablet, fingers flying over the screen. "Due west," he said finally, looking back at Reed. "Why?"

Kranch stepped closer, and asked, "Reed, what did Barry say to you?"

Reed hesitated, thoughts firing in every direction. The words Barry had whispered were like a riddle he couldn't untangle. He swallowed hard, "He said, 'Fine portraits require both light and shadow.'"

The three men exchanged a long, heavy look, each of them grasping the implications as the pieces clicked into place. The weight of realization settled over them like a lead blanket.

Carter broke the silence first, his tone grim. "That copter... it wasn't heading west, was it?"

Reed didn't answer immediately. He glanced toward the horizon, his thoughts focused. Finally, in a quiet, almost resigned voice, he said, "Have we just been played?"

Kranch's fist slammed against the nearest vehicle, the impact echoing across the compound. "Even in custody, he had a plan. Always another move, another angle."

Carter was already on his tablet, trying to track the trajectory. "If we mobilize now, maybe we can, "

"Wait." Reed held up his hand, his brow furrowing. Something about Barry's final words nagged at him. 'Fine portraits require both light and shadow.' The phrase felt loaded, deliberate, like everything else Barry did. But was it a taunt? A warning? Or something else entirely?

The media circus continued behind them, still celebrating a victory. Reed stared at the empty horizon. Barry Cox had proven time and again that nothing was ever quite what it seemed. Whether this was an escape or something else entirely, one thing was certain: the truth, like Barry himself, remained in the shadows.

27
REFLECTIONS

Thirty-eight days had passed since Barry Cox vanished into the eastern sky aboard an unmarked helicopter. In those five weeks, leads had gone cold, surveillance footage had revealed nothing, and Pro4uM.com had remained eerily silent. No cryptic messages had surfaced, no sightings had been reported, no bodies had been found. The media circus that once surrounded The Architect had subsided, his story fading into yesterday's news beneath an endless cycle of fresh scandals and distractions. Even PPI's most ardent watchdogs had gone quiet, leaving only questions and theories in their wake.

For Reed and his team, the silence had been both a relief and a torment. No more running, no more looking over their shoulders, but also no confirmation that their mission truly succeeded. The dust had settled, leaving them, like never before, completely still.

They had retreated to a quiet lakeside cabin, tucked far from the bustling cities and crowded conventions that once dictated their lives. The air was crisp, carrying the faint scent of pine and damp earth. The lake stretched out like glass, mirroring the burnt-orange hues of the setting sun. Golden light streamed through the wide cabin windows, bathing the room in warmth as the day surrendered to evening.

Outside, the team was gathered around a fire pit. Flames crackled and leapt, throwing dancing shadows across the cabin's exterior walls. The only sounds were the occasional rustle of leaves and the distant call of a loon echoing across the water. It was a beautiful thing. There was no rush, no immediate danger, just the hum of nature and the hypnotic roar of the flame.

Reed leaned forward, the firelight catching in his eyes, and poured bourbon into a tumbler, the amber liquid catching the last light of the day. The sound of it filled the silence, a soothing rhythm in the stillness. He passed the bottle to Grimes, who took it without a word. Kranch leaned back in his chair, arms crossed as usual, his typical scowl softened but not absent. Carter, perched on the edge of his seat, flipped lazily through his phone, though the screen's light barely held his attention. Grimes watched them all, sharp-eyed as ever but unusually still, his hands resting on his knees.

The weight of everything they had endured hung in the air, a silent, unspoken presence around the fire. Each man felt it, but no one rushed to fill the quiet. They had earned this moment of peace, however fleeting it might be.

The team spoke in hushed tones, the weight of taking down Barry hanging heavy in the air. The firelight danced across their faces, each word they shared laced with quiet vulnerability.

Kranch broke the silence first, saying, "I don't think I've got even one last fight in me... I'm done." He stared into the flame, his normally impenetrable expression softened with resignation. "Fieldwork's not just about strength, it's about heart. And mine's not in it anymore." His admission lingered in the air, surprising no one but still feeling heavy. "Maybe it's time I find something that doesn't involve dodging bullets."

Carter, always the joker, tried to lighten the mood. "Dodging bullets? No problem. But sleeping without a tablet buzzing next to my pillow? That's gonna take some getting used to." He chuckled, but the flicker in his eyes gave him away, restless unease that wouldn't disappear overnight. "Still... as much as I hated the chaos, the adrenaline? That's hard to let go."

Grimes leaned back, hands clasped over his stomach, ever the picture of calculated calm. "You can take the man out of the mission, but you can't take the mission out of the man," he said, his voice tinged with dry humor but underscored with sincerity. He looked out at the lake, his mind already moving to the next plan. "I'm not one for staying idle. Maybe consulting, maybe another convention. There's always something to fix, some system to build."

Reed snorted softly, shaking his head as he sipped his bourbon. "Yeah, well... I'm trying to prove you wrong on that one, Grimes." His words were light, but his tone was heavy. He swirled the bourbon in his glass, watching the liquid catch the firelight. "But I'm not gonna lie... it's not easy."

For a moment, silence took over again, each man lost in his own thoughts. The crackle of the fire and the soft rustle of the trees filled the space. It wasn't an uncomfortable quiet, it was the kind of stillness that came from shared experience, the bond of those who'd fought and bled together, even if they were on the brink of going their separate ways.

The conversation drifted into quieter waters, the blaze crackling softly as the team began to reflect on those who didn't make it through the chaos, Marcus, Seth, Dovere, and countless others whose lives had been consumed by Barry's shadow.

Kranch shifted forward, his elbows on his knees, staring into the flames as though seeking answers in their flickering dance. "Marcus," he muttered, his voice low. "He saw this coming before any of us did. He tried to warn us... left breadcrumbs for us to follow. Without him, we wouldn't have even gotten close to Barry."

Carter nodded, his expression uncharacteristically somber. "Marcus was the foundation, wasn't he? The guy saw things we didn't, connected dots no one else could. And Seth..." He trailed off, swallowing hard before continuing. "Seth cut Barry deep, but in the end... he knew it was all worth it. We wouldn't have had half the intel we did without him risking his life."

Reed exhaled slowly, the bourbon in his hand untouched now. "And Dovere," he said quietly, the name hanging in the air like a shadow. "He made the ultimate play, knowing Barry would take him down if he found out. But he still did it. He still took the risk."

Kranch shifted again in his seat, the firelight casting harsh lines across his face. "They all did. Marcus, Seth, Dovere... they sacrificed everything so we could be sitting here right now, nursing drinks instead of six feet under." His voice hardened, tinged with guilt. "We wouldn't have made it without them."

Their words lingered in the air, draping over the group like a heavy blanket. Grimes, trying to reassure the group, said, "They made their choices. We can't carry the weight of that, but we can remember them. Honor them by making sure this... all of this... wasn't for nothing."

Reed leaned back, tipping his head up to the sky, where the first stars were beginning to peek through the twilight. "I keep asking myself if it was worth it," he admitted. "Everything we've lost, everyone we've lost. And I don't have an answer. Not yet."

The group fell silent again, the only sounds the crackle of the fire and the distant hum of the lake. Each man was lost in his own thoughts, remembering the faces, the voices, the moments that brought them to this point. For a moment, they simply breathed, letting the memories settle like embers after the fire faded.

As the evening pressed on, an unspoken tension lingered in the air. Each man felt it, the same nagging question that had gnawed at them since the day Barry was taken away.

Carter finally said it, sitting sideways in his chair and staring at the stars overhead. "It doesn't sit right, does it?" he muttered, his voice low. "We saw him cuffed, loaded onto that chopper, flown out with all the fanfare. But... was that it? Was it really over?"

Kranch grunted. "The guy didn't earn the nickname 'The Architect' for nothing. He's slippery. Always two, three, five steps ahead. I mean, come on, how many times have we thought we had him, only for him to twist out of it like some Houdini act?"

Reed stared into the flames, the firelight dancing in his eyes as he mulled over their words. "It felt... off," he admitted quietly. "The unmarked chopper, the so-called international authorities, that smirk on his face as they took him away. It's like he wanted us to see it, like it was part of the show."

Grimes chimed in, his tone blunt. "You're not wrong to feel that way," he said, breaking the silence with a hard truth. "I've been digging, there's no official record of Barry's transfer. No flight plan logged for that chopper. No formal charges filed anywhere, not even a whisper from the international agencies that supposedly took him." His words landed heavily, each revelation deepening the unease that settled over the group.

Carter rubbed his face, letting out a heavy sigh. "So, what are you saying? We've been played?"

"Maybe," Grimes replied. "Or maybe he's in a hole so deep even we can't see it. Either way, we don't have the whole picture."

The uncertainty pressed down on them. Kranch spoke, with an insisting tone. "If he's out there, free, rebuilding... we'll know soon enough. Guys like Barry don't disappear. They leave fingerprints on everything."

Reed looked up from the fire, his expression grim. "But what if this time he does? What if he's finally figured out how to vanish completely? No smokescreens, no breadcrumbs, just gone?"

The group considered this concept proposed by Reed. For each member of the team, even the thought of such an idea was chilling. Not one of them wanted to accept this for a moment.

Carter shook his head. "I don't buy it. Barry's ego wouldn't let him just disappear. He's a puppet master, he thrives on control. He'd come back for the spotlight eventually. The question is when, and how hard he'll hit when he does."

Kranch leaned in, his gaze steady. "If he's out there, we'll be ready. But if we're wrong, if he's actually gone... then maybe we've finally won. Maybe."

Reed's uncertainty was gnawing at him. He glanced back at the fire, its light flickering across his face. "I've learned one thing about Barry," he said softly. "With him, nothing is ever what it seems."

The group fell silent once more, each man lost in the labyrinth of what-ifs and unanswered questions. The flame burned lower, its embers glowing faintly in the encroaching darkness. The weight of Barry's shadow might have lifted, but the doubt lingered, a haunting reminder that, even in defeat, The Architect's reach was long.

As the conversation lulled, Reed's phone buzzed sharply in his pocket, cutting through the quiet conversation. He glanced at the screen, *Secretary Kessler*. Without a word, he rose and stepped away, the sound of his boots muffled against the wooden planks of the wharf. The lake stretched out before him, its surface a mirror of the encroaching darkness as the sky faded into deep indigo.

"Kessler," Reed answered, his voice low. "What's the update?"

The Secretary's tone was calm but deliberately vague. "Reed, as promised, I'm following up with you. I apologize for the delay, it's been a busy time since we last spoke. You and your team did an outstanding job. Rest assured, Barry Cox is no longer a threat."

Reed tried to not let his frustration show. "That's great, sir. But where is he? How is he being held? When's the trial?"

There was a pause, and Kessler's voice took on an edge of practiced bureaucracy. "Reed, those details are classified. It's above your pay grade. Trust me when I say everything is being handled."

"Classified?" Reed snapped, stepping closer to the edge of the wharf, his reflection barely visible in the darkened water. "We risked everything to bring him in, and now you're telling me we don't even get to know where he is? How does that work?"

Kessler sighed, his tone growing firmer. "You did your part, Reed. Now it's time for us to do ours. I promise, some evidence related to

Barry will soon be declassified, and I'll make sure you get it when the time is right. But for now, you need to trust the system."

Reed stared out over the lake, his grip tightening around his phone. "Trust the system," he repeated, the disbelief heavy in his voice. "That's not exactly comforting, sir."

"Reed," Kessler replied, his tone softening just slightly, "I'm telling you, everything is under control. We'll be in touch."

The line went dead, leaving Reed alone in the quiet expanse of the wharf, the words *"under control"* ringing hollow in his ears. He stood there for a long moment, the cool night air brushing against his face as he processed the conversation.

When he returned, the team looked up expectantly. Kranch arched a brow, Carter leaned forward, and Grimes waited, his gaze sharp.

Reed sat with the team, exhaled heavily and shook his head. "He's saying everything is under control. But he won't tell me where Barry is. No trial date. No location. Nothing. Just keeps repeating 'Need to know' and 'Above your pay grade.'"

The group sat in reflective silence, the weight of Kessler's evasiveness lingering in the air. Reed stared into the burning embers, its crackling warmth a stark contrast to the cold uncertainty swirling in his mind.

They began to reason, speaking their thoughts out loud, voices low and cautious. Carter spoke first. "If Barry had escaped, Kessler would be in a full-blown panic. He'd be calling us back, throwing every resource at finding him again." Grimes nodded slightly. "Agreed. A guy like Kessler doesn't keep things quiet if the house is on fire. He'd need us back in play."

But doubt lingered, unspoken yet unmistakable. Reed rose and leaned against the wooden railing of the deck, the night air cool against his face. Finally, he voiced the thought that had been gnawing at the edges of his mind. "What if Kessler isn't telling us because he doesn't know? What if Barry slipped away again, leaving everyone, us, the agencies, the whole world, chasing shadows?"

Kranch unfolded his arms, the firelight casting harsh shadows across his hard, unreadable expression. His voice cut through the tension. "You all can believe whatever helps you sleep at night. Me? I'm not convinced."

His words hung in the air, heavy and final. A silence settled over the group, deeper than before, as night fully took hold outside. The firelight danced against the darkened windows, a fragile reminder that even in their moment of reflection, shadows still loomed large.

Reed remained standing, his gaze moving slowly over each of them. "I'm done," he said, his voice steady but carrying the weight of finality. "I'm walking away from all of it, the shadows, the hidden messages, the endless chase."

The words hung in the air, and the team watched him closely, waiting for him to continue. Reed drew a deep breath, as if unburdening himself. "I miss photography," he admitted, his tone softer now. "Real photography. Not surveillance, not hidden agendas. I want to take a photograph just because it's beautiful. No reason, no intelligence to gather, just light, composition, and a fleeting moment. Something simple. Honest."

Carter leaned forward, nodding in understanding. "I get it," he said, "It's about stepping out of the shadows. Finding clarity."

Kranch's expression was hard to read, but the faintest flicker of understanding crossed his features.

Grimes, always sharp and perceptive, gave Reed a small nod. He didn't say anything, he didn't need to. The gesture was enough.

Reed sighed, his shoulders relaxing finally after what felt like weeks of stress. "I don't know what's next," he admitted, looking out toward the dark lake beyond the cabin. "But I know it won't be this. No more secrets. No more running."

The fire burned softly, filling the space left by his words. It wasn't just an announcement; it was a declaration, a man reclaiming his life after years of living in the darkness.

Later that evening, Reed sat alone by the water's edge, the cool night air brushing against his face. His camera rested in his lap, its familiar weight grounding him in the moment. The moon hung high above, casting a silvery glow across the rippling surface of the lake, while the gentle lapping of the waves provided a quiet rhythm to his thoughts.

There were no orders to follow, no coded messages to decipher, no shadows lurking just out of sight. Reed was simply a photographer again. He lifted the camera, adjusting the lens with a practiced hand, instinct guiding his movements. The moonlight danced across the surface of the lake, shimmering like a thousand tiny stars. It wasn't perfect light, far from it, but Reed had worked with worse. His mind, trained by years of capturing fleeting moments under impossible conditions, kicked in automatically.

He dialed up the ISO, way up. The newer camera adjusted for excessive noise perfectly. Next came the shutter speed. He wanted to capture the softness of the night without overexposing the bright reflection of the moon. The f-stop... that was trickier. But Reed instinctively knew just what to do.

As he framed the shot, the years of training, countless hours spent perfecting his craft, came rushing back. It was muscle memory now, second nature. The feel of the camera, the way his fingers danced over the dials, the quiet rhythm of adjusting, composing, and waiting for just the right moment. It wasn't just technical skill... it was instinct.

Reed's breathing slowed as he focused. The silence around him deepened. No mission. No cover to maintain. No coded sequence to pass along. Just him, the camera, and the moonlight. He pressed the shutter. The soft click broke the stillness, echoing faintly across the water. For that brief moment, he wasn't a spy. He was just Reed Sawyer, a photographer capturing the beauty of a quiet night.

And for the first time in a long time, that was enough.

Reed lowered the camera, studying the image on the back of his camera. The dust had settled, the chaos of Barry Cox and PPI seemingly behind him. But somewhere, deep in his chest, a small ember of doubt refused to die, a quiet whisper that the shadows weren't entirely gone, and maybe they never would be.

For now, though, he focused on this single frame, this moment of clarity captured in perfect light, even as shadows lingered at the edges of his viewfinder.

28

AFTERIMAGE

Time marched on, indifferent to the chaos it left in its wake. Four months since Barry Cox vanished into the eastern sky, and the world of PPI had transformed beyond recognition. The once-shadowy organization now presented itself as nothing more than a photographer's networking site, its covert operations dissolved, its operatives scattered or reassigned. Pro4uM.com's hidden channels were stripped clean, the cryptic messages and coded assignments replaced by mundane discussions about camera gear and lighting techniques. Even the regional offices had been quietly shuttered, leaving only the New York headquarters to maintain the facade of normalcy.

The firestorm of Barry's capture had dwindled into silence, fading from headlines and conversations. No cryptic messages, no dead drops, no coded warnings flashed across secure channels. Not even a whisper of Barry's name echoed through the dark corners where operatives once traded secrets. It was as if PPI's shadow operations had never existed, scrubbed clean from history, leaving only the pristine surface of a professional photography organization behind.

Reed leaned back in his chair, his gaze wandered around his

small studio in New Orleans. The afternoon sun streamed through the window, its warmth a stark contrast to the cold knot of unease in his chest. On his desk sat his camera, a tool that had once been his sanctuary, now reduced to a reminder of times gone by. The framed photograph of a moonlit lake caught his eye. He had taken it months ago during a rare moment of peace, hoping to capture a sense of tranquility. Now, it felt like a taunt, its stillness mocking his restless thoughts.

PPI had gone silent, too. No assignments. No covert missions. Not even a routine photography gig. It was as if Reed no longer existed in their system. He had always thought the photography cover was a brilliant facade, PPI's way of blending operatives seamlessly into the world. But now, with the absence of missions, the line between facade and reality had blurred. Was PPI really just a photography organization now? Had the covert side dissolved, or was he being frozen out? The questions gnawed at him, feeding his growing frustration.

And then there was Secretary Kessler. After all Reed had done, risking his life, unraveling Barry's web, protecting Kessler from an assassin's bullet, there had been no acknowledgment, no updates. Every time Reed reached out for information about Barry's location or situation, he was met with the same empty platitudes: "Classified," "Above your pay grade," "Trust the process." Kessler's reassurances, once steadying, now felt hollow. Reed had given everything for the mission, and in return, he was left with a void.

Reed pushed away from his desk and started pacing the room. His footsteps echoed in the quiet studio, the rhythm as erratic as his thoughts. Barry's empire had crumbled. His operatives were scattered, arrested, or dead. And yet, the silence didn't feel like victory. Barry Cox was calculated, manipulative, always a step ahead. Reed couldn't shake the feeling that the quiet was part of Barry's design, a way to lull his enemies into complacency.

He stopped at the window, staring out at the street below. A delivery truck rumbled by, its engine drowning out the faint hum of the city. Life moved on, as if Barry Cox and PPI's shadows had never existed. Reed, however, felt trapped. His purpose, once so clear, now felt like smoke slipping through his fingers. He had spent years living in the margins, walking the line between photographer and operative, light and shadow. But now, without missions to anchor him, he was adrift.

The studio felt stifling. He grabbed his jacket and stepped outside, the cool breeze brushing against his face. As he walked aimlessly through the streets, his thoughts kept circling back to the same questions. Why hadn't Barry surfaced? Where was the trial Kessler had promised? Why was PPI treating him like a ghost?

He passed a café and caught a glimpse of his reflection in the window. The man staring back at him looked older, wearier. The once-bright red in his beard had dulled to a muted gray, and his eyes carried the weight of too many sleepless nights. He thought of his team, Kranch, Carter, Grimes. They had scattered, each trying to rebuild their lives.

Reed envied their ability to move on. He wanted to believe it was over, that Barry was truly gone, that PPI's covert side was dismantled. But the questions, the silence, they wouldn't let him rest. He reached into his pocket and pulled out his phone, scrolling aimlessly through old photos. Each image felt like a snapshot of a different life, a life where missions had purpose, where the shadows held answers.

His thumb hovered over Kessler's contact. He wanted to call, to demand the truth, to force the Secretary to give him something, anything, that would bring closure. But he knew the answer would be the same. Reed sighed, slipping the phone back into his pocket.

As he turned toward home, the breeze carried a faint whisper of hope, a reminder that, even in the silence, there was light to be found. Reed wasn't sure he believed it, but for now, it was enough to keep him moving.

Back at his studio, Reed tried to bury himself in the familiar. The sunlit space was a refuge, its tall windows casting golden light over the shelves of camera equipment and the worn wooden floors.

Framed prints adorned the walls, landscapes, candid portraits, and moments frozen in time that once represented the purest form of his craft. The faint, comforting aroma of freshly brewed coffee mingled with the metallic tang of camera gear, grounding him in a world far removed from the chaos he'd left behind.

Sitting at his desk, Reed adjusted the contrast on a set of images from a recent shoot. The rhythmic click of his mouse and the hum of his computer filled the silence. Each adjustment brought the photo closer to perfection, the act of editing a therapeutic escape. For a brief moment, it was just him, the light, and the frame, a reminder of why he'd fallen in love with photography in the first place.

But even as he focused on the images, his mind wandered. His hands moved automatically, sharpening edges and softening shadows, while the nagging unease gnawed at the edges of his thoughts. Was PPI really dismantled, or had it retreated further into the shadows, waiting for the dust to settle?

The buzz of his phone broke the quiet, vibrating against the desk. Reed reached for it without thinking, expecting a notification from Pro4uM.com, though the site had been eerily silent for months. Instead, the screen lit up with a message from Secretary Kessler.

Reed hesitated. Messages from Kessler were rare these days. His thumb hovered over the notification before tapping to open it. The message was brief, just a few words, but it hit like a hammer:

"Barry Cox is dead. Officially confirmed. This image has been declassified. Case closed."

Below the text was a single attachment. Reed tapped it, and the screen filled with an image that sent a chill down his spine. It was a photo of a helicopter, partially submerged, floating lifelessly in open waters off the coast of Puerto Rico. The once-pristine black paint was scorched and peeling, the tail section bent at an unnatural angle. The water around it was calm, deceptively serene, reflecting the broken machine like a mirror.

Reed stared at the image, his brow furrowed. The accompanying message was definitive, too definitive. There was no room for ambiguity, no mention of further investigation, no details about the circumstances of the crash. Just a blanket statement: *Barry Cox is dead.*

He leaned back in his chair, holding the phone at arm's length, as if putting distance between himself and the news would make it easier to process. A part of him wanted to believe it, to accept that the nightmare was over, that Barry's death marked the end of his manipulation, his schemes, his empire. But another part of him, the part honed by years of deception and shadow work, bristled at the finality of it. If anyone could fake a death convincingly, it was Barry Cox.

Reed zoomed in on the image, his photographer's eye scanning every detail. The markings on the helicopter were faint but still legible. There were no visible bodies, no debris field. Just the helicopter, floating in eerie isolation. The longer he stared, the more questions formed. How had this image been taken? Who had captured it? Why had it taken four months for this to surface?

He dropped the phone onto the desk, running a hand through his hair. The words *"Case closed"* echoed in his mind, but they felt hollow. He glanced at the photo he'd been editing on his monitor, a serene lakeside at dawn. It was a scene of calm, but in his chest, the storm raged on.

Reed grabbed his coffee cup, now lukewarm, and walked to the window. The street outside bustled with ordinary life, oblivious to the doubts and questions consuming him. The world moved on, as it always did, but Reed couldn't shake the feeling that he was having.

Reed couldn't let it go. Transferring the image from his phone to his computer, he stared at it on the larger screen. The wreckage seemed to taunt him, each pixel a whisper of something unresolved. Leaning forward, elbows resting on the desk, and fingers tapping against his lips, he scrutinized every detail. The image was haunting, the charred helicopter floating eerily on calm waters, its shattered frame a stark contrast against the placid surface. The shadow of the wreckage rippled faintly beneath the waves, almost ghostlike. But something didn't sit right.

"Four months of silence," Reed muttered under his breath. "Why hasn't this information shown up in the media?" He shook his head. Four months. That's how long the world had gone without hearing a whisper about Barry Cox. No sightings. No coded messages. No trails of influence left behind.

Reed leaned back, his chair creaking. "If Barry really died in that crash," he said aloud to no one, "why does this feel like a loose thread waiting to unravel?"

The thought circled in his mind like a vulture. Reed let his fingers fly across the keyboard with precision. He pulled the declassified image into his advanced forensic photo-enhancement software, the same tool he had used countless times during his covert missions to decode PPI's visual intelligence, hummed to life. The software was a gift and a curse, its capabilities were unparalleled, but it often fed his obsessive need to seek answers, even when none existed.

The helicopter image filled his screen as he began his methodical examination. It's glossy black paint was scarred and peeling, its tail section twisted at an unnatural angle.

First, he adjusted the chromatic values, isolating specific color channels. The software parsed through layers of digital information, breaking down the image's composite structure. Something about the water's reflection caught his eye, a subtle inconsistency in the light diffraction patterns.

"Level adjustment first," he muttered, fingers dancing across the keys. "Then wavelength isolation." The image shifted, its colors separating into distinct spectrums. Reed's eyes narrowed as he studied the histograms. The peaks weren't quite right, there were micro-variations in the shadow gradients that shouldn't be there.

He switched to dimensional analysis, examining the helicopter's position relative to the water line. The angle of the wreckage, the way it sat in the water, something felt off. Reed pulled up a reference diagram of the helicopter model, overlaying it against the crash photo. The proportions matched, but the distribution of weight suggested by the wreckage's position didn't align with the aircraft's center of gravity.

"Show me what you're hiding," Reed whispered, initiating a deep-scan pixel analysis. The software began isolating individual sections of the image, hunting for artifacts, compression abnormalities, or signs of digital manipulation. That's when he spotted it, a faint distortion pattern around the tail section, barely visible to the untrained eye.

His pulse quickened as he zoomed in, enhancing the resolution. There, almost lost in the pixelation, a faint logo, almost imperceptible was what appeared to be a military insignia. It flickered in and out of focus as he adjusted the contrast, like a ghost refusing to fully materialize. But why? And was it even real?

Reed's mind raced. "Was it there originally, or is it just a trick of the light?" He couldn't tell. He toggled different filters, sharpening edges and isolating colors, but the result was the same, a faint, almost ghostly mark that could mean everything or nothing.

He leaned closer, staring so intently that the screen seemed to blur. His mind, trained to question and analyze, couldn't help but run wild. Was this proof of a deeper conspiracy? A clue that Barry had connections to military operatives? Or was this just the last echoes of paranoia clinging to his thoughts after years of living in the shadows?

Reed sighed, his frustration mounting. "I'm chasing ghosts," he muttered, rubbing his temples. But even as he tried to dismiss the thought, the questions lingered. Why had it taken four months for this image to surface? Why was it released as "declassified" instead of announced publicly? And most of all, why did this feel so incomplete, so far from the definitive ending it was supposed to be?

He stared at the screen for hours, toggling the same adjustments, rechecking the same angles. His coffee had long since gone cold, the sun outside sinking behind the buildings. The faint glow of his monitor illuminated his tired face as his thoughts waged war between logic and instinct.

Finally, Reed exhaled deeply. "No!" he said emphatically. "I'm just being paranoid. Years of PPI training... it's got me questioning everything. Seeing patterns where none exist."

He stared at the image one last time before closing the program. "This loose end needs to be closed," he told himself. "It's over. Barry's dead. I'm walking away."

Reed switched off his monitor, plunging the room into darkness except for the faint light spilling through the windows. He stood and stretched, the weight of his decision settling on his shoulders, relief, finality, done. It wasn't peace, not truly, but it was the closest he'd come to it in months.

As he walked toward the window, gazing out at the quiet street below, a thought gnawed at the edge of his mind. He pushed it away, determined not to let it take root. "It's done," he whispered to himself, as if saying it enough times would make it true.

But deep down, in a part of him he couldn't silence, a single question remained, whispering just loud enough to be heard: *Is it over?*

A few months later, as Reed was sifting through his mail, he could hardly believe it when he opened the official looking envelope and found an Investigation and Legal Consultation document to appear at PPI Headquarters in New York. For a fleeting moment, he considered crumpling it up and tossing it in the trash. *Let them come and get me*, he thought bitterly. *All I ever did was follow orders*. But the more he stared at the summons, the more curiosity gnawed at him. What could they possibly want to discuss with him now? Could it be about Barry? Was there finally some closure to be found? Or was this just another game, another layer of bewilderment from an organization built on shadows?

The flight to New York felt surreal. Reed watched the landscape blur beneath him, each mile bringing him closer to a confrontation he'd been avoiding. He'd walked these halls before, but always as an operative, always with purpose. Now he was returning as... what? A loose end to be tied up? A liability to be managed?

Security was tighter than he remembered. The lobby of PPI headquarters gleamed with the same corporate sterility, but the guards' gazes lingered longer, their scrutiny more obvious. They escorted him through a maze of corridors he knew all too well.

Finally, they led him to a conference room deep within the building. The door clicked shut behind him with an ominous finality. Reed stood for a moment, taking in the sterile space.

As Reed settled into the chair facing the door, he couldn't help but appreciate the irony. He'd spent years living in PPI's shadows, and now here he was, about to face them in the cold light of day.

The air conditioning was set too cold, making the room feel more like an interrogation chamber than a corporate office. The walls were an uninspired shade of gray, stripped of any warmth or personality, while the fluorescent lights overhead buzzed faintly, casting an unflattering, clinical glow on everything in the room. The polished table stretched long and vast before him like a void, a chasm he knew better than to underestimate. Every detail in the room seemed designed to unsettle, to keep him on edge. It was working.

As Reed sat there, he couldn't help but remember how different this place had felt just a few months ago. Back then, he and Kranch had roamed these very halls, slipping past unsuspecting staff and accessing hidden corridors as they planted devices designed to expose PPI's darkest secrets. The adrenaline of those moments lingered in his memory, the sound of their hurried footsteps, the muffled beeps of their covert tech syncing with PPI's systems, and the faint tension in Kranch's voice as he muttered warnings about incoming patrols. They had turned this seemingly harmless corporate facade into a battlefield, unraveling the web of deceit that Barry Cox had spun so meticulously.

Even the faint hum of the fluorescent lights now reminded Reed of that night at SYNC, when everything came crashing down. The image of Barry's empire collapsing, piece by piece, flashed in his mind. The carefully planted devices, the encrypted files they'd pulled, the codes they'd deciphered, all of it had led to this moment. And yet, sitting here, anticipating the interrogation he thought would be coming, it felt like nothing had changed. The walls that had once hidden corruption now felt impenetrable, and the organization that claimed to have rebranded itself as a harmless professional network seemed as elusive and manipulative as ever.

Just then, they entered and sat across from him, three PPI lawyers, their tailored suits impeccable, their polished shoes gleaming. Two men and a woman. They radiated a quiet menace, their expressions unreadable, yet their eyes sharp and unyielding. It seemed to Reed that the woman was the lead lawyer. One of the lawyers, a silver-haired man with a voice as smooth as velvet, began. "Mr. Sawyer, let's begin by addressing the obvious: there is no Private Protection Initiative. Officially, it doesn't exist. It never existed."

Reed tilted his head slightly, letting the words hang in the air like an echo refusing to fade. His gaze moved slowly from one lawyer to the next, studying their faces. Each one sat with a practiced stillness, their expressions carefully neutral, professionals in the art of concealing intent. Their eyes were sharp, calculating, like lawyers.

"Is that so?" Reed's tone was calm, but there was a quiet edge to his voice, the kind that suggested a storm might follow. He leaned back in his chair, his fingers loosely interlaced, an air of deliberate nonchalance masking his simmering frustration. "Because I'd say my experiences tell a very different story."

One of the lawyers, the youngest of the trio, shifted ever so slightly in his seat, his polished façade wavering for a fraction of a second. Reed caught the movement, filing it away as if he'd won a small but significant point in an unseen game.

"Do they?" the lead lawyer asked, her tone smooth, almost too casual. The faintest hint of a smirk tugged at the corner of her lips, as if she were daring him to say more. Reed met her gaze head-on, the memory of SYNC and the chaos he'd helped unleash flashing in his mind. All of the encrypted messages, Pro4uM.com, Vienna. For a moment, the sterile conference room seemed to fade.

He shook off the memories, focusing on the present. "Oh, they do," he replied, his words deliberate. "And I'd wager if we compared notes, your version of reality would look pretty thin next to mine."

The room fell silent, the hum of the overhead lights filling the void. Reed didn't break eye contact, refusing to surrender any ground to the lawyers who thought they could rewrite the truth.

One of the lawyers, the silver-haired one with the smooth, oily voice, leaned forward slightly. His tone was steady, almost rehearsed, and his expression betrayed no hint of doubt. "We're not here to debate your experiences, Mr. Sawyer. We're here to clarify your involvement, or, rather, your lack thereof, with an organization that does not, and has never, existed."

Reed leaned forward, resting his arms on the table, his fingers laced together. "Right. Because an organization that doesn't exist somehow managed to recruit me, send me to Vienna, and nearly get me killed. But sure, let's pretend it's all a figment of my imagination."

The second lawyer, the younger man with horn-rimmed glasses and an unnervingly calm demeanor, cut in. "You're mistaken, Mr. Sawyer. What you're describing are merely coincidences. Misunderstandings. Professional Photographers Institute has always been, and will always remain, a legitimate organization supporting the craft of photography."

Reed's lips curled into a faint smirk. "Coincidences? You're telling me encrypted messages, covert assignments, and international chases were just me misinterpreting things?"

The horn-rimmed lawyer barely blinked, his tone laced with condescension. "What we're saying, Mr. Sawyer, is that you've tragically overestimated the importance of your little assignments. Any so-called connections to, oh, I don't know, *espionage,* are clearly the byproduct of your vivid and wildly overactive imagination. But hey, points for creativity."

Reed's eyes narrowed. "Why do you say that? Oh, I know, because I'm just a photographer. A man with a camera and nothing else." His tone was heavy with sarcasm, but the lawyers didn't bite. Instead, they exchanged glances, their silence louder than any argument.

The tension in the room thickened. Reed's pulse quickened, but he kept his breathing steady, his expression neutral. He needed to stay sharp. These weren't ordinary lawyers, they were trained for this. Deflect, deny, dismiss. That was their game. He leaned back in his chair again, forcing himself to appear relaxed. "So, let me get this straight," he said, his voice cutting through the quiet. "PPI never existed, and yet here I am, sitting across from three lawyers who seem very invested in convincing me otherwise."

The lead lawyer folded her hands on the table, her expression unyielding. "Mr. Sawyer, we're here to ensure that your... misconceptions don't create unnecessary complications. That's all."

"Right," Reed muttered, his fingers drumming against the table. "Typical lawyering."

The silver-haired lawyer, a sharp-eyed man spoke again. His voice was calm, almost disarmingly so. "Mr. Sawyer, let's not make this adversarial. You've had an exceptional career as a photographer. That's all this ever was, a career. Let's not complicate it with wild allegations."

Reed tilted his head, watching him carefully. He was good, too good. Every word he said was calculated, designed to disarm him. "Wild allegations?" he repeated. "Let me guess, next, you'll tell me I've imagined all the encrypted messages, the assignments, the near-death experiences?"

The man seemed like he was trying to smile, but it was very faint. "We're not saying you've imagined anything, Mr. Sawyer. We're simply saying that your interpretation of events may not align with reality."

Reed exhaled slowly. The room felt colder now, the air heavy with tension. Finally, he made his decision. "You know what? I'm done. I'm out. No more missions. No more encrypted messages. I'm walking away from all of it."

The lawyers exchanged brief glances. The lead lawyer broke the silence. "Walking away, Mr. Sawyer? From what, exactly?"

Reed met her gaze evenly. "From PPI. Or whatever you want to call it. I want to officially resign. I'm going back to photography. Real photography. No agendas. No shadows."

The lawyers exchanged another set of looks, and this time, faint smirks appeared on all their faces. The lead lawyer spoke, her tone dripping with condescension. "Mr. Sawyer, that's all PPI ever was, a tool for photographers. You're always welcome at the Professional Photographers Institute."

The words hit Reed like a gut punch, their double meaning hanging heavy in the air. He stood slowly, his gaze moving over each of them. "Right," he said quietly. "Well, you'll forgive me if I don't stick around for small talk."

The lead lawyer's smirk widened ever so slightly. "Of course. We wish you the best in your future endeavors, Mr. Sawyer."

Reed turned and got out of there as fast as he could, his footsteps echoing in the sterile corridor. The conversation replayed in his mind, every word a calculated move in a game he was no longer willing to play. As he stepped outside into the crisp New York air, he exhaled deeply, the weight of the encounter both pressing down and a relief at the same time. The lawyers had won the verbal sparring match, but Reed knew one thing for certain, he was done being their pawn.

Reed pushed open the massive glass doors of PPI Headquarters, stepping out into freedom at last. The heavy doors closed behind him with a muted *thud*, and for a moment, he stood still on the steps, staring ahead. This was it. The last time he would ever cross through these doors. The towering building loomed behind him, its sharp lines and mirrored glass catching the reflection of the city's ceaseless motion. But for Reed, this was a moment of stillness, a moment to sever himself from the life he'd lived within those walls.

Without hesitation, he started walking. His footsteps felt purposeful, even as his mind swirled with conflicting thoughts. The river. He didn't know why, but that's where his feet were carrying him. There was something final, something cleansing about the idea of standing by the water's edge, leaving everything behind, and letting it all drift away.

The city buzzed around him, taxis honking, pedestrians rushing past, snippets of conversations floating in the air. But Reed moved through it all like a ghost, detached and unaffected. The sound of the river grew louder as he approached, a low, steady hum that drowned out the city's chaos.

Reaching the edge of the water, Reed stopped. The river stretched before him, calm on the surface but full of hidden currents below, like his own life, he thought ironically. He pulled his phone from his pocket, holding it in his hand as if weighing its significance. This wasn't just a device; it was the lifeline that had tethered him to a world of secrets, lies, and shadows.

For a moment, Reed hesitated. He had to urge to hurl it into the river. Was this the right thing to do? Could he really walk away? His thumb hovered over the screen, and then, with a decisive breath, he began the process. Methodically, he wiped every trace, every log, every connection. Cryptic messaging apps were deleted one by one. He scrolled through the encrypted chats that had once buzzed with activity, silent now for months. Nothing. So, he deleted all of them as well.

Finally, he opened Pro4uM.com, his fingers moving instinctively through the familiar interface. He half-expected something to be there, some subtle hint, some last breadcrumb left behind. But the site looked normal. Innocent. Photography threads, lighting tips, lens reviews. No cryptic codes. No hidden messages. Just a thriving community of photographers sharing their passion. It was almost... jarring. Reed stared at the screen, his mind was confused. Could it all have been real?

"I know it was real!" he muttered under his breath, shaking his head. He knew what he knew. He'd lived it. He'd survived it. Barry's empire, PPI's covert operations, it was all too real to dismiss. But now, standing here, it felt like it had all dissolved into smoke. The shadows that once haunted every corner of his life seemed to have vanished.

The phone screen dimmed in his hand, pulling him back to the present. Reed gripped the device tightly, then flipped it over, staring at its black surface. This was it. The final act. The symbolic severing of his ties to the shadow world. He gripped the phone tightly, preparing to fling it into the deep water of the river. The river's edge lapped gently against the stones, as if urging him, do it, let go.

But before he did, Reed allowed himself one last thought: *Was it really over?* He stood there, the phone gripped tightly in his hands, its weight feeling far heavier than the sum of its parts. He whispered to no one, "No shadows. No whispers. Just light." His voice was quiet, almost swallowed by the gentle lapping of the water below. "Maybe it really is over."

Reed took a breath, his fingers gripping ever tighter. He could already picture the faint ripple spreading across the water, as the phone would sink to the bottom of the river. Broken, useless, destroyed, sinking and taking everything it represented with it. This was it, the final severance. His breath hitched. "Let's do it." He said to himself.

Then, *ping.*

The sound pierced the quiet like a gunshot. Reed froze. His eyes darted to the phone's screen, now glowing faintly in the dim light. One single notification. His pulse quickened as he brought the device closer. There, in bold letters, was an encrypted message. Familiar. Too familiar.

Reed's stomach churned. It was the exact same message he had received months ago on the flight to Vienna, sent in the same cryptic way. The message that had set everything in motion: *"Reed, we need to talk. Now."*

But this time, something was different. The message wasn't unsigned, anonymous, shrouded in mystery.

It bore a name. A signature.

Tammy Stark.

Reed stared at the screen, the glowing letters searing into his mind. His hand tightened around the phone, pulling it back from the edge. The shadows he had just convinced himself were gone? They were back. His thoughts raced, colliding with the memory of Tammy, the Pro4uM.com administrator, his brief romance, her quiet brilliance. She had always been in the background, part of the machinery of PPI, but never directly involved, or so he thought.

The river was forgotten. Reed's breath came shallow as a wave of questions swelled in his chest. *Why now? Why her? How much did Tammy know?*

The words on the screen pulled him back in: *"We need to talk. Now."*

29
SOFT FOCUS

Reed froze, the cold air from the river biting at his skin, his phone still poised over the water. The faint glow of the screen lit his face, reflecting the message that had stopped him in his tracks. His breath hung in the air, visible in the chill of the evening, as his eyes locked onto the name.

"Tammy Stark."

He said it aloud, the words escaping his lips without thought. The sound of her name against the quiet hum of the city felt out of place, like an answer he hadn't been looking for but now couldn't ignore. He blinked hard, his mind trying to make sense of the message. Slowly, he lowered the phone, pulling it closer to his face for another look, as if proximity might change what he was seeing.

The river lapped gently against the rocks below, a faint reminder of the decision he'd been about to make. Reed stared at the name on the screen, his voice breaking the stillness again. "Tammy Stark? The Pro4uM.com admin? That cannot be possible."

The words tumbled out in disbelief, yet they hung in the air, gaining weight with each passing second. Reed turned, pacing a few steps along the river's edge. The distant hum of traffic blending with the whisper of the water. Tammy Stark, the name was so ordinary, so familiar in its predictability. Yet, now, it loomed over him, casting a shadow on everything he thought he understood.

"Tammy Stark," he said again, louder this time, as if testing the reality of it. The name felt strange against the backdrop of all he had experienced, the chases, the cryptic messages, the betrayals. How could the seemingly unremarkable administrator of Pro4uM.com, the woman who managed discussions on lighting ratios and camera settings, be the one reaching out now, after months of silence?

Reed tightened his grip on the phone, the cold metal pressing against his palm. The message was there, undeniable, simple in its clarity: *Reed, we need to talk. Now.* And the signature, Tammy Stark, was unmistakable. The air around him seemed to thicken as memories flooded back: the cryptic posts, the carefully coded warnings, the calculated way every piece of this puzzle had fallen into place.

The river shimmered, its surface calm, mocking the storm building in Reed's chest. He paced back toward the railing, leaning against it, gripping the cold steel. His mind raced, trying to connect dots that had seemed scattered and unrelated. If Tammy Stark had been behind this all along, what did that mean for everything he thought he knew? And why now? Why, after months of silence, had she chosen this moment to reveal herself?

Reed stared at the message on his phone for another long moment, the urge to hurl it into the river fading with each second. His thumb quickly swiping to his contacts. A call to Tammy Stark was long overdue. Whatever this was, answers, closure, or yet another twist, he couldn't walk away now.

He tapped her name. The line barely buzzed once before a voice came through, crisp and direct.

"I see you got my message, Reed. Or should I say, *messages*?"

Reed paused, her words hitting like a jolt of electricity. "That's been you? All this time?" His tone was equal parts disbelief and accusation.

"Every last one," Tammy said, her voice calm but laced with

something unspoken. "But this isn't a conversation for the phone. We need to talk. Can you meet me now?"

Reed's grip on the phone tightened. "Yes," he said without hesitation. "Where are you?"

"Turn around," Tammy replied, her tone almost casual. After all, they were making plans to unravel months of chaos. "Go one block along the river. You can't miss it, The Cat Chat Café. I'm inside, on the right."

Reed glanced over his shoulder instinctively, scanning the shadowy stretch of the riverside as if he might spot her watching him. But there was nothing, just the quiet murmur of the city and the faint glow of distant streetlights.

"The Cat Chat Café?" he repeated, the name feeling absurd in the context of their cryptic exchange.

"You'll understand when you get here," Tammy said, her tone giving nothing away. Then, just as quickly as she'd answered, the line went dead.

Reed lowered the phone slowly, his heart pounding harder than he'd expected. He slipped the phone into his jacket pocket and started walking, his steps steady, though nothing in his head made sense. The Cat Chat Café? Of all the places for an endgame to begin, it had to be a café named after cats. The absurdity wasn't lost on him, but neither was the gravity of what he was walking into.

Reed pushed open the door to The Cat Chat Café, a soft chime announcing his entrance. The warm aroma of freshly brewed coffee mingled with the subtle scent of baked goods, creating an inviting atmosphere that contrasted sharply with the cold evening outside. His eyes scanned the room, quickly landing on Tammy Stark. She sat at a corner table, a laptop open before her and a kitten curled contentedly in her lap, its gentle purring visible even from a distance.

As he approached, Tammy looked up, a welcoming smile spreading across her face. "Reed," she greeted, her tone both familiar and mysterious.

"Well, hello Tammy," he replied, taking the seat opposite her.

Before he could say more, a beautiful red-haired woman wearing cute glasses appeared at their table, her demeanor cheerful.

"Hi there! Can I get you something to drink?" she asked.

"Yes, coffee, black," Reed responded, appreciating the simplicity amidst the complexity of his thoughts.

As the woman walked away, Tammy gestured towards her. "That's Scarlett. She owns this place. I love the vibe here, sometimes I sit here all day long doing Pro4uM duties."

Reed's focus returned to Tammy. She was relaxed, at ease, as though they were old friends catching up rather than participants in a high-stakes game of espionage.

Her smile grew wider, a glint of mischief in her green eyes. "Oh, by the way, nice move on the John Smith alias. I left that login active, just in case you want to use it again."

Reed raised an eyebrow, a mixture of surprise and curiosity flickering across his face. "You knew about that?"

Tammy chuckled softly, gently stroking the kitten in her lap. "Reed, there's a lot more I know. And this evening, it's time you knew too."

The casual, warm setting of the café, with its soft lighting and the gentle hum of quiet conversations, made Reed feel that this really was the perfect spot for the conversation that was about to take place. He took a deep breath, bracing himself for the answers he had long sought, now finally within reach.

"Okay, Tammy," he said urgently. "You have got to tell me the story. All this time, you knew everything?" His words came out in a rush, each one sharper than the last. "The messages, the Light and the Shadows, the code. It was like you were guiding me, step by step. Why? What's going on?" He leaned closer, his eyes narrowing. "I have to know."

Tammy tilted her head slightly, studying him with an almost amused expression. She took a slow sip of her tea, as though she had all the time in the world. But Reed could already feel his patience thinning. He was ready to know all of the answers.

"Reed," she began, her voice calm, measured, and maddeningly composed, "I always knew this conversation would happen, but I didn't expect it to be in a cat café." She chuckled lightly, rubbing the kitten's soft ears. "But you're right. You deserve answers. All of them."

The way she danced around the question made him a bit crazy, but he bit back the urge to push harder. He had waited months for this moment; a few more minutes wouldn't kill him.

Tammy set her tea down, the smile fading from her lips. Her tone shifted, taking on a gravity Reed hadn't heard before. "It's not as simple as you think. Guiding you... that's not exactly what I'd call it. Let's just say... I was there to make sure the pieces fell into place." She met his gaze directly, her eyes sharp and unwavering. "You were the one moving the chessboard, Reed. I just made sure you didn't miss the right moves."

Reed blinked, caught off guard. "Pieces? Moves? You're talking in riddles, Tammy."

"Am I?" She said softly, leaning back. "Or have I just been making sure you're ready for what you're about to learn?"

The cryptic response only deepened Reed's frustration, but it also fanned the flames of his curiosity. Whatever Tammy was holding back, it felt big, bigger than he'd realized. For months, he had tried to unravel layers of deception, but now, sitting across from the person who seemed to have orchestrated it all, he was finally close to the truth.

"Start from the beginning," Reed said, his voice steady, though every nerve in his body felt on edge. "Tell me everything."

Tammy shifted in her seat, as the kitten yawned and stretched in her lap. She took a deep breath, her gaze steady on Reed. "To understand this, Reed, you need to know that it started long before either of us realized. Long before you ever picked up a camera with PPI's agenda behind it."

She leaned forward slightly, her voice soft, as though unraveling a memory she hadn't revisited in years. "Marcus was married to Lisa, one of my closest friends from college. Lisa was the kind of friend you could tell anything to, your secrets, your fears, your wildest dreams, and know she'd never judge you for a second. She was like family. And when she married Marcus, it was clear she'd found someone just as brilliant and intuitive as she was. Marcus had this way of noticing things other people missed. He was sharp, always asking questions, always observing."

"Lisa and Sydney, Barry's third wife, were inseparable. And through them, the rest of us became this little circle. Marcus, Lisa, Sydney, and me. Even after Barry and Sydney divorced, we stayed connected. The four of us would get together from time to time, sharing meals, swapping stories, just... being friends. It felt easy, comfortable."

"They all knew my close ties to the professional photography industry, of course. Marcus was curious about the work I did with Pro4uM, and Barry, well, he never missed a chance to pick my brain about cameras or gear. And of course, he was always curious about the Admins and Moderator associated with the running of the Pro4uM. I thought nothing of it at the time. Friends ask questions, right? But looking back... it all feels so deliberate now, like every question was him gathering intel, assessing me."

She exhaled softly, with a sadness coming across her face. "Back then, I didn't see it. None of us did. It felt normal, until it didn't."

Tammy paused, her expression darkening as her fingers traced the rim of her tea cup, the memory visibly weighing on her. "Marcus started confiding in me about Barry, not all at once, but in bits and pieces, like he was testing the waters. At first, it was small things, quirks about how Barry ran his business. He had this unnerving way of always being ten steps ahead, like he already knew how a situation would play out before it even began. Marcus would talk about deals Barry closed that didn't feel clean, where too much money changed hands for too little explanation. And then there were the people, people who crossed Barry or got too close to something they shouldn't have. They didn't just fade into the background; they vanished, like they'd been erased."

She shook her head slowly, her voice dipping lower. "At first, I shrugged it off. Barry was powerful, sure. Everyone knew that. He had connections, influence, charisma, the kind of guy who could charm you into trusting him while robbing you blind. But every now and then, Marcus... well, let's just say he had a flair for overreacting. He saw patterns in things most people wouldn't notice, and I thought maybe he was reading too much into Barry's moves. I told myself it was just Marcus being Marcus. You know, little brother and all."

She took a deep breath and a sip of her tea. "And then, there was Barry's attitude about marriage. At the time, it didn't seem like a red flag, people get married and divorced all the time. No one gave it a second thought. Barry had this way of making his divorces seem almost... inevitable and normal, like they were just a natural progression. 'Irreconcilable differences,' he'd say with a shrug, and everyone would nod along, accepting it. It's only now, looking back, that it's so clear, every marriage ended when the wife got too close to something Barry didn't want her to see. Sydney talked about it later, how she'd started piecing together things that didn't add up, bank statements, meetings he'd leave for at odd hours, people he referred to in whispers. But hindsight is 20/20, right? At the time, we were just friends watching him move on to the next chapter, thinking, 'Well, that's just Barry.' No one saw the pattern until it was too late."

Tammy glanced at Reed, her eyes sharp, the weight of her words heavier than ever. "But then the details got darker. Marcus started talking about how Barry didn't just control people, he destroyed them. Financially, emotionally, even physically, if it came to that. He had no limits, no boundaries. Everything and everyone was expendable if it served his purpose. And Marcus? He'd started to realize he wasn't Barry's little brother anymore. And he wasn't his ally either. Marcus realized that, like so many others in Barry's world, he had become a liability."

She hesitated, her eyes distant, as if pulling the memory from a deep, hidden place. Her fingers fidgeted with the edge of her sleeve, betraying the weight of what she was about to say. "It was late, the kind of late where everything feels heavier, quieter. Marcus showed up at my house, pale, shaking, carrying this enormous file box. I remember teasing him, asking if he was moving in." A fleeting, hollow smile passed across her lips. "But he didn't laugh. Not even a little.

"He put the box on my kitchen counter and looked at me, Reed. Really looked at me, like he was trying to figure out if he could trust me with something he couldn't even say aloud. 'Tammy,' he said, his voice shaking, 'if something happens to me, if I go missing, Barry killed me.'"

Her voice cracked slightly as she continued. "I laughed. I actually laughed, Reed. I mean, Barry? Kill Marcus? His *brother*? It sounded so absurd, like something out of a bad crime novel. I even told him to stop being dramatic. But he didn't stop. He said it again, slower this time. 'If I disappear, Tammy, it's Barry. Don't trust anyone.'"

Tammy's expression darkened. "I still didn't believe him. Not then. But he made me promise to keep the box safe and to go through it if anything happened to him. And then…" Her voice dropped, her words slowing. "And then Marcus disappeared."

She exhaled shakily, her gaze dropping to the table. "That's when I realized, he wasn't joking. He was terrified. And I didn't see it until it was too late."

Reed's eyes widened, his gaze locking onto hers as if the room had shrunk around them. Tammy continued, her voice heavy with the weight of her words. "I didn't know what to do, Reed. I sat there with that box, just staring at it, wondering if opening it would make things worse. But then I did, and what I found inside…" She paused. "It changed everything."

Her voice laced with a quiet intensity. "There were documents, photos, financial statements that didn't add up, recordings, things

Marcus had clearly gathered over years. It was all circumstantial, nothing concrete enough to take to the police, nothing that screamed 'smoking gun.' But it painted a picture. Barry wasn't just some shrewd businessman. He was ruthless, manipulative, and dangerous. He didn't just crush his competition; he erased them."

Tammy's words slowed. "When I talked to Sydney, she confirmed it. She'd seen Barry's temper, his control, his absolute need to dominate everyone around him. She told me about the time he smashed a glass in his hand during an argument, just to prove a point. Blood everywhere, but he didn't flinch. He made her clean it up while he stood there, staring at her. She told me about the way he'd watch people, like he was dissecting them, figuring out how they ticked, how to break them if they got in his way."

She leaned forward, her voice quieter now but no less intense. "Sydney said she once overheard him on a call, threatening someone, calm, polite, like he was making dinner plans. But the things he said, Reed... 'If you don't sign, your family won't make it to the weekend.' Just like that, matter-of-fact. And when Sydney confronted him, he laughed. He actually laughed and said, 'It's business, sweetheart. Nothing personal.'"

Tammy exhaled shakily, her gaze dropping to the table. "It was horrifying. All of it. And the worst part? Sydney said he always had a way of making people feel like they were the crazy ones, like they were overreacting or imagining things. He made her doubt herself so much, she didn't even realize how trapped she was until after the divorce when she was finally free of him. She said it was constant gaslighting, never his fault."

She looked back up at Reed, her eyes focused on his. "That file box, those stories, it was enough to know Marcus wasn't imagining things. Barry was dangerous, and he had everyone around him walking on eggshells. And when Marcus disappeared, I knew I had to tread carefully."

She took a shaky breath before continuing. "That's when I knew I couldn't fight Barry alone. I didn't have the skills, the resources, or the connections. I needed someone who could play his game. And then you came along."

Tammy let her lips curling into a faint, knowing smile. "You and I... well, we didn't date long, but you impressed me. You were clever, resourceful, and confident in a way that didn't rely on arrogance. And that little John Smith stunt on Pro4uM?" She let out a soft laugh, shaking her head. "Oh, Reed, you thought you were so slick, didn't you?"

Her smile widened, but her eyes remained serious, intent. "You thought you were manipulating me, pulling the wool over my eyes, but all you really did was prove something I'd been wondering about. You proved that you had what it took, that you could do what Marcus couldn't, what I couldn't."

She leaned back slightly, her expression shifting to one of amused recollection. "I know you like to think the John Smith login was some genius move, a stroke of brilliance on your part. But honestly, Reed, you kind of telegraphed it. The way you suddenly started gushing about me, about how much you cared for me and how I meant more to you than PPI, come on. It was so transparent. I could see straight through it."

Tammy's grin grew, a glimmer of admiration flickering in her eyes. "But here's the thing, you still managed to impress me. Even while I saw what you were doing, I couldn't help but respect the way you went about it. You were bold, decisive, and you took a calculated risk. That's not something everyone can do. And that move? It told me everything I needed to know."

She paused, her tone softening. "It was right then and there that I decided you were the one. You were the person who could bring Barry Cox down. I mean, you had the skills, sure, the brains, the ability to think on your feet. But more than that, you had heart. You weren't just playing the game for yourself. Even back then, I could tell you genuinely cared about doing what was right, about people. And that's what made you different."

Tammy's voice grew quieter, her gaze steady. "After that, I started keeping a closer eye on you, on everything you did on Pro4uM. Every message, every move you made. I wanted to see if you'd slip up, if there was any crack in your armor. But you didn't, Reed. You were solid, dependable, and relentless. And I knew, I just knew, you were the only one who could take on Barry and actually win."

Reed leaned back slightly, still listening intently to every word she said. Tammy pressed on, her voice urgent. "So, when that job to photograph Secretary Kessler came up, it felt like fate, like the stars had aligned. I knew I could tweak your orders just enough to slip the Marcus code into the mix. The beauty of it was in its simplicity. To you, it was just another routine assignment. But that sequence buried in the shoot? It wasn't just numbers, it was Marcus's lifeline, a message meant for Kessler. Knowing their connection, I trusted Kessler would recognize it and act accordingly."

"But I also knew Barry wouldn't make it easy. He'd already planted Kranch and Carter to pull your strings, steering you exactly where he wanted. That's where I stepped in. I guided you in the background, nudging you to see their value, to trust them. And you did. You didn't just follow the mission; you turned it into something bigger. You brought them into the fold and made them allies when Barry expected them to be your enemies."

She paused, her smile fading. "Grimes, though... that was pure luck. I didn't see him coming. But you? You handled him brilliantly. You turned him against Barry. I knew you'd handle whatever Barry threw at you, and you did, just like I knew you would." Her voice softened. "But Reed, I'm so sorry I sent you the Code late. I feel like I almost got you killed." She looked away, regret in her eyes. "In my defense, though... by then, I was hoping you'd put two and two together and realize you'd had the Code all along."

Her tone darkened. "When Vienna fell apart, I thought I'd made a mistake. I wondered if I'd put too much faith in you, if I'd underestimated Barry. Him pulling that gun hidden in the lens, it was a curveball I didn't anticipate. I mean, who thinks to turn a piece of photography equipment into a weapon? It was brilliant in the most terrifying way, and for a moment, I thought everything had crumbled."

She paused, the memory clearly weighing on her. "But then SYNC happened. Unbelievable, I couldn't have scripted it better myself! Reed, you outdid yourself. You didn't just survive, you dismantled his empire on a public stage, in front of the entire industry, and even the world no less. Watching it all unfold, it felt... perfect, like justice served on a silver platter. I wish I could've been in the audience, front row, to see his face live."

Tammy leaned back in her chair, a flicker of frustration crossing her face. "But Barry being Barry, he found a way out. Again. It's infuriating, isn't it? Just when you think you've got him, he slips through the cracks. The man's like smoke, intangible, impossible to pin down. But even then, I knew you had shaken him. That public humiliation wasn't something he could brush off. You forced him into a corner, Reed, and that was a victory all on its own."

She smiled slyly, her eyes narrowing slightly. "What you didn't realize, Reed, is that I wasn't just sending *you* messages. Oh no, Barry was getting cryptic messages too, carefully designed to keep him off balance. You were playing the game out in the open, but I was playing him from the shadows. Every time he thought he had the upper hand, I'd drop a seed of doubt."

Tammy leaned forward, her grin widening. "Watching him squirm, knowing he was constantly second-guessing himself, it was like poetic justice."

Her tone turned darker, satisfaction creeping in. "Barry couldn't trust anyone. Every operative, every ally, he saw betrayal in every corner. He was so paranoid, he probably thought the walls had eyes. And let me tell you, Reed, for a man like Barry, doubt is a poison. I just kept feeding him more of it."

Reed stared at her, stunned.

She let her expression soften slightly. "He thought he was the architect of the game. But he was just another pawn. And I wanted him to feel it, to feel the shadows closing in, the walls caving. Because that's what he'd done to Marcus, to so many others. It was justice, Reed, even if it wasn't perfect."

Tammy took a sip of her tea. "And then Seth was killed. Dovere came into the picture. It felt like we were back at square one. But by then, you weren't just a player in the game. You were the one making the moves. You were running circles around Barry, and he didn't even realize it. I don't think I've ever been so nervous as I was watching you navigate those final days. And the way you handled Dovere..." She trailed off, shaking her head. "Reed, you did the impossible. You turned a career bad guy into a good guy."

She leaned back, her hands resting on the kitten in her lap. "And that's the story, Reed. Every cryptic message, every subtle nudge, it was me. Guiding you, helping you, because I knew you were the only one who could finish what Marcus started. So, what do you think? Any questions?"

Reed stared at her, his jaw wide open, trying to process the avalanche of revelations she'd just unloaded. He had to consciously close his mouth, feeling a little ridiculous as he did so. Finally, he managed, "Tammy, I have to ask... Are you a PPI agent? I mean, were you working for them all this time?"

Tammy burst into laughter, a genuine, carefree sound that felt completely at odds with the gravity of their conversation. She shook her head, wiping a tear of amusement from the corner of her eye. "Reed, seriously? Of course I'm a member of the Professional Photographers Institute! Aren't you?" Her grin widened, playful and knowing, and she even added a wink for good measure.

Reed rolled his eyes, groaning. "You know what I mean, Tammy. Don't dodge the question."

Her expression shifted slightly, becoming more serious, though the humor lingered in her eyes. "Alright, fine," she said, leaning back and crossing her arms. "Years and years ago, long before the likes of Barry Cox or even Luc Hudson, the PPI stuck its nose into Pro4uM.-

com. They thought they were so clever. To them, I was just some ditzy internet admin, stuck reading code and banning trolls. They had no idea who they were dealing with.”

Reed raised an eyebrow, intrigued. “So, you knew, even then?”

“Oh, I knew,” Tammy said, her tone sharper now. “I knew exactly what they were trying to do. They thought they were controlling things, monitoring every thread, every conversation, every encrypted post. And sure, I let it happen. I let them think they were in charge, that they were using *me* and my platform as a tool. But all the while, I was watching them. Monitoring *their* movements, *their* messages, *their* people. I had access to things they didn’t even realize I could see.”

Reed tapped his fingers on the table, his voice low. “So, what does that make you? A double agent? A rogue operative?”

Tammy shrugged, her lips curling into a faint smile as one eyebrow lifted. “Let’s just say... I’m nobody’s operative. I’m nobody’s pawn. I never worked for PPI, not officially. But probably, no one, and I mean no one, knows as much as I do about the backdoor dealings, the encrypted messages, and the shadowy plans they thought they were hiding so well. I’ve seen it all, Reed. Every dark little secret, every coded betrayal.”

She paused, her voice softening, the confidence in her tone faltering ever so slightly. “But I’ll admit, Barry had me fooled, too. He was so good at disguising his intent, those cryptic messages that seemed like everyday photography chatter. I missed so much. He used the Pro4uM like a playground, and I didn’t catch it until... until Marcus.” Her voice caught, the unspoken weight of Marcus’s fate hanging heavily in the air. She cleared her throat, forcing her composure back. “It wasn’t until after everything with him that I started piecing it together. Barry was always one step ahead, always hiding in plain sight. And that’s what made him so dangerous.”

Reed’s brow furrowed, the weight of her words sinking in. “So you’re saying, ”

“I’m saying,” Tammy interrupted, “there are now exactly two

people in this world who know what's really been going on with the Pro4uM and PPI. You... and me."

She leaned forward, her voice gaining a razor-sharp edge. "Now, Reed, I need to ask you something. Can we keep this little secret about Pro4uM and PPI between us? Just you and me. No one else."

Reed hesitated, feeling the weight of what she was asking. Her words hung in the air, a challenge wrapped in trust, daring him to answer. He understood why she was asking, but he couldn't help thinking about everyone on his team who had wrestled with the same questions. Then again... was this really such a big ask? How many other secrets, far more dangerous, would he be taking to his grave? This was nothing by comparison. So, he nodded, and at the same time, said softly, "Of course."

As Scarlett approached with Reed's coffee, a small kitten perched delicately on her arm, she paused at the table with a knowing smile. Her bright red hair glinted in the warm café light, catching Reed's attention. "Tammy tells me you're not a fan of cats," Scarlett said softly, setting the steaming cup of black coffee in front of him. Her tone carried a gentle challenge, her smile almost playful. "But this kitten's different. Just try it, right under her chin. She'll win you over."

Reed hesitated, his hand hovering awkwardly above the tiny creature. The kitten blinked up at him, wide-eyed and impossibly innocent. He glanced at Tammy, who raised an amused eyebrow, daring him without words. With a faint sigh and a slight shake of his head, Reed gave in. Slowly, he reached out and scratched under the kitten's chin as Scarlett suggested.

To his surprise, the kitten responded immediately, tilting its tiny head up, eyes half-closing in bliss. A deep, rumbling purr vibrated from the small body, filling the space between them with an unexpected warmth. The kitten nestled into Reed's hand, its soft fur brushing his fingers as it curled trustingly into his palm.

Scarlett chuckled lightly, the sound as warm as the ambiance of the café. "Told you," she said with a wink, before walking away, leaving the kitten and Reed to their moment.

Reed stared down at the small creature, now completely relaxed in his hand, and felt something he couldn't quite name. Tammy leaned in her chair, watching him with just a bit of a smile, as though she had orchestrated this small moment of peace.

Reed shook his head, his expression softening. The tension in his shoulders began to melt away as he sank back into his chair, absently stroking the kitten's fur. "You know," he said quietly, breaking the comfortable silence, "I've never been a cat person. But... this?" He gestured slightly with his free hand, coffee steaming on the table in front of him, the kitten nestled contentedly in his lap. "Sitting here, drinking coffee, petting a kitten, it's... nice. Normal."

Tammy nodded, her voice soft and thoughtful. "Normal's good, Reed. After everything, you deserve a little of it."

The moment lingered. The kitten purred softly in Reed's hand, its rhythmic vibration soothing. Around them, the faint hum of café chatter and the gentle clink of dishes being cleared blended into an ambiance Reed hadn't felt in years, calm, peace, and relief. He wasn't calculating his next move or watching shadows in the corners of the room. The weight of months, years, of paranoia and survival began to lift as he exhaled deeply.

Tammy tilted her head slightly. "It's ironic, isn't it? After all the chaos, the cryptic messages, the gun-lens in Vienna, and Barry's grand performance at SYNC... it all ends here. Coffee, kittens, and quiet."

Reed smirked faintly, the ghost of a smile flickering across his face as he scratched the kitten once more. "Yeah," he said. "It's almost poetic."

Tammy grinned, lifting her own cup to her lips. "Normal suits you, Reed," she said warmly. "Maybe you should try it more often."

Reed didn't reply immediately. He just looked down at the kitten, its tiny body curled trustingly in his palm.

Reed suddenly looked forward, like a memory just hit him, his curiosity piqued. "Alright, Tammy, here's one for you. How in the world did you pull off the message at the golf course in Cabo? 'Keep moving to the light.' That was... eerie. It felt like you were inside my head."

Tammy smirked, her fingers idly playing with the kitten nestled in her lap. She took a sip of her tea, her eyes drifting momentarily to her open laptop. "You guys think you're so smart," she began, her tone teasing but laced with knowing. "Meeting at different times, never staying in the same hotel, thinking you're untraceable. But Reed, the second I saw you'd secured a ticket to Cabo, I knew. Puerto Los Cabos Golf Club. It wasn't rocket science. When we were dating, you must've raved about that course at least five times. 'Best greens in Mexico,' you said. 'Unbeatable view of the Sea of Cortez.' It was like clockwork, obvious to anyone paying attention."

Reed tilted his head, with a faint grin. "Alright, fair point. But how'd you know the exact time and place? You couldn't have tracked us in real-time."

Tammy chuckled, the sound light and confident. "Oh, Reed. You underestimate the power of old-fashioned intuition, and a little local ingenuity. When I pieced it together, I figured you'd hit the course your first morning there. Routine, right? That's when I reached out to a contact. You'd be surprised what a crisp $100 bill can buy you in Cabo."

She leaned back, her grin widening as she let the memory settle between them. "A local caddy owed me a favor. He put me in touch with a young boy from the town who did odd jobs at the Golf Course. I told him to hang around and hand the note to the Golf Pro as soon as he saw the first gringo who looked like he had more on his mind than his golf swing. And voilà, message delivered. What can I say? It pays to have good friends."

Reed shook his head, equal parts impressed and bemused. "Unbelievable. So, you were basically orchestrating the entire thing from a distance?"

Tammy's smile softened. "I wouldn't say the whole thing, but yeah, I had my moments. You had enough on your plate, Reed. I just... nudged things along when I could. Like in Cabo. Sometimes it's the little breadcrumbs that keep you moving forward."

The kitten stretched lazily in her lap, its soft purr filling the momentary silence. Tammy glanced at Reed, her expression encouraging. "Come on, Reed. I know you've got more questions. Let's hear them."

Reed rubbed his chin thoughtfully, his brain pondering all the cryptic encounters and seemingly impossible moments from the past year. He took a deep breath and leaned forward again. "Alright, Tammy. Let's keep going. Here's one."

Reed's coffee was cooling in front of him, the steam had stopped rising. He looked Tammy straight in the eye, his voice low and serious. "Do you think Barry is dead?"

Tammy tilted her head, considering the question. A faint frown crossed her face as she spoke. "I want to think so, Reed. After everything he's done, after the chaos he's caused, I want to believe it's finally over. Knowing Barry the way I do... he was sneaky, manipulative, and dangerously cunning. He had these uncanny abilities. And he was so dedicated to his legacy, it was almost pathological."

She paused, her gaze distant as she sifted through her memories. "But faking a helicopter crash? Surviving something like that, just to orchestrate a grand escape and sell the illusion of his death? That's... ambitious, even for Barry. I mean, the logistics alone, how do you ensure it all looks convincing? The wreckage, the timing, the silence afterward. It's not impossible, but it would take an extraordinary amount of planning. Even for Barry, it feels... improbable."

Reed studied her, noting the hesitation in her voice. "So, you think he's gone?"

Tammy sighed, "I think so. I really do. But then again..." She hesitated, her words trailing off as she glanced at Reed, her eyes sharp with unease. "If you were to tell me he's alive, if you had proof or even just a gut feeling, I wouldn't be shocked. That's the thing with

Barry. He was a master of the unexpected. Just when you thought you had him cornered, he'd flip the script."

Tammy continued. "The thing is, Reed, people like Barry don't just disappear. They either burn out spectacularly or they go underground so completely that they might as well be dead. And Barry? He was too proud to just vanish. So, yea, I'm going with dead."

The kitten purred softly, its small, warm body nestled against Tammy's arm. But Reed's mind was miles away, racing through every encounter, every move Barry had made. Tammy's revelations were starting to uproot the seeds of doubt that had been planted deep in his mind, loosening their hold with each passing moment.

Tammy then said, "We can't chase ghosts forever, Reed. At some point, we have to believe it's over. Maybe it's not about Barry anymore. Maybe it's about moving forward."

Reed nodded slowly, but the doubt slightly lingered, an ever-present shadow in the back of his mind.

Reed let his fingers rest lightly on the coffee cup. He glanced at Tammy, her expression warm and relaxed.

He exhaled, "You know, I'm sure I have a ton more questions. About everything, Barry, PPI, the Pro4uM, all of it." He paused, running a hand through his hair. "But right now? I can't think of a single one. And honestly? I don't think I want to."

Tammy let a playful grin form. "Is this you taking a break, Reed? I didn't think you knew how to stop chasing answers."

He chuckled softly, a rare sound. "Maybe I'm learning." He hesitated, then added with a playful wink, "But just in case I do think of something later, can I buy you dinner tonight? I think I kinda owe you."

Tammy's grin widened, her eyes sparkling with a mix of amusement and something deeper, relief, perhaps, or a quiet acknowledgment of how far they'd both come. Or maybe, Reed thought, she just had a thing for prematurely graying, middle-aged, average-looking guys. "YES," she said, drawing out the word, her tone teasing and warm. "I thought you'd never ask!"

Reed stood, reaching for his jacket, the faintest trace of his usual sharpness returning. "Dinner, then. But don't think I'm letting you order the most expensive thing on the menu just because you saved my life. Twice." He winked again playfully.

As they walked toward the door, the evening air greeted them with a gentle breeze. Reed couldn't help but feel that, for once, the world seemed... still. And maybe, just maybe, this was the start of something normal, whatever that meant.

30

THE FINAL CLICK

Time had passed, smoothing the edges of chaos and replacing them with quiet. Reed Sawyer had fully stepped away from the clandestine world of espionage, covert operations, and the ever-looming shadows of PPI. The weight of encrypted messages, ticking clocks, and hidden agendas was gone, replaced by something simpler, something purer. His life now belonged to the moments in front of his lens, not for secrets, not for manipulation, but for the raw, unfiltered beauty of the world.

Today, Reed found himself in a serene, sunlit coastal town along the Mediterranean. The place seemed timeless, with cobblestone streets winding through pastel-colored buildings and fishing boats bobbing gently in the harbor. It was the kind of setting that didn't need to be chased; it simply existed, waiting to be noticed.

Reed stood atop a quiet overlook, his camera resting comfortably in his hands. The golden light of dawn spilled across the tranquil landscape, painting everything in hues of amber and rose. The air was still, carrying the faint scent of salt and the distant murmur of waves meeting the shore. He felt calm, centered, like he had finally found his place in the world.

This was his project now, one photo a day. Just one. No rush, no deadlines. The challenge wasn't in the shot itself, but in the discipline of waiting, searching for the moment that deserved to be immortalized. The act was meditative, almost ceremonial. It was about presence, about seeing the world as it was, not as someone wanted it to be.

Reed adjusted his settings, his fingers moving with ease. The soft click of the dials and the weight of the camera in his hands felt like old friends. He scanned the scene in front of him, the harbor reflecting the dawn, the distant mountains blushing with light, and a fisherman silhouetted against the horizon. Everything was perfectly imperfect, alive with possibility.

And then he saw it. The moment.

The light shifted, catching the fisherman's cast net in a golden halo as it arced gracefully through the air. A seagull glided into the frame, its wings outstretched in effortless balance. The scene was harmony itself, fleeting yet eternal. Reed steadied his breath, his finger hovering over the shutter.

Click.

The sound was soft, almost inaudible against the backdrop of the waking town. But to Reed, it was everything, a simple, honest moment frozen in time. He lowered the camera as a faint smile slipped over his face. This wasn't just a photograph. It was peace, purpose, a reminder of what life could be when stripped of its complications. Just light, truth, and the quiet satisfaction of capturing a moment worth remembering.

As Reed leaned against the stone railing of the overlook, his thoughts drifted. The chaos of SYNC played back in his mind like a fragmented film reel, the blinding flashes of cameras, the tension in every room, the calculated chaos that had brought Barry's empire crumbling down. He could almost hear the hum of overlapping conversations, the whispers of betrayal, the gun hidden in a camera lens back in Vienna, and the deafening silence that followed when it was all over.

Then came the cryptic messages. The codes, the signals buried in the most ordinary of places, the constant push and pull between clarity and deception. Each one had unraveled another thread of the web he'd been caught in, but not without a cost. Lives had been lost, Marcus, Seth, Dovere. People who had played their part, knowingly or unknowingly, in a game far larger than themselves. Their faces flickered through his memory, each one a reminder of the cost of exposing Barry and dismantling PPI.

The world itself had shifted. PPI, for all its layers of secrets, no longer existed in the form it once had. Reed had made sure of that. But what had risen from its ashes? Was it a true rebirth, stripped of its shadows, or just another mask, hiding the same games of power and manipulation? If it was left up to Reed, he would never know for sure, and that was a truth he had learned to accept.

Here, in this quiet coastal town, none of that mattered. The betrayals, the losses, the what-ifs, they felt distant, like echoes from a life that belonged to someone else. The air was fresh, the light golden, and the horizon endless. There was no need to look over his shoulder, no shadows lurking in the periphery. It was just Reed, his camera, and the light.

A genuine smile crossed his face. He looked out over the Mediterranean, watching the soft waves lap against the shore, the fishermen packing up their nets for the day, the faint chatter of locals exchanging greetings in a language Reed didn't understand but found comforting, nonetheless. Suddenly he realized it, he felt like a man untethered, free from the weight of survival and secrets.

Tomorrow, he would again rise with the sun, camera in hand, and continue his daily one-shot challenge. He would wait patiently for the perfect moment, the perfect light, the perfect truth to reveal itself.

Reed exhaled deeply, his shoulders relaxing as he turned from the overlook and began walking back toward the village. The thought crossed his mind, unbidden but welcome: maybe he had finally found peace, not in resolution but in letting go. And for now, that was enough.

As Reed strolled along the winding path toward the village, his thoughts turned to the team, each person who had stood with him through the chaos and uncertainty, each one who had played a critical role in dismantling Barry's empire. He smiled faintly, the memories of their camaraderie, their struggles, and their triumphs coming back to him in vivid detail. They had all gone their separate ways, finding new paths, but the bonds they had forged would remain with them forever.

Kranch, the gruff but steady presence, had retired from the field. Reed could picture him now, arms crossed as always, surveying a group of young recruits with that intense, no-nonsense expression that could silence a room. After leaving PPI, Kranch had poured his energy into consulting with military outlets, shaping the next generation of tacticians and operatives. Reed had heard through the grapevine that Kranch was even considering starting his own school to train civilians in tactical measures. It was a fitting evolution for a man who thrived in structure and discipline. Early mornings on the training field, barking commands and demonstrating maneuvers, it was the perfect place for him. Reed chuckled at the image. Even in retirement, Kranch wasn't one to take it easy.

Carter, on the other hand, had embraced the quiet. At long last, he was sleeping through the night without his tablet buzzing beside him. Reed remembered how Carter used to live on the edge of his nerves, constantly connected, his mind clicking with data and contingencies. Now, Carter had shifted his focus, still immersed in tech but without the life-or-death stakes. He had become a familiar face on Pro4uM.com, contributing thoughtful posts on SEO, marketing, and tech advice for up-and-coming photographers. Reed had to admit, Carter's tips had helped more than a few struggling artists refine their craft and their businesses. Recently, Carter had been approached by Google with an enticing offer to join their team, a position that promised security and challenge in equal measure. Reed wasn't sure which way Carter would lean, but whatever he chose, he knew Carter had finally found the balance he'd been searching for.

And then there was Grimes, the relentless operator. If anyone had been born to juggle high-stakes ventures, it was him. Grimes had decided to rebuild SYNC, the iconic photography convention, from the ground up. But, true to form, he wasn't content with just one massive project. He'd gone a step further, launching a new convention to rival SYNC: SNAP, the Society of Networked Artistic Photographers. Running one high-profile event was no small feat, but running two? That was Grimes at his finest. Reed had seen photos of him at the helm, surrounded by staff, his ever-present headset in place, his energy evident even through a camera lens. He was in his element, commanding rooms, bringing people together, and thriving on the energy of creativity and innovation. It was a world Grimes had built for himself, and Reed couldn't imagine him happier anywhere else.

Reed's smile deepened as he thought about each of them, the lives they had carved out for themselves after the storm. They had come through the fire together, and though they had gone their separate ways, they were still connected by the journey they had shared. Each of them had found their version of peace, their way of moving forward.

And now, here he was, doing the same. As the golden light of the Mediterranean surrounded him, Reed felt a rare, quiet sense of satisfaction. His camera hung at his side, and the weight of it was familiar and grounding. This was his world now. No shadows, no whispers, no second-guessing. Just moments to be captured and memories to be made.

At last, Reed could breathe without looking over his shoulder.

As the day stretched on, Reed sat quietly on a worn bench overlooking the calm Mediterranean waters. The bustling sounds of the coastal town faded into the background, leaving him with nothing but the soft rhythm of the waves and the occasional laughter of children in the distance. His camera rested comfortably in his lap, its strap coiled loosely around his wrist, a tool that once shielded him, defined him, and nearly destroyed him.

Reed scrolled through the images on his camera, pausing on one that caught his breath, a shot he took back at SYNC.

It was Barry Cox, mid-rehearsal on stage, illuminated by harsh stage lights. The image was raw, powerful. It captured the very essence of the man: commanding, manipulative, larger than life.

Reed's finger hovered over the delete button. For a moment, he hesitated, his thoughts spiraling. That chapter of his life had been chaotic, shadowed by betrayal and loss. This photograph was proof of that chaos, a tangible reminder of everything Barry had taken from him, from the world. But it was also proof of something else: survival. His survival.

Reed exhaled slowly, pressed delete, and watched as the image disappeared. The past is a photograph I'm no longer keeping in my portfolio, he thought, almost amused at the metaphor.

The sun began its descent, casting fiery streaks of orange and crimson across the horizon. Reed admired it for a moment, but he didn't reach for his camera. He had already taken his project image for the day. He told himself tomorrow, maybe, he would photograph the sunset. But today? Today, it was just for him.

As Reed zipped his camera bag, preparing to leave, his phone buzzed. He glanced at it reflexively, then stopped. Ignore it, he told himself. Not everything needs your attention anymore. But old habits die hard.

Slowly, he picked up the phone and unlocked the screen. The message was simple. Stark. No frills, no code, no context: **"Reed, we need to talk. Now."**

There was no signature. No sender information. Not even a time-stamp. Just the words.

Reed stared at the screen, his pulse quickening in a way it hadn't in months. His first thought was *Tammy*, but she wouldn't leave something this cryptic. Then, Barry. But *Barry* was gone. Wasn't he?

His grip on the phone tightened as he looked around instinctively, scanning the horizon, the streets, the windows above. Everything was serene. Peaceful. Normal. Yet the unease settled over him like a shadow, whispering the one question he thought he'd never have to ask again: *Is it really over?*

The sunset continued to blaze, its reflection painting the water in soft streaks of gold and pink. Reed let out a slow breath, pressed the power button on his phone, and slid it into his pocket. *Not today*, he thought. *Today, I'm not chasing shadows.*

But something lingered in his mind, a flicker of curiosity, or perhaps old instincts refusing to fade. Slowly, deliberately, he reached for his camera. Breaking his self-imposed one-shot-a-day rule, he raised the viewfinder to his eye. He framed the scene before him, a simple, unassuming shot of the sun melting into the water, the horizon aglow with warmth and peace.

The shutter clicked.

The image displayed in the viewfinder instantly, a frozen moment of light, simple clarity, and quiet reflection.

Reed lowered the camera, letting the silence settle around him. He told himself he was not going to look at the camera again. Not tonight. Maybe tomorrow.

But just as he moved to power down the camera, something caught his eye. A small detail, barely there. He zoomed in, adjusting the display.

Far in the distance, just above the horizon, a dark shape lingered, a helicopter, military-style, its rotors eerily still in the frozen frame. Too far to hear. Almost too far to see.

Reed exhaled slowly. He studied the image for a beat longer, then powered the camera off. He would take a closer look later.

As the waves lapped gently at the shore, Reed Sawyer picked up his bag, slung it over his shoulder, and walked away from the water. Behind him, the sun dipped below the horizon, leaving the world in a soft, lingering twilight.

And somewhere, out there in the growing dark, the shadows stirred.

Is it really over?

ABOUT THE AUTHOR

Kirk Voclain is a novelist and long-time professional photographer from South Louisiana. For more than forty years, he has made a living with a camera, creating senior portraits, real estate images, and commercial work for businesses that need results. He also runs Pro4uM.com, a respected community where working photographers share, learn, and level up.

Double Exposure is his debut thriller. Its hero, Reed Sawyer, is a photographer whose camera and confidence open doors that badges cannot. Kirk writes the way he shoots, fast and focused, with an eye for the telling detail. If a lens can find the truth, a lie cannot hide for long.

Kirk has taught classes and workshops across the country and around the world, and he has judged print competitions for years. He loves passing on practical craft, simple tools, and a push to keep going when the light is bad. He lives in Houma, Louisiana, with his family. When he is not writing, he is likely planning the next shoot, helping a fellow pro, or scouting a location that might turn into a chapter.

What comes next is already in motion. The prequel, Zero Exposure, reveals more about the world behind Double Exposure and how it came into existence. Negative Exposure, the sequel to Double Exposure, is on the way, along with a companion novel, Counter Exposure, told from Barry Cox's point of view. The worlds of art, access, and covert pressure continue to collide, and Kirk is right there with a notebook and a lens.

For news, extras, contact info, and social links, visit KirkVoclain.com.

amazon.com/author/kirkvoclain

facebook.com/kirkvoclainauthor

x.com/kirkvoclain

instagram.com/kirkvoclain

tiktok.com/@kirkvoclain

linkedin.com/in/kirkvoclain

youtube.com/kirkvoclain

goodreads.com/kirkvoclain

bookbub.com/authors/kirk-voclain

ALSO BY KIRK VOCLAIN

The Exposure Series

Double Exposure

Coming Soon

Zero Exposure

A prequel to Double Exposure

Counter Exposure

A companion novel told from Barry Cox's point of view

Negative Exposure

The sequel to Double Exposure

For updates, bonus content, and future promotions, visit KirkVoclain.com.

www.ingramcontent.com/pod-product-compliance
Lightning Source LLC
Chambersburg PA
CBHW071148100726
47908CB00002B/291